COLLECTED WORKS OF
RUDYARD KIPLING

COLLECTED WORKS OF RUDYARD KIPLING

VOLUME 2

Barrack Room Ballads,
The Story of the Gadsbys,
Under the Deodars and
France at War

BIBLIOBAZAAR

COLLECTED WORKS OF
RUDYARD KIPLING

CONTENTS

BARRACK-ROOM BALLADS...9

THE STORY OF THE GADSBY.. 79

UNDER THE DEODARS 189

FRANCE AT WAR 307

BARRACK-ROOM BALLADS

DEDICATION

To T. A.

    I have made for you a song,
    And it may be right or wrong,
But only you can tell me if it's true;
    I have tried for to explain
    Both your pleasure and your pain,
And, Thomas, here's my best respects to you!

    O there'll surely come a day
    When they'll give you all your pay,
And treat you as a Christian ought to do;
    So, until that day comes round,
    Heaven keep you safe and sound,
And, Thomas, here's my best respects to you!

R. K.

DANNY DEEVER

"What are the bugles blowin' for?" said Files-on-Parade.
"To turn you out, to turn you out", the Colour-Sergeant said.
"What makes you look so white, so white?" said Files-on-Parade.
"I'm dreadin' what I've got to watch", the Colour-Sergeant said.
> For they're hangin' Danny Deever, you can hear the Dead
> March play,
> The regiment's in 'ollow square—they're hangin' him to-day;
> They've taken of his buttons off an' cut his stripes away,
> An' they're hangin' Danny Deever in the mornin'.

"What makes the rear-rank breathe so 'ard?" said Files-on-Parade.
"It's bitter cold, it's bitter cold", the Colour-Sergeant said.
"What makes that front-rank man fall down?" said Files-on-
Parade.
"A touch o' sun, a touch o' sun", the Colour-Sergeant said.
> They are hangin' Danny Deever, they are marchin' of 'im
> round,
> They 'ave 'alted Danny Deever by 'is coffin on the ground;
> An' 'e'll swing in 'arf a minute for a sneakin' shootin'
> hound—
> O they're hangin' Danny Deever in the mornin'!

"'Is cot was right-'and cot to mine", said Files-on-Parade.
"'E's sleepin' out an' far to-night", the Colour-Sergeant said.
"I've drunk 'is beer a score o' times", said Files-on-Parade.
"'E's drinkin' bitter beer alone", the Colour-Sergeant said.
> They are hangin' Danny Deever, you must mark 'im
> place,
> For 'e shot a comrade sleepin'—you must look 'im
> face;

Nine 'undred of 'is county an' the regiment's disgrace,
While they're hangin' Danny Deever in the mornin'.

"What's that so black agin' the sun?" said Files-on-Parade.
"It's Danny fightin' 'ard for life", the Colour-Sergeant said.
"What's that that whimpers over'ead?" said Files-on-Parade.
"It's Danny's soul that's passin' now", the Colour-Sergeant said.
    For they're done with Danny Deever, you can 'ear the
       quickstep play,
    The regiment's in column, an' they're marchin' us away;
    Ho! the young recruits are shakin', an' they'll want their beer
       to-day,
    After hangin' Danny Deever in the mornin'.

Tommy

I went into a public-'ouse to get a pint o' beer,
The publican 'e up an' sez, "We serve no red-coats here."
The girls be'ind the bar they laughed an' giggled fit to die,
I outs into the street again an' to myself sez I:
    O it's Tommy this, an' Tommy that, an' "Tommy, go away";
    But it's "Thank you, Mister Atkins", when the band begins
       to play,
    The band begins to play, my boys, the band begins to play,
    ⊃ it's "Thank you, Mister Atkins", when the band begins to
       play.

      a theatre as sober as could be,
        drunk civilian room, but 'adn't none for me;
          to the gallery or round the music-'alls,
            nes to fightin', Lord! they'll shove me in the stalls!
   ⊃ 'is   mmy this, an' Tommy that, an' "Tommy, wait

  in the   l train for Atkins" when the trooper's on the

The troopship's on the tide, my boys, the troopship's on the
tide,
O it's "Special train for Atkins" when the trooper's on the
tide.

Yes, makin' mock o' uniforms that guard you while you sleep
Is cheaper than them uniforms, an' they're starvation cheap;
An' hustlin' drunken soldiers when they're goin' large a bit
Is five times better business than paradin' in full kit.
Then it's Tommy this, an' Tommy that, an' "Tommy, 'ow's yer
soul?"
But it's "Thin red line of 'eroes" when the drums begin to
roll,
The drums begin to roll, my boys, the drums begin to roll,
O it's "Thin red line of 'eroes" when the drums begin to
roll.

We aren't no thin red 'eroes, nor we aren't no blackguards too,
But single men in barricks, most remarkable like you;
An' if sometimes our conduck isn't all your fancy paints,
Why, single men in barricks don't grow into plaster saints;
While it's Tommy this, an' Tommy that, an' "Tommy, fall
be'ind",
But it's "Please to walk in front, sir", when there's trouble in
the wind,
There's trouble in the wind, my boys, there's trouble in the
wind,
O it's "Please to walk in front, sir", when there's trouble in
the wind.

You talk o' better food for us, an' schools, an' fires, an' all:
We'll wait for extry rations if you treat us rational.
Don't mess about the cook-room slops, but prove it to our face
The Widow's Uniform is not the soldier-man's disgrace.
For it's Tommy this, an' Tommy that, an' "Chuck him out, the
brute!"
But it's "Saviour of 'is country" when the guns begin to
shoot;

An' it's Tommy this, an' Tommy that, an' anything you
please;
An' Tommy ain't a bloomin' fool—you bet that Tommy sees!

Fuzzy-Wuzzy

(Soudan Expeditionary Force)

We've fought with many men acrost the seas,
    An' some of 'em was brave an' some was not:
The Paythan an' the Zulu an' Burmese;
    But the Fuzzy was the finest o' the lot.
We never got a ha'porth's change of 'im:
    'E squatted in the scrub an' 'ocked our 'orses,
'E cut our sentries up at Suakim,
    An' 'e played the cat an' banjo with our forces.
     So 'ere's to you, Fuzzy-Wuzzy, at your 'ome in the Soudan;
     You're a pore benighted 'eathen but a first-class fightin' man;
     We gives you your certificate, an' if you want it signed
     We'll come an' 'ave a romp with you whenever you're inclined.

We took our chanst among the Khyber 'ills,
    The Boers knocked us silly at a mile,
The Burman give us Irriwaddy chills,
    An' a Zulu impi dished us up in style:
But all we ever got from such as they
    Was pop to what the Fuzzy made us swaller;
We 'eld our bloomin' own, the papers say,
    But man for man the Fuzzy knocked us 'oller.
     Then 'ere's to you, Fuzzy-Wuzzy, an' the missis and the kid;
     Our orders was to break you, an' of course we went an' did.
     We sloshed you with Martinis, an' it wasn't 'ardly fair;
     But for all the odds agin' you, Fuzzy-Wuz, you broke the square.

'E 'asn't got no papers of 'is own,
    'E 'asn't got no medals nor rewards,
So we must certify the skill 'e's shown
    In usin' of 'is long two-'anded swords:
When 'e's 'oppin' in an' out among the bush
    With 'is coffin-'eaded shield an' shovel-spear,
An 'appy day with Fuzzy on the rush
    Will last an 'ealthy Tommy for a year.
        So 'ere's to you, Fuzzy-Wuzzy, an' your friends which are no
            more,
         If we 'adn't lost some messmates we would 'elp you to
            deplore;
        But give an' take's the gospel, an' we'll call the bargain fair,
        For if you 'ave lost more than us, you crumpled up the
            square!

'E rushes at the smoke when we let drive,
    An', before we know, 'e's 'ackin' at our 'ead;
'E's all 'ot sand an' ginger when alive,
    An' 'e's generally shammin' when 'e's dead.
'E's a daisy, 'e's a ducky, 'e's a lamb!
    'E's a injia-rubber idiot on the spree,
'E's the on'y thing that doesn't give a damn
    For a Regiment o' British Infantree!
        So 'ere's to you, Fuzzy-Wuzzy, at your 'ome in the Soudan;
        You're a pore benighted 'eathen but a first-class fightin' man;
        An' 'ere's to you, Fuzzy-Wuzzy, with your 'ayrick 'ead of
         'air—
        You big black boundin' beggar—for you broke a British
         square!

Soldier, Soldier

"Soldier, soldier come from the wars,
Why don't you march with my true love?"

"We're fresh from off the ship an' 'e's maybe give the slip,
An' you'd best go look for a new love."
    New love! True love!
    Best go look for a new love,
    The dead they cannot rise, an' you'd better dry your eyes,
    An' you'd best go look for a new love.

"Soldier, soldier come from the wars,
What did you see o' my true love?"
"I seed 'im serve the Queen in a suit o' rifle-green,
An' you'd best go look for a new love."

"Soldier, soldier come from the wars,
Did ye see no more o' my true love?"
"I seed 'im runnin' by when the shots begun to fly—
But you'd best go look for a new love."

"Soldier, soldier come from the wars,
Did aught take 'arm to my true love?"
"I couldn't see the fight, for the smoke it lay so white—
An' you'd best go look for a new love."

"Soldier, soldier come from the wars,
I'll up an' tend to my true love!"
"'E's lying on the dead with a bullet through 'is 'ead,
An' you'd best go look for a new love."

"Soldier, soldier come from the wars,
I'll down an' die with my true love!"
"The pit we dug'll 'ide 'im an' the twenty men beside 'im—
An' you'd best go look for a new love."

"Soldier, soldier come from the wars,
Do you bring no sign from my true love?"
"I bring a lock of 'air that 'e allus used to wear,
An' you'd best go look for a new love."

"Soldier, soldier come from the wars,
O then I know it's true I've lost my true love!"

"An' I tell you truth again—when you've lost the feel o' pain
You'd best take me for your true love."
    True love! New love!
    Best take 'im for a new love,
    The dead they cannot rise, an' you'd better dry your eyes,
    An' you'd best take 'im for your true love.

Screw-Guns

Smokin' my pipe on the mountings, sniffin' the mornin' cool,
I walks in my old brown gaiters along o' my old brown mule,
With seventy gunners be'ind me, an' never a beggar forgets
It's only the pick of the Army
        that handles the dear little pets—'Tss! 'Tss!
    For you all love the screw-guns—the screw-guns they all love
you!
    So when we call round with a few guns,
        o' course you will know what to do—hoo! hoo!
    Jest send in your Chief an' surrender—
        it's worse if you fights or you runs:
    You can go where you please, you can skid up the trees,
        but you don't get away from the guns!

They sends us along where the roads are, but mostly we goes where
    they ain't:
We'd climb up the side of a sign-board an' trust to the stick o' the
    paint:
We've chivied the Naga an' Looshai, we've give the Afreedeeman fits,
For we fancies ourselves at two thousand,
        we guns that are built in two bits—'Tss! 'Tss!
    For you all love the screw-guns . . .

If a man doesn't work, why, we drills 'im an' teaches 'im 'ow to
    behave;
If a beggar can't march, why, we kills 'im an' rattles 'im into 'is grave.

You've got to stand up to our business an' spring without snatchin'
    or fuss.
D'you say that you sweat with the field-guns?
        By God, you must lather with us—'Tss! 'Tss!
    For you all love the screw-guns . . .

The eagles is screamin' around us, the river's a-moanin' below,
We're clear o' the pine an' the oak-scrub,
        we're out on the rocks an' the snow,
An' the wind is as thin as a whip-lash what carries away to the plains
The rattle an' stamp o' the lead-mules—
        the jinglety-jink o' the chains—'Tss! 'Tss!
    For you all love the screw-guns . . .

There's a wheel on the Horns o' the Mornin',
        an' a wheel on the edge o' the Pit,
An' a drop into nothin' beneath you as straight as a beggar can spit:
With the sweat runnin' out o' your shirt-sleeves,
        an' the sun off the snow in your face,
An' 'arf o' the men on the drag-ropes
        to hold the old gun in 'er place—'Tss! 'Tss!
    For you all love the screw-guns . . .

Smokin' my pipe on the mountings, sniffin' the mornin' cool,
I climbs in my old brown gaiters along o' my old brown mule.
The monkey can say what our road was—
        the wild-goat 'e knows where we passed.
Stand easy, you long-eared old darlin's!
        Out drag-ropes! With shrapnel! Hold fast—'Tss! 'Tss!
    For you all love the screw-guns—the screw-guns they all love
you!
So when we take tea with a few guns,
        o' course you will know what to do—hoo! hoo!
Jest send in your Chief an' surrender—
        it's worse if you fights or you runs:
You may hide in the caves, they'll be only your graves,
        but you can't get away from the guns!

Cells

I've a head like a concertina: I've a tongue like a button-stick:
I've a mouth like an old potato, and I'm more than a little sick,
But I've had my fun o' the Corp'ral's Guard: I've made the cinders
    fly,
And I'm here in the Clink for a thundering drink
       and blacking the Corporal's eye.
    With a second-hand overcoat under my head,
    And a beautiful view of the yard,
O it's pack-drill for me and a fortnight's C.B.
    For "drunk and resisting the Guard!"
    Mad drunk and resisting the Guard—
    'Strewth, but I socked it them hard!
So it's pack-drill for me and a fortnight's C.B.
    For "drunk and resisting the Guard."

I started o' canteen porter, I finished o' canteen beer,
But a dose o' gin that a mate slipped in, it was that that brought
    me here.
'Twas that and an extry double Guard that rubbed my nose in the
    dirt;
But I fell away with the Corp'ral's stock
       and the best of the Corp'ral's shirt.

I left my cap in a public-house, my boots in the public road,
And Lord knows where, and I don't care, my belt and my tunic
    goed;
They'll stop my pay, they'll cut away the stripes I used to wear,
But I left my mark on the Corp'ral's face, and I think he'll keep it
    there!

My wife she cries on the barrack-gate, my kid in the barrack-yard,
It ain't that I mind the Ord'ly room—it's that that cuts so hard.
I'll take my oath before them both that I will sure abstain,
But as soon as I'm in with a mate and gin, I know I'll do it again!
    With a second-hand overcoat under my head,
    And a beautiful view of the yard,

Yes, it's pack-drill for me and a fortnight's C.B.
    For "drunk and resisting the Guard!"
    Mad drunk and resisting the Guard—
    'Strewth, but I socked it them hard!
So it's pack-drill for me and a fortnight's C.B.
    For "drunk and resisting the Guard."

Gunga Din

You may talk o' gin and beer
When you're quartered safe out 'ere,
An' you're sent to penny-fights an' Aldershot it;
But when it comes to slaughter
You will do your work on water,
An' you'll lick the bloomin' boots of 'im that's got it.
Now in Injia's sunny clime,
Where I used to spend my time
A-servin' of 'Er Majesty the Queen,
Of all them blackfaced crew
The finest man I knew
Was our regimental bhisti, Gunga Din.
      He was "Din! Din! Din!
   You limpin' lump o' brick-dust, Gunga Din!
     Hi! slippery hitherao!
     Water, get it! Panee lao!
   You squidgy-nosed old idol, Gunga Din."

The uniform 'e wore
Was nothin' much before,
An' rather less than 'arf o' that be'ind,
For a piece o' twisty rag
An' a goatskin water-bag
Was all the field-equipment 'e could find.
When the sweatin' troop-train lay
In a sidin' through the day,

Where the 'eat would make your bloomin' eyebrows crawl,
We shouted "Harry By!"
Till our throats were bricky-dry,
Then we wopped 'im 'cause 'e couldn't serve us all.
      It was "Din! Din! Din!
   You 'eathen, where the mischief 'ave you been?
         You put some juldee in it
         Or I'll marrow you this minute
      If you don't fill up my helmet, Gunga Din!"

'E would dot an' carry one
Till the longest day was done;
An' 'e didn't seem to know the use o' fear.
If we charged or broke or cut,
You could bet your bloomin' nut,
'E'd be waitin' fifty paces right flank rear.
With 'is mussick on 'is back,
'E would skip with our attack,
An' watch us till the bugles made "Retire",
An' for all 'is dirty 'ide
'E was white, clear white, inside
When 'e went to tend the wounded under fire!
      It was "Din! Din! Din!"
   With the bullets kickin' dust-spots on the green.
         When the cartridges ran out,
         You could hear the front-files shout,
      "Hi! ammunition-mules an' Gunga Din!"

I shan't forgit the night
When I dropped be'ind the fight
With a bullet where my belt-plate should 'a' been.
I was chokin' mad with thirst,
An' the man that spied me first
Was our good old grinnin', gruntin' Gunga Din.
'E lifted up my 'ead,
An' he plugged me where I bled,
An' 'e guv me 'arf-a-pint o' water-green:
It was crawlin' and it stunk,
But of all the drinks I've drunk,

I'm gratefullest to one from Gunga Din.
    It was "Din! Din! Din!
  'Ere's a beggar with a bullet through 'is spleen;
    'E's chawin' up the ground,
    An' 'e's kickin' all around:
  For Gawd's sake git the water, Gunga Din!"

'E carried me away
To where a dooli lay,
An' a bullet come an' drilled the beggar clean.
'E put me safe inside,
An' just before 'e died,
"I 'ope you liked your drink", sez Gunga Din.
So I'll meet 'im later on
At the place where 'e is gone—
Where it's always double drill and no canteen;
'E'll be squattin' on the coals
Givin' drink to poor damned souls,
An' I'll get a swig in hell from Gunga Din!
    Yes, Din! Din! Din!
  You Lazarushian-leather Gunga Din!
    Though I've belted you and flayed you,
    By the livin' Gawd that made you,
  You're a better man than I am, Gunga Din!

Oonts

(Northern India Transport Train)

Wot makes the soldier's 'eart to penk, wot makes 'im to perspire?
It isn't standin' up to charge nor lyin' down to fire;
But it's everlastin' waitin' on a everlastin' road
For the commissariat camel an' 'is commissariat load.
    O the oont, O the oont, O the commissariat oont!

With 'is silly neck a-bobbin' like a basket full o' snakes;
We packs 'im like an idol, an' you ought to 'ear 'im grunt,
    An' when we gets 'im loaded up 'is blessed girth-rope
breaks.

Wot makes the rear-guard swear so 'ard when night is drorin' in,
An' every native follower is shiverin' for 'is skin?
It ain't the chanst o' being rushed by Paythans from the 'ills,
It's the commissariat camel puttin' on 'is bloomin' frills!
    O the oont, O the oont, O the hairy scary oont!
        A-trippin' over tent-ropes when we've got the night alarm!
    We socks 'im with a stretcher-pole an' 'eads 'im off in front,
        An' when we've saved 'is bloomin' life 'e chaws our bloomin'
arm.

The 'orse 'e knows above a bit, the bullock's but a fool,
The elephant's a gentleman, the battery-mule's a mule;
But the commissariat cam-u-el, when all is said an' done,
'E's a devil an' a ostrich an' a orphan-child in one.
    O the oont, O the oont, O the Gawd-forsaken oont!
        The lumpy-'umpy 'ummin'-bird a-singin' where 'e lies,
    'E's blocked the whole division from the rear-guard to the
front,
        An' when we get him up again—the beggar goes an' dies!

'E'll gall an' chafe an' lame an' fight—'e smells most awful vile;
'E'll lose 'isself for ever if you let 'im stray a mile;
'E's game to graze the 'ole day long an' 'owl the 'ole night through,
An' when 'e comes to greasy ground 'e splits 'isself in two.
    O the oont, O the oont, O the floppin', droppin' oont!
        When 'is long legs give from under an' 'is meltin' eye is dim,
    The tribes is up be'ind us, and the tribes is out in front—
        It ain't no jam for Tommy, but it's kites an' crows for 'im.

So when the cruel march is done, an' when the roads is blind,
An' when we sees the camp in front an' 'ears the shots be'ind,
Ho! then we strips 'is saddle off, and all 'is woes is past:
'E thinks on us that used 'im so, and gets revenge at last.
    O the oont, O the oont, O the floatin', bloatin' oont!

The late lamented camel in the water-cut 'e lies;
We keeps a mile be'ind 'im an' we keeps a mile in front,
But 'e gets into the drinkin'-casks, and then o' course we dies.

Loot

If you've ever stole a pheasant-egg be'ind the keeper's back,
If you've ever snigged the washin' from the line,
If you've ever crammed a gander in your bloomin' 'aversack,
　　You will understand this little song o' mine.
But the service rules are 'ard, an' from such we are debarred,
　　For the same with English morals does not suit.
　　　　　(Cornet: Toot! toot!)
W'y, they call a man a robber if 'e stuffs 'is marchin' clobber
　　With the—
(Chorus) Loo! loo! Lulu! lulu! Loo! loo! Loot! loot! loot!
　　　　　Ow the loot!
　　　　　Bloomin' loot!
　　　　That's the thing to make the boys git up an' shoot!
　　　　　It's the same with dogs an' men,
　　　　　If you'd make 'em come again
　　　　　Clap 'em forward with a Loo! loo! Lulu! Loot!
　　(ff) Whoopee! Tear 'im, puppy! Loo! loo! Lulu! Loot! loot! loot!

If you've knocked a nigger edgeways when 'e's thrustin' for your
　　life,
　　You must leave 'im very careful where 'e fell;
An' may thank your stars an' gaiters if you didn't feel 'is knife
　　That you ain't told off to bury 'im as well.
Then the sweatin' Tommies wonder as they spade the beggars
　　under
　　Why lootin' should be entered as a crime;
So if my song you'll 'ear, I will learn you plain an' clear
　　'Ow to pay yourself for fightin' overtime.
(Chorus) With the loot, . . .

Now remember when you're 'acking round a gilded Burma god
    That 'is eyes is very often precious stones;
An' if you treat a nigger to a dose o' cleanin'-rod
    'E's like to show you everything 'e owns.
When 'e won't prodooce no more, pour some water on the floor
    Where you 'ear it answer 'ollow to the boot
        (Cornet: Toot! toot!)—
When the ground begins to sink, shove your baynick down the chink,
    An' you're sure to touch the—
(Chorus) Loo! loo! Lulu! Loot! loot! loot!
        Ow the loot! . . .

When from 'ouse to 'ouse you're 'unting, you must always work in
    pairs—
    It 'alves the gain, but safer you will find—
For a single man gets bottled on them twisty-wisty stairs,
    An' a woman comes and clobs 'im from be'ind.
When you've turned 'em inside out, an' it seems beyond a doubt
    As if there weren't enough to dust a flute
        (Cornet: Toot! toot!)—
Before you sling your 'ook, at the 'ousetops take a look,
    For it's underneath the tiles they 'ide the loot.
(Chorus) Ow the loot! . . .

You can mostly square a Sergint an' a Quartermaster too,
    If you only take the proper way to go;
I could never keep my pickin's, but I've learned you all I knew—
    An' don't you never say I told you so.
An' now I'll bid good-bye, for I'm gettin' rather dry,
    An' I see another tunin' up to toot
        (Cornet: Toot! toot!)—
So 'ere's good-luck to those that wears the Widow's clo'es,
    An' the Devil send 'em all they want o' loot!
(Chorus)   Yes, the loot,
           Bloomin' loot!
           In the tunic an' the mess-tin an' the boot!
           It's the same with dogs an' men,
           If you'd make 'em come again

(fff) Whoop 'em forward with a Loo! loo! Lulu! Loot! loot! loot!

        Heeya! Sick 'im, puppy! Loo! loo! Lulu! Loot! loot! loot!

'Snarleyow'

This 'appened in a battle to a batt'ry of the corps
Which is first among the women an' amazin' first in war;
An' what the bloomin' battle was I don't remember now,
But Two's off-lead 'e answered to the name o' Snarleyow.
    Down in the Infantry, nobody cares;
    Down in the Cavalry, Colonel 'e swears;
    But down in the lead with the wheel at the flog
    Turns the bold Bombardier to a little whipped dog!

They was movin' into action, they was needed very sore,
To learn a little schoolin' to a native army corps,
They 'ad nipped against an uphill, they was tuckin' down the brow,
When a tricky, trundlin' roundshot give the knock to Snarleyow.

They cut 'im loose an' left 'im—'e was almost tore in two—
But he tried to follow after as a well-trained 'orse should do;
'E went an' fouled the limber, an' the Driver's Brother squeals:
"Pull up, pull up for Snarleyow—'is head's between 'is 'eels!"

The Driver 'umped 'is shoulder, for the wheels was goin' round,
An' there ain't no "Stop, conductor!" when a batt'ry's changin' ground;
Sez 'e: "I broke the beggar in, an' very sad I feels,
But I couldn't pull up, not for you—your 'ead between your 'eels!"

'E 'adn't 'ardly spoke the word, before a droppin' shell
A little right the batt'ry an' between the sections fell;
An' when the smoke 'ad cleared away, before the limber wheels,
There lay the Driver's Brother with 'is 'ead between 'is 'eels.

Then sez the Driver's Brother, an' 'is words was very plain,
"For Gawd's own sake get over me, an' put me out o' pain."
They saw 'is wounds was mortial, an' they judged that it was best,
So they took an' drove the limber straight across 'is back an' chest.

The Driver 'e give nothin' 'cept a little coughin' grunt,
But 'e swung 'is 'orses 'andsome when it came to "Action Front!"
An' if one wheel was juicy, you may lay your Monday head
'Twas juicier for the niggers when the case begun to spread.

The moril of this story, it is plainly to be seen:
You 'avn't got no families when servin' of the Queen—
You 'avn't got no brothers, fathers, sisters, wives, or sons—
If you want to win your battles take an' work your bloomin' guns!
 Down in the Infantry, nobody cares;
 Down in the Cavalry, Colonel 'e swears;
 But down in the lead with the wheel at the flog
 Turns the bold Bombardier to a little whipped dog!

The Widow at Windsor

'Ave you 'eard o' the Widow at Windsor
 With a hairy gold crown on 'er 'ead?
She 'as ships on the foam—she 'as millions at 'ome,
 An' she pays us poor beggars in red.
  (Ow, poor beggars in red!)
There's 'er nick on the cavalry 'orses,
 There's 'er mark on the medical stores—
An' 'er troopers you'll find with a fair wind be'ind
 That takes us to various wars.
  (Poor beggars!—barbarious wars!)
   Then 'ere's to the Widow at Windsor,
    An' 'ere's to the stores an' the guns,

The men an' the 'orses what makes up the forces
    O' Missis Victorier's sons.
      (Poor beggars! Victorier's sons!)

Walk wide o' the Widow at Windsor,
    For 'alf o' Creation she owns:
We 'ave bought 'er the same with the sword an' the flame,
    An' we've salted it down with our bones.
      (Poor beggars!—it's blue with our bones!)
Hands off o' the sons o' the Widow,
    Hands off o' the goods in 'er shop,
For the Kings must come down an' the Emperors frown
    When the Widow at Windsor says "Stop"!
      (Poor beggars!—we're sent to say "Stop"!)
        Then 'ere's to the Lodge o' the Widow,
          From the Pole to the Tropics it runs—
        To the Lodge that we tile with the rank an' the file,
          An' open in form with the guns.
        (Poor beggars!—it's always they guns!)

We 'ave 'eard o' the Widow at Windsor,
    It's safest to let 'er alone:
For 'er sentries we stand by the sea an' the land
    Wherever the bugles are blown.
      (Poor beggars!—an' don't we get blown!)
Take 'old o' the Wings o' the Mornin',
    An' flop round the earth till you're dead;
But you won't get away from the tune that they play
    To the bloomin' old rag over'ead.
      (Poor beggars!—it's 'ot over'ead!)
        Then 'ere's to the sons o' the Widow,
          Wherever, 'owever they roam.
        'Ere's all they desire, an' if they require
          A speedy return to their 'ome.
        (Poor beggars!—they'll never see 'ome!)

Belts

There was a row in Silver Street that's near to Dublin Quay,
Between an Irish regiment an' English cavalree;
It started at Revelly an' it lasted on till dark:
The first man dropped at Harrison's, the last forninst the Park.
    For it was:—"Belts, belts, belts, an' that's one for you!"
    An' it was "Belts, belts, belts, an' that's done for you!"
    O buckle an' tongue
    Was the song that we sung
    From Harrison's down to the Park!

There was a row in Silver Street—the regiments was out,
They called us "Delhi Rebels", an' we answered "Threes
    about!"
That drew them like a hornet's nest—we met them good an' large,
The English at the double an' the Irish at the charge.
    Then it was:—"Belts . . .

There was a row in Silver Street—an' I was in it too;
We passed the time o' day, an' then the belts went whirraru!
I misremember what occurred, but subsequint the storm
A Freeman's Journal Supplemint was all my uniform.
    O it was:—"Belts . . .

There was a row in Silver Street—they sent the Polis there,
The English were too drunk to know, the Irish didn't care;
But when they grew impertinint we simultaneous rose,
Till half o' them was Liffey mud an' half was tatthered clo'es.
    For it was:—"Belts . . .

There was a row in Silver Street—it might ha' raged till now,
But some one drew his side-arm clear, an' nobody knew how;
'Twas Hogan took the point an' dropped; we saw the red blood
    run:
An' so we all was murderers that started out in fun.
    While it was:—"Belts . . .

There was a row in Silver Street—but that put down the shine,
Wid each man whisperin' to his next: "'Twas never work o'
    mine!"
We went away like beaten dogs, an' down the street we bore him,
The poor dumb corpse that couldn't tell the bhoys were sorry for
    him.
    When it was:—"Belts . . .

There was a row in Silver Street—it isn't over yet,
For half of us are under guard wid punishments to get;
'Tis all a merricle to me as in the Clink I lie:
There was a row in Silver Street—begod, I wonder why!
    But it was:—"Belts, belts, belts, an' that's one for you!"
    An' it was "Belts, belts, belts, an' that's done for you!"
    O buckle an' tongue
    Was the song that we sung
    From Harrison's down to the Park!

The Young British Soldier

When the 'arf-made recruity goes out to the East
'E acts like a babe an' 'e drinks like a beast,
An' 'e wonders because 'e is frequent deceased
    Ere 'e's fit for to serve as a soldier.
        Serve, serve, serve as a soldier,
        Serve, serve, serve as a soldier,
        Serve, serve, serve as a soldier,
            So-oldier of the Queen!

Now all you recruities what's drafted to-day,
You shut up your rag-box an' 'ark to my lay,
An' I'll sing you a soldier as far as I may:
    A soldier what's fit for a soldier.
        Fit, fit, fit for a soldier . . .

First mind you steer clear o' the grog-sellers' huts,
For they sell you Fixed Bay'nets that rots out your guts—
Ay, drink that 'ud eat the live steel from your butts—
    An' it's bad for the young British soldier.
      Bad, bad, bad for the soldier . . .

When the cholera comes—as it will past a doubt—
Keep out of the wet and don't go on the shout,
For the sickness gets in as the liquor dies out,
    An' it crumples the young British soldier.
      Crum-, crum-, crumples the soldier . . .

But the worst o' your foes is the sun over'ead:
You must wear your 'elmet for all that is said:
If 'e finds you uncovered 'e'll knock you down dead,
    An' you'll die like a fool of a soldier.
      Fool, fool, fool of a soldier . . .

If you're cast for fatigue by a sergeant unkind,
Don't grouse like a woman nor crack on nor blind;
Be handy and civil, and then you will find
    That it's beer for the young British soldier.
      Beer, beer, beer for the soldier . . .

Now, if you must marry, take care she is old—
A troop-sergeant's widow's the nicest I'm told,
For beauty won't help if your rations is cold,
    Nor love ain't enough for a soldier.
      'Nough, 'nough, 'nough for a soldier . . .

If the wife should go wrong with a comrade, be loath
To shoot when you catch 'em—you'll swing, on my oath!—
Make 'im take 'er and keep 'er: that's Hell for them both,
    An' you're shut o' the curse of a soldier.
      Curse, curse, curse of a soldier . . .

When first under fire an' you're wishful to duck,
Don't look nor take 'eed at the man that is struck,
Be thankful you're livin', and trust to your luck

And march to your front like a soldier.
        Front, front, front like a soldier . . .

When 'arf of your bullets fly wide in the ditch,
Don't call your Martini a cross-eyed old bitch;
She's human as you are—you treat her as sich,
        An' she'll fight for the young British soldier.
        Fight, fight, fight for the soldier . . .

When shakin' their bustles like ladies so fine,
The guns o' the enemy wheel into line,
Shoot low at the limbers an' don't mind the shine,
        For noise never startles the soldier.
        Start-, start-, startles the soldier . . .

If your officer's dead and the sergeants look white,
Remember it's ruin to run from a fight:
So take open order, lie down, and sit tight,
        And wait for supports like a soldier.
        Wait, wait, wait like a soldier . . .

When you're wounded and left on Afghanistan's plains,
And the women come out to cut up what remains,
Jest roll to your rifle and blow out your brains
        An' go to your Gawd like a soldier.
        Go, go, go like a soldier,
        Go, go, go like a soldier,
        Go, go, go like a soldier,
                So-oldier of the Queen!

Mandalay

By the old Moulmein Pagoda, lookin' eastward to the sea,
There's a Burma girl a-settin', and I know she thinks o' me;
For the wind is in the palm-trees, and the temple-bells they say:

"Come you back, you British soldier; come you back to Mandalay!"
　　Come you back to Mandalay,
　　Where the old Flotilla lay:
　　Can't you 'ear their paddles chunkin' from Rangoon to Mandalay?
　　On the road to Mandalay,
　　Where the flyin'-fishes play,
　　An' the dawn comes up like thunder outer China 'crost the Bay!

'Er petticoat was yaller an' 'er little cap was green,
An' 'er name was Supi-yaw-lat—jes' the same as Theebaw's Queen,
An' I seed her first a-smokin' of a whackin' white cheroot,
An' a-wastin' Christian kisses on an 'eathen idol's foot:
　　Bloomin' idol made o'mud—
　　Wot they called the Great Gawd Budd—
　　Plucky lot she cared for idols when I kissed 'er where she stud!
　　On the road to Mandalay . . .

When the mist was on the rice-fields an' the sun was droppin' slow,
She'd git 'er little banjo an' she'd sing "Kulla-lo-lo!"
With 'er arm upon my shoulder an' 'er cheek agin' my cheek
We useter watch the steamers an' the hathis pilin' teak.
　　Elephints a-pilin' teak
　　In the sludgy, squdgy creek,
　　Where the silence 'ung that 'eavy you was 'arf afraid to speak!
　　On the road to Mandalay . . .

But that's all shove be'ind me—long ago an' fur away,
An' there ain't no 'busses runnin' from the Bank to Mandalay;
An' I'm learnin' 'ere in London what the ten-year soldier tells:
"If you've 'eard the East a-callin', you won't never 'eed naught else."
　　No! you won't 'eed nothin' else
　　But them spicy garlic smells,
　　An' the sunshine an' the palm-trees an' the tinkly temple-bells;
　　On the road to Mandalay . . .

I am sick o' wastin' leather on these gritty pavin'-stones,
An' the blasted Henglish drizzle wakes the fever in my bones;
Tho' I walks with fifty 'ousemaids outer Chelsea to the Strand,
An' they talks a lot o' lovin', but wot do they understand?

Beefy face an' grubby 'and—
Law! wot do they understand?
I've a neater, sweeter maiden in a cleaner, greener land!
On the road to Mandalay . . .

Ship me somewheres east of Suez, where the best is like the worst,
Where there aren't no Ten Commandments an' a man can raise a
    thirst;
For the temple-bells are callin', an' it's there that I would be—
By the old Moulmein Pagoda, looking lazy at the sea;
    On the road to Mandalay,
    Where the old Flotilla lay,
    With our sick beneath the awnings when we went to Mandalay!
    On the road to Mandalay,
    Where the flyin'-fishes play,
    An' the dawn comes up like thunder outer China 'crost the Bay!

Troopin'

(Our Army in the East)

Troopin', troopin', troopin' to the sea:
'Ere's September come again—the six-year men are free.
O leave the dead be'ind us, for they cannot come away
To where the ship's a-coalin' up that takes us 'ome to-day.
    We're goin' 'ome, we're goin' 'ome,
        Our ship is at the shore,
    An' you must pack your 'aversack,
        For we won't come back no more.
    Ho, don't you grieve for me,
        My lovely Mary-Ann,
    For I'll marry you yit on a fourp'ny bit
        As a time-expired man.

The Malabar's in 'arbour with the Jumner at 'er tail,
An' the time-expired's waitin' of 'is orders for to sail.
Ho! the weary waitin' when on Khyber 'ills we lay,
But the time-expired's waitin' of 'is orders 'ome to-day.

They'll turn us out at Portsmouth wharf in cold an' wet an' rain,
All wearin' Injian cotton kit, but we will not complain;
They'll kill us of pneumonia—for that's their little way—
But damn the chills and fever, men, we're goin' 'ome to-day!

Troopin', troopin', winter's round again!
See the new draf's pourin' in for the old campaign;
Ho, you poor recruities, but you've got to earn your pay—
What's the last from Lunnon, lads? We're goin' there to-day.

Troopin', troopin', give another cheer—
'Ere's to English women an' a quart of English beer.
The Colonel an' the regiment an' all who've got to stay,
Gawd's mercy strike 'em gentle—Whoop! we're goin' 'ome to-
        day.
        We're goin' 'ome, we're goin' 'ome,
            Our ship is at the shore,
        An' you must pack your 'aversack,
            For we won't come back no more.
        Ho, don't you grieve for me,
            My lovely Mary-Ann,
        For I'll marry you yit on a fourp'ny bit
            As a time-expired man.

The Widow's Party

"Where have you been this while away,
        Johnnie, Johnnie?"
'Long with the rest on a picnic lay,
        Johnnie, my Johnnie, aha!

They called us out of the barrack-yard
To Gawd knows where from Gosport Hard,
And you can't refuse when you get the card,
    And the Widow gives the party.
        (Bugle: Ta—rara—ra-ra-rara!)

"What did you get to eat and drink,
    Johnnie, Johnnie?"
Standing water as thick as ink,
    Johnnie, my Johnnie, aha!
A bit o' beef that were three year stored,
A bit o' mutton as tough as a board,
And a fowl we killed with a sergeant's sword,
    When the Widow give the party.

"What did you do for knives and forks,
    Johnnie, Johnnie?"
We carries 'em with us wherever we walks,
    Johnnie, my Johnnie, aha!
And some was sliced and some was halved,
And some was crimped and some was carved,
And some was gutted and some was starved,
    When the Widow give the party.

"What ha' you done with half your mess,
    Johnnie, Johnnie?"
They couldn't do more and they wouldn't do less,
    Johnnie, my Johnnie, aha!
They ate their whack and they drank their fill,
And I think the rations has made them ill,
For half my comp'ny's lying still
    Where the Widow give the party.

"How did you get away—away,
    Johnnie, Johnnie?"
On the broad o' my back at the end o' the day,
    Johnnie, my Johnnie, aha!
I comed away like a bleedin' toff,
For I got four niggers to carry me off,

As I lay in the bight of a canvas trough,
  When the Widow give the party.

"What was the end of all the show,
    Johnnie, Johnnie?"
Ask my Colonel, for I don't know,
    Johnnie, my Johnnie, aha!
We broke a King and we built a road—
A court-house stands where the reg'ment goed.
And the river's clean where the raw blood flowed
    When the Widow give the party.
        (Bugle: Ta—rara—ra-ra-rara!)

Ford o' Kabul River

Kabul town's by Kabul river—
  Blow the bugle, draw the sword—
There I lef' my mate for ever,
  Wet an' drippin' by the ford.
    Ford, ford, ford o' Kabul river,
      Ford o' Kabul river in the dark!
    There's the river up and brimmin', an' there's 'arf a squadron swimmin'
      'Cross the ford o' Kabul river in the dark.

Kabul town's a blasted place—
  Blow the bugle, draw the sword—
'Strewth I sha'n't forget 'is face
  Wet an' drippin' by the ford!
    Ford, ford, ford o' Kabul river,
      Ford o' Kabul river in the dark!
    Keep the crossing-stakes beside you, an' they will surely guide you
      'Cross the ford o' Kabul river in the dark.

Kabul town is sun and dust—
    Blow the bugle, draw the sword—
I'd ha' sooner drownded fust
    'Stead of 'im beside the ford.
        Ford, ford, ford o' Kabul river,
            Ford o' Kabul river in the dark!
        You can 'ear the 'orses threshin', you can 'ear the men a-splashin',
            'Cross the ford o' Kabul river in the dark.

Kabul town was ours to take—
    Blow the bugle, draw the sword—
I'd ha' left it for 'is sake—
    'Im that left me by the ford.
        Ford, ford, ford o' Kabul river,
            Ford o' Kabul river in the dark!
        It's none so bloomin' dry there; ain't you never comin' nigh there,
            'Cross the ford o' Kabul river in the dark?

Kabul town'll go to hell—
    Blow the bugle, draw the sword—
'Fore I see him 'live an' well—
    'Im the best beside the ford.
        Ford, ford, ford o' Kabul river,
            Ford o' Kabul river in the dark!
        Gawd 'elp 'em if they blunder, for their boots'll pull 'em under,
            By the ford o' Kabul river in the dark.

Turn your 'orse from Kabul town—
    Blow the bugle, draw the sword—
'Im an' 'arf my troop is down,
    Down an' drownded by the ford.
        Ford, ford, ford o' Kabul river,
            Ford o' Kabul river in the dark!
        There's the river low an' fallin', but it ain't no use o' callin'
            'Cross the ford o' Kabul river in the dark.

Gentlemen-Rankers

To the legion of the lost ones, to the cohort of the damned,
    To my brethren in their sorrow overseas,
Sings a gentleman of England cleanly bred, machinely crammed,
    And a trooper of the Empress, if you please.
Yea, a trooper of the forces who has run his own six horses,
    And faith he went the pace and went it blind,
And the world was more than kin while he held the ready tin,
    But to-day the Sergeant's something less than kind.
      We're poor little lambs who've lost our way,
        Baa! Baa! Baa!
      We're little black sheep who've gone astray,
        Baa—aa—aa!
      Gentlemen-rankers out on the spree,
      Damned from here to Eternity,
      God ha' mercy on such as we,
        Baa! Yah! Bah!

Oh, it's sweet to sweat through stables, sweet to empty kitchen slops,
    And it's sweet to hear the tales the troopers tell,
To dance with blowzy housemaids at the regimental hops
    And thrash the cad who says you waltz too well.
Yes, it makes you cock-a-hoop to be "Rider" to your troop,
    And branded with a blasted worsted spur,
When you envy, O how keenly, one poor Tommy being cleanly
    Who blacks your boots and sometimes calls you "Sir".

If the home we never write to, and the oaths we never keep,
    And all we know most distant and most dear,
Across the snoring barrack-room return to break our sleep,
    Can you blame us if we soak ourselves in beer?
When the drunken comrade mutters and the great guard-lantern
    gutters
    And the horror of our fall is written plain,
Every secret, self-revealing on the aching white-washed ceiling,
    Do you wonder that we drug ourselves from pain?

We have done with Hope and Honour, we are lost to Love and Truth,
    We are dropping down the ladder rung by rung,
And the measure of our torment is the measure of our youth.
    God help us, for we knew the worst too young!
Our shame is clean repentance for the crime that brought the
    sentence,
    Our pride it is to know no spur of pride,
And the Curse of Reuben holds us till an alien turf enfolds us
    And we die, and none can tell Them where we died.
        We're poor little lambs who've lost our way,
            Baa! Baa! Baa!
        We're little black sheep who've gone astray,
            Baa—aa—aa!
        Gentlemen-rankers out on the spree,
        Damned from here to Eternity,
        God ha' mercy on such as we,
            Baa! Yah! Bah!

Route Marchin'

We're marchin' on relief over Injia's sunny plains,
A little front o' Christmas-time an' just be'ind the Rains;
Ho! get away you bullock-man, you've 'eard the bugle blowed,
There's a regiment a-comin' down the Grand Trunk Road;
        With its best foot first
        And the road a-sliding past,
        An' every bloomin' campin'-ground exactly like the last;
        While the Big Drum says,
        With 'is "rowdy-dowdy-dow!"—
        "Kiko kissywarsti don't you hamsher argy jow?"
Oh, there's them Injian temples to admire when you see,
There's the peacock round the corner an' the monkey up the tree,
An' there's that rummy silver grass a-wavin' in the wind,
An' the old Grand Trunk a-trailin' like a rifle-sling be'ind.
        While it's best foot first, . . .

At half-past five's Revelly, an' our tents they down must come,
Like a lot of button mushrooms when you pick 'em up at 'ome.
But it's over in a minute, an' at six the column starts,
While the women and the kiddies sit an' shiver in the carts.
  An' it's best foot first, . . .

Oh, then it's open order, an' we lights our pipes an' sings,
An' we talks about our rations an' a lot of other things,
An' we thinks o' friends in England, an' we wonders what they're
  at,
An' 'ow they would admire for to hear us sling the bat.
  An' it's best foot first, . . .
It's none so bad o' Sunday, when you're lyin' at your ease,
To watch the kites a-wheelin' round them feather-'eaded trees,
For although there ain't no women, yet there ain't no barrick-
  yards,
So the orficers goes shootin' an' the men they plays at cards.
  Till it's best foot first, . . .

So 'ark an' 'eed, you rookies, which is always grumblin' sore,
There's worser things than marchin' from Umballa to Cawnpore;
An' if your 'eels are blistered an' they feels to 'urt like 'ell,
You drop some tallow in your socks an' that will make 'em well.
  For it's best foot first, . . .

We're marchin' on relief over Injia's coral strand,
Eight 'undred fightin' Englishmen, the Colonel, and the Band;
Ho! get away you bullock-man, you've 'eard the bugle blowed,
There's a regiment a-comin' down the Grand Trunk Road;
  With its best foot first
  And the road a-sliding past,
  An' every bloomin' campin'-ground exactly like the last;
  While the Big Drum says,
  With 'is "rowdy-dowdy-dow!"—
  "Kiko kissywarsti don't you hamsher argy jow?"

Shillin' a Day

My name is O'Kelly, I've heard the Revelly
From Birr to Bareilly, from Leeds to Lahore,
Hong-Kong and Peshawur,
Lucknow and Etawah,
And fifty-five more all endin' in "pore".
Black Death and his quickness, the depth and the thickness,
Of sorrow and sickness I've known on my way,
But I'm old and I'm nervis,
I'm cast from the Service,
And all I deserve is a shillin' a day.
    (Chorus) Shillin' a day,
                Bloomin' good pay—
                Lucky to touch it, a shillin' a day!

Oh, it drives me half crazy to think of the days I
Went slap for the Ghazi, my sword at my side,
When we rode Hell-for-leather
Both squadrons together,
That didn't care whether we lived or we died.
But it's no use despairin', my wife must go charin'
An' me commissairin' the pay-bills to better,
So if me you be'old
In the wet and the cold,
By the Grand Metropold, won't you give me a letter?
    (Full chorus) Give 'im a letter—
                'Can't do no better,
                Late Troop-Sergeant-Major an'—runs with a letter!
                Think what 'e's been,
                Think what 'e's seen,
                Think of his pension an'—

                Gawd save the Queen

'Bobs'

There's a little red-faced man,
    Which is Bobs,
Rides the tallest 'orse 'e can-
    Our Bobs,
If it bucks or kicks or rears,
'E can sit for twenty years
With a smile round both 'is ears-
    Can't yer, Bobs?

Then 'ere's to Bobs Bahadur-
    Little Bobs, Bobs, Bobs!
'E's or pukka Kandaharder-
    Fightin' Bobs, Bobs, Bobs!
'E's the Dook of Aggy Chel;
'E's the man that done us well,
An' we'll follow 'im to 'ell-
    Won't we Bobs?

If a limber's slipped a trace,
    'Ook on Bobs.
If a marker's lost 'is place,
    Dress by Bobs.
For 'e's eyes all up 'is coat,
An' a bugle in 'is throat,
An' you will not play the goat
    Under Bobs.

'E's a little down on drink,
    Chaplain Bobs;
But it keeps us outer Clink-
    Don't it Bobs?
So we will not complain
Tho' 'e's water on the brain,

If 'e leads us straight again-
      Blue-light Bobs.

If you stood 'im on 'is head
      Father Bobs,
You could spill a quart o' lead
      Outer Bobs.
'E's been at it thirty years,
An' amassin souveneers
In the way o' slugs an' spears-
      Ain't yer, Bobs?

What 'e does not Know o' war,
      Gen'ral Bobs,
You can arst the shop next door-
      Can't they, Bobs?
Oh, 'e's little, but he's wise;
'E's a terror for 'is size,
An'-'e-does-not-advertise-
      Do yer, Bobs?

Now they've made a bloomin' Lord
      Outer Bobs,
Which was but 'is fair reward-
      Weren't it Bobs?
So 'e'll wear a coronet
Where 'is 'elmet used to set;
But we know you won't forget-
      Will yer, Bobs?

Then 'ere's to Bobs Bahadur-
      Little Bobs, Bobs, Bobs!
Pocket-Wellin'ton an' arder -
      Fightin' Bobs, Bobs, Bobs!
This ain't no bloomin' ode,
But you've 'elped the soldier's load,
An' for benefits bestowed,
      Bless yer, Bobs!

'Back to the Army Again'

I'm 'ere in a ticky ulster an' a broken billycock 'at,
A-layin' on to the sergeant I don't know a gun from a bat;
My shirt's doin' duty for jacket, my sock's stickin' out o' my boots,
An' I'm learnin' the damned old goose-step along o' the new
recruits!

Back to the Army again, sergeant,
   Back to the Army again.
Don't look so 'ard, for I 'aven't no card,
   I'm back to the Army again!

I done my six years' service. 'Er Majesty sez: "Good-day—
You'll please to come when you're rung for, an' 'ere's your 'ole
back-pay;
An' fourpence a day for baccy—an' bloomin' gen'rous, too;
An' now you can make your fortune—the same as your orf'cers
do."

Back to the Army again, sergeant,
   Back to the Army again;
'Ow did I learn to do right-about turn?
   I'm back to the Army again!

A man o' four-an'-twenty that 'asn't learned of a trade—
Beside "Reserve" agin' him—'e'd better be never made.
I tried my luck for a quarter, an' that was enough for me,
An' I thought of 'Er Majesty's barricks, an' I thought I'd go an'
see.

Back to the Army again, sergeant,
   Back to the Army again;
'Tisn't my fault if I dress when I 'alt—
   I'm back to the Army again!

The sergeant arst no questions, but 'e winked the other eye,
'E sez to me, "'Shun!" an' I shunted, the same as in days gone by;

47

For 'e saw the set o' my shoulders, an' I couldn't 'elp 'oldin' straight
When me an' the other rookies come under the barrick-gate.

> Back to the Army again, sergeant,
>> Back to the Army again;
> 'Oo would ha' thought I could carry an' port?
>> I'm back to the Army again!

I took my bath, an' I wallered—for, Gawd, I needed it so!
I smelt the smell o' the barricks, I 'eard the bugles go.
I 'eard the feet on the gravel—the feet o' the men what drill—
An' I sez to my flutterin' 'eart-strings, I sez to 'em, "Peace, be still!"

> Back to the Army again, sergeant,
>> Back to the Army again;
> 'Oo said I knew when the Jumner was due?
>> I'm back to the Army again!

I carried my slops to the tailor; I sez to 'im, "None o' your lip!
You tight 'em over the shoulders, an' loose 'em over the 'ip,
For the set o' the tunic's 'orrid." An' 'e sez to me, "Strike me dead,
But I thought you was used to the business!" an' so 'e done what
I said.

> Back to the Army again, sergeant,
>> Back to the Army again.
> Rather too free with my fancies? Wot—me?
>> I'm back to the Army again!

Next week I'll 'ave 'em fitted; I'll buy me a swagger-cane;
They'll let me free o' the barricks to walk on the Hoe again
In the name o' William Parsons, that used to be Edward Clay,
An'—any pore beggar that wants it can draw my fourpence a day!

> Back to the Army again, sergeant,
>> Back to the Army again:
> Out o' the cold an' the rain, sergeant,
>> Out o' the cold an' the rain.

'Oo's there?
A man that's too good to be lost you,
A man that is 'andled an' made—
A man that will pay what 'e cost you
In learnin' the others their trade—parade!
You're droppin' the pick o' the Army
Because you don't 'elp 'em remain,
But drives 'em to cheat to get out o' the street
An' back to the Army again!

'Birds of Prey' March

March! The mud is cakin' good about our trousies.
    Front!—eyes front, an' watch the Colour-casin's drip.
Front! The faces of the women in the 'ouses
    Ain't the kind o' things to take aboard the ship.

    Cheer! An' we'll never march to victory.
    Cheer! An' we'll never live to 'ear the cannon roar!
        The Large Birds o' Prey
        They will carry us away,
    An' you'll never see your soldiers any more!

Wheel! Oh, keep your touch; we're goin' round a corner.
    Time!—mark time, an' let the men be'ind us close.
Lord! the transport's full, an' 'alf our lot not on 'er—
    Cheer, O cheer! We're going off where no one knows.

March! The Devil's none so black as 'e is painted!
    Cheer! We'll 'ave some fun before we're put away.
'Alt, an' 'and 'er out—a woman's gone and fainted!
    Cheer! Get on—Gawd 'elp the married men to-day!

Hoi! Come up, you 'ungry beggars, to yer sorrow.
    ('Ear them say they want their tea, an' want it quick!)

You won't have no mind for slingers, not to-morrow—
    No; you'll put the 'tween-decks stove out, bein' sick!

'Alt! The married kit 'as all to go before us!
    'Course it's blocked the bloomin' gangway up again!
Cheer, O cheer the 'Orse Guards watchin' tender o'er us,
    Keepin' us since eight this mornin' in the rain!

Stuck in 'eavy marchin'-order, sopped and wringin'—
    Sick, before our time to watch 'er 'eave an' fall,
'Ere's your 'appy 'ome at last, an' stop your singin'.
    'Alt! Fall in along the troop-deck! Silence all!

    Cheer! For we'll never live to see no bloomin' victory!
    Cheer! An' we'll never live to 'ear the cannon roar! (One cheer
    more!)
        The jackal an' the kite
        'Ave an 'ealthy appetite,
    An' you'll never see your soldiers any more! ('Ip! Urroar!)
        The eagle an' the crow
        They are waitin' ever so,
    An' you'll never see your soldiers any more! ('Ip! Urroar!)
        Yes, the Large Birds o' Prey
        They will carry us away,
    An' you'll never see your soldiers any more!

'Soldier an' Salor Too'

As I was spittin' into the Ditch aboard o' the Crocodile,
I seed a man on a man-o'-war got up in the Reg'lars' style.
'E was scrapin' the paint from off of 'er plates,
    an' I sez to 'im, "'Oo are you?"
Sez 'e, "I'm a Jolly—'Er Majesty's Jolly—soldier an' sailor too!"
Now 'is work begins by Gawd knows when, and 'is work is never
    through;

'E isn't one o' the reg'lar Line, nor 'e isn't one of the crew.
'E's a kind of a giddy harumfrodite—soldier an' sailor too!

An' after I met 'im all over the world, a-doin' all kinds of things,
Like landin' 'isself with a Gatlin' gun to talk to them 'eathen kings;
'E sleeps in an 'ammick instead of a cot,
      an' 'e drills with the deck on a slew,
An' 'e sweats like a Jolly—'Er Majesty's Jolly—soldier an' sailor
      too!
For there isn't a job on the top o' the earth the beggar don't know,
      nor do—
You can leave 'im at night on a bald man's 'ead, to paddle 'is own
      canoe—
'E's a sort of a bloomin' cosmopolouse—soldier an' sailor too.

We've fought 'em in trooper, we've fought 'em in dock,
      and drunk with 'em in betweens,
When they called us the seasick scull'ry-maids,
      an' we called 'em the Ass Marines;
But, when we was down for a double fatigue, from Woolwich to
      Bernardmyo,
We sent for the Jollies—'Er Majesty's Jollies—soldier an' sailor too!
They think for 'emselves, an' they steal for 'emselves,
      and they never ask what's to do,
But they're camped an' fed an' they're up an' fed before our bugle's
      blew.
Ho! they ain't no limpin' procrastitutes—soldier an' sailor too.

You may say we are fond of an 'arness-cut, or 'ootin' in barrick-yards,
Or startin' a Board School mutiny along o' the Onion Guards;
But once in a while we can finish in style for the ends of the earth
      to view,
The same as the Jollies—'Er Majesty's Jollies—soldier an' sailor too!
They come of our lot, they was brothers to us;
      they was beggars we'd met an' knew;
Yes, barrin' an inch in the chest an' the arm, they was doubles o'
      me an' you;
For they weren't no special chrysanthemums—soldier an' sailor too!

To take your chance in the thick of a rush, with firing all about,
Is nothing so bad when you've cover to 'and, an' leave an' likin' to
    shout;
But to stand an' be still to the Birken'ead drill
    is a damn tough bullet to chew,
An' they done it, the Jollies—'Er Majesty's Jollies—
    soldier an' sailor too!
Their work was done when it 'adn't begun; they was younger nor
    me an' you;
Their choice it was plain between drownin' in 'eaps
    an' bein' mopped by the screw,
So they stood an' was still to the Birken'ead drill, soldier an' sailor too!

We're most of us liars, we're 'arf of us thieves,
    an' the rest are as rank as can be,
But once in a while we can finish in style
    (which I 'ope it won't 'appen to me).
But it makes you think better o' you an' your friends,
    an' the work you may 'ave to do,
When you think o' the sinkin' Victorier's Jollies—soldier an' sailor
    too!
Now there isn't no room for to say ye don't know—
    they 'ave proved it plain and true—
That whether it's Widow, or whether it's ship, Victorier's work is
    to do,
An' they done it, the Jollies—'Er Majesty's Jollies—
    soldier an' sailor too!

Sappers

When the Waters were dried an' the Earth did appear,
    ("It's all one," says the Sapper),
The Lord He created the Engineer,
    Her Majesty's Royal Engineer,
    With the rank and pay of a Sapper!

When the Flood come along for an extra monsoon,
'Twas Noah constructed the first pontoon
    To the plans of Her Majesty's, etc.

But after fatigue in the wet an' the sun,
Old Noah got drunk, which he wouldn't ha' done
    If he'd trained with, etc.

When the Tower o' Babel had mixed up men's bat,
Some clever civilian was managing that,
    An' none of, etc.

When the Jews had a fight at the foot of a hill,
Young Joshua ordered the sun to stand still,
    For he was a Captain of Engineers, etc.

When the Children of Israel made bricks without straw,
They were learnin' the regular work of our Corps,
    The work of, etc.

For ever since then, if a war they would wage,
Behold us a-shinin' on history's page—
    First page for, etc.

We lay down their sidings an' help 'em entrain,
An' we sweep up their mess through the bloomin' campaign,
    In the style of, etc.

They send us in front with a fuse an' a mine
To blow up the gates that are rushed by the Line,
    But bent by, etc.

They send us behind with a pick an' a spade,
To dig for the guns of a bullock-brigade
    Which has asked for, etc.

We work under escort in trousers and shirt,
An' the heathen they plug us tail-up in the dirt,
    Annoying, etc.

We blast out the rock an' we shovel the mud,
We make 'em good roads an'—they roll down the khud,
　　Reporting, etc.

We make 'em their bridges, their wells, an' their huts,
An' the telegraph-wire the enemy cuts,
　　An' it's blamed on, etc.

An' when we return, an' from war we would cease,
They grudge us adornin' the billets of peace,
　　Which are kept for, etc.

We build 'em nice barracks—they swear they are bad,
That our Colonels are Methodist, married or mad,
　　Insultin', etc.

They haven't no manners nor gratitude too,
For the more that we help 'em, the less will they do,
　　But mock at, etc.

Now the Line's but a man with a gun in his hand,
An' Cavalry's only what horses can stand,
　　When helped by, etc.

Artillery moves by the leave o' the ground,
But we are the men that do something all round,
　　For we are, etc.

I have stated it plain, an' my argument's thus
　　("It's all one," says the Sapper),
There's only one Corps which is perfect—that's us;
　　An' they call us Her Majesty's Engineers,
　　Her Majesty's Royal Engineers,
　　With the rank and pay of a Sapper!

That Day

It got beyond all orders an' it got beyond all 'ope;
    It got to shammin' wounded an' retirin' from the 'alt.
'Ole companies was lookin' for the nearest road to slope;
    It were just a bloomin' knock-out—an' our fault!

    Now there ain't no chorus 'ere to give,
        Nor there ain't no band to play;
    An' I wish I was dead 'fore I done what I did,
        Or seen what I seed that day!

We was sick o' bein' punished, an' we let 'em know it, too;
    An' a company-commander up an' 'it us with a sword,
An' some one shouted "'Ook it!" an' it come to sove-ki-poo,
    An' we chucked our rifles from us—O my Gawd!

There was thirty dead an' wounded on the ground we wouldn't
    keep—
    No, there wasn't more than twenty when the front begun to go;
But, Christ! along the line o' flight they cut us up like sheep,
    An' that was all we gained by doin' so.

I 'eard the knives be'ind me, but I dursn't face my man,
    Nor I don't know where I went to, 'cause I didn't 'alt to see,
Till I 'eard a beggar squealin' out for quarter as 'e ran,
    An' I thought I knew the voice an'—it was me!

We was 'idin' under bedsteads more than 'arf a march away;
    We was lyin' up like rabbits all about the countryside;
An' the major cursed 'is Maker 'cause 'e lived to see that day,
    An' the colonel broke 'is sword acrost, an' cried.

We was rotten 'fore we started—we was never disciplined;
    We made it out a favour if an order was obeyed;
Yes, every little drummer 'ad 'is rights an' wrongs to mind,
    So we had to pay for teachin'—an' we paid!

The papers 'id it 'andsome, but you know the Army knows;
 We was put to groomin' camels till the regiments withdrew,
An' they gave us each a medal for subduin' England's foes,
 An' I 'ope you like my song—because it's true!

  An' there ain't no chorus 'ere to give,
   Nor there ain't no band to play;
  But I wish I was dead 'fore I done what I did,
   Or seen what I seed that day!

'The Men that fought at Minden'

A Song of Instruction

The men that fought at Minden, they was rookies in their time—
 So was them that fought at Waterloo!
All the 'ole command, yuss, from Minden to Maiwand,
 They was once dam' sweeps like you!

  Then do not be discouraged, 'Eaven is your 'elper,
   We'll learn you not to forget;
  An' you mustn't swear an' curse, or you'll only catch it worse,
  For we'll make you soldiers yet!

The men that fought at Minden, they 'ad stocks beneath their chins,
 Six inch 'igh an' more;
But fatigue it was their pride, and they would not be denied
 To clean the cook-'ouse floor.

The men that fought at Minden, they had anarchistic bombs
 Served to 'em by name of 'and-grenades;
But they got it in the eye (same as you will by-an'-by)
 When they clubbed their field-parades.

The men that fought at Minden, they 'ad buttons up an' down,
    Two-an'-twenty dozen of 'em told;
But they didn't grouse an' shirk at an hour's extry work,
    They kept 'em bright as gold.

The men that fought at Minden, they was armed with musketoons,
    Also, they was drilled by 'alberdiers;
I don't know what they were, but the sergeants took good care
    They washed be'ind their ears.

The men that fought at Minden, they 'ad ever cash in 'and
    Which they did not bank nor save,
But spent it gay an' free on their betters—such as me—
    For the good advice I gave.

The men that fought at Minden, they was civil—yuss, they was—
    Never didn't talk o' rights an' wrongs,
But they got it with the toe (same as you will get it—so!)—
    For interrupting songs.

The men that fought at Minden, they was several other things
    Which I don't remember clear;
But that's the reason why, now the six-year men are dry,
    The rooks will stand the beer!

    Then do not be discouraged, 'Eaven is your 'elper,
        We'll learn you not to forget;
    An' you mustn't swear an' curse, or you'll only catch it worse,
        For we'll make you soldiers yet!

    Soldiers yet, if you've got it in you—
        All for the sake of the Core;
    Soldiers yet, if we 'ave to skin you—
        Run an' get the beer, Johnny Raw—Johnny Raw!
    Ho! run an' get the beer, Johnny Raw!

Cholera Camp

We've got the cholerer in camp—it's worse than forty fights;
　　We're dyin' in the wilderness the same as Isrulites;
It's before us, an' be'ind us, an' we cannot get away,
　　An' the doctor's just reported we've ten more to-day!

　　　Oh, strike your camp an' go, the Bugle's callin',
　　　　The Rains are fallin'—
　　　The dead are bushed an' stoned to keep 'em safe below;
　　　The Band's a-doin' all she knows to cheer us;
　　　The Chaplain's gone and prayed to Gawd to 'ear us—
　　　　To 'ear us—
　　　O Lord, for it's a-killin' of us so!

Since August, when it started, it's been stickin' to our tail,
Though they've 'ad us out by marches an' they've 'ad us back by rail;
But it runs as fast as troop-trains, and we cannot get away;
An' the sick-list to the Colonel makes ten more to-day.

There ain't no fun in women nor there ain't no bite to drink;
It's much too wet for shootin', we can only march and think;
An' at evenin', down the nullahs, we can 'ear the jackals say,
"Get up, you rotten beggars, you've ten more to-day!"

'Twould make a monkey cough to see our way o' doin' things—
Lieutenants takin' companies an' captains takin' wings,
An' Lances actin' Sergeants—eight file to obey—
For we've lots o' quick promotion on ten deaths a day!

Our Colonel's white an' twitterly—'e gets no sleep nor food,
But mucks about in 'orspital where nothing does no good.
'E sends us 'eaps o' comforts, all bought from 'is pay—
But there aren't much comfort 'andy on ten deaths a day.

Our Chaplain's got a banjo, an' a skinny mule 'e rides,
An' the stuff 'e says an' sings us, Lord, it makes us split our sides!
With 'is black coat-tails a-bobbin' to Ta-ra-ra Boom-der-ay!

'E's the proper kind o' padre for ten deaths a day.

An' Father Victor 'elps 'im with our Roman Catholicks—
He knows an 'eap of Irish songs an' rummy conjurin' tricks;
An' the two they works together when it comes to play or pray;
So we keep the ball a-rollin' on ten deaths a day.

We've got the cholerer in camp—we've got it 'ot an' sweet;
It ain't no Christmas dinner, but it's 'elped an' we must eat.
We've gone beyond the funkin', 'cause we've found it doesn't pay,
An' we're rockin' round the Districk on ten deaths a day!

    Then strike your camp an' go, the Rains are fallin',
        The Bugle's callin'!
    The dead are bushed an' stoned to keep 'em safe below!
    An' them that do not like it they can lump it,
    An' them that cannot stand it they can jump it;
    We've got to die somewhere—some way—some'ow—
    We might as well begin to do it now!
    Then, Number One, let down the tent-pole slow,
    Knock out the pegs an' 'old the corners—so!
    Fold in the flies, furl up the ropes, an' stow!
    Oh, strike—oh, strike your camp an' go!
        (Gawd 'elp us!)

The Ladies

I've taken my fun where I've found it;
    I've rogued an' I've ranged in my time;
I've 'ad my pickin' o' sweet'earts,
    An' four o' the lot was prime.
One was an 'arf-caste widow,
    One was a woman at Prome,
One was the wife of a jemadar-sais,
    An' one is a girl at 'ome.

Now I aren't no 'and with the ladies,
    For, takin' 'em all along,
You never can say till you've tried 'em,
    An' then you are like to be wrong.
There's times when you'll think that you mightn't,
    There's times when you'll know that you might;
But the things you will learn from the Yellow an' Brown,
    They'll 'elp you a lot with the White!

I was a young un at 'Oogli,
    Shy as a girl to begin;
Aggie de Castrer she made me,
    An' Aggie was clever as sin;
Older than me, but my first un—
    More like a mother she were—
Showed me the way to promotion an' pay,
    An' I learned about women from 'er!

Then I was ordered to Burma,
    Actin' in charge o' Bazar,
An' I got me a tiddy live 'eathen
    Through buyin' supplies off 'er pa.
Funny an' yellow an' faithful—
    Doll in a teacup she were,
But we lived on the square, like a true-married pair,
    An' I learned about women from 'er!

Then we was shifted to Neemuch
    (Or I might ha' been keepin' 'er now),
An' I took with a shiny she-devil,
    The wife of a nigger at Mhow;
'Taught me the gipsy-folks' bolee;
    Kind o' volcano she were,
For she knifed me one night 'cause I wished she was white,
    And I learned about women from 'er!

Then I come 'ome in the trooper,
    'Long of a kid o' sixteen—
Girl from a convent at Meerut,

The straightest I ever 'ave seen.
Love at first sight was 'er trouble,
　　She didn't know what it were;
An' I wouldn't do such, 'cause I liked 'er too much,
　　But—I learned about women from 'er!

I've taken my fun where I've found it,
　　An' now I must pay for my fun,
For the more you 'ave known o' the others
　　The less will you settle to one;
An' the end of it's sittin' and thinkin',
　　An' dreamin' Hell-fires to see;
So be warned by my lot (which I know you will not),
　　An' learn about women from me!

　　　　What did the Colonel's Lady think?
　　　　　　Nobody never knew.
　　　　Somebody asked the Sergeant's wife,
　　　　　　An' she told 'em true!
　　　　When you get to a man in the case,
　　　　　　They're like as a row of pins—
　　　　For the Colonel's Lady an' Judy O'Grady
　　　　　　Are sisters under their skins!

Bill 'Awkins

　　　"'As anybody seen Bill 'Awkins?"
　　　　　"Now 'ow in the devil would I know?"
　　　"'E's taken my girl out walkin',
　　　　　　An' I've got to tell 'im so—
　　　　　　　Gawd—bless—'im!
　　　　　I've got to tell 'im so."

　　　　"D'yer know what 'e's like, Bill 'Awkins?"
　　　　　　"Now what in the devil would I care?"
　　　"'E's the livin', breathin' image of an organ-grinder's monkey,
　　　　　With a pound of grease in 'is 'air—
　　　　　　　Gawd—bless—'im!
　　　　An' a pound o' grease in 'is 'air."

"An' s'pose you met Bill 'Awkins,
    Now what in the devil 'ud ye do?"
"I'd open 'is cheek to 'is chin-strap buckle,
    An' bung up 'is both eyes, too—
        Gawd—bless—'im!
    An' bung up 'is both eyes, too!"

"Look 'ere, where 'e comes, Bill 'Awkins!
    Now what in the devil will you say?"
"It isn't fit an' proper to be fightin' on a Sunday,
    So I'll pass 'im the time o' day—
        Gawd—bless—'im!
    I'll pass 'im the time o' day!"

The Mother-Lodge

There was Rundle, Station Master,
    An' Beazeley of the Rail,
An' 'Ackman, Commissariat,
    An' Donkin' o' the Jail;
An' Blake, Conductor-Sargent,
    Our Master twice was 'e,
With 'im that kept the Europe-shop,
    Old Framjee Eduljee.

        Outside—"Sergeant! Sir! Salute! Salaam!"
        Inside—"Brother", an' it doesn't do no 'arm.
        We met upon the Level an' we parted on the Square,
        An' I was Junior Deacon in my Mother-Lodge out there!

We'd Bola Nath, Accountant,
    An' Saul the Aden Jew,
An' Din Mohammed, draughtsman
    Of the Survey Office too;
There was Babu Chuckerbutty,

An' Amir Singh the Sikh,
An' Castro from the fittin'-sheds,
    The Roman Catholick!

We 'adn't good regalia,
    An' our Lodge was old an' bare,
But we knew the Ancient Landmarks,
    An' we kep' 'em to a hair;
An' lookin' on it backwards
    It often strikes me thus,
There ain't such things as infidels,
    Excep', per'aps, it's us.

For monthly, after Labour,
    We'd all sit down and smoke
(We dursn't give no banquits,
    Lest a Brother's caste were broke),
An' man on man got talkin'
    Religion an' the rest,
An' every man comparin'
    Of the God 'e knew the best.

So man on man got talkin',
    An' not a Brother stirred
Till mornin' waked the parrots
    An' that dam' brain-fever-bird;
We'd say 'twas 'ighly curious,
    An' we'd all ride 'ome to bed,
With Mo'ammed, God, an' Shiva
    Changin' pickets in our 'ead.

Full oft on Guv'ment service
    This rovin' foot 'ath pressed,
An' bore fraternal greetin's
    To the Lodges east an' west,
Accordin' as commanded
    From Kohat to Singapore,
But I wish that I might see them
    In my Mother-Lodge once more!

I wish that I might see them,
     My Brethren black an' brown,
With the trichies smellin' pleasant
     An' the hog-darn passin' down;
An' the old khansamah snorin'
     On the bottle-khana floor,
Like a Master in good standing
     With my Mother-Lodge once more!

          Outside—"Sergeant! Sir! Salute! Salaam!"
          Inside—"Brother", an' it doesn't do no 'arm.
          We met upon the Level an' we parted on the Square,
          An' I was Junior Deacon in my Mother-Lodge out there!

'Follow Me 'Ome'

     There was no one like 'im, 'Orse or Foot,
          Nor any o' the Guns I knew;
An' because it was so, why, o' course 'e went an' died,
          Which is just what the best men do.

     So it's knock out your pipes an' follow me!
          An' it's finish up your swipes an' follow me!
               Oh, 'ark to the big drum callin',
               Follow me—follow me 'ome!

     'Is mare she neighs the 'ole day long,
          She paws the 'ole night through,
An' she won't take 'er feed 'cause o' waitin' for 'is step,
          Which is just what a beast would do.

     'Is girl she goes with a bombardier
          Before 'er month is through;
An' the banns are up in church, for she's got the beggar hooked,
          Which is just what a girl would do.

We fought 'bout a dog—last week it were—
　　No more than a round or two;
But I strook 'im cruel 'ard, an' I wish I 'adn't now,
　　Which is just what a man can't do.

'E was all that I 'ad in the way of a friend,
　　An' I've 'ad to find one new;
But I'd give my pay an' stripe for to get the beggar back,
　　Which it's just too late to do.

So it's knock out your pipes an' follow me!
An' it's finish off your swipes an' follow me!
　　　Oh, 'ark to the fifes a-crawlin'!
　　Follow me—follow me 'ome!

　　　Take 'im away! 'E's gone where the best men go.
　　　Take 'im away! An' the gun-wheels turnin' slow.
　　　Take 'im away! There's more from the place 'e come.
　　　Take 'im away, with the limber an' the drum.

For it's "Three rounds blank" an' follow me,
An' it's "Thirteen rank" an' follow me;
　　　Oh, passin' the love o' women,
　　Follow me—follow me 'ome!

The Sergeant's Weddin'

'E was warned agin' 'er—
　　That's what made 'im look;
She was warned agin' 'im—
　　That is why she took.
'Wouldn't 'ear no reason,
　　'Went an' done it blind;
We know all about 'em,
　　They've got all to find!

Cheer for the Sergeant's weddin'—
    Give 'em one cheer more!
Grey gun-'orses in the lando,
    An' a rogue is married to, etc.

What's the use o' tellin'
    'Arf the lot she's been?
'E's a bloomin' robber,
    An' 'e keeps canteen.
'Ow did 'e get 'is buggy?
    Gawd, you needn't ask!
'Made 'is forty gallon
    Out of every cask!

Watch 'im, with 'is 'air cut,
    Count us filin' by—
Won't the Colonel praise 'is
    Pop—u—lar—i—ty!
We 'ave scores to settle—
    Scores for more than beer;
She's the girl to pay 'em—
    That is why we're 'ere!

See the chaplain thinkin'?
    See the women smile?
Twig the married winkin'
    As they take the aisle?
Keep your side-arms quiet,
    Dressin' by the Band.
Ho! You 'oly beggars,
    Cough be'ind your 'and!

Now it's done an' over,
    'Ear the organ squeak,
"'Voice that breathed o'er Eden"—
    Ain't she got the cheek!
White an' laylock ribbons,
    Think yourself so fine!

I'd pray Gawd to take yer
      'Fore I made yer mine!

Escort to the kerridge,
      Wish 'im luck, the brute!
Chuck the slippers after—
      (Pity 'tain't a boot!)
Bowin' like a lady,
      Blushin' like a lad—
'Oo would say to see 'em
      Both is rotten bad?

            Cheer for the Sergeant's weddin'—
            Give 'em one cheer more!
            Grey gun-'orses in the lando,
            An' a rogue is married to, etc.

The Jacket

Through the Plagues of Egyp' we was chasin' Arabi,
      Gettin' down an' shovin' in the sun;
An' you might 'ave called us dirty, an' you might ha' called us dry,
      An' you might 'ave 'eard us talkin' at the gun.
But the Captain 'ad 'is jacket, an' the jacket it was new—
      ('Orse Gunners, listen to my song!)
An' the wettin' of the jacket is the proper thing to do,
      Nor we didn't keep 'im waitin' very long.

One day they gave us orders for to shell a sand redoubt,
      Loadin' down the axle-arms with case;
But the Captain knew 'is dooty, an' he took the crackers out
      An' he put some proper liquor in its place.
An' the Captain saw the shrapnel, which is six-an'-thirty clear.
      ('Orse Gunners, listen to my song!)
"Will you draw the weight," sez 'e, "or will you draw the beer?"

An' we didn't keep 'im waitin' very long.
For the Captain, etc.

Then we trotted gentle, not to break the bloomin' glass,
 Though the Arabites 'ad all their ranges marked;
But we dursn't 'ardly gallop, for the most was bottled Bass,
 An' we'd dreamed of it since we was disembarked:
So we fired economic with the shells we 'ad in 'and,
 ('Orse Gunners, listen to my song!)
But the beggars under cover 'ad the impidence to stand,
 An' we couldn't keep 'em waitin' very long.
And the Captain, etc.

So we finished 'arf the liquor (an' the Captain took champagne),
 An' the Arabites was shootin' all the while;
An' we left our wounded 'appy with the empties on the plain,
 An' we used the bloomin' guns for pro-jec-tile!
We limbered up an' galloped—there were nothin' else to do—
 ('Orse Gunners, listen to my song!)
An' the Battery came a-boundin' like a boundin' kangaroo,
 But they didn't watch us comin' very long.
As the Captain, etc.

We was goin' most extended—we was drivin' very fine,
 An' the Arabites were loosin' 'igh an' wide,
Till the Captain took the glassy with a rattlin' right incline,
 An' we dropped upon their 'eads the other side.
Then we give 'em quarter—such as 'adn't up and cut,
 ('Orse Gunners, listen to my song!)
An' the Captain stood a limberful of fizzy—somethin' Brutt,
 But we didn't leave it fizzing very long.
For the Captain, etc.

We might ha' been court-martialled, but it all come out all right
 When they signalled us to join the main command.
There was every round expended, there was every gunner tight,
 An' the Captain waved a corkscrew in 'is 'and.
But the Captain 'ad 'is jacket, etc.

The 'Eathen

The 'eathen in 'is blindness bows down to wood an' stone;
'E don't obey no orders unless they is 'is own;
'E keeps 'is side-arms awful: 'e leaves 'em all about,
An' then comes up the regiment an' pokes the 'eathen out.

    All along o' dirtiness, all along o' mess,
    All along o' doin' things rather-more-or-less,
    All along of abby-nay, kul, an' hazar-ho,
    Mind you keep your rifle an' yourself jus' so!
The young recruit is 'aughty—'e draf's from Gawd knows where;
They bid 'im show 'is stockin's an' lay 'is mattress square;
'E calls it bloomin' nonsense—'e doesn't know no more—
An' then up comes 'is Company an' kicks 'im round the floor!

The young recruit is 'ammered—'e takes it very 'ard;
'E 'angs 'is 'ead an' mutters—'e sulks about the yard;
'E talks o' "cruel tyrants" 'e'll swing for by-an'-by,
An' the others 'ears an' mocks 'im, an' the boy goes orf to cry.

The young recruit is silly—'e thinks o' suicide;
'E's lost 'is gutter-devil; 'e 'asn't got 'is pride;
But day by day they kicks 'im, which 'elps 'im on a bit,
Till 'e finds 'isself one mornin' with a full an' proper kit.

    Gettin' clear o' dirtiness, gettin' done with mess,
    Gettin' shut o' doin' things rather-more-or-less;
    Not so fond of abby-nay, kul, nor hazar-ho,
    Learns to keep 'is rifle an' 'isself jus' so!

The young recruit is 'appy—'e throws a chest to suit;
You see 'im grow mustaches; you 'ear 'im slap 'is boot;
'E learns to drop the "bloodies" from every word 'e slings,
An' 'e shows an 'ealthy brisket when 'e strips for bars an' rings.

The cruel-tyrant-sergeants they watch 'im 'arf a year;
They watch 'im with 'is comrades, they watch 'im with 'is beer;

They watch 'im with the women at the regimental dance,
And the cruel-tyrant-sergeants send 'is name along for "Lance".

An' now 'e's 'arf o' nothin', an' all a private yet,
'Is room they up an' rags 'im to see what they will get;
They rags 'im low an' cunnin', each dirty trick they can,
But 'e learns to sweat 'is temper an' 'e learns to sweat 'is man.

An', last, a Colour-Sergeant, as such to be obeyed,
'E schools 'is men at cricket, 'e tells 'em on parade;
They sees 'em quick an' 'andy, uncommon set an' smart,
An' so 'e talks to orficers which 'ave the Core at 'eart.

'E learns to do 'is watchin' without it showin' plain;
'E learns to save a dummy, an' shove 'im straight again;
'E learns to check a ranker that's buyin' leave to shirk;
An' 'e learns to make men like 'im so they'll learn to like their
    work.

An' when it comes to marchin' he'll see their socks are right,
An' when it comes to action 'e shows 'em 'ow to sight;
'E knows their ways of thinkin' and just what's in their mind;
'E knows when they are takin' on an' when they've fell be'ind.

'E knows each talkin' corpril that leads a squad astray;
'E feels 'is innards 'eavin', 'is bowels givin' way;
'E sees the blue-white faces all tryin' 'ard to grin,
An' 'e stands an' waits an' suffers till it's time to cap 'em in.

An' now the hugly bullets come peckin' through the dust,
An' no one wants to face 'em, but every beggar must;
So, like a man in irons which isn't glad to go,
They moves 'em off by companies uncommon stiff an' slow.

Of all 'is five years' schoolin' they don't remember much
Excep' the not retreatin', the step an' keepin' touch.
It looks like teachin' wasted when they duck an' spread an' 'op,
But if 'e 'adn't learned 'em they'd be all about the shop!

An' now it's "'Oo goes backward?" an' now it's "'Oo comes on?"
And now it's "Get the doolies," an' now the captain's gone;
An' now it's bloody murder, but all the while they 'ear
'Is voice, the same as barrick drill, a-shepherdin' the rear.

'E's just as sick as they are, 'is 'eart is like to split,
But 'e works 'em, works 'em, works 'em till he feels 'em take the
    bit;
The rest is 'oldin' steady till the watchful bugles play,
An' 'e lifts 'em, lifts 'em, lifts 'em through the charge that wins the
    day!

    The 'eathen in 'is blindness bows down to wood an' stone;
    'E don't obey no orders unless they is 'is own;
    The 'eathen in 'is blindness must end where 'e began,
    But the backbone of the Army is the non-commissioned
    man!

    Keep away from dirtiness—keep away from mess.
    Don't get into doin' things rather-more-or-less!
    Let's ha' done with abby-nay, kul, an' hazar-ho;
    Mind you keep your rifle an' yourself jus' so!

The Shut-Eye Sentry

Sez the Junior Orderly Sergeant
    To the Senior Orderly Man:
"Our Orderly Orf'cer's hokee-mut,
    You 'elp 'im all you can.
For the wine was old and the night is cold,
    An' the best we may go wrong,
So, 'fore 'e gits to the sentry-box,
    You pass the word along."

    So it was "Rounds! What Rounds?" at two of a frosty night,
      'E's 'oldin' on by the sergeant's sash, but, sentry, shut your
    eye.
    An' it was "Pass! All's well!" Oh, ain't 'e drippin' tight!
      'E'll need an affidavit pretty badly by-an'-by.

The moon was white on the barricks,
    The road was white an' wide,
An' the Orderly Orf'cer took it all,
    An' the ten-foot ditch beside.
An' the corporal pulled an' the sergeant pushed,
    An' the three they danced along,
But I'd shut my eyes in the sentry-box,
    So I didn't see nothin' wrong.

    Though it was "Rounds! What Rounds?" O corporal, 'old 'im up!
        'E's usin' 'is cap as it shouldn't be used, but, sentry, shut your eye.
    An' it was "Pass! All's well!" Ho, shun the foamin' cup!
        'E'll need, etc.

'Twas after four in the mornin';
    We 'ad to stop the fun,
An' we sent 'im 'ome on a bullock-cart,
    With 'is belt an' stock undone;
But we sluiced 'im down an' we washed 'im out,
    An' a first-class job we made,
When we saved 'im, smart as a bombardier,
    For six-o'clock parade.

    It 'ad been "Rounds! What Rounds?" Oh, shove 'im straight
    again!
        'E's usin' 'is sword for a bicycle, but, sentry, shut your
        eye.
    An' it was "Pass! All's well!" 'E's called me "Darlin' Jane"!
        'E'll need, etc.

The drill was long an' 'eavy,
    The sky was 'ot an' blue,
An' 'is eye was wild an' 'is 'air was wet,
    But 'is sergeant pulled 'im through.
Our men was good old trusties—
    They'd done it on their 'ead;
But you ought to 'ave 'eard 'em markin' time
    To 'ide the things 'e said!

For it was "Right flank—wheel!" for "'Alt, an' stand at ease!"
    An' "Left extend!" for "Centre close!" O marker, shut your eye!
An' it was, "'Ere, sir, 'ere! before the Colonel sees!"
    So he needed affidavits pretty badly by-an'-by.

There was two-an'-thirty sergeants,
    There was corp'rals forty-one,
There was just nine 'undred rank an' file
    To swear to a touch o' sun.
There was me 'e'd kissed in the sentry-box,
    As I 'ave not told in my song,
But I took my oath, which were Bible truth,
    I 'adn't seen nothin' wrong.

There's them that's 'ot an' 'aughty,
    There's them that's cold an' 'ard,
But there comes a night when the best gets tight,
    And then turns out the Guard.
I've seen them 'ide their liquor
    In every kind o' way,
But most depends on makin' friends
    With Privit Thomas A.!

    When it is "Rounds! What Rounds?" 'E's breathin' through 'is nose.
        'E's reelin', rollin', roarin' tight, but, sentry, shut your eye.
    An' it is "Pass! All's well!" An' that's the way it goes:
        We'll 'elp 'im for 'is mother, an' 'e'll 'elp us by-an'-by!

'Mary, Pity Women!'

You call yourself a man,
    For all you used to swear,
An' leave me, as you can,

My certain shame to bear?
I 'ear! You do not care—
　　You done the worst you know.
I 'ate you, grinnin' there . . .
　　Ah, Gawd, I love you so!

　　　Nice while it lasted, an' now it is over—
　　　Tear out your 'eart an' good-bye to your lover!
　　　What's the use o' grievin', when the mother that bore you
　　　(Mary, pity women!) knew it all before you?

It aren't no false alarm,
　　The finish to your fun;
You—you 'ave brung the 'arm,
　　An' I'm the ruined one;
An' now you'll off an' run
　　With some new fool in tow.
Your 'eart? You 'aven't none . . .
　　Ah, Gawd, I love you so!

　　　When a man is tired there is naught will bind 'im;
　　　All 'e solemn promised 'e will shove be'ind 'im.
　　　What's the good o' prayin' for The Wrath to strike 'im
　　　(Mary, pity women!), when the rest are like 'im?

What 'ope for me or—it?
　　What's left for us to do?
I've walked with men a bit,
　　But this—but this is you.
So 'elp me Christ, it's true!
　　Where can I 'ide or go?
You coward through and through! . . .
　　Ah, Gawd, I love you so!

　　　All the more you give 'em the less are they for givin'—
　　　Love lies dead, an' you cannot kiss 'im livin'.
　　　Down the road 'e led you there is no returnin'
　　　(Mary, pity women!), but you're late in learnin'!

You'd like to treat me fair?
 You can't, because we're pore?
We'd starve? What do I care!
 We might, but this is shore!
I want the name—no more—
 The name, an' lines to show,
An' not to be an 'ore . . .
 Ah, Gawd, I love you so!

  What's the good o' pleadin', when the mother that bore you
  (Mary, pity women!) knew it all before you?
  Sleep on 'is promises an' wake to your sorrow
  (Mary, pity women!), for we sail to-morrow!

For to Admire

The Injian Ocean sets an' smiles
 So sof', so bright, so bloomin' blue;
There aren't a wave for miles an' miles
 Excep' the jiggle from the screw.
The ship is swep', the day is done,
 The bugle's gone for smoke and play;
An' black agin' the settin' sun
 The Lascar sings, "Hum deckty hai!"

  For to admire an' for to see,
  For to be'old this world so wide—
  It never done no good to me,
  But I can't drop it if I tried!

I see the sergeants pitchin' quoits,
 I 'ear the women laugh an' talk,
I spy upon the quarter-deck
 The orficers an' lydies walk.
I thinks about the things that was,

An' leans an' looks acrost the sea,
Till spite of all the crowded ship
    There's no one lef' alive but me.

The things that was which I 'ave seen,
    In barrick, camp, an' action too,
I tells them over by myself,
    An' sometimes wonders if they're true;
For they was odd—most awful odd—
    But all the same now they are o'er,
There must be 'eaps o' plenty such,
    An' if I wait I'll see some more.

Oh, I 'ave come upon the books,
    An' frequent broke a barrick rule,
An' stood beside an' watched myself
    Be'avin' like a bloomin' fool.
I paid my price for findin' out,
    Nor never grutched the price I paid,
But sat in Clink without my boots,
    Admirin' 'ow the world was made.

Be'old a crowd upon the beam,
    An' 'umped above the sea appears
Old Aden, like a barrick-stove
    That no one's lit for years an' years!
I passed by that when I began,
    An' I go 'ome the road I came,
A time-expired soldier-man
    With six years' service to 'is name.

My girl she said, "Oh, stay with me!"
    My mother 'eld me to 'er breast.
They've never written none, an' so
    They must 'ave gone with all the rest—
With all the rest which I 'ave seen
    An' found an' known an' met along.
I cannot say the things I feel,
    And so I sing my evenin' song:

For to admire an' for to see,
For to be'old this world so wide—
It never done no good to me,
But I can't drop it if I tried!

THE STORY OF THE GADSBY

PREFACE

To THE ADDRESS OF
CAPTAIN J. MAFFLIN,
Duke of Derry's (Pink) Hussars.

DEAR MAFFLIN,-You will remember that I wrote this story as an Awful Warning. None the less you have seen fit to disregard it and have followed Gadsby's example—as I betted you would. I acknowledge that you paid the money at once, but you have prejudiced the mind of Mrs. Mafflin against myself, for though I am almost the only respectable friend of your bachelor days, she has been darwaza band to me throughout the season. Further, she caused you to invite me to dinner at the Club, where you called me "a wild ass of the desert," and went home at half-past ten, after discoursing for twenty minutes on the responsibilities of housekeeping. You now drive a mail-phaeton and sit under a Church of England clergyman. I am not angry, Jack. It is your kismet, as it was Gaddy's, and his kismet who can avoid? Do not think that I am moved by a spirit of revenge as I write, thus publicly, that you and you alone are responsible for this book. In other and more expansive days, when you could look at a magnum without flushing and at a cheroot without turning white, you supplied me with most of the material. Take it back again-would that I could have preserved your fatherless speech in the telling-take it back, and by your slippered hearth read it to the late Miss Deercourt. She will not be any the more willing to receive my cards, but she will admire you immensely, and you, I feel sure, will love me. You may even invite me to another very bad dinner-at the Club, which, as you and your wife know, is a safe neutral ground for the entertainment of wild asses. Then, my very dear hypocrite, we shall be quits.

Yours always,
RUDYARD KIPLING.

P. S.-On second thoughts I should recommend you to keep the book away from Mrs. Mafflin.

POOR DEAR MAMMA

The wild hawk to the wind-swept sky, The deer to the wholesome wold, And the heart of a man to the heart of a maid, As it was in the days of old. Gypsy Song.

SCENE.-Interior of Miss MINNIE THREEGAN'S Bedroom at Simla. Miss THREEGAN, in window-seat, turning over a drawerful of things. Miss EMMA DEERCOURT, bosom-friend, who has come to spend the day, sitting on the bed, manipulating the bodice of a ballroom frock, and a bunch of artificial lilies of the valley. Time, 5:30 P. M. on a hot May afternoon.

Miss DEERCOURT. And he said: "I shall never forget this dance," and, of course, I said: "Oh, how can you be so silly!" Do you think he meant any-thing, dear?

Miss THREEGAN. (Extracting long lavender silk stocking from the rubbish.) You know him better than I do.

Miss D. Oh, do be sympathetic, Minnie! I'm sure he does. At least I would be sure if he wasn't always riding with that odious Mrs. Hagan.

Miss T. I suppose so. How does one manage to dance through one's heels first? Look at this-isn't it shameful? (Spreads stocking-heel on open hand for inspection.)

Miss D. Never mind that! You can't mend it. Help me with this hateful bodice. I've run the string so, and I've run the string so, and I can't make the fulness come right. Where would you put this? (Waves lilies of the valley.)

Miss T. As high up on the shoulder as possible.

Miss D. Am I quite tall enough? I know it makes May Older look lopsided.

Miss T. Yes, but May hasn't your shoulders. Hers are like a hock-bottle.

BEARER. (Rapping at door.) Captain Sahib aya.

Miss D. (Jumping up wildly, and hunting for bodice, which she has discarded owing to the heat of the day.) Captain Sahib! What Captain Sahib? Oh, good gracious, and I'm only half dressed! Well, I sha'n't bother.

Miss T. (Calmly.) You needn't. It isn't for us. That's Captain Gadsby. He is going for a ride with Mamma. He generally comes five days out of the seven.

AGONIZED VOICE. (Prom an inner apartment.) Minnie, run out and give Captain Gadsby some tea, and tell him I shall be ready in ten minutes; and, O Minnie, come to me an instant, there's a dear girl!

Miss T. Oh, bother! (Aloud.) Very well, Mamma.

Exit, and reappears, after five minutes, flushed, and rubbing her fingers.

Miss D. You look pink. What has happened?

Miss T. (In a stage whisper.) A twenty-four-inch waist, and she won't let it out. Where are my bangles? (Rummager on the toilet-table, and dabs at her hair with a brush in the interval.)

Miss D. Who is this Captain Gadsby? I don't think I've met him.

Miss T. You must have. He belongs to the Harrar set. I've danced with him, but I've never talked to him. He's a big yellow man, just like a newly-hatched chicken, with an enormous moustache. He walks like this (imitates Cavalry swagger), and he goes "Ha-Hmmm!" deep down in his throat when he can't think of anything to say. Mamma likes him. I don't.

Miss D. (Abstractedly.) Does he wax that moustache?

Miss T. (Busy with Powder-puff.) Yes, I think so. Why?

Miss D. (Bending over the bodice and sewing furiously.) Oh, nothing-only-Miss T. (Sternly.) Only what? Out with it, Emma.

Miss D. Well, May Olger-she's engaged to Mr. Charteris, you know-said-Promise you won't repeat this?

Miss T. Yes, I promise. What did she say?

Miss D. That-that being kissed (with a rush) with a man who didn't wax his moustache was-like eating an egg without salt.

Miss T. (At her full height, with crushing scorn.) May Olger is a horrid, nasty Thing, and you can tell her I said so. I'm glad she doesn't belong to my set-I must go and feed this man! Do I look presentable?

Miss D. Yes, perfectly. Be quick and hand him over to your Mother, and then we can talk. I shall listen at the door to hear what you say to him.

Miss T. 'Sure I don't care. I'm not afraid of Captain Gadsby.

In proof of this swings into the drawing-room with a mannish stride followed by two short steps, which Produces the effect of a restive horse entering. Misses CAPTAIN GADSBY, who is sitting in the shadow of the window-curtain, and gazes round helplessly.

CAPTAIN GADSBY. (Aside.) The filly, by Jove! 'Must ha' picked up that action from the sire. (Aloud, rising.) Good evening, Miss Threegan.

Miss T. (Conscious that she is flushing.) Good evening, Captain Gadsby. Mamma told me to say that she will be ready in a few minutes. Won't you have some tea? (Aside.) I hope Mamma will be quick. What am I to say to the creature? (Aloud and abruptly.) Milk and sugar?

CAPT. G. No sugar, tha-anks, and very little milk. Ha-Hmmm.

Miss T. (Aside.) If he's going to do that, I'm lost. I shall laugh. I know I shall!

CAPT. G. (Pulling at his moustache and watching it sideways down his nose.) Ha-Hamm. (Aside.) 'Wonder what the little beast can talk about. 'Must make a shot at it.

Miss T. (Aside.) Oh, this is agonizing. I must say something.

Both Together. Have you Been-CAPT. G. I beg your pardon. You were going to say-Miss T. (Who has been watching the moustache with awed fascination.) Won't you have some eggs?

CAPT. G. (Looking bewilderedly at the tea-table.) Eggs! (Aside.) O Hades! She must have a nursery-tea at this hour. S'pose they've wiped her mouth and sent her to me while the Mother is getting on her duds. (Aloud.) No, thanks.

Miss T. (Crimson with confusion.) Oh! I didn't mean that. I wasn't thinking of mou-eggs for an instant. I mean salt. Won't you have some sa-sweets? (Aside.) He'll think me a raving lunatic. I wish Mamma would come.

CAPT. G. (Aside.) It was a nursery-tea and she's ashamed of it. By Jove! She doesn't look half bad when she colors up like that. (Aloud, helping himself from the dish.) Have you seen those new chocolates at Peliti's?

Miss T. No, I made these myself. What are they like?

CAPT. G. These! De-licious. (Aside.) And that's a fact.

Miss T. (Aside.) Oh, bother! he'll think I'm fishing for compliments. (Aloud.) No, Peliti's of course.

CAPT. G. (Enthusiastically.) Not to compare with these. How d'you make them? I can't get my khansamah to understand the simplest thing beyond mutton and fowl.

Miss T. Yes? I'm not a khansamah, you know. Perhaps you frighten him. You should never frighten a servant. He loses his head. It's very bad policy.

CAPT. G. He's so awf'ly stupid.

Miss T. (Folding her hands in her Zap.) You should call him quietly and say: "O khansamah jee!"

CAPT. G. (Getting interested.) Yes? (Aside.) Fancy that little featherweight saying, "O khansamah jee" to my bloodthirsty Mir Khan!

Miss T Then you should explain the dinner, dish by dish.

CAPT. G. But I can't speak the vernacular.

Miss T. (Patronizingly.) You should pass the Higher Standard and try.

CAPT. G. I have, but I don't seem to be any the wiser. Are you?

Miss T. I never passed the Higher Standard. But the khansamah is very patient with me. He doesn't get angry when I talk about sheep's topees, or order maunds of grain when I mean seers.

CAPT. G. (Aside with intense indignation.) I'd like to see Mir Khan being rude to that girl! Hullo! Steady the Buffs! (Aloud.) And do you understand about horses, too?

Miss T. A little-not very much. I can't doctor them, but I know what they ought to eat, and I am in charge of our stable.

CAPT. G. Indeed! You might help me then. What ought a man to give his sais in the Hills? My ruffian says eight rupees, because everything is so dear.

Miss T. Six rupees a month, and one rupee Simla allowance-neither more nor less. And a grass-cut gets six rupees. That's better than buying grass in the bazar.

CAPT. G. (Admiringly.) How do you know?

Miss T. I have tried both ways.

CAPT. G. Do you ride much, then? I've never seen you on the Mall.

Miss T. (Aside.) I haven't passed him more than fifty times. (Aloud.) Nearly every day.

CAPT. G. By Jove! I didn't know that. Ha-Hamm (Pulls at his mousache and is silent for forty seconds.) Miss T. (Desperately, and wondering what will happen next.) It looks beautiful. I shouldn't touch it if I were you. (Aside.) It's all Mamma's fault for not coming before. I will be rude!

CAPT. G. (Bronzing under the tan and bringing down his hand very quickly.) Eh! What-at! Oh, yes! Ha! Ha! (Laughs uneasily.)

(Aside.) Well, of all the dashed cheek! I never had a woman say that to me yet. She must be a cool hand or else-Ah! that nursery-tea!

VOICE PROM THE UNKNOWN. Tchk! Tchk! Tchk!

CAPT. G. Good gracious! What's that?

Miss T. The dog, I think. (Aside.) Emma has been listening, and I'll never forgive her!

CAPT. G. (Aside.) They don't keep dogs here. (Aloud.) 'Didn't sound like a dog, did it?

Miss T. Then it must have been the cat. Let's go into the veranda. What a lovely evening it is!

Steps into veranda and looks out across the hills into sunset. The CAPTAIN follows.

CAPT. G. (Aside.) Superb eyes! I wonder that I never noticed them before! (Aloud.) There's going to he a dance at Viceregal Lodge on Wednesday. Can you spare me one?

Miss T. (Shortly.) No! I don't want any of your charity-dances. You only ask me because Mamma told you to. I hop and I bump. You know I do!

CAPT. G. (Aside.) That's true, but little girls shouldn't understand these things. (Aloud.) No, on my word, I don't. You dance beautifully.

Miss T. Then why do you always stand out after half a dozen turns? I thought officers in the Army didn't tell fibs.

CAPT. G. It wasn't a fib, believe me. I really do want the pleasure of a dance with you.

Miss T. (Wickedly.) Why? Won't Mamma dance with you any more?

CAPT. G. (More earnestly than the necessity demands.) I wasn't thinking of your Mother. (Aside.) You little vixen!

Miss T. (Still looking out of the window.) Eh? Oh, I beg your pardon. I was thinking of something else.

CAPT. G. (Aside.) Well! I wonder what she'll say next. I've never known a woman treat me like this before. I might be—Dash it, I might be an Infantry subaltern! (Aloud.) Oh, please don't trouble. I'm not worth thinking about. Isn't your Mother ready yet?

Miss T. I should think so; but promise me, Captain Gadsby, you won't take poor dear Mamma twice round Jakko any more. It tires her so.

CAPT. G. She says that no exercise tires her.

Miss T. Yes, but she suffers afterward. You don't know what rheumatism is, and you oughtn't to keep her out so late, when it gets chill in the evenings.

CAPT. G. (Aside.) Rheumatism. I thought she came off her horse rather in a bunch. Whew! One lives and learns. (Aloud.) I'm sorry to hear that. She hasn't mentioned it to me.

Miss T. (Flurried.) Of course not! Poor dear Mamma never would. And you mustn't say that I told you either. Promise me that you won't. Oh, CAPTAIN Gadsby, promise me you won't I

CAPT. G. I am dumb, or-I shall be as soon as you've given me that dance, and another-if you can trouble yourself to think about me for a minute.

Miss T. But you won't like it one little bit. You'll be awfully sorry afterward.

CAPT. G. I shall like it above all things, and I shall only be sorry that I didn't get more. (Aside.) Now what in the world am I saying?

Miss T. Very well. You will have only yourself to thank if your toes are trodden on. Shall we say Seven?

CAPT. G. And Eleven. (Aside.) She can't be more than eight stone, but, even then, it's an absurdly small foot. (Looks at his own riding boots.)

Miss T. They're beautifully shiny. I can almost see my face in them.

CAPT. G. I was thinking whether I should have to go on crutches for the rest of my life if you trod on my toes.

Miss T. Very likely. Why not change Eleven for a square?

CAPT. G. No, please! I want them both waltzes. Won't you write them down?

Miss T. J don't get so many dances that I shall confuse them. You will be the offender.

CAPT. G. Wait and see! (Aside.) She doesn't dance perfectly, perhaps, but

Miss T. Your tea must have got cold by this time. Won't you have another cup?

CAPT. G. No, thanks. Don't you think it's pleasanter out in the veranda? (Aside.) I never saw hair take that color in the sunshine before. (Aloud.) It's like one of Dicksee's pictures.

Miss T. Yes I It's a wonderful sunset, isn't it? (Bluntly.) But what do you know about Dicksee's pictures?

CAPT. G. I go Home occasionally. And I used to know the Galleries. (Nervously.) You mustn't think me only a Philistine with-a moustache.

Miss T. Don't! Please don't. I'm so sorry for what I said then. I was horribly rude. It slipped out before j thought. Don't you know the temptation to say frightful and shocking things just for the mere sake of saying them? I'm afraid I gave way to it.

CAPT. G. (Watching the girl as she flushes.) I think I know the feeling. It would be terrible if we all yielded to it, wouldn't it? For instance, I might say-POOR DEAR MAMMA. (Entering, habited, hatted, and booted.) Ah, Captain Gadsby? 'Sorry to keep you waiting. 'Hope you haven't been bored. 'My little girl been talking to you?

Miss T. (Aside.) I'm not sorry I spoke about the rheumatism. I'm not! I'm NOT! I only wished I'd mentioned the corns too.

CAPT. G. (Aside.) What a shame! I wonder how old she is. It never occurred to me before. (Aloud.) We've been discussing "Shakespeare and the musical glasses" in the veranda.

Miss T. (Aside.) Nice man! He knows that quotation. He isn't a Philistine with a moustache. (Aloud.) Good-bye, Captain Gadsby. (Aside.) What a huge hand and what a squeeze! I don't suppose he meant it, but he has driven the rings into my fingers.

POOR DEAR MAMMA. Has Vermillion come round yet? Oh, yes! Captain Gadsby, don't you think that the saddle is too far forward? (They pass into the front veranda.)

CAPT. G. (Aside.) How the dickens should I know what she prefers? She told me that she doted on horses. (Aloud.) I think it is.

Miss T. (Coming out into front veranda.) Oh! Bad Buldoo! I must speak to him for this. He has taken up the curb two links, and Vermillion bates that. (Passes out and to horse's head.)

CAPT. G. Let me do it!

Miss. T. No, Vermillion understands me. Don't you, old man? (Looses curb-chain skilfully, and pats horse on nose and throttle.) Poor Vermillion! Did they want to cut his chin off? There!

Captain Gadsby watches the interlude with undisguised admiration.

POOR DEAR MAMMA. (Tartly to Miss T.) You've forgotten your guest, I think, dear.

Miss T. Good gracious! So I have! Good-bye. (Retreats indoors hastily.)

POOR DEAR MAMMA. (Bunching reins in fingers hampered by too tight gauntlets.) CAPTAIN Gadsby!

CAPTAIN GADSBY stoops and makes the foot-rest. POOR DEAR MAMMA blunders, halts too long, and breaks through it.

CAPT. G. (Aside.) Can't hold up even stone forever. It's all your rheumatism. (Aloud.) Can't imagine why I was so clumsy. (Aside.) Now Little Featherweight would have gone up like a bird.

They ride oat of the garden. The Captain falls back.

CAPT. G. (Aside.) How that habit catches her under the arms! Ugh!

POOR DEAR MAMMA. (With the worn smile of sixteen seasons, the worse for exchange.) You're dull this afternoon, CAPTAIN Gadsby.

CAPT. G. (Spurring up wearily.) Why did you keep me waiting so long?

Et cetera, et cetera, et cetera.

(AN INTERVAL OF THREE WEEKS.)

GILDED YOUTH. (Sitting on railings opposite Town Hall.) Hullo, Gandy! 'Been trotting out the Gorgonzola! We all thought it was the Gorgan you're mashing.

CAPT. G. (With withering emphasis.) You young cub! What the-does it matter to you?

Proceeds to read GILDED YOUTH a lecture on discretion and deportment, which crumbles latter like a Chinese Lantern. Departs fuming.

(FURTHER INTERVAL OF FIVE WEEKS.)
SCENE.-Exterior of New Simla Library

on a foggy evening. Miss THREECAN and Miss DEERCOURT meet among the 'rickshaws. Miss T. is carrying a bundle of books under her left arm.

Miss D. (Level intonation.) Well?

Miss 'T'. (Ascending intonation.) Well?

Miss D. (Capturing her friend's left arm, taking away all the books, placing books in 'rickshaw, returning to arm, securing hand by third finger and investigating.) Well! You bad girl! And you never told me.

Miss T. (Demurely.) He-he-he only spoke yesterday afternoon.

Miss D. Bless you, dear! And I'm to be bridesmaid, aren't I? You know you promised ever so long ago.

Miss T. Of course. I'll tell you all about it to-morrow. (Gets into 'rickshaw.) O Emma!

Miss D. (With intense interest.) Yes, dear?

Miss T. (Piano.) It's quite true——about-the-egg.

Miss D. What egg?

Miss T. (Pianissimo prestissimo.) The egg without the salt. (Porte.) Chalo ghar ko jaldi, jhampani! (Go home, jhampani.)

THE WORLD WITHOUT

Certain people of importance.

SCENE.-Smoking-room of the Degchi Club. Time, 10.30 P. M. of a stuffy night in the Rains. Four men dispersed in picturesque attitudes and easy-chairs. To these enter BLAYNE of the Irregular Moguls, in evening dress.

BLAYNE. Phew! The Judge ought to be hanged in his own store-godown. Hi, khitmatgarl Poora whiskey-peg, to take the taste out of my mouth.

CURTISS. (Royal Artillery.) That's it, is it? What the deuce made you dine at the Judge's? You know his bandobust.

BLAYNE. 'Thought it couldn't be worse than the Club, but I'll swear he buys ullaged liquor and doctors it with gin and ink (looking round the room.) Is this all of you to-night?

DOONE. (P.W.D.) Anthony was called out at dinner. Mingle had a pain in his tummy.

CURTISS. Miggy dies of cholera once a week in the Rains, and gets drunk on chlorodyne in between. 'Good little chap, though. Any one at the Judge's, Blayne?

BLAYNE. Cockley and his memsahib looking awfully white and fagged. 'F('.male girl-couldn't catch the name-on her way to the

Hills, under the Cockleys' charge-the Judge, and Markyn fresh from Simla-disgustingly fit.

CURTISS. Good Lord, how truly magnificent! Was there enough ice? When I mangled garbage there I got one whole lump-nearly as big as a walnut. What had Markyn to say for himself?

BLAYNE. 'Seems that every one is having a fairly good time up there in spite of the rain. By Jove, that reminds me! I know I hadn't come across just for the pleasure of your society. News! Great news! Markyn told me.

DOONE. Who's dead now?

BLAYNE. No one that I know of; but Gandy's hooked at last!

DROPPING CHORUS. How much? The Devil! Markyn was pulling your leg. Not GANDY!

BLAYNE. (Humming.) "Yea, verily, verily, verily! Verily, verily, I say unto thee." Theodore, the gift o' God! Our Phillup! It's been given out up above.

MACKESY. (Barrister-at-Law.) Huh! Women will give out anything. What does accused say?

BLAYNE. Markyn told me that he congratulated him warily-one hand held out, t'other ready to guard. Gandy turned pink and said it was so.

CURTISS. Poor old Caddy! They all do it. Who's she? Let's hear the details.

BLAYNE. She's a girl-daughter of a Colonel Somebody.

DOONE. Simla's stiff with Colonels' daughters. Be more explicit.

BLAYNE. Wait a shake. What was her name? Thresomething. Three-

CURTISS. Stars, perhaps. Caddy knows that brand.

BLAYNE. Threegan-Minnie Threegan.

MACKESY. Threegan Isn't she a little bit of a girl with red hair?

BLAYNE. 'Bout that-from what from what Markyn said.

MACKESY. Then I've met her. She was at Lucknow last season. 'Owned a permanently juvenile Mamma, and danced damnably. I say, Jervoise, you knew the Threegans, didn't you?

JERVOISE. (Civilian of twenty-five years' service, waking up from his doze.) Eh? What's that? Knew who? How? I thought I was at Home, confound you!

MACKESY. The Threegan girl's engaged, so Blayne says.

JERVOISE. (Slowly.) Engaged-en-gaged! Bless my soul! I'm getting an old man! Little Minnie Threegan engaged. It was only the other day I went home with them in the Surat-no, the Massilia-and she was crawling about on her hands and knees among the ayahs. 'Used to call me the "Tick Tack Sakib" because I showed her my watch. And that was in Sixty-Seven-no, Seventy. Good God, how time flies! I'm an old man. I remember when Threegan married Miss Derwent-daughter of old Hooky Derwent-but that was before your time. And so the little baby's engaged to have a little baby of her own! Who's the other fool?

MACKESY. Gadsby of the Pink Hussars.

JERVOISE. 'Never met him. Threegan lived in debt, married in debt, and 'll die in debt. 'Must be glad to get the girl off his hands.

BLAYNE. Caddy has money-lucky devil. Place at Home, too.

DOONE. He comes of first-class stock. 'Can't quite understand his being caught by a Colonel's daughter, and (looking cautiously round room.) Black Infantry at that! No offence to you, Blayne.

BLAYNE. (Stiffly.) Not much, thaanks.

CURTISS. (Quoting motto of Irregular Moguls.) "We are what we are," eh, old man? But Gandy was such a superior animal as a rule. Why didn't he go Home and pick his wife there?

MACKESY. They are all alike when they come to the turn into the straight. About thirty a man begins to get sick of living alone.

CURTISS. And of the eternal muttony-chop in the morning.

DOONE. It's a dead goat as a rule, but go on, Mackesy.

MACKESY. If a man's once taken that way nothing will hold him, Do you remember Benoit of your service, Doone? They transferred him to Tharanda when his time came, and he married a platelayer's daughter, or something of that kind. She was the only female about the place.

DONE. Yes, poor brute. That smashed Benoit's chances of promotion altogether. Mrs. Benoit used to ask "Was you gem' to the dance this evenin'?"

CURTISS. Hang it all! Gandy hasn't married beneath him. There's no tarbrush in the family, I suppose.

JERVOISE. Tar-brush! Not an anna. You young fellows talk as though the man was doing the girl an honor in marrying her. You're all too conceited-nothing's good enough for you.

BLAYNE. Not even an empty Club, a dam' bad dinner at the Judge's, and a Station as sickly as a hospital. You're quite right. We're a set of Sybarites.

DOONE. Luxurious dogs, wallowing in-

CURTISS. Prickly heat between the shoulders. I'm covered with it. Let's hope Beora will be cooler.

BLAYNE. Whew! Are you ordered into camp, too? I thought the Gunners had a clean sheet.

CURTISS. No, worse luck. Two cases yesterday-one died-and if we have a third, out we go. Is there any shooting at Beora, Doone?

DOONE. The country's under water, except the patch by the Grand Trunk Road. I was there yesterday, looking at a bund, and came across four poor devils in their last stage. It's rather bad from here to Kuchara.

CURTISS. Then we're pretty certain to have a heavy go of it. Heigho! I shouldn't mind changing places with Gaddy for a while. 'Sport with Amaryllis in the shade of the Town Hall, and all that. Oh, why doesn't somebody come and marry me, instead of letting me go into cholera-camp?

MACKESY. Ask the Committee.

CURTISS. You ruffian! You'll stand me another peg for that. Blayne, what will you take? Mackesy is fine on moral grounds. Done, have you any preference?

DONE. Small glass Kummel, please. Excellent carminative, these days. Anthony told me so.

MACKESY. (Signing voucher for four drinks.) Most unfair punishment. I only thought of Curtiss as Actaeon being chivied round the billiard tables by the nymphs of Diana.

BLAYNE. Curtiss would have to import his nymphs by train. Mrs. Cockley's the only woman in the Station. She won't leave Cockley, and he's doing his best to get her to go.

CURTISS. Good, indeed! Here's Mrs. Cockley's health. To the only wife in the Station and a damned brave woman!

OMNES. (Drinking.) A damned brave woman

BLAVNE. I suppose Gandy will bring his wife here at the end of the cold weather. They are going to be married almost immediately, I believe.

CURTISS. Gandy may thank his luck that the Pink Hussars are all detachment and no headquarters this hot weather, or he'd be torn from the arms of his love as sure as death. Have you ever noticed the thorough-minded way British Cavalry take to cholera? It's because they are so expensive. If the Pinks had stood fast here, they would have been out in camp a. month ago. Yes, I should decidedly like to be Gandy.

MACKESY. He'll go Home after he's married, and send in his papers-see if he doesn't.

BLAYNE. Why shouldn't he? Hasn't he money? Would any one of us be here if we weren't paupers?

DONE. Poor old pauper! What has become of the six hundred you rooked from our table last month?

BLAYNE. It took unto itself wings. I think an enterprising tradesman got some of it, and a shroff gobbled the rest-or else I spent it.

CURTISS. Gandy never had dealings with a shroff in his life.

DONE. Virtuous Gandy! If I had three thousand a month, paid from England, I don't think I'd deal with a shroff either.

MACKESY. (Yawning.) Oh, it's a sweet life! I wonder whether matrimony would make it sweeter.

CURTISS. Ask Cockley-with his wife dying by inches!

BLAYNE. Go home and get a fool of a girl to come out to-what is it Thackeray says?-"the splendid palace of an Indian pro-consul."

DOONE. Which reminds me. My quarters leak like a sieve. I had fever last night from sleeping in a swamp. And the worst of it is, one can't do anything to a roof till the Rains are over.

CURTISS. What's wrong with you? You haven't eighty rotting Tommies to take into a running stream.

DONE. No: but I'm mixed boils and bad language. I'm a regular Job all over my body. It's sheer poverty of blood, and I don't see any chance of getting richer-either way.

BLAYNE. Can't you take leave? DONE. That's the pull you Army men have over us. Ten days are nothing in your sight. I'm so important that Government can't find a substitute if I go away. Ye-es, I'd like to be Gandy, whoever his wife may be.

CURTISS. You've passed the turn of life that Mackesy was speaking of.

DONE. Indeed I have, but I never yet had the brutality to ask a woman to share my life out here.

BLAvNE. On my soul I believe you're right. I'm thinking of Mrs. Cockley. The woman's an absolute wreck.

DONE. Exactly. Because she stays down here. The only way to keep her fit would be to send her to the Hills for eight months-and the same with any woman. I fancy I see myself taking a wife on those terms.

MACKESY. With the rupee at one and sixpence. The little Doones would be little Debra Doones, with a fine Mussoorie chi-chi anent to bring home for the holidays.

CURTISS. And a pair of be-ewtiful sambhur-horns for Done to wear, free of expense, presented by-DONE. Yes, it's an enchanting prospect. By the way, the rupee hasn't done falling yet. The time will come when we shall think ourselves lucky if we only lose half our pay.

CURTISS. Surely a third's loss enough. Who gains by the arrangement? That's what I want to know.

BLAYNE. The Silver Question! I'm going to bed if you begin squabbling Thank Goodness, here's Anthony-looking like a ghost.

Enter ANTHONY, Indian Medical Staff, very white and tired.

ANTHONY. 'Evening, Blayne. It's raining in sheets. Whiskey peg lao, khitmatgar. The roads are something ghastly.

CURTISS. How's Mingle?

ANTHONY. Very bad, and more frightened. I handed him over to Few-ton. Mingle might just as well have called him in the first place, instead of bothering me.

BLAYNE. He's a nervous little chap. What has he got, this time?

ANTHONY. 'Can't quite say. A very bad tummy and a blue funk so far. He asked me at once if it was cholera, and I told him not to be a fool. That soothed him.

CURTIS. Poor devil! The funk does half the business in a man of that build.

ANTHONY. (Lighting a cheroot.) I firmly believe the funk will kill him if he stays down. You know the amount of trouble he's been giving Fewton for the last three weeks. He's doing his very best to frighten himself into the grave.

GENERAL CHORUS. Poor little devil! Why doesn't he get away?

ANTHONY. 'Can't. He has his leave all right, but he's so dipped he can't take it, and I don't think his name on paper would raise four annas. That's in confidence, though.

MACKESY. All the Station knows it.

ANTHONY. "I suppose I shall have to die here," he said, squirming all across the bed. He's quite made up his mind to Kingdom Come. And I know he has nothing more than a wet-weather tummy if he could only keep a hand on himself.

BLAYNE. That's bad. That's very bad. Poor little Miggy. Good little chap, too. I say-

ANTHONY. What do you say?

BLAYNE. Well, look here-anyhow. If it's like that-as you say-I say fifty.

CURTISS. I say fifty.

MACKESY. I go twenty better.

DONE. Bloated Croesus of the Bar! I say fifty. Jervoise, what do you say? Hi! Wake up!

JERVOISE. Eh? What's that? What's that?

CURTISS. We want a hundred rupees from you. You're a bachelor drawing a gigantic income, and there's a man in a hole.

JERVOISE. What man? Any one dead?

BLAYNE. No, hut he'll die if you don't give the hundred. Here! Here's a peg-voucher. You can see what we've signed for, and Anthony's man will come round to-morrow to collect it. So there will be no trouble.

JERVOISE. (Signing.) One hundred, E. M. J. There you are (feebly). It isn't one of your jokes, is it?

BLAYNE. No, it really is wanted. Anthony, you were the biggest poker-winner last week, and you've defrauded the tax-collector too long. Sign!

ANTHONY. Let's see. Three fifties and a seventy-two twenty-three twenty-say four hundred and twenty. That'll give him a month clear at the Hills. Many thanks, you men. I'll send round the chaprassi to-morrow.

CURTISS. You must engineer his taking the stuff, and of course you mustn't-

ANTHONY. Of course. It would never do. He'd weep with gratitude over his evening drink.

BLAYNE. That's just what he would do, damn him. Oh! I say, Anthony, you pretend to know everything. Have you heard about Gandy?

ANTHONY. No. Divorce Court at last?

BLAYNE. Worse. He's engaged!

ANTHONY. How much? He can't be!

BLAYNE. He is. He's going to be married in a few weeks. Markyn told me at the Judge's this evening. It's pukka.

ANTHONY. You don't say so? Holy Moses! There'll be a shine in the tents of Kedar.

CURTISS. 'Regiment cut up rough, think you?

ANTHONY. 'Don't know anything about the Regiment.

MACKESY. It is bigamy, then?

ANTHONY. Maybe. Do you mean to say that you men have forgotten, or is there more charity in the world than I thought?

DONE. You don't look pretty when you are trying to keep a secret. You bloat. Explain.

ANTHONY. Mrs. Herriott!

BLAYNE. (After a long pause, to the room generally.) It's my notion that we are a set of fools.

MACKESY. Nonsense. That business was knocked on the head last season. Why, young Mallard-

ANTHONY. Mallard was a candlestick, paraded as such. Think awhile. Recollect last season and the talk then. Mallard or no Mallard, did Gandy ever talk to any other woman?

CURTISS. There's something in that. It was slightly noticeable now you come to mention it. But she's at Naini Tat and he's at Simla.

ANTHONY. He had to go to Simla to look after a globe-trotter relative of his-a person with a title. Uncle or aunt.

BLAYNE And there he got engaged. No law prevents a man growing tired of a woman.

ANTHONY. Except that he mustn't do it till the woman is tired of him. And the Herriott woman was not that.

CURTISS. She may be now. Two months of Naini Tal works wonders.

DONE. Curious thing how some women carry a Fate with them. There was a Mrs. Deegie in the Central Provinces whose men invariably fell away and got married. It became a regular proverb with us when I was down there. I remember three men desperately devoted to her, and they all, one after another, took wives.

CURTISS. That's odd. Now I should have thought that Mrs. Deegie's influence would have led them to take other men's wives. It ought to have made them afraid of the judgment of Providence.

ANTHONY. Mrs. Herriott will make Gandy afraid of something more than the judgment of Providence, I fancy.

BLAYNE. Supposing things are as you say, he'll be a fool to face her. He'll sit tight at Simla.

ANTHONY. 'Shouldn't be a bit surprised if he went off to Naini to explain. He's an unaccountable sort of man, and she's likely to be a more than unaccountable woman.

DONE. What makes you take her character away so confidently?

ANTHONY. Primum tern pus. Caddy was her first and a woman doesn't allow her first man to drop away without expostulation. She justifies the first transfer of affection to herself by swearing that it is forever and ever. Consequently-

BLAYNE. Consequently, we are sitting here till past one o'clock, talking scandal like a set of Station cats. Anthony, it's all your fault. We were perfectly respectable till you came in Go to bed. I'm off, Good-night all.

CURTISS. Past one! It's past two by Jove, and here's the khit coming for the late charge. Just Heavens! One, two, three, four, five rupees to pay for the pleasure of saying that a poor little beast of a woman is no better than she should be. I'm ashamed of myself. Go to bed, you slanderous villains, and if I'm sent to Beora to-morrow, be prepared to hear I'm dead before paying my card account!

THE TENTS OF KEDAR

Only why should it be with pain at all Why must I 'twix the leaves of corona! Put any kiss of pardon on thy brow? Why should the other women know so much, And talk together-Such the look and such The smile he used to love with, then as now.-Any Wife to any Husband.

SCENE-A Naini Tal dinner for thirty-four. Plate, wines, crockery, and khitmatgars care fully calculated to scale of Rs. 6000 per mensem, less Exchange. Table split lengthways by bank of flowers.

MRS. HERRIOTT. (After conversation has risen to proper pitch.) Ah! 'Didn't see you in the crush in the drawing-room. (Sotto voce.) Where have you been all this while, Pip?

CAPTAIN GADSBY. (Turning from regularly ordained dinner partner and settling hock glasses.) Good evening. (Sotto voce.) Not quite so loud another time. You've no notion how your voice carries. (Aside.) So much for shirking the written explanation. It'll have to be a verbal one now. Sweet prospect! How on earth am I to tell her that I am a respectable, engaged member of society and it's all over between us?

MRS. H. I've a heavy score against you. Where were you at the Monday Pop? Where were you on Tuesday? Where were you at the Lamonts' tennis? I was looking everywhere.

CAPT. G. For me! Oh, I was alive somewhere, I suppose. (Aside.) It's for Minnie's sake, but it's going to be dashed unpleasant.

MRS. H. Have I done anything to offend you? I never meant it if I have. I couldn't help going for a ride with the Vaynor man. It was promised a week before you came up.

CAPT. G. I didn't know-

MRS. H. It really was.

CAPT. G. Anything about it, I mean.

MRS. H. What has upset you today? All these days? You haven't been near me for four whole days-nearly one hundred hours. Was it kind of you, Pip? And I've been looking forward so much to your coming.

CAPT. G. Have you?

MRS. H. You know I have! I've been as foolish as a schoolgirl about it. I made a little calendar and put it in my card-case, and every time the twelve o'clock gun went off I scratched out a square and said: "That brings me nearer to Pip. My Pip!"

CAPT. G. (With an uneasy laugh). What will Mackler think if you neglect him so?

MRS. H. And it hasn't brought you nearer. You seem farther away than ever. Are you sulking about something? I know your temper.

CAPT. G. No.

MRS. H. Have I grown old in' the last few months, then? (Reaches forward to bank of flowers for menu-card.)

PARTNER ON LEFT. Allow me. (Hands menu-card. MRS. H. keeps her arm at full stretch for three seconds.)

MRS. H. (To partner.) Oh, thanks. I didn't see. (Turns right again.) Is anything in me changed at all?

CAPT. G. For Goodness's sake go on with your dinner! You must eat something. Try one of those cutlet arrangements. (Aside.) And I fancied she had good shoulders, once upon a time! What an ass a man can make of himself!

MRS. H. (Helping herself to a paper frill, seven peas, some stamped carrots and a spoonful of gravy.) That isn't an answer. Tell me whether I have done anything.

CAPT. G. (Aside.) If it isn't ended here there will be a ghastly scene some-where else. If only I'd written to her and stood the racket-at long range! (To Khitmatgar.) Han! Simpkin do. (Aloud.) I'll tell you later on.

MRS. H. Tell me now. It must be some foolish misunderstanding, and you know that there was to be nothing of that sort between us. We) of all people in the world, can't afford it. Is it the Vaynor man, and don't you like to say so? On my honor-CAPT. G. I haven't given the Vaynor man a thought.

MRS. H. But how d'you know that I haven't?

CAPT. G. (Aside.) Here's my chance and may the Devil help me through with it. (Aloud and measuredly.) Believe me, I do not care how often or how tenderly you think of the Vaynor man.

MRS. H. I wonder if you mean that! Oh, what is the good of squabbling and pretending to misunderstand when you are only up for so short a time? Pip, don't be a stupid!

Follows a pause, during which he crosses his left leg over his right and continues his dinner.

CAPT. G. (In answer to the thunderstorm in her eyes.) Corns-my worst.

MRS. H. Upon my word, you are the very rudest man in the world! I'll never do it again.

CAPT. G. (Aside.) No, I don't think you will; but I wonder what you will do before it's all over. (To Khitmatgar.) Thorah ur Simpkin do.

MRS. H. Well! Haven't you the grace to apologize, bad man?

CAPT. G. (Aside.) I mustn't let it drift back now. Trust a woman for being as blind as a bat when she won't see.

MRS. H. I'm waiting; or would you like me to dictate a form of apology?

CAPT. G. (Desperately.) By all means dictate.

MRS. H. (Lightly.) Very well. Rehearse your several Christian names after me and go on: "Profess my sincere repentance."

CAPT. G. "Sincere repentance."

MRS. H. "For having behaved"-

CAPT. G. (Aside.) At last! I wish to Goodness she'd look away. "For having behaved"-as I have behaved, and declare that I am thoroughly and heartily sick of the whole business, and take this opportunity of making clear my intention of ending it, now, henceforward, and forever. (Aside.) If any one had told me I should be such a blackguard!-

MRS. H. (Shaking a spoonful of potato chips into her plate.) That's not a pretty joke.

CAPT. G. No. It's a reality. (Aside.) I wonder if smashes of this kind are always so raw.

MRS. H. Really, Pip, you're getting more absurd every day.

CAPT. G. I don't think you quite understand me. Shall I repeat it?

MRS. H. No! For pity's sake don't do that. It's too terrible, even in fur.

CAPT. G. I'll let her think it over for a while. But I ought to be horsewhipped.

MRS. H. I want to know what you meant by what you said just now.

CAPT. G. Exactly what I said. No less.

MRS. H. But what have I done to deserve it? What have I done?

CAPT. G. (Aside.) If she only wouldn't look at me. (Aloud and very slowly, his eyes on his plate.) D'you remember that evening in July, before the Rains broke, when you said that the end would have to come sooner or later-and you wondered for which of US it would come first?

MRS. H. Yes! I was only joking. And you swore that, as long as there was breath in your body, it should never come. And I believed you.

CAPT. G. (Fingering menu-card.) Well, it has. That's all.

A long pause, during which MRS. H. bows her head and rolls the bread-twist into little pellets; G. stares at the oleanders.

MRS. H. (Throwing back her head and laughing naturally.) They train us women well, don't they, Pip?

CAPT. G. (Brutally, touching shirt-stud.) So far as the expression goes. (Aside.) It isn't in her nature to take things quietly. There'll be an explosion yet.

MRS. H. (With a shudder.) Thank you. B-but even Red Indians allow people to wriggle when they're being tortured, I believe. (Slips fan from girdle and fans slowly: rim of fan level with chin.)

PARTNER ON LEFT. Very close tonight, isn't it? 'You find it too much for you?

MRS. H. Oh, no, not in the least. But they really ought to have punkahs, even in your cool Naini Tal, oughtn't they? (Turns, dropping fan and raising eyebrows.)

CAPT. G. It's all right. (Aside.) Here comes the storm!

MRS. H. (Her eyes on the tablecloth: fan ready in right hand.) It was very cleverly managed, Pip, and I congratulate you. You swore-you never contented yourself with merely Saying a thing-you swore that, as far as lay in your power, you'd make my wretched life pleasant for me. And you've denied me the consolation of breaking down. I should have done it-indeed I should. A woman would hardly have thought of this refinement, my kind, considerate friend. (Fan-guard as before.) You have explained things so tenderly and truthfully, too! You haven't spoken or written a word of warning, and you have let me believe in you till the last minute. You haven't condescended to give me your reason yet. No! A woman could not have managed it half so well. Are there many men like you in the world?

CAPT. G. I'm sure I don't know. (To Khitmatgar.) Ohe! Simpkin do.

MRS. H. You call yourself a man of the world, don't you? Do men of the world behave like Devils when they a woman the honor to get tired of her?

CAPT. G. I'm sure I don't know. Don't speak so loud!

MRS. H. Keep us respectable, O Lord, whatever happens. Don't be afraid of my compromising you. You've chosen your ground far too well, and I've been properly brought up. (Lowering fan.) Haven't you any pity, Pip, except for yourself?

CAPT. G. Wouldn't it be rather impertinent of me to say that I'm sorry for you?

MRS. H. I think you have said it once or twice before. You're growing very careful of my feelings. My God, Pip, I was a good woman once! You said I was. You've made me what I am. What are you going to do with me? What are you going to do with me? Won't you say that you are sorry? (Helps herself to iced asparagus.)

CAPT. G. I am sorry for you, if you Want the pity of such a brute as I am. I'm awf'ly sorry for you.

MRS. H. Rather tame for a man of the world. Do you think that that admission clears you?

CAPT. G. What can I do? I can only tell you what I think of myself. You can't think worse than that?

MRS. H. Oh, yes, I can! And now, will you tell me the reason of all this? Remorse? Has Bayard been suddenly conscience-stricken?

CAPT. G. (Angrily, his eyes still lowered.) No! The thing has come to an end on my side. That's all. Mafisch!

MRS. H. "That's all. Mafisch!" As though I were a Cairene Dragoman. You used to make prettier speeches. D'you remember when you said?-

CAPT. G. For Heaven's sake don't bring that back! Call me anything you like and I'll admit it-

MRS. H. But you don't care to be reminded of old lies? If I could hope to hurt you one-tenth as much as you have hurt me to-night-No, I wouldn't-I couldn't do it-liar though you are.

CAPT. G. I've spoken the truth.

MRS. H. My dear Sir, you flatter yourself. You have lied over the reason. Pip, remember that I know you as you don't know yourself. You have heen everything to me, though you are-(Fan-guard.) Oh, what a contemptible Thing it is! And so you are merely tired of me?

CAPT. G. Since you insist upon my repeating it-Yes.

Mas. H. Lie the first. I wish I knew a coarser word. Lie seems so in-effectual in your case. The fire has just died out and there is no fresh one? Think for a minute, Pip, if you care whether I despise you more than I do. Simply Mafisch, is it?

CAPT. G. Yes. (Aside.) I think I deserve this.

MRS. H. Lie number two. Before the next glass chokes you, tell me her name.

CAPT. G. (Aside.) I'll make her pay for dragging Minnie into the business! (Aloud.) Is it likely?

MRS. H. Very likely if you thought that it would flatter your vanity. You'd cry my name on the house-tops to make people turn round.

CAPT. G. I wish I had. There would have been an end to this business.

MRS. H. Oh, no, there would not-And so you were going to be virtuous and blase', were you? To come to me and say: "I've done with you. The incident is clo-osed." I ought to be proud of having kept such a man so long.

CAPT. G. (Aside.) It only remains to pray for the end of the dinner. (Aloud.) You know what I think of myself.

MRS. H. As it's the only person in he world you ever do think of, and as I know your mind thoroughly, I do. Vou want to get it all over and-Oh, I can't keep you back! And you're going-think of it, Pip-to throw me over for another woman. And you swore that all other women were-Pip, my Pip! She can't care for you as I do. Believe me, she can't. Is it any one that I know?

CAPT. G. Thank Goodness it isn't. (Aside.) I expected a cyclone, but not an earthquake.

MRS. H. She can't! Is there anything that I wouldn't do for you-or haven't done? And to think that I should take this trouble over you, knowing what you are! Do you despise me for it?

CAPT. G. (Wiping his mouth to hide a smile.) Again? It's entirely a work of charity on your part.

MRS. H. Ahhh! But I have no right to resent it.-Is she better-looking than I? Who was it said?-

CAPT. G. No-not that!

MRS. H. I'll be more merciful than you were. Don't you know that all women are alike?

CAPT. G. (Aside.) Then this is the exception that proves the rule.

MRS. H. All of them! I'll tell you anything you like. I will, upon my word! They only want the admiration-from anybody-no matter who-anybody! But there is always one man that they care for more than any one else in the world, and would sacrifice all the others to. Oh, do listen! I've kept the Vaynor man trotting after me like a poodle, and he believes that he is the only man I am interested in. I'll tell you what he said to me.

CAPT. G. Spare him. (Aside.) I wonder what his version is.

MRS. H. He's been waiting for me to look at him all through dinner. Shall I do it, and you can see what an idiot he looks?

CAPT. G. "But what imports the nomination of this gentleman?"

MRS. H. Watch! (Sends a glance to the Vaynor man, who tries vainly to combine a mouthful of ice pudding, a smirk of self-satisfaction, a glare of intense devotion, and the stolidity of a Bntish dining countenance.)

CAPT. G. (Critically.) He doesn't look pretty. Why didn't you wait till the spoon was out of his mouth?

MRS. H. To amuse you. She'll make an exhibition of you as I've made of him; and people will laugh at you. Oh, Pip, can't you see that? It's as plain as the noonday Sun. You'll be trotted about and told lies, and made a fool of like the others. j never made a fool of you, did I?

CAPT. G. (Aside.) What a clever little woman it is!

MRS. H. Well, what have you to say?

CAPT. G. I feel better.

MRS. H. Yes, I suppose so, after I have come down to your level. I couldn't have done it if I hadn't cared for you so much. I have spoken the truth.

CAPT. G. It doesn't alter the situation.

MRS. H. (Passionately.) Then she has said that she cares for you! Don't believe her, Pip. It's a lie-as bad as yours to me!

CAPT. G. Ssssteady! I've a notion that a friend of yours is looking at you.

MRS. H. He! I hate him. He introduced you to me.

CAPT. G. (Aside.) And some people would like women to assist in making the laws. Introduction to imply condonement. (Aloud.) Well, you see, if you can remember so far back as that, I couldn't, in' common politeness, refuse the offer.

MRS. H. In common politeness I We have got beyond that!

CAPT. G. (Aside.) Old ground means fresh trouble. (Aloud.) On my honor

MRS. H. Your what? Ha, ha!

CAPT. G. Dishonor, then. She's not what you imagine. I meant to-

MRS. H. Don't tell me anything about her! She won't care for you, and when you come back, after having made an exhibition of yourself, you'll find me occupied with-

CAPT. G. (Insolently.) You couldn't while I am alive. (Aside.) If that doesn't bring her pride to her rescue, nothing will.

MRS. H. (Drawing herself up.) Couldn't do it? I' (Softening.) You're right. I don't believe I could-though you are what you are-a coward and a liar in grain.

CAPT. G. It doesn't hurt so much after your little lecture-with demonstrations.

MRS. H. One mass of vanity! Will nothing ever touch you in this life? There must be a Hereafter if it's only for the benefit of- But you will have it all to yourself.

CAPT. G. (Under his eyebrows.) Are you certain of that?

MRS. H. I shall have had mine in this life; and it will serve me right,

CAPT. G. But the admiration that you insisted on so strongly a moment ago? (Aside.) Oh, I am a brute!

MRS. H. (Fiercely.) Will that con-sole me for knowing that you will go to her with the same words, the same arguments, and the- the same pet names you used to me? And if she cares for you, you two will laugh over my story. Won't that be punishment heavy enough even for me-even for me?-And it's all useless. That's another punishment.

CAPT. G. (Feebly.) Oh, come! I'm not so low as you think.

MRS. H. Not now, perhaps, but you will be. Oh, Pip, if a woman flatters your vanity, there's nothing on earth that you would not tell her; and no meanness that you would not do. Have I known you so long without knowing that?

CAPT. G. If you can trust me in nothing else-and I don't see why I should be trusted-you can count upon my holding my tongue.

MRS. H. If you denied everything you've said this evening and declared it was all in' fun (a long pause), I'd trust you. Not otherwise. All I ask is, don't tell her my name. Please don't. A man might forget: a woman never would. (Looks up table and sees hostess beginning to collect eyes.) So it's all ended, through no fault of mine-Haven't I behaved beautifully? I've accepted your dismissal, and you managed it as cruelly as you could, and I have made you respect my sex, haven't I? (Arranging gloves and fan.) I only pray that she'll know you some day as I know you now. I wouldn't be you then, for I think even your conceit will be hurt. I hope she'll pay you back the humiliation you've brought on me. I hope-No. I don't! I can't give you up! I must have something to look forward to or I shall go crazy. When it's all over, come back to me, come back to me, and you'll find that you're my Pip still!

CAPT. G. (Very clearly.) False move, and you pay for it. It's a girl!

MRS. H. (Rising.) Then it was true! They said-but I wouldn't insult you by asking. A girl! I was a girl not very long ago. Be good to her, Pip. I daresay she believes in' you.

Goes out with an uncertain smile. He watches her through the door, and settles into a chair as the men redistribute themselves.

CAPT. G. Now, if there is any Power who looks after this world, will He kindly tell me what I have done? (Reaching out for the claret, and half aloud.) What have I done?

WITH ANY AMAZEMENT

And are not afraid with any amazement.-Marriage Service.

SCENE.-A bachelor's bedroom-toilet-table arranged with unnatural neat-ness. CAPTAIN GADSBY asleep and snoring heavily. Time, 10:30 A. M.-a glorious autumn day at Simla. Enter delicately Captain MAFFLIN of GADSBY's regiment. Looks at sleeper, and shakes his head murmuring "Poor Gaddy." Performs violent fantasia with hair-brushes on chairback.

CAPT. M. Wake up, my sleeping beauty! (Roars.)

"Uprouse ye, then, my merry merry men! It is our opening day! It is our opening da-ay!"

Gaddy, the little dicky-birds have been billing and cooing for ever so long; and I'm here!

CAPT. G. (Sitting up and yawning.) 'Mornin'. This is awf'ly good of you, old fellow. Most awf'ly good of you. 'Don't know what I should do without you. 'Pon my soul, I don't. 'Haven't slept a wink all night.

CAPT. M. I didn't get in till half-past eleven. 'Had a look at you then, and you seemed to be sleeping as soundly as a condemned criminal.

CAPT. G. Jack, if you want to make those disgustingly worn-out jokes, you'd better go away. (With portentous gravity.) It's the happiest day in my life.

CAPT. M. (Chuckling grimly.) Not by a very long chalk, my son. You're going through some of the most refined torture you've ever known. But be calm. I am with you. 'Shun! Dress!

CAPT. G. Eh! Wha-at?

CAPT. M. Do you suppose that you are your own master for the next twelve hours? If you do, of course-(Makes for the door.)

CAPT. G. No! For Goodness' sake, old man, don't do that! You'll see through, won't you? I've been mugging up that beastly drill, and can't remember a line of it.

CAPT. M. (Overturning G.'s uniform.) Go and tub. Don't bother me. I'll give you ten minutes to dress in.

interval, filled by the noise as O/ one splashing in the bathroom..

CAPT. G. (Emerging from dressing-room.) What time is it?

CAPT. M. Nearly eleven.

CAPT. G. Five hours more. O Lord!

CAPT. M. (Aside.) 'First sign of funk, that. 'Wonder if it's going to spread. (Aloud.) Come along to breakfast.

CAPT. G. I can't eat anything. I don't want any breakfast.

CAPT. M. (Aside.) So early! (Aloud) CAPTAIN Gadsby, I order you to eat breakfast, and a dashed good break-fast, too. None of your bridal airs and graces with me!

Leads G. downstairs and stands over him while he eats two chops.

CAPT. G. (Who has looked at his watch thrice in the last five minutes.) What time is it?

CAPT. M. Time to come for a walk. Light up.

CAPT. G. I haven't smoked for ten days, and I won't now. (Takes cheroot which M. has cut for him, and blows smoke through his nose luxuriously.) We aren't going down the Mall, are we?

CAPT. M. (Aside.) They're all alike in these stages. (Aloud.) No, my Vestal. We're going along the quietest road we can find.

CAPT. G. Any chance of seeing Her? CAPT. M. Innocent! No! Come along, and, if you want me for the final obsequies, don't cut my eye out with your stick.

CAPT. G. (Spinning round.) I say, isn't She the dearest creature that ever walked? What's the time? What comes after "wilt thou take this woman"?

CAPT. M. You go for the ring. R'clect it'll be on the top of my right-hand little finger, and just be careful how you draw it off, because I shall have the Verger's fees somewhere in my glove.

CAPT. G. (Walking forward hastily.) D-the Verger! Come along! It's past twelve and I haven't seen Her since yesterday evening. (Spinning round again.) She's an absolute angel, Jack, and She's a dashed deal too good for me. Look here, does She come up the aisle on my arm, or how?

CAPT. M. If I thought that there was the least chance of your remembering anything for two consecutive minutes, I'd tell you. Stop passaging about like that!

CAPT. G. (Halting in *he middle of the road.) I say, Jack.

CAPT. M. Keep quiet for another ten minutes if you can, you lunatic; and walk!

The two tramp at five miles an hour for fifteen minutes.

CAPT. G. What's the time? How about the cursed wedding-cake and the slippers? They don't throw 'em about in church, do they?

CAPT. M. In-variably. The Padre leads off with his boots.

CAPT. G. Confound your silly soul! Don't make fun of me. I can't stand it, and I won't!

CAPT. M. (Untroubled.) So-ooo, old horse You'll have to sleep for a couple of hours this afternoon.

CAPT. G. (Spinning round.) I'm not going to be treated like a dashed child. understand that

CAPT. M. (Aside.) Nerves gone to fiddle-strings. What a day we're having! (Tenderly putting his hand on G.'s shoulder.) My David, how long have you known this Jonathan? Would I come up here to make a fool of you-after all these years?

CAPT. G. (Penitently.) I know, I know, Jack-but I'm as upset as I can be. Don't mind what I say. Just hear me run through the drill and see if I've got it all right:-"To have and to hold for better or worse, as it was in the beginning, is now, and ever shall be, world without end, so help me God. Amen."

CAPT. M. (Suffocating with suppressed laughter.) Yes. That's about the gist of it. I'll prompt if you get into a hat.

CAPT. G. (Earnestly.) Yes, you'll stick by me, Jack, won't you? I'm awfully happy, but I don't mind telling you that I'm in a blue funk!

CAPT. M. (Gravely.) Are you? I should never have noticed it. You don't look like it.

CAPT. G. Don't I? That's all right. (Spinning round.) On my soul and honor, Jack, She's the sweetest little angel that ever came down from the sky. There isn't a woman on earth fit to speak to Her.

CAPT. M. (Aside.) And this is old Gandy! (Aloud.) Go on if it relieves you.

CAPT. G. You can laugh! That's all you wild asses of bachelors are fit for.

CAPT. M. (Drawling.) You never would wait for the troop to come up. You aren't quite married yet, y'know.

CAPT. G. Ugh! That reminds me. I don't believe I shall be able to get into any boots Let's go home and try 'em on (Hurries forward.)

CAPT. M. 'Wouldn't be in your shoes for anything that Asia has to offer.

CAPT. G. (Spinning round.) That just shows your hideous blackness of soul-your dense stupidity-your brutal narrow-mindedness. There's only one fault about you. You're the best of good fellows, and I don't know what [should have done without you, but-you aren't married. (Wags his head gravely.) Take a wife, Jack.

CAPT. M. (With a face like a wall.) Va-as. Whose for choice?

CAPT. G. If you're going to be a blackguard, I'm going on-What's the time?

CAPT. M. (Hums.)-

An' since 'twas very clear we drank only ginger-beer, Faith, there must ha' been some stingo in the ginger."

Come back, you maniac. I'm going to take you home, and you're going to lie down.

CAPT. G. What on earth do I want to lie down for?

CAPT. M. Give me a light from your cheroot and see.

CAPT. G. (Watching cheroot-butt quiver like a tuning-fork.) Sweet state I'm in!

CAPT. M. You are. I'll get you a peg and you'll go to sleep.

They return and M. compounds a four-finger peg.

CAPT. G. O bus! bus! It'll make me as drunk as an owl.

CAPT. M. 'Curious thing, 'twon't have the slightest effect on you. Drink it off, chuck yourself down there, and go to bye-bye.

CAPT. G. It's absurd. I sha'n't sleep, I know I sha'n't!

Falls into heavy doze at end of seven minutes. CAPT. M. watches him tenderly.

CAPT. M. Poor old Gandy! I've seen a few turned off before, but never one who went to the gallows in this condition. 'Can't tell how it affects 'em, though. It's the thoroughbreds that sweat when they're backed into double-harness.-And that's the man who went through the guns at Amdheran like a devil possessed of devils. (Leans over G.) But this is worse than the guns, old pal-worse than the guns, isn't it? (G. turns in his sleep, and M. touches him clumsily on the forehead.) Poor, dear old Gaddy I Going like the rest of 'em-going like the rest of 'em-Friend that sticketh closer than a brother-eight years. Dashed bit of a slip of a girl-eight weeks! And-where's your friend? (Smokes disconsolately till church clock strikes three.)

CAPT. M. Up with you! Get into your kit.

CAPT. C. Already? Isn't it too soon? Hadn't I better have a shave?

CAPT. M. No! You're all right. (Aside.) He'd chip his chin to pieces.

CAPT. C. What's the hurry?

CAPT. M. You've got to be there first.

CAPT. C. To be stared at?

CAPT. M. Exactly. You're part of the show. Where's the burnisher? Your spurs are in a shameful state.

CAPT. G. (Gruffly.) Jack, I be damned if you shall do that for me.

CAPT. M. (More gruffly.) Dry' up and get dressed! If I choose to clean your spurs, you're under my orders.

CAPT. G. dresses. M. follows suit.

CAPT. M. (Critically, walking round.) M'yes, you'll do. Only don't look so like a criminal. Ring, gloves, fees-that's all right for me. Let your moustache alone. Now, if the ponies are ready, we'll go.

CAPT. G. (Nervously.) It's much too soon. Let's light up! Let's have a peg! Let's-CAPT. M. Let's make bally asses of ourselves!

BELLS. (Without.)-

"Good-peo-ple-all To prayers-we call."

CAPT. M. There go the bells! Come an-unless you'd rather not. (They ride off.)

BELLS.-

"We honor the King And Brides joy do bring-Good tidings we tell, And ring the Dead's knell."

CAPT. G. (Dismounting at the door of the Church.) I say, aren't we much too soon? There are no end of people inside. I say, aren't we much too late? Stick by me, Jack! What the devil do I do?

CAPT. M. Strike an attitude at the bead of the aisle and wait for Her. (G. groans as M. wheels him into position he/ore three hundred eyes.)

CAPT. M. (Imploringly.) Gaddy, if you love me, for pity's sake, for the Honor of the Regiment, stand up! Chuck yourself into your uniform! Look like a man! I've got to speak to the Padre a minute. (G. breaks into a gentle Perspiration.) your face I'll never man again. Stand up! visibly.) If you wipe your face I'll never be your best man again. Stand up! (G. Trembles visibly.)

CAPT. M. (Returning.) She's commg now. Look out when the music starts. There's the organ beginning to clack.

Bride steps out of 'rickshaw at Church door. G. catches a glimpse o/ her and takes heart.

ORGAN.-

"The Voice that breathed o'er Eden, That earliest marriage day, The primal marriage-blessing, It hath not passed away."

CAPT. M. (Watching G.) By Jove! He is looking well. 'Didn't think he had it in him.

CAPT. G. How long does this hymn go on for?

CAPT. M. It will be over directly. (Ansiously.) Beginning to vleach and gulp. Hold on, Gabby, and think o' the Regiment.

CAPT. G. (Measuredly.) I say there's a big brown lizard crawling up that wall.

CAPT. M. My Sainted Mother! The last stage of collapse!

Bride comes Up to left of altar, lifts her eyes once to G., who is suddenly smitten mad.

CAPT. G. (TO himself again and again.) Little Featherweight's a woman-a woman! And I thought she was a little girl.

CAPT. M. (In a whisper.) Form the halt-inward wheel.

CAPT. G. obeys mechanically and the ceremony proceeds.

PADRE . . . only unto her as ye both shall live?

CAPT. G. (His throat useless.) Ha-hmmm!

CAPT. M. Say you will or you won't. There's no second deal here.

Bride gives response with perfect coomess, and is given away by the father.

CAPT. G. (Thinking to show his learning.) Jack give me away now, quick!

CAPT. M. You've given yourself away quite enough. Her right hand, man! Repeat! Repeat! "Theodore Philip." Have you forgotten your own name?

CAPT. G. stumbles through Affirmation, which Bride repeats without a tremor.

CAPT. M. Now the ring! Follow the Padre! Don't pull off my glove! Here it is! Great Cupid, he's found his voice.

CAPT. G. repeats Troth in a voice to be heard to the end of the Church and turns on his heel.

CAPT. M. (Desperately.) Rein back! Back to your troop! 'Tisn't half legal yet.

PADRE . . . joined together let no man put asunder.

CAPT. G. paralyzed with fear jibs after Blessing.

CAPT. M. (Quickly.) On your own front-one length. Take her with you. I don't come. You've nothing to say. (CAPT. G. jingles up to altar.)

CAPT. M. (In a piercing rattle meant to be a whisper.) Kneel, you stiff-necked ruffian! Kneel!

PADRE . . . whose daughters are ye so long as ye do well and are not afraid with any amazement.

CAPT. M. Dismiss! Break off! Left wheel!

All troop to vestry. They sign.

CAPT. M. Kiss Her, Gaddy.

CAPT. G. (Rubbing the ink into his glove.) Eh! Wha-at?

CAPT. M. (Taking one pace to Bride.) If you don't, I shall.

CAPT. G. (Interposing an arm.) Not this journey!

General kissing, in which CAPT. G. is pursued by unknown female.

CAPT. G. (Faintly to M.) This is Hades! Can I wipe my face now?

CAPT. M. My responsibility has ended. Better ask Misses GADSAY.

CAPT. G. winces as though shot and procession is Mendelssohned out of Church to house, where usual tortures take place over the wedding-cake.

CAPT. M. (At table.) Up with you, Gaddy. They expect a speech.

CAPT. G. (After three minutes' agony.) Ha-hmmm. (Thunders Of applause.)

CAPT. M. Doocid good, for a first attempt. Now go and change your kit while Mamma is weeping over_"the Missus." (CAPT. G. disappears. CAPT. M. starts up tearing his hair.) It's not half legal. Where are the shoes? Get an ayah.

AVAH. Missie Captain Sahib done gone band karo all the jutis.

CAPT. M. (Brandishing scab larded sword.) Woman, produce those shoes Some one lend me a bread-knife. We mustn't crack Gaddy's head more than it is. (Slices heel off white satin slipper and puts slipper up his sleeve.)

Where is the Bride? (To the company at large.) Be tender with that rice. It's a heathen custom. Give me the big bag.

* * * * *

Bride slips out quietly into 'rickshaw and departs toward the sun-set.

CAPT. M. (In the open.) Stole away, by Jove! So much the worse for Gaddy! Here he is. Now Gaddy, this'll be livelier than Amdberan! Where's your horse?

CAPT. G. (Furiously, seeing that the women are out of an earshot.) Where the-is my Wife?

CAPT. M. Half-way to Mahasu by this
    Young Lochinvar.

    Horse comes round on his hind legs; re
him.

CAPT. G. Oh you will, will you? Get 'round, you
    you beast! Get round!

    Wrenches horse's head over, nearly breaking lower jaw
himself into saddle, and sends home both spurs in the mids
spattering gale of Best Patna.

CAPT. M. For your life and your love-ride, Gaddy-And God bless
    you!

    Throws half a pound of rice at G. who disappears, bowed
forward on the saddle, in a cloud of sun-lit dust.

CAPT. M. I've lost old Gaddy. (Lights cigarette and strolls off,
    singing absently):-

    "You may carve it on his tombstone, you may cut it on his
card, That a young man married is a young man marred!"

Miss DEERCOURT. (From her horse.) Really, Captain Mafflin!
    You are more plain spoken than polite!

CAPT. M. (Aside.) They say marriage is like cholera. 'Wonder who'll
    be the next victim.

    White satin slipper slides from his sleeve and falls at his feet.
Left wondering.

time. You'll have to ride like

...uses to let G. handle

...rute-you hog-

...swings

...of a

...Mahasu dak-bungalow, ...on the left, glimpse of the Dead ...right, Simla Hills. In background, line of ...TAIN GADSBY, now three weeks a husband, is ...ng the pipe of peace on a rug in the sunshine. Banjo and tobacco-pouch on rug. Overhead the Fagoo eagles. MRS. G. comes out of bungalow.

MRS. G. My husband! CAPT. G. (Lazily, with intense enjoyment.) Eb, wha-at? Say that again.

MRS. G. I've written to Mamma and told her that we shall be back on the 17th.

CAPT. G. Did you give her my love?

MRS. G. No, I kept all that for myself. (Sitting down by his side.) I thought you wouldn't mind.

CAPT. G. (With mock sternness.) I object awf'ly. How did you know that it was yours to keep?

MRS. G. I guessed, Phil.

CAPT. G. (Rapturously.) Lit-tle Featherweight!

MRS. G. I won' t be called those sporting pet names, bad boy.

CAPT. G. You'll be called anything I choose. Has it ever occurred to you, Madam, that you are my Wife?

MRS. G. It has. I haven't ceased wondering at it yet.

CAPT. G. Nor I. It seems so strange; and yet, somehow, it doesn't. (Confidently.) You see, it could have been no one else.

MRS. G. (Softly.) No. No one else-for me or for you. It must have been all arranged from the beginning. Phil, tell me again what made you care for me.

CAPT. G. How could I help it? You were you, you know.

MRS. G. Did you ever want to help it? Speak the truth!

CAPT. G. (A twinkle in his eye.) I did, darling, just at the first. Rut only at the very first. (Chuckles.) I called you-stoop low and I'll whisper-"a little beast." Ho! Ho! Ho!

MRS. G. (Taking him by the mous'ache and making him sit up.) "A-little-beast!" Stop laughing over your crime! And yet you had the-the-awful cheek to propose to me!

CAPT. C. I'd changed my mind then. And you weren't a little beast any more.

MRS. G. Thank you, sir! And when was I ever?

CAPT. G. Never! But that first day, when you gave me tea in that peach-colored muslin gown thing, you looked-you did indeed, dear-such an absurd little mite. And I didn't know what to say to you.

MRS. G. (Twisting moustache.) So you said "little beast." Upon my word, Sir! I called you a "Crrrreature," but I wish now I had called you something worse.

CAPT. G. (Very meekly.) I apologize, but you're hurting me awf'ly. (Interlude.) You're welcome to torture me again on those terms.

MRS. G. Oh, why did you let me do it?

CAPT. G. (Looking across valley.) No reason in particular, but-if it amused you or did you any good-you might-wipe those dear little boots of yours on me.

MRS. G. (Stretching out her hands.) Don't! Oh, don't! Philip, my King, please don't talk like that. It's how I feel. You're so much too good for me. So much too good!

CAPT. G. Me! I'm not fit to put my arm around you. (Puts it round.)

MRS. C. Yes, you are. But I-what have I ever done?

CAPT. G. Given me a wee bit of your heart, haven't you, my Queen!

MRS. G. That's nothing. Any one would do that. They cou-couldn't help it.

CAPT. G. Pussy, you'll make me horribly conceited. Just when I was beginning to feel so humble, too.

MRS. G. Humble! I don't believe it's in your character.

CAPT. G. What do you know of my character, Impertinence?

MRS. G. Ah, but I shall, shan't I, Phil? I shall have time in all the years and years to come, to know everything about you; and there will be no secrets between us.

CAPT. G. Little witch! I believe you know me thoroughly already.

MRS. G. I think I can guess. You're selfish?

CAPT. G. Yes.

MRS. G. Foolish?

CAPT. G. Very.

MRS. G. And a dear?

CAPT. G. That is as my lady pleases.

MRS. G. Then your lady is pleased. (A pause.) D'you know that we're two solemn, serious, grown-up people-CAPT. G. (Tilting her straw hat over her eyes.) You grown-up! Pooh! You're a baby.

MRS. G. And we're talking nonsense.

CAPT. G. Then let's go on talking nonsense. I rather like it. Pussy, I'll tell you a secret. Promise not to repeat?

MRS. G. Ye-es. Only to you.

CAPT. G. I love you.

MRS. G. Re-ally! For how long?

CAPT. G. Forever and ever.

MRS. G. That's a long time.

CAPT. G. 'Think so? It's the shortest I can do with.

MRS. G. You're getting quite clever.

CAPT. G. I'm talking to you.

MRS. G. Prettily turned. Hold up your stupid old head and I'll pay you for it.

CAPT. G. (Affecting supreme contempt.) Take it yourself if you want it.

MRS. G. I've a great mind to-and I will! (Takes it and is repaid with interest.)

CAPT. G, Little Featherweight, it's my opinion that we are a couple of idiots.

MRS. G. We're the only two sensible people in the world. Ask the eagle. He's coming by.

CAPT. G. Ah! I dare say he's seen a good many sensible people at Mahasu. They say that those birds live for ever so long.

MRS. G. How long?

CAPT. G. A hundred and twenty years.

MRS. G. A hundred and twenty years! O-oh! And in a hundred and twenty years where will these two sensible people be?

CAPT. G. What does it matter so long as we are together now?

MRS. G. (Looking round the horizon.) Yes. Only you and I-I and you-in the whole wide, wide world until the end. (Sees the line of the Snows.) How big and quiet the hills look! D'you think they care for us?

CAPT. G. 'Can't say I've consulted em particularly. I care, and that's enough for me.

MRS. G. (Drawing nearer to him.) Yes, now-but afterward. What's that little black blur on the Snows?

CAPT. G. A snowstorm, forty miles away. You'll see it move, as the wind carries it across the face of that spur and then it will be all gone.

MRS. G. And then it will be all gone. (Shivers.)

CAPT. G. (Anriously.) 'Not chilled, pet, are you? 'Better let me get your cloak.

MRS. G. No. Don't leave me, Phil. Stay here. I believe I am afraid. Oh, why are the hills so horrid! Phil, promise me that you'll always love me.

CAPT. G. What's the trouble, darling? I can't promise any more than I have; but I'll promise that again and again if you like.

MRs. G. (Her head on his shoulder.) Say it, then-say it! N-no-don't! The-the-eagles would laugh. (Recovering.) My husband, you've married a little goose.

CAPT. G. (Very tenderly.) Have I? I am content whatever she is, so long as she is mine.

MRS. G. (Quickly.) Because she is yours or because she is me mineself?

CAPT. G. Because she is both. (Piteously.) I'm not clever, dear, and I don't think I can make myself understood properly.

MRS. G. I understand. Pip, will you tell me something?

CAPT. G. Anything you like. (Aside.) I wonder what's coming now.

MRS. G. (Haltingly, her eyes 'owered.) You told me once in the old days-centunes and centuries ago-that you had been engaged before. I didn't say anything-then.

CAPT. G. (Innocently.) Why not?

MRS. G. (Raising her eyes to his.) Because-because I was afraid of losing you, my heart. But now-tell about it-please.

CAPT. G. There's nothing to tell. I was awf'ly old then-nearly two and twenty-and she was quite that.

MRS. G. That means she was older than you. I shouldn't like her to have been younger. Well?

CAPT. G. Well, I fancied myself in love and raved about a bit, and-oh, yes, by Jove! I made up poetry. Ha! Ha!

MRS. G. You never wrote any for me! What happened?

CAPT. G. I came out here, and the whole thing went phut. She wrote to say that there had been a mistake, and then she married.

Mas. G. Did she care for you much?

CAPT. G. No. At least she didn't show it as far as I remember.

MRS. G. As far as you rememberl Do you remember her name? (Hears it and bows her head.) Thank you, my husband.

CAPT. G. Who but you had the right? Now, Little Featherweight, have you ever been mixed up in any dark and dismal tragedy?

MRS. G. If you call me Mrs. Gadsby, p'raps I'll tell.

CAPT. G. (Throwing Parade rasp into his voice.) Mrs. Gadsby, confessl

MRS. G. Good Heavens, Phil! I never knew that you could speak in that terrible voice.

CAPT. G. You don't know half my accomplishments yet. Wait till we are settled in the Plains, and I'll show you how I bark at my troop. You were going to say, darling?

MRS. G. I-I don't like to, after that voice. (Tremulously.) Phil, never you dare to speak to me in that tone, whatever I may do!

CAPT. G. My poor little love! Why, you're shaking all over. I am so sorry. Of course I never meant to upset you Don't tell me anything, I'm a brute.

MRS. G. No, you aren't, and I will tell-There was a man.

CAPT. G. (Lightly.) Was there? Lucky man!

MRS. G. (In a whisper.) And I thougbt I cared for him.

CAPT. G. Still luckier man! Well?

MRS. G. And I thought I cared for him-and I didn't-and then you came-and I cared for you very, very much indeed. That's all. (Face hidden.) You aren't angry, are you?

CAPT. G. Angry? Not in the least. (Aside.) Good Lord, what have I done to deserve this angel?

MRS. G. (Aside.) And he never asked for the name! How funny men are! But perhaps it's as well.

CAPT. G. That man will go to heaven because you once thought you cared for him. 'Wonder if you'll ever drag me up there?

MRS. G. (Firmly.) 'Sha'n't go if you don't.

CAPT. G. Thanks. I say, Pussy, I don't know much about your religious beliefs. You were brought up to believe in a heaven and all that, weren't you?

MRS. G. Yes. But it was a pincushion heaven, with hymn-books in all the pews.

CAPT. G. (Wagging his head with intense conviction.) Never mind. There is a pukka heaven.

MRS. G. Where do you bring that message from, my prophet?

CAPT. G. Here! Because we care for each other. So it's all right.

Mrs. G. (As a troop of langurs crash through the branches.) So it's all right. But Darwin says that we came from those!

CAPT. G. (Placidly.) Ah! Darwin was never in love with an angel. That settles it. Sstt, you brutes! Monkeys, indeed! You shouldn't read those books.

MRS. G. (Folding her hands.) If it pleases my Lord the King to issue proclamation.

CAPT. G. Don't, dear one. There are no orders between us. Only I'd rather you didn't. They lead to nothing, and bother people's heads.

MRS. G. Like your first engagement.

CAPT. G. (With an immense calm.) That was a necessary evil and led to you. Are you nothing?

MRS. G. Not so very much, am I?

CAPT. G. All this world and the next to me.

MRS. G. (Very softly.) My boy of boys! Shall I tell you something?

CAPT. G. Yes, if it's not dreadful-about other men.

MRS. G. It's about my own bad little self.

CAPT. G. Then it must be good. Go on, dear.

MRS. G. (Slowly.) I don't know why I'm telling you, Pip; but if ever you marry again-(Interlude.) Take your hand from my mouth or I'll bite! In the future, then remember-I don't know quite how to put it!

CAPT. G. (Snorting indignantly.) Don't try. "Marry again," indeed!

MRS. G. I must. Listen, my husband. Never, never, never tell your wife anything that you do not wish her to remember and think over all her life. Because a woman-yes, I am a woman-can't forget.

CAPT. G. By Jove, how do you know that?

MRS. G. (Confusedly.) I don't. I'm only guessing. I am-I was-a silly little girl; but I feel that I know so much, oh, so very much more than you, dearest. To begin with, I'm your wife.

CAPT. G. So I have been led to believe.

MRS. G. And I shall want to know every one of your secrets-to share everything you know with you. (Stares round desperately.)

CAPT. G. So you shall, dear, so you shall-but don't look like that.

MRS. G. For your own sake don't stop me, Phil. I shall never talk to you in this way again. You must not tell me! At least, not now.

Later on, when I'm an old matron it won't matter, but if you love me, be very good to me now; for this part of my life I shall never forget! Have I made you understand?

CAPT. G. I think so, child. Have I said anything yet that you disapprove of?

MRS. G. Will you be very angry? That-that voice, and what you said about the engagement-

CAPT. G. But you asked to be told that, darling.

MRS. G. And that's why you shouldn't have told me! You must be the Judge, and, oh, Pip, dearly as I love you, I shan't be able to help you! I shall hinder you, and you must judge in spite of me!

CAPT. G. (Meditatively.) We have a great many things to find out together, God help us both-say so, Pussy-but we shall understand each other better every day; and I think I'm beginning to see now. How in the world did you come to know just the importance of giving me just that lead?

MRS. G. I've told you that I don't know. Only somehow it seemed that, in all this new life, I was being guided for your sake as well as my own.

CAPT. G. (Aside.) Then Mafilin was right! They know, and we-we're blind all of us. (Lightly.) 'Getting a little beyond our depth, dear, aren't we? I'll remember, and, if I fail, let me be punished as I deserve.

MRS. G. There shall be no punishment. We'll start into life together from here-you and I-and no one else.

CAPT. G. And no one else. (A pause.) Your eyelashes are all wet, Sweet? Was there ever such a quaint little Absurdity?

MAS. G. Was there ever such nonsense talked before?

CAPT. G. (Knocking the ashes out of his pipe.) 'Tisn't what we say, it's what we don't say, that helps. And it's all the profoundest philosophy. But no one would understand-even if it were put into a book.

MRS. G. The idea! No-only we ourselves, or people like ourselves-if there are any people like us.

CAPT. G. (Magisterially.) All people, not like ourselves, are blind idiots.

MRS. G. (Wiping her eyes.) Do you think, then, that there are any people as happy as we are?

CAPT. G. 'Must be-unless we've appropriated all the happiness in the world.

MRS. G'. (Looking toward Simla.) Poor dears! Just fancy if we have!

CAPT. G. Then we'll hang on to the whole show, for it's a great deal too jolly to lose-eh, wife o' mine?

MRS. G. O Pip! Pip! How much of you is a solemn, married man and how much a horrid slangy schoolboy?

CAPT. G. When you tell me how much of you was eighteen last birthday and how much is as old as the Sphinx and twice as mysterious, perhaps I'll attend to you. Lend me that banjo. The spirit moveth me to jowl at the sunset.

MRS. G. Mind! It's not tuned. Ah! How that jars!

CAPT G. (Turning pegs.) It's amazingly different to keep a banjo to proper pitch.

MRS. G. It's the same with all musical instruments, What shall it be?

CAPT. G. "Vanity," and let the hills hear. (Sings through the first and hal' of the second verse. Turning to MRS. G.) Now, chorus! Sing, Pussy!

BOTH TOGETHRR. (Con brio, to the horror of the monkeys who are settling for the night.)-

"Vanity, all is Vanity," said Wisdom. scorning me-I clasped my true Love's tender hand and answered frank and free-ee "If this be Vanity who'd be wise? If this be Vanity who'd be wise? If this be Vanity who'd be wi-ise (Crescendo.) Vanity let it be!"

MRS. G. (Defiantly to the grey of the evening sky.) "Vanity let it be!"

ECHO. (Prom the Fagoo spur.) Let it be!

FATIMA

And you may go in every room of the house and see everything that is there, but into the Blue Room you must not go.-The Story of Blue Beard.

SCENE.-The GADSBYS' bungalow in the Plains. Time, 11 A. M. on a Sunday morning. Captain GADSBY, in his shirt-sleeves, is bending over a complete set of Hussar's equipment, from saddle to picketing-rope, which is neatly spread over the floor of his study. He is smoking an unclean briar, and his forehead is puckered with thought.

CAPT. G. (To himself, fingering a headstall.) Jack's an ass. There's enough brass on this to load a mule-and, if the Americans know anything about anything, it can be cut down to a bit only. 'Don't want the watering-bridle, either. Humbug!-Half a dozen sets of chains and pulleys for one horse! Rot! (Scratching his head.) Now, let's consider it all over from the he-ginning. By Jove, I've forgotten the scale of weights! Ne'er mind. 'Keep the bit only, and eliminate every boss from the crupper to breastplate. No breastplate at all. Simple leather strap across the breast-like the Russians. Hi! Jack never thought of that!

MRS. G. (Entering hastily, her hand bound in a cloth.) Oh, Pip, I've scalded my hand over that horrid, horrid Tiparee jam!

CAPT. G. (Absently.) Eh! Wha-at?

MRS. G. (With round-eyed reproach.) I've scalded it aw-fully! Aren't you sorry? And I did so want that jam to jam properly.

CAPT. G. Poor little woman! Let me kiss the place and make it well. (Unrolling bandage.) You small sinner! Where's that scald? I can't see it.

MRS. G. On the top of the little finger. There!-It's a most 'normous big burn!

CAPT. G. (Kissing little finger.) Baby! Let Hyder look after the jam. You know I don't care for sweets.

Mas. G. In-deed?-Pip!

CAPT. G. Not of that kind, anyhow. And now run along, Minnie, and leave me to my own base devices. I'm busy.

MRS. G. (Calmly settling herself in long chair.) So I see. What a mess you're making! Why have you brought all that smelly leather stuff into the house?

CAPT. G. To play with. Do you mind, dear?

MRS. G. Let me play too. I'd like it.

CAPT. G. I'm afraid you wouldn't. Pussy-Don't you think that jam will burn, or whatever it is that jam does when it's not looked after by a clever little housekeeper?

MRS. G. I thought you said Hyder could attend to it. I left him in the veranda, stirring-when I hurt myself so.

CAPT. G. (His eye returning to the equipment.) Po-oor little woman!-Three pounds four and seven is three eleven, and that can be cut down to two eight, with just a lee-tie care, with-out weakening anything. Farriery is all rot in incompetent hands.

What's the use of a shoe-case when a man's scouting? He can't stick it on with a lick-like a stamp-the shoe! Skittles

MRS. G. What's skittles? Pah! What is this leather cleaned with?

CAPT. G. Cream and champagne and-Look here, dear, do you really want to talk to me about anything important?

MRS. G. No. I've done my accounts, and I thought I'd like to see what you're doing.

CAPT. G. Well, love, now you've seen and-Would you mind?-That is to say-Minnie, I really am busy.

MRS. G. You want me to go?

CAPT. G, Yes, dear, for a little while. This tobacco will hang in your dress, and saddlery doesn't interest you.

MRS. G. Everything you do interests me, Pip.

CAPT. G. Yes, I know, I know, dear. I'll tell you all about it some day when I've put a head on this thing. In the meantime-

MRS. G. I'm to be turned out of the room like a troublesome child?

CAPT. G. No-o. I don't mean that exactly. But, you see, I shall be tramping up and down, shifting these things to and fro, and I shall be in your way. Don't you think so?

MRS. G. Can't I lift them about? Let me try. (Reaches forward to trooper's saddle.)

CAPT. G. Good gracious, child, don't touch it. You'll hurt yourself. (Picking up saddle.) Little girls aren't expected to handle numdahs. Now, where would you like it put? (Holds saddle above his head.)

MRS. G. (A break in her voice.) Nowhere. Pip, how good you are-and how strong! Oh, what's that ugly red streak inside your arm?

CAPT. G. (Lowering saddle quickly.) Nothing. It's a mark of sorts. (Aside.) And Jack's coming to tiffin with his notions all cut and dried!

MRS. G. I know it's a mark, but I've never seen it before. It runs all up the arm. What is it?

CAPT. G. A cut-if you want to know.

MRS. G. Want to know! Of course I do! I can't have my husband cut to pieces in this way. How did it come? Was it an accident? Tell me, Pip.

CAPT. G. (Grimly.) No. 'Twasn't an accident. I got it-from a man-in Afghanistan.

MRS. G. In action? Oh, Pip, and you never told me!

CAPT. G. I'd forgotten all about it.

MRS. G. Hold up your arm! What a horrid, ugly scar! Are you sure it doesn't hurt now! How did the man give it you?

CAPT. G. (Desperately looking at his watch.) With a knife. I came down-old Van Loo did, that's to say-and fell on my leg, so I couldn't run. And then this man came up and began chopping at me as I sprawled.

MRS. G. Oh, don't, don't! That's enough!-Well, what happened?

CAPT. G. I couldn't get to my holster, and Mafflin came round the corner and stopped the performance.

MRS. G. How? He's such a lazy man, I don't believe he did.

CAPT. G. Don't you? I don't think the man had much doubt about it. Jack cut his head off.

Mas. G. Cut-his-head-off! "With one blow," as they say in the books?

CAPT. G. I'm not sure. I was too interested in myself to know much about it. Anyhow, the head was off, and Jack was punching old Van Loo in the ribs to make him get up. Now you know all about it, dear, and now-

MRS. G. You want me to go, of course. You never told me about this, though I've been married to you for ever so long; and you never would have told me if I hadn't found out; and you never do tell me anything about yourself, or what you do, or what you take an interest in.

CAPT. G. Darling, I'm always with you, aren't I?

MRS. G. Always in my pocket, you were going to say. I know you are; but you are always thinking away from me.

CAPT. G. (Trying to hide a smile.) Am I? I wasn't aware of it. I'm awf'ly sorry.

MRS. G. (Piteously.) Oh, don't make fun of me! Pip, you know what I mean. When you are reading one of those things about Cavalry, by that idiotic Prince-why doesn't he be a Prince instead of a stable-boy?

CAPT. G. Prince Kraft a stable-boy-Oh, my Aunt! Never mind, dear. You were going to say?

MRS. G. It doesn't matter; you don't care for what I say. Only-only you get up and walk about the room, staring in front of you, and then Mafflin comes in to dinner, and after I'm in the drawmg-room I can hear you and him talking, and talking, and talking, about things I can't understand, and-oh, I get so tired and feel so lonely!-I don't want to complain and be a trouble, Pip; but I do indeed I do!

CAPT. G. My poor darling! I never thought of that. Why don't you ask some nice people in to dinner?

MRS. G. Nice people! Where am I to find them? Horrid frumps! And if I did, I shouldn't be amused. You know I only want you.

CAPT, G. And you have me surely, Sweetheart?

MRS. G. I have not! Pip why don't you take me into your life?

CAPT. G. More than I do? That would be difficult, dear.

MRS. G. Yes, I suppose it would-to you. I'm no help to you-no companion to you; and you like to have it so.

CAPT. G. Aren't you a little unreasonable, Pussy?

MRS. G. (Stamping her foot.) I'm the most reasonable woman in the world-when I'm treated properly.

CAPT. G. And since when have I been treating you improperly?

MRS. G. Always-and since the beginning. You know you have.

CAPT. G. I don't; but I'm willing to be convinced.

MRS. G. (Pointing to saddlery.) There!

CAPT. G. How do you mean?

MRS. G. What does all that mean? Why am I not to be told? Is it so precious?

CAPT. G. I forget its exact Government value just at present. It means that it is a great deal too heavy.

MRS. G. Then why do you touch it?

CAPT. G. To make it lighter. See here, little love, I've one notion and Jack has another, but we are both agreed that all this equipment is about thirty pounds too heavy. The thing is how to cut it down without weakening any part of it, and, at the same time, allowing the trooper to carry everything he wants for his own comfort-socks and shirts and things of that kind.

MRS. G. Why doesn't he pack them in a little trunk?

CAPT. G. (Kissing her.) Oh, you darling! Pack them in a little trunk, indeed! Hussars don't carry trunks, and it's a most important thing to make the horse do all the carrying.

MRS. G. But why need you bother about it? You're not a trooper.

CAPT. G. No; but I command a few score of him; and equipment is nearly everything in these days.

MRS. G. More than me?

CAPT. G. Stupid! Of course not; but it's a matter that I'm tremendously interested in, because if I or Jack, or I and Jack, work out some sort of lighter saddlery and all that. it's possible that we may get it adopted.

MRS. G. How?

CAPT. G. Sanctioned at Home, where they will make a sealed pattern-a pattern that all the saddlers must copy-and so it will be used by all the regiments.

MRS. G. And that interests you?

CAPT. G. It's part of my profession, y'know, and my profession is a good deal to me. Everything in a soldier's equipment is important, and if we can improve that equipment, so much the better for the soldiers and for us.

Mas. G. Who's "us"?

CAPT. G. Jack and I; only Jack's notions are too radical. What's that big sigh for, Minnie?

MRS. G. Oh, nothing-and you've kept all this a secret from me! Why?

CAPT. G. Not a secret, exactly, dear. I didn't say anything about it to you because I didn't think it would amuse you.

MRS. G. And am I only made to be amused?

CAPT. G. No, of course. I merely mean that it couldn't interest you.

MRS. G. It's your work and-and if you'd let me, I'd count all these things up. If they are too heavy, you know by how much they are too heavy, and you must have a list of things made out to your scale of lightness, and-

CAPT. G. I have got both scales somewhere in my head; hut it's hard to tell how light you can make a head-stall, for instance, until you've actually had a model made.

MRS. G. But if you read out the list, I could copy it down, and pin it up there just above your table. Wouldn't that do?

CAPT. G. It would be awf'ly nice, dear, but it would be giving you trouble for nothing. I can't work that way. I go by rule of thumb. I know the present scale of weights, and the other one-the one that I'm trying to work to-will shift and vary so much that I couldn't be certain, even if I wrote it down.

MRS. G. I'm so sorry. I thought I might help. Is there anything else that I could be of use in?

CAPT. G. (Looking round the room.) I can't think of anything. You're always helping me you know.

MRS. G. Am I? How?

CAPT. G. You are of course, and as long as you're near me-I can't explain exactly, but it's in the air.

MRS. G. And that's why you wanted to send me away?

CAPT. G. That's only when I'm trying to do work-grubby work like this.

MRS. G. Mafflin's better, then, isn't he?

CAPT. G. (Rashly.) Of course he is. Jack and I have been thinking along the same groove for two or three years about this equipment. It's our hobby, and it may really be useful some day.

MRS. G. (After a pause.) And that's all that you have away from me?

CAPT. G. It isn't very far away from you now. Take care the oil on that bit doesn't come off on your dress.

MRS. G. I wish-I wish so much that I could really help you. I believe I could-if I left the room. But that's not what I mean.

CAPT. G. (Aside.) Give me patience! I wish she would go. (Aloud.) I as-sure you you can't do anything for me, Minnie, and I must really settle down to this. Where's my pouch?

MRS. G. (Crossing to writing-table.) Here you are, Bear. What a mess you keep your table in!

CAPT. G. Don't touch it. There's a method in my madness, though you mightn't think of it.

MRS. G. (At table.) I want to look-Do you keep accounts, Pip?

CAPT. G. (Bending over saddlery.) Of a sort. Are you rummaging among the Troop papers? Be careful.

MRs. G. Why? I sha'n't disturb anything. Good gracious! I had no idea that you had anything to do with so many sick horses.

CAPT. G. 'Wish I hadn't, but they insist on falling sick. Minnie, if 1 were you I really should not investigate those papers. You may come across something that you won't like.

MRS. G. Why will you always treat me like a child? I know I'm not displacing the horrid things.

CAPT. G. (Resignedly.) Very well, then. Don't blame me if anything happens. Play with the table and let me go on with the saddlery. (Slipping hand into trousers-pocket.) Oh, the deuce!

MRS. G. (Her back to G.) What's that for?

CAPT. G. Nothing. (Aside.) There's not much in it, but I wish I'd torn it up.

MRS. G. (Turning over contents of table.) I know you'll hate me for this; but I do want to see what your work is like. (A pause.) Pip, what are "farcybuds"?

CAPT. G. Hab! Would you really like to know? They aren't pretty things.

MRS. G. This Journal of Veterinary Science says they are of "absorbing interest." Tell me.

CAPT. G. (Aside.) It may turn her attention.

Gives a long and designedly loathsome account of glanders and farcy.

MRS. G. Oh, that's enough. Don't go on!

CAPT. G. But you wanted to know-Then these things suppurate and matterate and spread-

MRS. G. Pin, you're making me sick! You're a horrid, disgusting schoolboy.

CAPT. G. (On his knees among the bridles.) You asked to be told. It's not my fault if you worry me into talking about horrors.

Mas. G. Why didn't you say-No?

CAPT. G. Good Heavens, child! Have you come in here simply to bully me?

Mas. G. I bully you? How could I! You're so strong. (Hysterically.) Strong enough to pick me up and put me outside the door and leave me there to cry. Aren't you?

CAPT. G. It seems to me that you're an irrational little baby. Are you quite well?

MRS. G. Do I look ill? (Returning to table). Who is your lady friend with the big grey envelope and the fat monogram outside?

CAPT. G. (Aside.) Then it wasn't locked up, confound it. (Aloud.) "God made her, therefore let her pass for a woman." You remember what farcybuds are like?

Mas. G. (Showing envelope.) This has nothing to do with them. I'm going to open it. May I?

CAPT. G. Certainly, if you want to. I'd sooner you didn't though. I don't ask to look at your letters to the Deer-court girl.

Mas. G. You'd better not, Sir! (Takes letter from envelope.) Now, may I look? If you say no, I shall cry.

CAPT. G. You've never cried in my knowledge of you, and I don't believe you could.

Mas. G. I feel very like it to-day, Pip. Don't be hard on me. (Reads letter.) It begins in the middle, with-out any "Dear Captain Gadsby," or anything. How funny!

CAPT. G. (Aside.) No, it's not Dear Captain Gadsby, or anything, now. How funny!

Mas. G. What a strange letter! (Reads.) "And so the moth has come too near the candle at last, and has been singed into-shall I say Respectability? I congratulate him, and hope he will be as happy as he deserves to be." What does that mean? Is she congratulating you about our marriage?

CAPT. G. Yes, I suppose so.

Mas. G. (Still r'ading letter.) She seems to be a particular friend of yours.

CAPT. G. Yes. She was an excellent matron of sorts-a Mrs. Herriott-wife of a Colonel Herriott. I used to know some of her people at Home long ago-before I came out.

Mas. G. Some Colonel's wives are young-as young as me. I knew one who was younger.

CAPT. G. Then it couldn't have been Mrs. Herriott. She was old enough to have been ycur mother, dear.

Mas. G. I remember now. Mrs. Scargill was talking about her at the Dutfins' tennis, before you came for me, on Tuesday. Captain Mafflin said she was a "dear old woman." Do you know, I think Mafilin is a very clumsy man with his feet.

CAPT. G. (Aside.) Good old Jack! (Aloud.) Why, dear?

Mas. G. He had put his cup down on the ground then, and he literally stepped into it. Some of the tea spirted over my dress-the grey one. I meant to tell you about it before.

CAPT. G. (Aside.) There are the makings of a strategist about Jack though his methods are coarse. (Aloud.) You'd better get a new dress, then. (Aside.) Let us pray that that will turn her.

Mas. G. Oh, it isn't stained in the least. I only thought that I'd tell you. (Returning to letter.) What an extraordinary person! (Reads.) "But need I remind you that you have taken upon yourself a charge of wardship"-what in the world is a charge of wardship?-"which as you yourself know, may end in Consequences"-

CAPT. G. (Aside.) It's safest to let em see everything as they come across it; but 'seems to me that there are exceptions to the rule. (Aloud.) I told you that there was nothing to be gained from rearranging my table.

Mas. G. (Absently.) What does the woman mean? She goes on talking about Consequences-' 'almost inevitable Consequences" with a capital C-for half a page. (Flushing scarlet.) Oh, good gracious! How abominable!

CAPT. G. (Promptly.) Do you think so? Doesn't it show a sort of motherly interest in us? (Aside.) Thank Heaven. Harry always wrapped her meaning up safely! (Aloud.) Is it absolutely necessary to go on with the letter, darling?

Mas. G. It's impertinent-it's simply horrid. What right has this woman to write in this way to you? She oughtn't to.

CAPT. G. When you write to the Deercourt girl, I notice that you generally fill three or four sheets. Can't you let an old woman babble on paper once in a way? She means well.

MRS. G. I don't care. She shouldn't write, and if she did, you ought to have shown me her letter.

CAPT. G. Can't you understand why I kept it to myself, or must I explain at length-as I explained the farcybuds?

Mas. G. (Furiously.) Pip I hate you! This is as bad as those idiotic saddle-bags on the floor. Never mind whether it would please me or not, you ought to have given it to me to read.

CAPT. G. It comes to the same thing. You took it yourself.

MRS. G. Yes, but if I hadn't taken it, you wouldn't have said a word. I think this Harriet Herriott-it's like a name in a book-is an interfering old Thing.

CAPT. G. (Aside.) So long as you thoroughly understand that she is old, I don't much care what you think. (Aloud.) Very good, dear. Would you like to write and tell her so? She's seven thousand miles away.

MRS. G. I don't want to have any-thing to do with her, but you ought to have told me. (Turning to last page of letter.) And she patronizes me, too. I've never seen her! (Reads.) "I do not know how the world stands with you; in all human probability I shall never know; but whatever I may have said before, I pray for her sake more than for yours that all may be well. I have learned what misery means, and I dare not wish that any one dear to you should share my knowledge."

CAPT. G. Good God! Can't you leave that letter alone, or, at least, can't you refrain from reading it aloud? I've been through it once. Put it back on 'he desk. Do you hear me?

Mas. G. (Irresolutely.) I sh-sha'n't! (Looks at G.'s eyes.) Oh, Pip, please! I didn't mean to make you angry-'Deed, I didn't. Pip, I'm so sorry. I know I've wasted your time-CAPT. G. (Grimly.) You have. Now, will you be good enough to go-if there is nothing more in my room that you are anxious to pry into?

Mas. G. (Putting out her hands.) Oh, Pip, don't look at me like that! I've never seen you look like that before and it hu-urts me! I'm sorry. I oughtn't to have been here at all, and-and-and-(sobbing.) Oh, be good to me! Be good to me! There's only you-anywhere! Breaks down in long chair, hiding face in cushions.

CAPT. G. (Aside.) She doesn't know how she flicked me on the raw. (Aloud, bending over chair.) I didn't mean to be harsh, dear-I didn't really. You can stay here as long as you please, and do what you please. Don't cry like that. You'll make yourself sick. (Aside.) What on earth has come over her? (Aloud.) Darling, what's the matter with you?

Mrs. G. (Her face still hidden.) Let me go-let me go to my own room. Only-only say you aren't angry with me.

CAPT. G. Angry with you, love! Of course not. I was angry with myself. I'd lost my temper over the saddlery-Don't hide your face, Pussy. I want to kiss it.

Bends lower, Mas. G. slides right arm round his neck. Several interludes and much sobbing.

Mas. G. (In a whisper.) I didn't mean about the jam when I came in to tell you-

CAPT'. G. Bother the jam and the equipment! (Interlude.)

Mas. G. (Still more faintly.) My finger wasn't scalded at all. I-[wanted to speak to you about-about-something else, and-I didn't know how.

CAPT. G. Speak away, then. (Looking into her eyes.) Eb! Wha-at? Minnie! Here, don't go away! You don't mean?

Mas. G. (Hysterically, backing to portiere and hiding her face in its fold's.) The-the Almost Inevitable Consequences! (Flits through portiere as G. attempts to catch her, and bolts her self in her own room.)

CAPT. G. (His arms full of portiere.) Oh! (Sitting down heavily in chair.) I'm a brutea pig-a bully, and a blackguard. My poor, poor little darling! "Made to be amused only?"-

THE VALLEY OF THE SHADOW
KNOWING GOOD AND EVIL.

SCENE.-The GADSBYS' bungalow in the Plains, in June.

Punkah-coolies asleep in veranda where Captain GADBY is walking up and down. DOCTOR'S trap in porch. JUNIOR CHAPLAIN drifting generally and uneasily through the house. Time, 3:4O A. M. Heat 94 degrees in veranda.

DOCTOR. (Coming into veranda and touching G. on the shoulder.) You had better go in and see her now.

CAPT. G. (The color of good cigar-ash.) Eb, wha-at? Oh, yes, of course. What did you say?

DOCTOR. (Syllable by syllable.) Go-in-to-the-room-and-see-her. She wants to speak to you. (Aside, testily.) I shall have him on my hands next.

JUNIOR CHAPLAIN. (In half-lighted dining room.) Isn't there any?-

DOCTOR. (Savagely.) Hsb, you little fool!

JUNIOR CHAPLAIN. Let me do my work. Gadsby, stop a minute I (Edges after G.)

DOCTOR. Wait till she sends for you at least-at least. Man alive, he'll kill you if you go in there! What are you bothering him for?

JUNIOR CHAPLAIN. (Coming into veranda.) I've given him a stiff brandy-peg. He wants it. You've forgotten him for the last ten hours and-forgotten yourself too.

CAPT. G. enters bedroom, which is lit by one night-lamp. Ayak on the floor pretending to be asleep.

VOICE. (From the bed.) All down the street-such bonfires! Ayah, go and put them out! (Appealingly.) How can I sleep with an installation of the C.I.E. in my room? No-not C.I.E. Something else. What was it?

CAPT. G. (Trying to control his voice.) Minnie, I'm here. (Bending over bed.) Don't you know me, Mmnie? It's me-it's Phil-it's your husband.

VOICE. (Mechanically.) It's me-it's Phil-it's your husband.

CAPT. G. She doesn't know mel-It's your own husband, darling.

VOICE. Your own husband, darling. AYAH. (With an inspiration.) Memsahib understanding all I saying.

CAPT. G. Make her understand me then-quick!

AYAH. (Hand on Mas. G.'s fore-head.) Memsahib! Captain Sahib here.

VOICE. Salaem do. (Fretfully.) I know I'm not fit to be seen.

AYAH. (Aside to G.) Say "marneen" same as breakfash.

CAPT. G. Good-morning, little woman. How are we to-day?

VOICE. That's Phil. Poor old Phil. (Viciously.) Phil, you fool, I can't see you. Come nearer.

CAPT. G. Minnie! Minnie! It's me-you know me?

VOICE. (Mockingly.) Of course I do. Who does not know the man who was so cruel to his wife-almost the only one he ever had?

CAPT. G. Yes, dear. Yes-of course, of course. But won't you speak to bim? He wants to speak to you so much.

VOICE. They'd never let him in. The Doctor would give darwaza bund even if he were in the house. He'll never come. (Despairingly.) O Judas! Judas! Judas!

CAPT. G. (Putting out his arms.) They have let him in, and he always was in the house Oh, my love-don't you know me?

VOrCE. (In a half chant.) "And it came to pass at the eleventh hour that this poor soul repented." It knocked at the gates, but they were shut-tight as a plaster-a great, burning plaster They had pasted our marriage certificate all across the door, and it was made of red-hot iron-people really ought to be more careful, you know.

CAPT. G. What am I to do? (Taking her in his arms.) Minnie! speak to me-to Phil.

VOICE. What shall I say? Oh, tell me what to say before it's too late! They are all going away and I can't say anything.

CAPT. G. Say you know me! Only say you know me!

DOCTOR. (Who has entered quietly.) For pity's sake don't take it too much to heart, Gadsby. It's this way sometimes. They won't recognize. They say all sorts of queer things-don't you see?

CAPT. G. All right! All right! Go away now; she'll recognize me; you're bothering her. She must-mustn't she?

DOCTOR. She will before-Have I your leave to try?-

CAPT. G. Anything you please, so long as she'll know me. It's only a question of-hours, isn't it?

DOCTOR. (Professionally.) While there's life there's hope y'know. But don't build on it.

CAPT. G. I don't. Pull her together if it's possible. (Aside.) What have I done to deserve this?

DOCTOR. (Bending over bed.) Now, Mrs. Gadsby! We shall be all right tomorrow. You must take it, or I sha'n't let Phil see you. It isn't nasty, is it?

Voice. Medicines! Always more medicines! Can't you leave me alone?

CAPT. G. Oh, leave her in peace, Doc!

DOCTOR. (Stepping back,-aside.) May I be forgiven if I've none wrong. (Aloud.) In a few minutes she ought to be sensible; but I daren't tell you to look for anything. It's only-

CAPT. G. What? Go on, man.

DOCTOR. (In a whisper.) Forcing the last rally.

CAPT. G. Then leave us alone.

DOCTOR. Don't mind what she says at first, if you can. They-they-they turn against those they love most sometimes in this.- It's hard, but-

CAPT. G. Am I her husband or are you? Leave us alone for what time we have together.

VOICE. (Confidentially.) And we were engaged quite suddenly, Emma. I assure you that I never thought of it for a moment; but, oh, my little Me!-I don't know what I should have done if he hadn't proposed.

CAPT. G. She thinks of that Deercourt girl before she thinks of me. (Aloud.) Minnie!

VOICE. Not from the shops, Mummy dear. You can get the real leaves from Kaintu, and (laughing weakly) never mind about the blossoms-Dead white silk is only fit for widows, and I won't wear it. It's as bad as a winding sheet. (A long pause.)

CAPT. G. I never asked a favor yet. If there is anybody to listen to me, let her know me-even if I die too!

VOICE. (Very faintly.) Pip, Pip dear.

CAPT. G. I'm here, darling.

VOICE. What has happened? They've been bothering me so with medicines and things, and they wouldn't let you come and see me. I was never ill before. Am I ill now?

CAPT. G. You-you aren't quite well.

VOICE. How funny! Have I been ill long?

CAPT. G. Some day; but you'll be all right in a little time.

VOICE. Do you think so, Pip? I don't feel well and-Oh! what have they done to my hair?

CAPT. G. I d-d-on't know.

VOICE. They've cut it off. What a shame!

CAPT. G. It must have been to make your head cooler.

VOICE. Just like a boy's wig. Don't I look horrid?

CAPT. G. Never looked prettier in your life, dear. (Aside.) How am I to ask her to say good-bye?

VOICE. I don't feel pretty. I feel very ill. My heart won't work. It's nearly dead inside me, and there's a funny feeling in my eyes. Everything seems the same distance-you and the almirah and the table inside my eyes or miles away. What does it mean, Pip?

CAPT. G. You're a little feverish, Sweetheart-very feverish. (Breaking down.) My love! my love! How can I let you go?

VOICE. I thought so. Why didn't you tell me that at first?

CAPT. G. What?

VOICE. That I am going to-die.

CAPT. G. But you aren't! You sha'n't.

AYAH to punkah-coolie. (Stepping into veranda after a glance at the bed.). Punkah chor do! (Stop pulling the punkah.)

VOICE. It's hard, Pip. So very, very hard after one year-just one year.

(Wailing.) And I'm only twenty. Most girls aren't even married at twenty. Can't they do anything to help me? I don't want to die.

CAPT. G. Hush, dear. You won't.

VOICE. What's the use of talking? Help me! You've never failed me yet. Oh, Phil, help me to keep alive. (Feverishly.) I don't believe you wish me to live. You weren't a bit sorry when that horrid Baby thing died. I wish I'd killed it!

CAPT. G. (Drawing his hand across his forehead.) It's more than a man's meant to bear-it's not right. (Aloud.) Minnie, love, I'd die for you if it would help.

VOICE. No more death. There's enough already. Pip, don't you die too.

CAPT. G. I wish I dared.

VOICE. It says: "Till Death do us part." Nothing after that-and so it would be no use. It stops at the dying. Why does it stop there? Only such a very short life, too. Pip, I'm sorry we married.

CAPT. G. No! Anything but that, Mm!

VOICE. Because you'll forget and I'll forget. Oh, Pip, don't forget! I always loved you, though I was cross sometimes. If I ever did anything that you didn't like, say you forgive me now.

CAPT. G. You never did, darling. On my soul and honor you never did. I haven't a thing to forgive you.

VOICE. I sulked for a whole week about those petunias. (With a laugh.) What a little wretch I was, and how grieved you were! Forgive me that, Pp.

CAPT. G. There's nothing to forgive. It was my fault. They were too near the drive. For God's sake don't talk so, Minnie! There's such a lot to say and so little time to say it in.

VOICE. Say that you'll always love me-until the end.

CAPT. G. Until the end. (Carried away.) It's a lie. It must be, because we've loved each other. This isn't the end.

VOICE. (Relapsing into semi-delirium.) My Church-service has an ivory-cross on the back, and it says so, so it must be true. "Till Death do us part."-but that's a lie. (With a parody of G.'s manner.) A damned lie! (Recklessly.) Yes, I can swear as well as a Trooper, Pip. I can't make my head think, though. That's because they cut off my hair. How can one think with one's head all fuzzy?

(Pleadingly.) Hold me, Pip! Keep me with you always and always. (Relapsing.) But if you marry the Thorniss girl when I'm dead, I'll come back and howl under our bedroom window all night. Oh, bother! You'll think I'm a jackall. Pip, what time is it?

CAPT. G. A little before the dawn, dear.

VOICE. I wonder where I shall be this time to-morrow?

CAPT. G. Would you like to see the Padre?

VOICE. Why should I? He'd tell me that I am going to heaven; and that wouldn't be true, because you are here. Do you recollect when he upset the cream-ice all over his trousers at the Gassers' tennis?

CAPT. G. Yes, dear.

VOICE. I often wondered whether he got another pair of trousers; but then his are so shiny all over that you really couldn't tell unless you were told. Let's call him in and ask.

CAPT. G. (Gravely.) No. I don't think he'd like that. 'Your head comfy, Sweetheart?'

VOICE. (Faintly with a sigh of contentment.) Yeth! Gracious, Pip, when did you shave last? Your chin's worse than the barrel of a musical box.-No, don't lift it up. I like it. (A pause.) You said you've never cried at all. You're crying all over my cheek.

CAPT. G. I-I-I can't help it, dear.

VOICE. How funny! I couldn't cry now to save my life. (G. shivers.) I want to sing.

CAPT. G. Won't it tire you? 'Better not, perhaps.

VOICE. Why? I won't be bothered about. (Begins in a hoarse quaver)

"Minnie bakes oaten cake, Minnie brews ale, All because her Johnnie's coming home from the sea. (That's parade, Pip.) And she grows red as a rose, who was so pale; And 'Are you sure the church-clock goes?' says she."

(Pettishly.) I knew I couldn't take the last note. How do the bass chords run? (Puts out her hands and begins playing piano on the sheet.)

CAPT. G. (Catching up hands.) Ahh! Don't do that, Pussy, if you love me.

VOICE. Love you? Of course I do. Who else should it be? (A pause.)

VOICE. (Very clearly.) Pip, I'm gomg now. Something's choking me cruelly. (Indistinctly.) Into the dark-without you, my heart-But it's a lie, dear-we mustn't believe it.-Forever and ever, living or dead. Don't let me go, my husband-hold me tight.-They can't-whatever happens. (A cough.) Pip-my Pip! Not for always-and-so-soon! (Voice ceases.)

Pause of ten minutes. G. buries his face in the side of the bed while AYAH bends over bed from opposite side and feels Mas. G.'s breast and forehead.

CAPT. G. (Rising.) Doctor Sahib ko salaam do.

AYAH. (Still by bedside, with a shriek.) Ail Ail Tuta-phuta! My Memsahib! Not getting-not have got!-Pusseena agyal (The sweat has come.) (Fiercely to G.) TUM jao Doctor Sahib ko jaldi! (You go to the doctor.) Oh, my Memsahib!

DOCTOR. (Entering hastily.) Come away, Gadsby. (Bends over bed.) Eb! The Dev-What inspired you to stop the punkab? Get out, man-go away-wait outside! Go! Here, Ayab! (Over his shoulder to G.) Mind I promise nothing.

The dawn breaks as G. stumbles into the garden.

CAPT. M. (Rehung up at the gate on his way to parade and very soberly.) Old man, how goes?

CAPT. G. (Dazed.) I don't quite know. Stay a bit. Have a drink or something. Don't run away. You're just getting amusing. Ha! ha!

CAPT. M. (Aside.) What am I let in for? Gaddy has aged ten years in the night.

CAPT. G. (Slowly, fingering charger's headstall.) Your curb's too loose.

CAPT. M. So it is. Put it straight, will you? (Aside.) I shall be late for parade. Poor Gaddy.

CAPT. G. links and unlinks curb-chain aimlessly, and finally stands staring toward the veranda. The day brightens.

DOCTOR. (Knocked out of professional gravity, tramping across flower-beds and shaking G's hands.) It'-it's-it's !-Gadsby, tbere's a fair chance-a dashed fair chance. The flicker, y'know. The sweat, y'know I saw how it would be. The punkab, y'know. Deuced clever woman that Ayah of yours. Stopped the punkab just at the right time. A dashed good chance! No-you don't go in. We'll pull her through yet I promise on my reputation-under Providence. Send a man with this note to Bingle. Two heads better than one. 'Specially the Ayah! We'll pull her round. (Retreats hastily to house.)

CAPT. G. (His head on neck of M.'s charger.) Jack! I bub-bu-believe, I'm going to make a bu-bub-bloody exhibitiod of byself.

CAPT. M. (Sniffing openly and feelmg in his left cuff.) I b-b-believe, I'b doing it already. Old bad, what cad I say? I'b as pleased as-Cod dab you, Gaddy! You're one big idiot and I'b adother. (Pulling himself together.) Sit tight! Here comes the Devil-dodger.

JUNIOR CHAPLAIN. (Who is not in the Doctor's confidence.) We-we are only men in these things, Gadsby. I know that I can say nothing now to help

CAPT. M. (fealously.) Then don't say it Leave him alone. It's not bad enough to croak over. Here, Gaddy, take the chit to Bingle and ride hell-for-leather. It'll do you good. I can't go.

JUNIOR CHAPLAIN. Do him good! (Smiling.) Give me the chit and I'll drive. Let him lie down. Your horse is blocking my cart-please!

CAPT. M. (Slowly without reining back.) I beg your pardon-I'll apologize. On paper if you like.

JUNIOR CHAPLAIN. (Flicking M.'s charger.) That'll do, thanks. Turn in, Gadsby, and I'll bring Bingle back-ahem-"hell-for-leather."

CAPT. M. (Solus.) It would have served me right if he'd cut me across the face. He can drive too. I shouldn't care to go that pace in a bamboo cart. What a faith he must have in his Maker-of harness! Come hup, you brute! (Gallops off to parade, blowing his nose, as the sun rises.)

(INTERVAL OF' FIVE WEEKS.)

MRS. G. (Very white and pinched, in morning wrapper at break fast table.) How big and strange the room looks, and how glad I am to see it again! What dust, though! I must talk to the servants. Sugar, Pip? I've almost forgotten. (Seriously.) Wasn't I very ill?

CAPT. G. Iller than I liked. (Tenderly.) Oh, you bad little Pussy, what a start you gave me'

MRS. G. I'll never do it again.

CAPT. G. You'd better not. And now get those poor pale cheeks pink again, or I shall be angry. Don't try to lift the urn. You'll upset it. Wait. (Comes round to head of table and lifts urn.)

Mas. G. (Quickly.) Khitmatgar, howarchikhana see kettly lao. Butler, get a kettle from the cook-house. (Drawing down G.'s face to her own.) Pip dear, I remember.

CAPT. G. What?

Mas. G. That last terrible night.

CAPT'. G. Then just you forget all about it.

Mas. G. (Softly, her eyes filling.) Never. It has brought us very close together, my husband. There! (Interlude.) I'm going to give Junda a saree.

CAPT. G. I gave her fifty dibs.

Mas. G. So she told me. It was a 'normous reward. Was I worth it? (Several interludes.) Don't! Here's the khitmatgar.-Two lumps or one Sir?

THE SWELLING OF JORDAN

If thou hast run with the footmen and they have wearied thee, then how canst thou contend with horses? And if in the land of peace wherein thou trustedst they wearied thee, then how wilt thou do in the swelling of Jordan?

SCENE.-The GADSBYS' bungalow in the Plains, on a January morning. Mas. G. arguing with bearer in back veranda.

CAPT. M. rides up.

CAPT. M. 'Mornin', Mrs. Gadsby. How's the Infant Phenomenon and the Proud Proprietor?

Mas. G. You'll find them in the front veranda; go through the house. I'm Martha just now.

CAPT. M, 'Cumbered about with cares of Khitmatgars? I fly.

Passes into front veranda, where GADSBV is watching GADSBY JUNIOR, aged ten months, crawling about the matting.

CAPT. M. What's the trouble, Gaddy-spoiling an honest man's Europe morning this way? (Seeing G. JUNIOR.) By Jove, that yearling's comm' on amaxingly! Any amount of bone below the knee there.

CAPT. G. Yes, he's a healthy little scoundrel. Don't you think his hair's growing?

CAPT. M. Let's have a look. Hi! Hst Come here, General Luck, and we'll report on you.

MRS. G. (Within.) What absurd name will you give him next? Why do you call him that?

CAPT. M. Isn't he our Inspector-General of Cavalry? Doesn't he come down in his seventeen-two perambulator every morning the Pink Hussars parade? Don't wriggle, Brigadier. Give us your private opinion on the way the third squadron went past. 'Trifle ragged, weren t they?

CAPT. G. A bigger set of tailors than the new draft I don't wish to see. They've given me more than my fair share-knocking the squadron out of shape. It's sickening!

CAPT. M. When you're in command, you'll do better, young 'un. Can't you walk yet? Grip my finger and try. (To G.) 'Twon't hurt his hocks, will it?

CAPT. G. Oh, no. Don't let him flop, though, or he'll lick all the blacking off your boots.

MRS. G. (Within.) Who's destroy mg my son's character?

CAPT. M. And my Godson's. I'm ashamed of you, Gaddy. Punch your father in the eye, Jack! Don't you stand it! Hit him again I

CAPT. G. (Sotto voce.) Put The Butcha down and come to the end of the veranda. I'd rather the Wife didn't hear-just now.

CAPT. M. You look awf'ly serious. Anything wrong?

CAPT. G. 'Depends on your view entirely. I say, Jack, you won't think more hardly of me than you can help, will you? Come further this way.-The fact of the matter is, that I've made up my mind-at least I'm thinking seriously of-cutting the Service.

CAPT. M. Hwhatt?

CAPT. G. Don't shout. I'm going to send in my papers.

CAPT. M. You! Are you mad?

CAPT. G. No-only married.

CAPT. M. Look here! What's the meaning of it all? You never intend to leave us. You can't. Isn't the best squadron of the best regiment of the best cavalry in all the world good enough for you?

CAPT. G. (Jerking his head over his shoulder.) She doesn't seem to thrive in this God-forsaken country, and there's The Butcha to be considered and all that, you know.

CAPT. M. Does she say that she doesn't like India?

CAPT. G. That's the worst of it. She won't for fear of leaving me.

CAPT. M. What are the Hills made for?

CAPT. G. Not for my wife, at any rate.

CAPT. M. You know too much, Gaddy, and-I don't like you any the better for it!

CAPT. G. Never mind that. She wants England, and The Butcha would be all the better for it. I'm going to chuck. You don't understand.

CAPT. M. (Hotly.) I understand this One hundred and thirty-seven new horse to be licked into shape somehow before Luck comes round again; a hairy-heeled draft who'll give more trouble than the horses; a camp next cold weather for a certainty; ourselves the first on the roster; the Russian shindy ready to come to a head at five minutes' notice, and you, the best of us all, backing out of it all! Think a little, Gaddy. You won't do it.

CAPT. G. Hang it, a man has some duties toward his family, I suppose.

CAPT. M. I remember a man, though, who told me, the night after Amdheran, when we were picketed under Jagai, and he'd left his sword-by the way, did you ever pay Ranken for that sword?-in an Utmanzai's head-that man told me that he'd stick by me and the Pinks as long as he lived. I don't blame him for not sticking by me-I'm not much of a man-but I do blame him for not sticking by the Pink Hussars.

CAPT. G. (Uneasily.) We were little more than boys then. Can't you see, Jack, how things stand? 'Tisn't as if we were serving for our bread. We've all of us, more or less, got the filthy lucre. I'm luckier than some, perhaps. There's no call for me to serve on.

CAPT. M. None in the world for you or for us, except the Regimental. If you don't choose to answer to that, of course-

CAPT. G. Don't be too hard on a man. You know that a lot of us only take up the thing for a few years and then go back to Town and catch on with the rest.

CAPT. M. Not lots, and they aren't some of Us.

CAPT. G. And then there are one's affairs at Home to be considered-my place and the rents, and all that. I don't suppose my father can last much longer, and that means the title, and so on.

CAPT. M. 'Fraid you won't be entered in the Stud Book correctly unless you go Home? Take six months, then, and come out in October. If I could slay off a brother or two, I s'pose I should be a Marquis of sorts. Any fool can be that; but it needs men, Gaddy-men like you-to lead flanking squadrons properly. Don't you delude yourself into the belief that you're going Home to take your place and prance about among pink-nosed Kabuli dowagers. You aren't built that way. I know better.

CAPT. G. A man has a right to live his life as happily as he can. You aren't married.

CAPT. M. No-praise be to Providence and the one or two women who have had the good sense to jawab me.

CAPT. G. Then you don't know what it is to go into your own room and see your wife's head on the pillow, and when everything else is safe and the house shut up for the night, to wonder whether the roof-beams won't give and kill her.

CAPT. M. (Aside.) Revelations first and second! (Aloud.) So-o! I knew a man who got squiffy at our Mess once and confided to me that he never helped his wife on to her horse without praymg that she'd break her neck before she came back. All husbands aren't alike, you see.

CAPT. G. What on earth has that to do with my case? The man must ha' been mad, or his wife as bad as they make 'em.

CAPT. M. (Aside.) 'No fault of yours if either weren't all you say. You've forgotten the time when you were insane about the Herriott woman. You always were a good hand at forgetting. (Aloud.) Not more mad than men who go to the other extreme. Be reasonable, Gaddy. Your roof-beams are sound enough.

CAPT. G. That was only a way of speaking. I've been uneasy and worried about the Wife ever since that awful business three years ago-when-I nearly lost her. Can you wonder?

CAPT. M. Oh, a shell never falls twice in the same place. You've paid your toll to misfortune-why should your Wife be picked out more than anybody else's?

CAPT. G. I can talk just as reasonably as you can, but you don't understand-you don't understand. And then there's The Butcha. Deuce knows where the Ayah takes him to sit in the evening! He has a bit of a cough. Haven't you noticed it?

CAPT. M. Bosh! The Brigadier's jumping out of his skin with pure condition. He's got a muzzle like a rose-leaf and the chest of a two-year-old. What's demoralized you?

CAPT. G. Funk. That's the long and the short of it. Funk!

CAPT. M. But what is there to funk?

CAPT. G. Everything. It's ghastly.

CAPT. M. Ah! I see.

You don't want to fight, And by Jingo when we do, You've got the kid, you've got the Wife, You've got the money, too.

That's about the case, eh?

CAPT. G. I suppose that's it. But it's not br myself. It's because of them. At least I think it is.

CAPT. M. Are you sure? Looking at the matter in a cold-blooded light, the Wife is provided for even if you were wiped out tonight. She has an ancestral home to go to, money and the Brigadier to carry on the illustrious name.

CAPT. G. Then it is for myself or because they are part of me. You don't see it. My life's so good, so pleasant, as it is, that I want to make it quite safe. Can't you understand?

CAPT. M. Perfectly. "Shelter-pit for the Off'cer's charger," as they say in the Line.

CAPT. G. And I have everything to my hand to make it so. I'm sick of the strain and the worry for their sakes out here; and there isn't a single real difficulty to prevent my dropping it altogether. It'll only cost me-Jack, I hope you'll never know the shame that I've been going through for the past six months.

CAPT. M. Hold on there! I don't wish to he told. Every man has his moods and tenses sometimes.

CAPT. G. (Laughing brtterly.) Has he? What do you call craning over to see where your near-fore lands?

CAPT. M. In my case it means that I have been on the Considerable Bend, and have come to parade with a Head and a Hand. It passes in three strides.

CAPT. G. (Lowering voice.) It never passes w'th me, Jack. I'm always thinking about it. Phil Gadsby funking a fall on parade! Sweet picture, isn't it! Draw it for me.

CAPT. M. (Gravely.) Heaven forbid! A man like you can't be as bad as that. A fall is no nice thing, but one never gives it a thought.

CAPT. G. Doesn't one? Wait till you've got a wife and a youngster of your own, and then you'll know how the roar of the squadron behind you turns you cold all up the back.

CAPT. M. (Aside.) And this man led at Amdheran after Bagal Deasin went under, and we were all mixed up together, and he came out of the snow dripping like a butcher. (Aloud.) Skittles! The men can always open out, and you can always pick your way more or less. We haven't the dust to bother us, as the men have, and whoever heard of a horse stepping on a man?

CAPT. G. Never-as long as he can see. But did they open out for poor Errington?

CAPT. M. Oh, this is childish!

CAPT. G. I know it is, worse than that. I don't care. You've ridden Van Loo. Is he the sort of brute to pick his way-'specially when we're coming up in column of troop with any pace on?

CAPT. M. Once in a Blue Moon do we gallop in column of troop, and then only to save time. Aren't three lengths enough for you?

CAPT. G. Yes-quite enough. They just allow for the full development of the smash. I'm talking like a cur, I know: but I tell you that, for the past three months, I've felt every hoof of the squadron in the small of my back every time that I've led.

CAPT. M. But, Gaddy, this is awful!

CAPT. G. Isn't it lovely? Isn't it royal? A Captain of the Pink Hussars watering up his charger before parade like the blasted boozing Colonel of a Black Regiment!

CAPT. M. You never did!

CAPT. G. Once Only. He squelched like a mussuck, and the Troop-Sergeant-Major cocked his eye at me. You know old Haffy's eye. I was afraid to do it again.

CAPT. M. I should think so. That was the best way to rupture old Van Loo's tummy, and make him crumple you up. You knew that.

CAPT. G. I didn't care. It took the edge off him.

CAPT. M. "Took the edge off him"? Gaddy, you-you-you mustn't, you know! Think of the men.

CAPT. G. That's another thing I am afraid of. D'you s'pose they know?

CAPT. M. Let's hope not; but they're deadly quick to spot skirm-little things of that kind. See here, old man, send the Wife Home for the hot weather and come to Kashmir with me. We'll start a boat on the Dal or cross the Rhotang-shoot ibex or loaf-which you please. Only come! You're a bit off your oats and you're talking nonsense. Look at the Colonel-swag-bellied rascal that he is. He has a wife and no end of a bow-window of his own. Can any one of us ride round him-chalkstones and all? I can't, and I think I can shove a crock along a bit.

CAPT. G. Some men are different. I haven't any nerve. Lord help me, I haven't the nerve! I've taken up a hole and a half to get my knees well under the wallets. I can't help it. I'm so afraid of anything happening to me. On my soul, I ought to be broke in front of the squadron, for cowardice.

CAPT. M. Ugly word, that. I should never have the courage to own up.

CAPT. G. I meant to lie about my reasons when I began, but-I've got out of the habit of lying to you, old man. Jack, you won't?-But I know you won't.

CAPT. M. Of course not. (Half aloud.) The Pinks are paying dearly for their Pride.

CAPT. G. Eh! What-at?

CAPT. M. Don't you know? The men have called Mrs. Gadsby the Pride of the Pink Hussars ever since she came to us.

CAPT. G. 'Tisn't her fault. Don't think that. It's all mine.

CAPT. M. What does she say?

CAPT. G. I haven't exactly put it before her. She's the best little woman in the world, Jack, and all that-but she wouldn't counsel a man to stick to his calling if it came between him and her. At least, I think-

CAPT. M. Never mind. Don't tell her what you told me. Go on the Peerage and Landed-Gentry tack.

CAPT. G. She'd see through it. She's five times cleverer than I am.

CAPT. M. (Aside.) Then she'll accept the sacrifice and think a little bit worse of him for the rest of her days.

CAPT. G. (Absentl'y.) I say, do you despise me?

CAPT. M. 'Queer way of putting it. Have you ever been asked that question? Think a minute. What answer used you to give?

CAPT. G. So bad as that? I'm not entitled to expect anything more, but it's a bit hard when one's best friend turns round and-

CAPT. M. So ! have found But you will have consolations-Bailiffs and Drains and Liquid Manure and the Primrose League, and, perhaps, if you're lucky, the Colonelcy of a Yeomanry Cav-al-ry Regiment-all uniform and no riding, I believe. How old are you?

CAPT. G. Thirty-three. I know it's-

CAPT. M. At forty you'll be a fool of a J. P. landlord. At fifty you'll own a bath-chair, and The Brigadier, if he takes after you, will be fluttering the dovecotes of-what's the particular dunghill you're going to? Also, Mrs. Gadsby will be fat.

CAPT. G. (Limply.) This is rather more than a joke.

CAPT. M. D'you think so? Isn't cutting the Service a joke? It generally takes a man fifty years to arrive at it. You're quite right, though. It is more than a joke. You've managed it in thirty-three.

CAPT. G. Don't make me feel worse than I do. Will it satisfy you if I own that I am a shirker, a skrim-shanker, and a coward?

CAPT. M. It will not, because I'm the only man in the world who can talk to you like this without being knocked down. You mustn't take all that I've said to heart in this way. I only spoke-a lot of it at least-out of pure selfishness, because, because-Oh, damn it all, old man,-I don't know what I shall do without you. Of course, you've got the money and the place and all that-and there are two very good reasons why you should take care of yourself.

CAPT. G. 'Doesn't make it any sweeter. I'm backing out-I know I am. I always had a soft drop in me somewhere-and I daren't risk any danger to them.

CAPT. M. Why in the world should you? You're bound to think of your family-bound to think. Er-hmm. If I wasn't a younger son I'd go too-be shot if I wouldn't I!

CAPT. G. Thank you, Jack. It's a kind lie, but it's the blackest you've told for some time. I know what I'm doing, and I'm going into it with my eyes open. Old man, I can't help it. What would you do if you were in my place?

CAPT. M. (Aside.) 'Couldn't conceive any woman getting permanently between me and the Regiment. (Aloud.) 'Can't say. 'Very likely I should do no better. I'm sorry for you-awf'ly sorry-but "if them's your sentiments," I believe, I really do, that you are acting wisely.

CAPT. G. Do you? I hope you do. (In a whisper.) Jack, be very sure of yourself before you marry. I'm an ungrateful ruffian to say this, but marriage-even as good a marriage as mine has been-hampers a man's work, it cripples his sword-arm, and oh, it plays Hell with his notions of duty. Sometimes-good and sweet as she is-sometimes I could wish that I had kept my freedom-No, I don't mean that exactly.

MRS. G. (Coming down veranda.) What are you wagging your head ove; Pip?

CAPT. M. (Turning quickly.) Me, as usual. The old sermon. Your husband is recommending me to get married. 'Never saw such a one-ideaed man.

MRS. G. Well, why don't you? I dare say you would make some woman very happy.

CAPT. G. There's the Law and the Prophets, Jack. Never mind the Regiment. Make a woman happy. (Aside.) O Lord!

CAPT. M. We'll see. I must be off to make a Troop Cook desperately unhappy. I won't have the wily Hussar fed on Government Bullock Train shinbones-(Hastily.) Surely black ants can't be good for The Brigadier. He's picking em off the matting and eating 'em. Here, Senor Comandante Don Grubbynuse, come and talk to me. (Lifts G. JUNIOR in his arms.) 'Want my watch? You won't be able to put it into your mouth, but you can try. (G. JUNIOR drops watch, breaking dial and hands.)

MRS. G. Oh, Captain Mafflin, I am so sorry! Jack, you bad, bad little villain. Ahhh!

CAPT. M. It's not the least consequence, I assure you. He'd treat the world in the same way if he could get it into his hands. Everything's made to be played, with and broken, isn't it, young 'un?

* * * * *

MRS. G. Mafflin didn't at all like his watch being broken, though he was too polite to say so. It was entirely his fault for giving it to the child. Dem little puds are werry, werry feeble, aren't dey, by Jack-in-de-box? (To G.) What did he want to see you for?

CAPT. G. Regimental shop as usual.

MRS. G. The Regiment! Always the Regiment. On my word, I sometimes feel jealous of Mafflin.

CAPT. G. (Wearily.) Poor old Jack? I don't think you need. Isn't it time for The Butcha to have his nap? Bring a chair out here, dear. I've got some thing to talk over with you.

AND THIS IS THE END OF
THE STORY OF THE GADSBYS

UNDER THE DEODARS

THE EDUCATION OF OTIS YEERE

I

> In the pleasant orchard-closes
> 'God bless all our gains,' say we;
> But 'May God bless all our losses,'
> Better suits with our degree.
> The Lost Bower.

This is the history of a failure; but the woman who failed said that it might be an instructive tale to put into print for the benefit of the younger generation. The younger generation does not want instruction, being perfectly willing to instruct if any one will listen to it. None the less, here begins the story where every right-minded story should begin, that is to say at Simla, where all things begin and many come to an evil end.

The mistake was due to a very clever woman making a blunder and not retrieving it. Men are licensed to stumble, but a clever woman's mistake is outside the regular course of Nature and Providence; since all good people know that a woman is the only infallible thing in this world, except Government Paper of the '79 issue, bearing interest at four and a half per cent. Yet, we have to remember that six consecutive days of rehearsing the leading part of The Fallen Angel, at the New Gaiety Theatre where the plaster is not yet properly dry, might have brought about an unhingement of spirits which, again, might have led to eccentricities.

Mrs. Hauksbee came to 'The Foundry' to tiffin with Mrs. Mallowe, her one bosom friend, for she was in no sense 'a woman's woman.' And it was a woman's tiffin, the door shut to all the world; and they both talked chiffons, which is French for Mysteries.

'I've enjoyed an interval of sanity,' Mrs. Hauksbee announced, after tiffin was over and the two were comfortably settled in the little writing-room that opened out of Mrs. Mallowe's bedroom.

'My dear girl, what has he done?' said Mrs. Mallowe sweetly. It is noticeable that ladies of a certain age call each other 'dear girl,' just as commissioners of twenty-eight years' standing address their equals in the Civil List as 'my boy.'

'There's no he in the case. Who am I that an imaginary man should be always credited to me? Am I an Apache?'

'No, dear, but somebody's scalp is generally drying at your wigwam-door. Soaking rather.'

This was an allusion to the Hawley Boy, who was in the habit of riding all across Simla in the Rains, to call on Mrs. Hauksbee. That lady laughed.

'For my sins, the Aide at Tyrconnel last night told me off to The Mussuck. Hsh! Don't laugh. One of my most devoted admirers. When the duff came some one really ought to teach them to make puddings at Tyrconnel The Mussuck was at liberty to attend to me.'

'Sweet soul! I know his appetite,' said Mrs. Mallowe. 'Did he, oh did he, begin his wooing?'

'By a special mercy of Providence, no. He explained his importance as a Pillar of the Empire. I didn't laugh.'

'Lucy, I don't believe you.'

'Ask Captain Sangar; he was on the other side. Well, as I was saying, The Mussuck dilated.'

'I think I can see him doing it,' said Mrs. Mallowe pensively, scratching her fox-terrier's ears.

'I was properly impressed. Most properly. I yawned openly. "Strict supervision, and play them off one against the other," said The Mussuck, shovelling down his ice by tureenfuls, I assure you. "That, Mrs. Hauksbee, is the secret of our Government." '

Mrs. Mallowe laughed long and merrily. 'And what did you say?'

'Did you ever know me at loss for an answer yet? I said: "So I have observed in my dealings with you." The Mussuck swelled with pride. He is coming to call on me to-morrow. The Hawley Boy is coming too.'

' "Strict supervision and play them off one against the other. That, Mrs. Hauksbee, is the secret of our Government." And I daresay if we could get to The Mussuck's heart, we should find that he considers himself a man of the world.'

'As he is of the other two things. I like The

Mussuck, and I won't have you call him names. He amuses me.'

'He has reformed you, too, by what appears. Explain the interval of sanity, and hit Tim on the nose with the paper-cutter, please. That dog is too fond of sugar. Do you take milk in yours?'

'No, thanks. Polly, I'm wearied of this life. It's hollow.'

'Turn religious, then. I always said that Rome would be your fate.'

'Only exchanging half-a-dozen attach,s in red for one in black, and if I fasted, the wrinkles would come, and never, never go. Has it ever struck you, dear, that I'm getting old?'

'Thanks for your courtesy. I'll return it. Ye-es, we are both not exactly how shall I put it?'

'What we have been. "I feel it in my bones," as Mrs. Crossley says. Polly, I've wasted my life.'

'As how?'

'Never mind how. I feel it. I want to be a Power before I die.'

'Be a Power then. You've wits enough for anything and beauty!'

Mrs. Hauksbee pointed a teaspoon straight at her hostess. 'Polly, if you heap compliments on me like this, I shall cease to believe that you're a woman. Tell me how I am to be a Power.'

'Inform The Mussuck that he is the most fascinating and slimmest man in Asia, and he'll tell you anything and everything you please.'

'Bother The Mussuck! I mean an intellectual Power not a gas-power. Polly, I'm going to start a salon.'

Mrs. Mallowe turned lazily on the sofa and rested her head on her hand. 'Hear the words of the Preacher, the son of Baruch,' she said.

'Will you talk sensibly?'

'I will, dear, for I see that you are going to make a mistake.'

'I never made a mistake in my life at least, never one that I couldn't explain away afterwards.'

'Going to make a mistake,' went on Mrs. Mallowe composedly. 'It is impossible to start a salon in Simla. A bar would be much more to the point.'

'Perhaps, but why? It seems so easy.'

'Just what makes it so difficult. How many clever women are there in Simla?'

'Myself and yourself,' said Mrs. Hauksbee, without a moment's hesitation.

'Modest woman! Mrs. Feardon would thank you for that. And how many clever men?'

'Oh er hundreds,' said Mrs. Hauksbee vaguely.

'What a fatal blunder! Not one. They are all bespoke by the Government. Take my husband, for instance. Jack was a clever man, though I say so who shouldn't. Government has eaten him up. All his ideas and powers of conversation he really used to be a good talker, even to his wife in the old days are taken from him by this this kitchen-sink of a Government. That's the case with every man up here who is at work. I don't suppose a Russian convict under the knout is able to amuse the rest of his gang; and all our men-folk here are gilded convicts.'

'But there are scores '

'I know what you're going to say. Scores of idle men up on leave. I admit it, but they are all of two objectionable sets. The Civilian who'd be delightful if he had the military man's knowledge of the world and style, and the military man who'd be adorable if he had the Civilian's culture.'

'Detestable word! Have Civilians culchaw? I never studied the breed deeply.'

'Don't make fun of Jack's Service. Yes. They're like the teapoys in the Lakka Bazar good material but not polished. They can't help themselves, poor dears. A Civilian only begins to be tolerable after he has knocked about the world for fifteen years.'

'And a military man?'

'When he has had the same amount of service. The young of both species are horrible. You would have scores of them in your salon.'

'I would not!' said Mrs. Hauksbee fiercely.

'I would tell the bearer to darwaza band them. I'd put their own colonels and commissioners at the door to turn them away. I'd give them to the Topsham Girl to play with.'

'The Topsham Girl would be grateful for the gift. But to go back to the salon. Allowing that you had gathered all your men and women together, what would you do with them? Make them talk? They would all with one accord begin to flirt. Your salon would become a glorified Peliti's a "Scandal Point" by lamplight.'

'There's a certain amount of wisdom in that view.'

'There's all the wisdom in the world in it. Surely, twelve Simla seasons ought to have taught you that you can't focus anything in India; and a salon, to be any good at all, must be permanent. In two seasons your roomful would be scattered all over Asia. We are only little bits of dirt on the hillsides here one day and blown down the khud the next. We have lost the art of talking at least our men have. We have no cohesion '

'George Eliot in the flesh,' interpolated Mrs. Hauksbee wickedly.

'And collectively, my dear scoffer, we, men and women alike, have no influence. Come into the verandah and look at the Mall!'

The two looked down on the now rapidly filling road, for all Simla was abroad to steal a stroll between a shower and a fog.

'How do you propose to fix that river? Look! There's The Mussuck head of goodness knows what. He is a power in the land, though he does eat like a costermonger. There's Colonel Blone, and General Grucher, and Sir Dugald Delane, and Sir Henry Haughton, and Mr. Jellalatty. All Heads of Departments, and all powerful.'

'And all my fervent admirers,' said Mrs. Hauksbee piously. 'Sir Henry Haughton raves about me. But go on.'

'One by one, these men are worth something. Collectively, they're just a mob of Anglo-Indians. Who cares for what Anglo-Indians say? Your salon won't weld the Departments together and make you mistress of India, dear. And these creatures won't talk administrative "shop" in a crowd your salon because they are so afraid of the men in the lower ranks overhearing it. They have forgotten what of Literature and Art they ever knew, and the women '

'Can't talk about anything except the last Gymkhana, or the sins of their last nurse. I was calling on Mrs. Derwills this morning.'

'You admit that? They can talk to the subalterns though, and the subalterns can talk to them. Your salon would suit their views admirably, if you respected the religious prejudices of the country and provided plenty of kala juggahs.'

'Plenty of kala juggahs. Oh my poor little idea! Kala juggahs in a salon! But who made you so awfully clever?'

'Perhaps I've tried myself; or perhaps I know a woman who has. I have preached and expounded the whole matter and the conclusion thereof'

'You needn't go on. "Is Vanity." Polly, I thank you. These vermin' Mrs. Hauksbee waved her hand from the verandah to two men in the crowd below who had raised their hats to her 'these vermin shall not rejoice in a new Scandal Point or an extra Peliti's. I will abandon the notion of a salon. It did seem so tempting, though. But what shall I do? I must do something.'

'Why? Are not Abana and Pharpar'

'Jack has made you nearly as bad as himself! I want to, of course. I'm tired of everything and everybody, from a moonlight picnic at Seepee to the blandishments of The Mussuck.'

'Yes that comes, too, sooner or later. Have you nerve enough to make your bow yet?'

Mrs. Hauksbee's mouth shut grimly. Then she laughed. 'I think I see myself doing it. Big pink placards on the Mall: "Mrs. Hauksbee! Positively her last appearance on any stage! This is to give notice!" No more dances; no more rides; no more luncheons; no more theatricals with supper to follow; no more sparring with one's dearest, dearest friend; no more fencing with an inconvenient man who hasn't wit enough to clothe what he's pleased to call his sentiments in passable speech; no more parading of The Mussuck while Mrs. Tarkass calls all round Simla, spreading horrible stories about me! No more of anything that is thoroughly wearying, abominable, and detestable, but, all the same, makes life worth the having. Yes! I see it all! Don't interrupt, Polly, I'm inspired. A mauve and white striped "cloud" round my excellent shoulders, a seat in the fifth row of the Gaiety, and both horses sold. Delightful vision! A comfortable arm-chair, situated in three different draughts, at every ball-room; and nice, large, sensible shoes for all the couples to stumble over as they go into the verandah! Then at supper. Can't you imagine the scene? The greedy mob gone away. Reluctant subaltern, pink all over like a newly-powdered baby, they really ought to tan subalterns before they are exported, Polly, sent back by the hostess to do his duty. Slouches up to me across the room, tugging at a glove two sizes too large for him I hate a man who wears gloves like overcoats and trying to look as if he'd thought of it from the first. "May I ah-have the pleasure 'f takin' you 'nt' supper?" Then I get up with a hungry smile. Just like this.'

'Lucy, how can you be so absurd?'

'And sweep out on his arm. So! After supper I shall go away early, you know, because I shall be afraid of catching cold. No one will look for my 'rickshaw. Mine, so please you! I shall stand, always with that mauve and white "cloud" over my head, while the wet soaks into my dear, old, venerable feet, and Tom swears and shouts for the mem-sahib's gharri. Then home to bed at half-past eleven! Truly excellent life helped out by the visits of the Padri, just fresh from burying somebody down below there.' She pointed through the pines toward the Cemetery, and continued with vigorous dramatic gesture

'Listen! I see it all down, down even to the stays! Such stays! Six-eight a pair, Polly, with red flannel or list, is it? that they put into the tops of those fearful things. I can draw you a picture of them.'

'Lucy, for Heaven's sake, don't go waving your arms about in that idiotic manner! Recollect every one can see you from the Mall.'

'Let them see! They'll think I am rehearsing for The Fallen Angel. Look! There's The Mussuck. How badly he rides. There!'

She blew a kiss to the venerable Indian administrator with infinite grace.

'Now,' she continued, 'he'll be chaffed about that at the Club in the delicate manner those brutes of men affect, and the Hawley Boy will tell me all about it softening the details for fear of shocking me. That boy is too good to live, Polly. I've serious thoughts of recommending him to throw up his commission and go into the Church. In his present frame of mind he would obey me. Happy, happy child!'

'Never again,' said Mrs. Mallowe, with an affectation of indignation, 'shall you tiffin here! "Lucindy your behaviour is scand'lus." '

'All your fault,' retorted Mrs. Hauksbee, 'for suggesting such a thing as my abdication. No! jamais! nevaire! I will act, dance, ride, frivol, talk scandal, dine out, and appropriate the legitimate captives of any woman I choose, until I d-r-r-rop, or a better woman than I puts me to shame before all Simla, and it's dust and ashes in my mouth while I'm doing it!'

She swept into the drawing-room. Mrs. Mallowe followed and put an arm round her waist.

'I'm not!' said Mrs. Hauksbee defiantly, rummaging for her handkerchief. 'I've been dining out the last ten nights, and rehearsing in the afternoon. You'd be tired yourself. It's only because I'm tired.'

Mrs. Mallowe did not offer Mrs. Hauksbee any pity or ask her to lie down, but gave her another cup of tea, and went on with the talk.

'I've been through that too, dear,' she said.

'I remember,' said Mrs. Hauksbee, a gleam of fun on her face. 'In '84, wasn't it? You went out a great deal less next season.'

Mrs. Mallowe smiled in a superior and Sphinx-like fashion.

'I became an Influence,' said she.

'Good gracious, child, you didn't join the Theosophists and kiss Buddha's big toe, did you? I tried to get into their set once, but they cast me out for a sceptic without a chance of improving my poor little mind, too.'

'No, I didn't Theosophilander. Jack says '

'Never mind Jack. What a husband says is known before. What did you do?'

'I made a lasting impression.'

'So have I for four months. But that didn't console me in the least. I hated the man. Will you stop smiling in that inscrutable way and tell me what you mean?'

Mrs. Mallowe told.

'And you mean to say that it is absolutely Platonic on both sides?'

'Absolutely, or I should never have taken it up.'

'And his last promotion was due to you?'

Mrs. Mallowe nodded.

'And you warned him against the Topsham Girl?'

Another nod.

'And told him of Sir Dugald Delane's private memo about him?'

A third nod.

'Why?'

'What a question to ask a woman! Because it amused me at first. I am proud of my property now. If I live, he shall continue to be successful. Yes, I will put him upon the straight road to Knighthood, and everything else that a man values. The rest depends upon himself.'

'Polly, you are a most extraordinary woman.'

'Not in the least. I'm concentrated, that's all. You diffuse yourself, dear; and though all Simla knows your skill in managing a team '

'Can't you choose a prettier word?'

'Team, of half-a-dozen, from The Mussuck to the Hawley Boy, you gain nothing by it. Not even amusement.'

'And you?'

'Try my recipe. Take a man, not a boy, mind, but an almost mature, unattached man, and be his guide, philosopher, and friend. You'll find it the most interesting occupation that you ever embarked on. It can be done you needn't look like that because I've done it.'

'There's an element of risk about it that makes the notion attractive. I'll get such a man and say to him, "Now, understand that there must be no flirtation. Do exactly what I tell you, profit by my instruction and counsels, and all will yet be well." Is that the idea?'

'More or less,' said Mrs. Mallowe, with an unfathomable smile. 'But be sure he understands.'

II

Dribble-dribble trickle-trickle
What a lot of raw dust!
My dollie's had an accident
And out came all the sawdust!
Nursery Rhyme.

So Mrs. Hauksbee, in 'The Foundry' which overlooks Simla Mall, sat at the feet of Mrs. Mallowe and gathered wisdom. The end of the Conference was the Great Idea upon which Mrs. Hauksbee so plumed herself.

'I warn you,' said Mrs. Mallowe, beginning to repent of her suggestion, 'that the matter is not half so easy as it looks. Any woman even the Topsham Girl can catch a man, but very, very few know how to manage him when caught.'

'My child,' was the answer, 'I've been a female St. Simon Stylites looking down upon men for these these years past. Ask The Mussuck whether I can manage them.'

Mrs. Hauksbee departed humming, 'I'll go to him and say to him in manner most ironical.' Mrs. Mallowe laughed to herself. Then she grew suddenly sober. 'I wonder whether I've done well in advising that amusement? Lucy's a clever woman, but a thought too careless.'

A week later the two met at a Monday Pop. 'Well?' said Mrs. Mallowe.

'I've caught him!' said Mrs. Hauksbee: her eyes were dancing with merriment.

'Who is it, mad woman? I'm sorry I ever spoke to you about it.'

'Look between the pillars. In the third row; fourth from the end. You can see his face now. Look!'

'Otis Yeere! Of all the improbable and impossible people! I don't believe you.'

'Hsh! Wait till Mrs. Tarkass begins murdering Milton Wellings; and I'll tell you all about it. S-s-ss! That woman's voice always reminds me of an Underground train coming into Earl's Court with the brakes on. Now listen. It is really Otis Yeere.'

'So I see, but does it follow that he is your property!'

'He is! By right of trove. I found him, lonely and unbefriended, the very next night after our talk, at the Dugald Delanes' burra-khana. I liked his eyes, and I talked to him. Next day he called. Next day we went for a ride together, and to-day he's tied to my 'richshaw-wheels hand and foot. You'll see when the concert's over. He doesn't know I'm here yet.'

'Thank goodness you haven't chosen a boy. What are you going to do with him, assuming that you've got him?'

'Assuming, indeed! Does a woman do I ever make a mistake in that sort of thing? First' Mrs. Hauksbee ticked off the items ostentatiously on her little gloved fingers 'First, my dear, I shall dress him properly. At present his raiment is a disgrace, and he wears a dress-shirt like a crumpled sheet of the Pioneer. Secondly, after I have made him presentable, I shall form his manners his morals are above reproach.'

'You seem to have discovered a great deal about him considering the shortness of your acquaintance.'

'Surely you ought to know that the first proof a man gives of his interest in a woman is by talking to her about his own sweet self. If the woman listens without yawning, he begins to like her. If she flatters the animal's vanity, he ends by adoring her.'

'In some cases.'

'Never mind the exceptions. I know which one you are thinking of. Thirdly, and lastly, after he is polished and made pretty, I shall, as you said, be his guide, philosopher, and friend, and he shall become a success as great a success as your friend. I always wondered how that man got on. Did The Mussuck come to you with the Civil List and, dropping on one knee no, two knees, ˆ la Gibbon hand it to you and say, "Adorable angel, choose your friend's appointment"?'

'Lucy, your long experiences of the Military Department have demoralised you. One doesn't do that sort of thing on the Civil Side.'

'No disrespect meant to Jack's Service, my dear. I only asked for information. Give me three months, and see what changes I shall work in my prey.'

'Go your own way since you must. But I'm sorry that I was weak enough to suggest the amusement.'

' "I am all discretion, and may be trusted to an in-fin-ite extent," ' quoted Mrs. Hauksbee from The Fallen Angel; and the conversation ceased with Mrs. Tarkass's last, long-drawn war-whoop.

Her bitterest enemies and she had many could hardly accuse Mrs. Hauksbee of wasting her time. Otis Yeere was one of those wandering 'dumb' characters, foredoomed through life to be nobody's property. Ten years in Her Majesty's Bengal Civil Service, spent, for the most part, in undesirable Districts, had given him little to be proud of, and nothing to bring confidence. Old enough to have lost the first fine careless rapture that showers on the immature 'Stunt imaginary Commissionerships and Stars, and sends him into the collar with coltish earnestness and abandon; too young to be yet able to look back upon the progress he had made, and thank Providence that under the conditions of the day he had come even so far, he stood upon the dead-centre of his career. And when a man stands still he feels the slightest impulse from without. Fortune had ruled that Otis Yeere should be, for the first part of his service, one of the rank and file who are ground up in the wheels of the Administration; losing heart and soul, and mind and strength, in the process. Until steam replaces manual power in the working of the Empire, there must always be this percentage must always be the men who are used up, expended, in the mere mechanical routine. For these promotion is far off and the mill-grind of every day very instant. The Secretariats know them only by name; they are not the picked men of the Districts with Divisions and Collectorates awaiting them. They are simply the rank and file the food for fever sharing with the ryot and the plough-bullock the honour of being the plinth on which the State rests. The older ones have lost their aspirations; the younger are putting theirs aside with a sigh. Both learn to endure patiently until the end of the day. Twelve years in the rank and file, men say, will sap the hearts of the bravest and dull the wits of the most keen.

Out of this life Otis Yeere had fled for a few months; drifting, in the hope of a little masculine society, into Simla. When his leave was over he would return to his swampy, sour-green, under-manned Bengal district; to the native Assistant, the native Doctor, the native Magistrate, the steaming, sweltering Station, the ill-kempt City, and the undisguised insolence of the Municipality that babbled away the lives of men. Life was cheap, however. The soil spawned humanity, as it bred frogs in the Rains, and the gap of the sickness of one season was filled to overflowing by the fecundity of the next. Otis was unfeignedly thankful to lay down his work for a little while and escape from the seething, whining, weakly hive, impotent to help itself, but strong in its power to cripple, thwart, and annoy the sunkeneyed man who, by official irony, was said to be 'in charge' of it.

'I knew there were women-dowdies in Bengal. They come up here sometimes. But I didn't know that there were men-dowds, too.'

Then, for the first time, it occurred to Otis Yeere that his clothes wore rather the mark of the ages. It will be seen that his friendship with Mrs. Hauksbee had made great strides.

As that lady truthfully says, a man is never so happy as when he is talking about himself. From Otis Yeere's lips Mrs. Hauksbee, before long, learned everything that she wished to know about the subject of her experiment: learned what manner of life he had led in what she vaguely called 'those awful cholera districts'; learned, too, but this knowledge came later, what manner of life he had purposed to lead and what dreams he had dreamed in the year of grace '77, before the reality had knocked the heart out of him. Very pleasant are the shady bridle-paths round Prospect Hill for the telling of such confidences.

'Not yet,' said Mrs. Hauksbee to Mrs. Maliowe. 'Not yet. I must wait until the man is properly dressed, at least. Great heavens, is it possible that he doesn't know what an honour it is to be taken up by Me!'

Mrs. Hauksbee did not reckon false modesty as one of her failings.

'Always with Mrs. Hauksbee!' murmured Mrs. Mallowe, with her sweetest smile, to Otis. 'Oh you men, you men! Here are our Punjabis growling because you've monopolised the nicest woman in Simla. They'll tear you to pieces on the Mall, some day, Mr. Yeere.'

Mrs. Mallowe rattled downhill, having satisfied herself, by a glance through the fringe of her sunshade, of the effect of her words.

The shot went home. Of a surety Otis Yeere was somebody in this bewildering whirl of Simla had monopolised the nicest woman in it, and the Punjabis were growling. The notion justified a mild glow of vanity. He had never looked upon his acquaintance with Mrs. Hauksbee as a matter for general interest.

The knowledge of envy was a pleasant feeling to the man of no account. It was intensified later in the day when a luncher at the Club said spitefully, 'Well, for a debilitated Ditcher, Yeere, you are going it. Hasn't any kind friend told you that she's the most dangerous woman in Simla?'

Yeere chuckled and passed out. When, oh, when would his new clothes be ready? He descended into the Mall to inquire; and Mrs. Hauksbee, coming over the Church Ridge in her 'rickshaw, looked down upon him approvingly. 'He's learning to carry himself as if he were a man, instead of a piece of furniture, and,' she screwed up her eyes to see the better through the sunlight 'he is a man when he holds himself like that. O blessed Conceit, what should we be without you?'

With the new clothes came a new stock of self-confidence. Otis Yeere discovered that he could enter a room without breaking into a gentle perspiration could cross one, even to talk to Mrs. Hauksbee, as though rooms were meant to be crossed. He was for the first time in nine years proud of himself, and contented with his life, satisfied with his new clothes, and rejoicing in the friendship of Mrs. Hauksbee.

'Conceit is what the poor fellow wants,' she said in confidence to Mrs. Mallowe. 'I believe they must use Civilians to plough the fields with in Lower Bengal. You see I have to begin from the very beginning haven't I? But you'll admit, won't you, dear, that he is immensely improved since I took him in hand. Only give me a little more time and he won't know himself.'

Indeed, Yeere was rapidly beginning to forget what he had been. One of his own rank and file put the matter brutally when he asked Yeere, in reference to nothing, 'And who has been making you a Member of Council, lately? You carry the side of half-a-dozen of 'em.'

'I I'm awf'ly sorry. I didn't mean it, you know,' said Yeere apologetically.

'There'll be no holding you,' continued the old stager grimly. 'Climb down, Otis climb down, and get all that beastly affectation knocked out of you with fever! Three thousand a month wouldn't support it.'

Yeere repeated the incident to Mrs. Hauksbee. He had come to look upon her as his Mother Confessor.

'And you apologised!' she said. 'Oh, shame! I hate a man who apologises. Never apologise for what your friend called "side." Never! It's a man's business to be insolent and overbearing until he meets with a stronger. Now, you bad boy, listen to me.'

Simply and straightforwardly, as the 'rickshaw loitered round Jakko, Mrs. Hauksbee preached to Otis Yeere the Great Gospel of Conceit, illustrating it with living pictures encountered during their Sunday afternoon stroll.

'Good gracious!' she ended with the personal argument, 'you'll apologise next for being my attach,!'

'Never!' said Otis Yeere. 'That's another thing altogether. I shall always be '

'What's coming?' thought Mrs. Hauksbee.

'Proud of that,' said Otis.

'Safe for the present,' she said to herself.

'But I'm afraid I have grown conceited. Like Jeshurun, you know. When he waxed fat, then he kicked. It's the having no worry on one's mind and the Hill air, I suppose.'

'Hill air, indeed!' said Mrs. Hauksbee to herself. 'He'd have been hiding in the Club till the last day of his leave, if I hadn't discovered him.' And aloud

'Why shouldn't you be? You have every right to.'

'I! Why?'

'Oh, hundreds of things. I'm not going to waste this lovely afternoon by explaining; but I know you have. What was that heap of manuscript you showed me about the grammar of the aboriginal what's their names?'

'Gullals. A piece of nonsense. I've far too much work to do to bother over Gullals now. You should see my District. Come down with your husband some day and I'll show you round. Such a lovely place in the Rains! A sheet of water with the railway-embankment and the snakes sticking out, and, in the summer, green flies and green squash. The people would die of fear if you shook a dogwhip at 'em. But they know you're forbidden to do that, so they conspire to make your life a burden to you. My District's worked by some man at Darjiling, on the strength of a native pleader's false reports. Oh, it's a heavenly place!'

Otis Yeere laughed bitterly.

'There's not the least necessity that you should stay in it. Why do you?'

'Because I must. How'm I to get out of it?'

'How! In a hundred and fifty ways. If there weren't so many people on the road I'd like to box your ears. Ask, my dear boy, ask! Look! There is young Hexarly with six years' service and half your talents. He asked for what he wanted, and he got it. See, down by the Convent! There's McArthurson, who has come to his present position by asking sheer, downright asking after he had pushed himself out of the rank and file. One man is as good as another in your service believe me. I've seen Simla for more seasons than I care to think about. Do you suppose men are chosen for appointments because of their special fitness beforehand? You have all passed a high test what do you call it? in the beginning, and, except for the few who have gone altogether to the bad, you can all work hard. Asking does the rest. Call it cheek, call it insolence, call it anything you like, but ask! Men argue yes, I know what men say that a man, by the mere audacity of his request, must have some good in him. A weak man doesn't say: "Give me this and that." He whines: "Why haven't I been given this and that?" If you were in the Army, I should say learn to spin plates or play a tambourine with your toes. As it is ask! You belong to a Service that ought to be able to command the Channel Fleet, or set a leg at twenty minutes' notice, and yet you hesitate over asking to escape from a squashy green district where you admit you are not master. Drop the Bengal Government altogether. Even Darjiling is a little out-of-the-way hole. I was there once, and the rents were extortionate. Assert yourself. Get the Government of India to take you over. Try to get on the Frontier, where every man has a grand chance if he can trust himself. Go somewhere! Do something! You have twice the wits and three times the presence of the men up here, and, and' Mrs. Hauksbee paused for breath; then continued 'and in any way you look at it, you ought to. You who could go so far!'

'I don't know,' said Yeere, rather taken aback by the unexpected eloquence. 'I haven't such a good opinion of myself.'

It was not strictly Platonic, but it was Policy. Mrs. Hauksbee laid her hand lightly upon the ungloved paw that rested on the turned-back 'rickshaw hood, and, looking the man full in the face, said tenderly, almost too tenderly, 'I believe in you if you mistrust yourself. Is that enough, my friend?'

'It is enough,' answered Otis very solemnly.

He was silent for a long time, redreaming the dreams that he had dreamed eight years ago, but through them all ran, as sheet-lightning through golden cloud, the light of Mrs. Hauksbee's violet eyes.

Curious and impenetrable are the mazes of Simla life the only existence in this desolate land worth the living. Gradually it went abroad among men and women, in the pauses between dance, play, and Gymkhana, that Otis Yeere, the man with the newly-lit light of self-confidence in his eyes, had 'done something decent' in the wilds whence he came. He had brought an erring Municipality to reason, appropriated the funds on his own responsibility, and saved the lives of hundreds. He knew more about the Gullals than any living man. Had a vast knowledge of the aboriginal tribes; was, in spite of his juniority, the greatest authority on the aboriginal Gullals. No one quite knew who or what the Gullals were till The Mussuck, who had been calling on Mrs. Hauksbee, and prided himself upon picking people's brains, explained they were a tribe of ferocious hillmen, somewhere near Sikkim, whose friendship even the Great Indian Empire would find it worth her while to secure. Now we know that Otis Yeere had showed Mrs. Hauksbee his MS. notes of six years' standing on these same Gullals. He had told her, too, how, sick and shaken with the fever their negligence had bred, crippled by the loss of his pet clerk, and savagely angry at the desolation in his charge, he had once damned the collective eyes of his 'intelligent local board' for a set of haramzadas. Which act of 'brutal and tyrannous oppression' won him a Reprimand Royal from the Bengal Government; but in the anecdote as amended for Northern consumption we find no record of this. Hence we are forced to conclude that Mrs. Hauksbee edited his reminiscences before sowing them in idle ears, ready, as she well knew, to exaggerate good or evil. And Otis Yeere bore himself as befitted the hero of many tales.

'You can talk to me when you don't fall into a brown study. Talk now, and talk your brightest and best,' said Mrs. Hauksbee.

Otis needed no spur. Look to a man who has the counsel of a woman of or above the world to back him. So long as he keeps his head, he can meet both sexes on equal ground an advantage never intended by Providence, who fashioned Man on one day and Woman on another, in sign that neither should know more than a very little of the other's life. Such a man goes far, or, the counsel being withdrawn, collapses suddenly while his world seeks the reason.

Generalled by Mrs. Hauksbee, who, again, had all Mrs. Mallowe's wisdom at her disposal, proud of himself and, in the end, believing in himself because he was believed in, Otis Yeere stood ready for any fortune that might befall, certain that it would be good. He would fight for his own hand, and intended that this second struggle should lead to better issue than the first helpless surrender of the bewildered 'Stunt.

What might have happened it is impossible to say. This lamentable thing befell, bred directly by a statement of Mrs. Hauksbee that she would spend the next season in Darjiling.

'Are you certain of that?' said Otis Yeere.

'Quite. We're writing about a house now.'

Otis Yeere 'stopped dead,' as Mrs. Hauksbee put it in discussing the relapse with Mrs. Mallowe.

'He has behaved,' she said angrily, 'just like Captain Kerrington's pony only Otis is a donkey at the last Gymkhana. Planted his forefeet and refused to go on another step. Polly, my man's going to disappoint me. What shall I do?'

As a rule, Mrs. Mallowe does not approve of staring, but on this occasion she opened her eyes to the utmost.

'You have managed cleverly so far,'she said. 'Speak to him, and ask him what he means.'

'I will at to-night's dance.'

'No o, not at a dance,' said Mrs. Mallowe cautiously. 'Men are never themselves quite at dances. Better wait till to-morrow morning.'

'Nonsense. If he's going to 'vert in this insane way there isn't a day to lose. Are you going? No? Then sit up for me, there's a dear. I shan't stay longer than supper under any circumstances.'

Mrs. Mallowe waited through the evening, looking long and earnestly into the fire, and sometimes smiling to herself.

'Oh! oh! oh! The man's an idiot! A raving, positive idiot! I'm sorry I ever saw him!'

Mrs. Hauksbee burst into Mrs. Mallowe's house, at midnight, almost in tears.

'What in the world has happened?' said Mrs. Mallowe, but her eyes showed that she had guessed an answer.

'Happened! Everything has happened! He was there. I went to him and said, "Now, what does this nonsense mean?" Don't laugh, dear, I can't bear it. But you know what I mean I said. Then it was a square, and I sat it out with him and wanted an explanation, and he said Oh! I haven't patience with such idiots! You know what I said about going to Darjiling next year? It doesn't matter to me where

I go. I'd have changed the Station and lost the rent to have saved this. He said, in so many words, that he wasn't going to try to work up any more, because because he would be shifted into a province away from Darjiling, and his own District, where these creatures are,is within a day's journey '

'Ah hh!' said Mrs. Mallowe, in a tone of one who has successfully tracked an obscure word through a large dictionary.

'Did you ever hear of anything so mad so absurd? And he had the ball at his feet. He had only to kick it! I would have made him anything! Anything in the wide world. He could have gone to the world's end. I would have helped him. I made him, didn't I, Polly? Didn't I create that man? Doesn't he owe everything to me? And to reward me, just when everything was nicely arranged, by this lunacy that spoilt everything!'

'Very few men understand your devotion thoroughly.'

'Oh, Polly, don't laugh at me! I give men up from this hour. I could have killed him then and there. What right had this man this Thing I had picked out of his filthy paddy-fields to make love to me?'

'He did that, did he?'

'He did. I don't remember half he said, I was so angry. Oh, but such a funny thing happened! I can't help laughing at it now, though I felt nearly ready to cry with rage. He raved and I stormed I'm afraid we must have made an awful noise in our kala juggah. Protect my character, dear, if it's all over Simla by to-morrow and then he bobbed forward in the middle of this insanity I firmly believe the man's demented and kissed me.'

'Morals above reproach,' purred Mrs. Mallowe.

'So they were so they are! It was the most absurd kiss. I don't believe he'd ever kissed a woman in his life before. I threw my head back, and it was a sort of slidy, pecking dab, just on the end of the chin here.' Mrs. Hauksbee tapped her masculine little chin with her fan. 'Then, of course, I was furiously angry, and told him that he was no gentleman, and I was sorry I'd ever met him, and so on. He was crushed so easily then I couldn't be very angry. Then I came away straight to you.'

'Was this before or after supper?'

'Oh! before oceans before. Isn't it perfectly disgusting?'

'Let me think. I withhold judgment till tomorrow. Morning brings counsel.'

But morning brought only a servant with a dainty bouquet of Annandale roses for Mrs. Hauksbee to wear at the dance at Viceregal Lodge that night.

'He doesn't seem to be very penitent,' said Mrs. Mallowe. 'What's the billet-doux in the centre?'

Mrs. Hauksbee opened the neatly-folded note, another accomplishment that she had taught Otis, read it, and groaned tragically.

'Last wreck of a feeble intellect! Poetry! Is it his own, do you think? Oh, that I ever built my hopes on such a maudlin idiot!'

'No. It's a quotation from Mrs. Browning, and in view of the facts of the case, as Jack says, uncommonly well chosen. Listen

Sweet, thou hast trod on a heart,
    Pass! There's a world full of men;
And women as fair as thou art
    Must do such things now and then.
Thou only hast stepped unaware
    Malice not one can impute;
And why should a heart have been there,
    In the way of a fair woman's foot?

'I didn't I didn't I didn't!' said Mrs. Hauksbee angrily, her eyes filling with tears; 'there was no malice at all. Oh, it's too vexatious!'

'You've misunderstood the compliment,' said Mrs. Mallowe. 'He clears you completely and ahem I should think by this, that he has cleared completely too. My experience of men is that when they begin to quote poetry they are going to flit. Like swans singing before they die, you know.'

'Polly, you take my sorrows in a most unfeeling way.'

'Do I? Is it so terrible? If he's hurt your vanity, I should say that you've done a certain amount of damage to his heart.'

'Oh, you can never tell about a man!' said Mrs. Hauksbee.

AT THE PIT'S MOUTH

Men say it was a stolen tide
    The Lord that sent it He knows all,
But in mine ear will aye abide
    The message that the bells let fall-
And awesome bells they were to me,
That in the dark rang, 'Enderby.'

                   —Jean Ingelow

Once upon a time there was a Man and his Wife and a Tertium Quid.

All three were unwise, but the Wife was the unwisest. The Man should have looked after his Wife, who should have avoided the Tertium Quid, who, again, should have married a wife of his own, after clean and open flirtations, to which nobody can possibly object, round Jakko or Observatory Hill. When you see a young man with his pony in a white lather and his hat on the back of his head, flying downhill at fifteen miles an hour to meet a girl who will be properly surprised to meet him, you naturally approve of that young man, and wish him Staff appointments, and take an interest in his welfare, and, as the proper time comes, give them sugar-tongs or side-saddles according to your means and generosity.

The Tertium Quid flew downhill on horseback, but it was to meet the Man's Wife; and when he flew uphill it was for the same end. The Man was in the Plains, earning money for his Wife to spend on dresses and four-hundred-rupee bracelets, and inexpensive luxuries of that kind. He worked very hard, and sent her a letter or a post-card daily. She also wrote to him daily, and said that she was longing for him to come up to Simla. The Tertium Quid used to lean over her shoulder and laugh as she wrote the notes. Then the two would ride to the Post-office together.

Now, Simla is a strange place and its customs are peculiar; nor is any man who has not spent at least ten seasons there qualified to pass judgment on circumstantial evidence, which is the most untrustworthy in the Courts. For these reasons, and for others which need not appear, I decline to state positively whether there was anything irretrievably wrong in the relations between the Man's Wife and the Tertium Quid. If there was, and hereon you must form your own opinion, it was the Man's Wife's fault. She was kittenish in her manners, wearing generally an air of soft and fluffy innocence. But she was deadlily learned and evil-instructed; and, now and again, when the mask dropped, men saw this, shuddered and almost drew back. Men are occasionally particular, and the least particular men are always the most exacting.

Simla is eccentric in its fashion of treating friendships. Certain attachments which have set and crystallised through half-a-dozen seasons acquire almost the sanctity of the marriage bond, and are revered as such. Again, certain attachments equally old, and, to all appearance, equally venerable, never seem to win any recognised official status; while a chance-sprung acquaintance, not two months born, steps into the place which by right belongs to the senior. There is no law reducible to print which regulates these affairs.

Some people have a gift which secures them infinite toleration, and others have not. The Man's Wife had not. If she looked over the garden wall, for instance, women taxed her with stealing their husbands. She complained pathetically that she was not allowed to choose her own friends. When she put up her big white muff to her lips, and gazed over it and under her eyebrows at you as she said this thing, you felt that she had been infamously misjudged, and that all the other women's instincts were all wrong; which was absurd. She was not allowed to own the Tertium Quid in peace; and was so strangely constructed that she would not have enjoyed peace had she been so permitted. She preferred some semblance of intrigue to cloak even her most commonplace actions.

After two months of riding, first round Jakko, then Elysium, then Summer Hill, then Observatory Hill, then under Jutogh, and lastly up and down the Cart Road as far as the Tara Devi gap in the dusk, she said to the Tertium Quid, 'Frank, people say we are too much together, and people are so horrid.'

The Tertium Quid pulled his moustache, and replied that horrid people were unworthy of the consideration of nice people.

'But they have done more than talk they have written written to my hubby I'm sure of it,' said the Man's Wife, and she pulled a letter from her husband out of her saddle-pocket and gave it to the Tertium Quid.

It was an honest letter, written by an honest man, then stewing in the Plains on two hundred rupees a month (for he allowed his wife eight hundred and fifty), and in a silk banian and cotton trousers. It said that, perhaps, she had not thought of the unwisdom of allowing her name to be so generally coupled with the Tertium Quid's; that she was too much of a child to understand the dangers of that sort of thing; that he, her husband, was the last man in the world to interfere jealously with her little amusements and interests, but that it would be better were she to drop the Tertium Quid quietly and for her husband's sake. The letter was sweetened with many pretty little pet names, and it amused the Tertium Quid considerably. He and She laughed over it, so that you, fifty yards away, could see their shoulders shaking while the horses slouched along side by side.

Their conversation was not worth reporting. The upshot of it was that, next day, no one saw the Man's Wife and the Tertium Quid together. They had both gone down to the Cemetery, which, as a rule, is only visited officially by the inhabitants of Simla.

A Simla funeral with the clergyman riding, the mourners riding, and the coffin creaking as it swings between the bearers, is one of the most depressing things on this earth, particularly when the procession passes under the wet, dank dip beneath the Rockcliffe Hotel, where the sun is shut out, and all the hill streams are wailing and weeping together as they go down the valleys.

Occasionally folk tend the graves, but we in India shift and are transferred so often that, at the end of the second year, the Dead have no friend only acquaintances who are far too busy amusing themselves up the hill to attend to old partners. The idea of using a Cemetery as a rendezvous is distinctly a feminine one. A man would have said simply, 'Let people talk. We'll go down the Mall.' A woman is made differently, especially if she be such a woman as the Man's Wife. She and the Tertium Quid enjoyed each other's society among the graves of men and women whom they had known and danced with aforetime.

They used to take a big horse-blanket and sit on the grass a little to the left of the lower end, where there is a dip in the ground, and where the occupied graves stop short and the ready-made ones are not ready. Each well-regulated Indian Cemetery keeps half-a-dozen graves permanently open for contingencies and incidental wear and tear. In the Hills these are more usually baby's size, because children who come up weakened and sick from the Plains often succumb to the effects of the Rains in the Hills or get pneumonia from their ayahs taking them through damp pine-woods after the sun has set. In Cantonments, of course, the man's size is more in request; these arrangements varying with the climate and population.

One day when the Man's Wife and the Tertium Quid had just arrived in the Cemetery, they saw some coolies breaking ground. They had marked out a full-size grave, and the Tertium Quid asked them whether any Sahib was sick. They said that they did not know; but it was an order that they should dig a Sahib's grave.

'Work away,' said the Tertium Quid, 'and let's see how it's done.'

The coolies worked away, and the Man's Wife and the Tertium Quid watched and talked for a couple of hours while the grave was being deepened. Then a coolie, taking the earth in baskets as it was thrown up, jumped over the grave.

'That's queer,' said the Tertium Quid. 'Where's my ulster?'

'What's queer?' said the Man's Wife.

'I have got a chill down my back just as if a goose had walked over my grave.'

'Why do you look at the thing, then?' said the Man's Wife. 'Let us go.'

The Tertium Quid stood at the head of the grave, and stared without answering for a space. Then he said, dropping a pebble down, 'It is nasty and cold: horribly cold. I don't think I shall come to the Cemetery any more. I don't think grave-digging is cheerful.'

The two talked and agreed that the Cemetery was depressing. They also arranged for a ride next day out from the Cemetery through the Mashobra Tunnel up to Fagoo and back, because all the world was going to a garden-party at Viceregal Lodge, and all the people of Mashobra would go too.

Coming up the Cemetery road, the Tertium Quid's horse tried to bolt uphill, being tired with standing so long, and managed to strain a back sinew.

'I shall have to take the mare to-morrow,' said the Tertium Quid, 'and she will stand nothing heavier than a snaffle.'

They made their arrangements to meet in the Cemetery, after allowing all the Mashobra people time to pass into Simla. That night it rained heavily, and, next day, when the Tertium Quid came to the trysting-place, he saw that the new grave had a foot of water in it, the ground being a tough and sour clay.

"Jove! That looks beastly,' said the Tertium Quid. 'Fancy being boarded up and dropped into that well!'

They then started off to Fagoo, the mare playing with the snaffle and picking her way as though she were shod with satin, and the sun shining divinely. The road below Mashobra to Fagoo is officially styled the Himalayan-Thibet road; but in spite of its name it is not much more than six feet wide in most places, and the drop into the valley below may be anything between one and two thousand feet.

'Now we're going to Thibet,' said the Man's Wife merrily, as the horses drew near to Fagoo. She was riding on the cliff-side.

'Into Thibet,' said the Tertium Quid, 'ever so far from people who say horrid things, and hubbies who write stupid letters. With you to the end of the world!'

A coolie carrying a log of wood came round a corner, and the mare went wide to avoid him forefeet in and haunches out, as a sensible mare should go.

'To the world's end,' said the Man's Wife, and looked unspeakable things over her near shoulder at the Tertium Quid.

He was smiling, but, while she looked, the smile froze stiff as it were on his face, and changed to a nervous grin the sort of grin men wear when they are not quite easy in their saddles. The mare seemed to be sinking by the stern, and her nostrils cracked while she was trying to realise what was happening. The rain of the night before had rotted the drop-side of the Himalayan-Thibet Road, and it was giving way under her. 'What are you doing?' said the Man's Wife. The Tertium Quid gave no answer. He grinned nervously and set his spurs into the mare, who rapped with her forefeet on the road, and the struggle began. The Man's Wife screamed, 'Oh, Frank, get off!'

But the Tertium Quid was glued to the saddle his face blue and white and he looked into the Man's Wife's eyes. Then the Man's Wife clutched at the mare's head and caught her by the nose instead of the bridle. The brute threw up her head and went down with a scream, the Tertium Quid upon her, and the nervous grin still set on his face.

The Man's Wife heard the tinkle-tinkle of little stones and loose earth falling off the roadway, and the sliding roar of the man and horse going down. Then everything was quiet, and she called on Frank to leave his mare and walk up. But Frank did not answer. He was underneath the mare, nine hundred feet below, spoiling a patch of Indian corn.

As the revellers came back from Viceregal Lodge in the mists of the evening, they met a temporarily insane woman, on a temporarily mad horse, swinging round the corners, with her eyes and her mouth open, and her head like the head of a Medusa. She was stopped by a man at the risk of his life, and taken out of the saddle, a limp heap, and put on the bank to explain herself. This wasted twenty minutes, and then she was sent home in a lady's 'rickshaw, still with her mouth open and her hands picking at her riding-gloves.

She was in bed through the following three days, which were rainy; so she missed attending the funeral of the Tertium Quid, who was lowered into eighteen inches of water, instead of the twelve to which he had first objected.

A WAYSIDE COMEDY

Because to every purpose there is time and judgment,
therefore the misery of man is great upon him.

—Eccles. viii. 6.

Fate and the Government of India have turned the Station of Kashima into a prison; and, because there is no help for the poor souls who are now lying there in torment, I write this story, praying that the Government of India may be moved to scatter the European population to the four winds.

Kashima is bounded on all sides by the rocktipped circle of the Dosehri hills. In Spring, it is ablaze with roses; in Summer, the roses die and the hot winds blow from the hills; in Autumn, the white mists from the jhils cover the place as with water, and in Winter the frosts nip everything young and tender to earth-level. There is but one view in Kashima a stretch of perfectly flat pasture and plough-land, running up to the gray-blue scrub of the Dosehri hills.

There are no amusements, except snipe and tiger shooting; but the tigers have been long since hunted from their lairs in the rock-caves, and the snipe only come once a year. Narkarra one hundred and forty-three miles by road is the nearest station to Kashima. But Kashima never goes to Narkarra, where there are at least twelve English people. It stays within the circle of the Dosehri hills.

All Kashima acquits Mrs. Vansuythen of any intention to do harm; but all Kashima knows that she, and she alone, brought about their pain.

Boulte, the Engineer, Mrs. Boulte, and Captain Kurrell know this. They are the English population of Kashima, if we except

Major Vansuythen, who is of no importance whatever, and Mrs. Vansuythen, who is the most important of all.

You must remember, though you will not understand, that all laws weaken in a small and hidden community where there is no public opinion. When a man is absolutely alone in a Station he runs a certain risk of falling into evil ways. This risk is multiplied by every addition to the population up to twelve the Jury-number. After that, fear and consequent restraint begin, and human action becomes less grotesquely jerky.

There was deep peace in Kashima till Mrs. Vansuythen arrived. She was a charming woman, every one said so everywhere; and she charmed every one. In spite of this, or, perhaps, because of this, since Fate is so perverse, she cared only for one man, and he was Major Vansuythen. Had she been plain or stupid, this matter would have been intelligible to Kashima. But she was a fair woman, with very still gray eyes, the colour of a lake just before the light of the sun touches it. No man who had seen those eyes could, later on, explain what fashion of woman she was to look upon. The eyes dazzled him. Her own sex said that she was 'not bad-looking, but spoilt by pretending to be so grave.' And yet her gravity was natural. It was not her habit to smile. She merely went through life, looking at those who passed; and the women objected while the men fell down and worshipped.

She knows and is deeply sorry for the evil she has done to Kashima; but Major Vansuythen cannot understand why Mrs. Boulte does not drop in to afternoon tea at least three times a week. 'When there are only two women in one Station, they ought to see a great deal of each other,' says Major Vansuythen.

Long and long before ever Mrs. Vansuythen came out of those far-away places where there is society and amusement, Kurrell had discovered that Mrs. Boulte was the one woman in the world for him and you dare not blame them. Kashima was as out of the world as Heaven or the Other Place, and the Dosehri hills kept their secret well. Boulte had no concern in the matter. He was in camp for a fortnight at a time. He was a hard, heavy man, and neither Mrs. Boulte nor Kurrell pitied him. They had all Kashima and each other for their very, very own; and Kashima was the Garden of Eden in those days. When Boulte returned from his wanderings he would slap Kurrell between the shoulders and call him 'old fellow,' and the three would dine together. Kashima was happy then when the judgment of God seemed almost as distant as Narkarra or the railway that ran down to the sea. But the Government sent Major Vansuythen to Kashima, and with him came his wife.

The etiquette of Kashima is much the same as that of a desert island. When a stranger is cast away there, all hands go down to the shore to make him welcome. Kashima assembled at the masonry platform close to the Narkarra Road, and spread tea for the Vansuythens. That ceremony was reckoned a formal call, and made them free of the Station, its rights and privileges. When the Vansuythens settled down they gave a tiny house-warming to all Kashima; and that made Kashima free of their house, according to the immemorial usage of the Station.

Then the Rains came, when no one could go into camp, and the Narkarra Road was washed away by the Kasun River, and in the cup-like pastures of Kashima the cattle waded knee-deep. The clouds dropped down from the Dosehri hills and covered everything.

At the end of the Rains Boulte's manner towards his wife changed and became demonstratively affectionate. They had been married twelve years, and the change startled Mrs. Boulte, who hated her husband with the hate of a woman who has met with nothing but kindness from her mate, and, in the teeth of this kindness, has done him a great wrong. Moreover, she had her own trouble to fight with her watch to keep over her own property, Kurrell. For two months the Rains had hidden the Dosehri hills and many other things besides; but, when they lifted, they showed Mrs. Boulte that her man among men, her Ted for she called him Ted in the old days when Boulte was out of earshot was slipping the links of the allegiance.

'The Vansuythen Woman has taken him,' Mrs. Boulte said to herself; and when Boulte was away, wept over her belief, in the face of the over-vehement blandishments of Ted. Sorrow in Kashima is as fortunate as Love because there is nothing to weaken it save the flight of Time. Mrs. Boulte had never breathed her suspicion to Kurrell because she was not certain; and her nature led her to be very certain before she took steps in any direction. That is why she behaved as she did.

Boulte came into the house one evening, and leaned against the door-posts of the drawing-room, chewing his moustache. Mrs. Boulte was putting some flowers into a vase. There is a pretence of civilisation even in Kashima.

'Little woman,' said Boulte quietly, 'do you care for me?'

'Immensely,' said she, with a laugh. 'Can you ask it?'

'But I'm serious,' said Boulte. 'Do you care for me?'

Mrs. Boulte dropped the flowers, and turned round quickly. 'Do you want an honest answer?'

'Ye-es, I've asked for it.'

Mrs. Boulte spoke in a low, even voice for five minutes, very distinctly, that there might be no misunderstanding her meaning. When Samson broke the pillars of Gaza, he did a little thing, and one not to be compared to the deliberate pulling down of a woman's homestead about her own ears. There was no wise female friend to advise Mrs. Boulte, the singularly cautious wife, to hold her hand. She struck at Boulte's heart, because her own was sick with suspicion of Kurrell, and worn out with the long strain of watching alone through the Rains. There was no plan or purpose in her speaking. The sentences made themselves; and Boulte listened, leaning against the door-post with his hands in his pockets. When all was over, and Mrs. Boulte began to breathe through her nose before breaking out into tears, he laughed and stared straight in front of him at the Dosehri hills.

'Is that all?' he said. 'Thanks, I only wanted to know, you know.'

'What are you going to do?' said the woman, between her sobs.

'Do! Nothing. What should I do? Kill Kurrell, or send you Home, or apply for leave to get a divorce? It's two days' d f k into Narkarra.' He laughed again and went on: 'I'll tell you what you can do. You can ask Kurrell to dinner tomorrow no, on Thursday, that will allow you time to pack and you can bolt with him. I give you my word I won't follow.'

He took up his helmet and went out of the room, and Mrs. Boulte sat till the moonlight streaked the floor, thinking and thinking and thinking. She had done her best upon the spur of the moment to pull the house down; but it would not fall. Moreover, she could not understand her husband, and she was afraid. Then the folly of her useless truthfulness struck her, and she was ashamed to write to Kurrell, saying, 'I have gone mad and told everything. My husband says that I am free to elope with you. Get a d f k for Thursday, and we will fly after dinner.' There was a cold-bloodedness about that procedure which did not appeal to her. So she sat still in her own house and thought.

At dinner-time Boulte came back from his walk, white and worn and haggard, and the woman was touched at his distress. As the evening wore on she muttered some expression of sorrow, something approaching to contrition. Boulte came out of a brown study and said, 'Oh, that! I wasn't thinking about that. By the way, what does Kurrell say to the elopement?'

'I haven't seen him,' said Mrs. Boulte. 'Good God, is that all?'

But Boulte was not listening and her sentence ended in a gulp.

The next day brought no comfort to Mrs. Boulte, for Kurrell did not appear, and the new lift that she, in the five minutes' madness of the previous evening, had hoped to build out of the ruins of the old, seemed to be no nearer.

Boulte ate his breakfast, advised her to see her Arab pony fed in the verandah, and went out. The morning wore through, and at mid-day the tension became unendurable. Mrs. Boulte could not cry. She had finished her crying in the night, and now she did not want to be left alone. Perhaps the Vansuythen Woman would talk to her; and, since talking opens the heart, perhaps there might be some comfort to be found in her company. She was the only other woman in the Station.

In Kashima there are no regular calling-hours. Every one can drop in upon every one else at pleasure. Mrs. Boulte put on a big terai hat, and walked across to the Vansuythens' house to borrow last week's Queen. The two compounds touched, and instead of going up the drive, she crossed through the gap in the cactus-hedge, entering the house from the back. As she passed through the dining-room, she heard, behind the purdah that cloaked the drawing-room door, her husband's voice, saying

'But on my Honour! On my Soul and Honour, I tell you she doesn't care for me. She told me so last night. I would have told you then if Vansuythen hadn't been with you. If it is for her sake that you'll have nothing to say to me, you can make your mind easy. It's Kurrell '

'What?' said Mrs. Vansuythen, with a hysterical little laugh. 'Kurrell! Oh, it can't be! You two must have made some horrible mistake. Perhaps you you lost your temper, or misunderstood, or something. Things can't be as wrong as you say.'

Mrs. Vansuythen had shifted her defence to avoid the man's pleading, and was desperately trying to keep him to a side-issue.

'There must be some mistake,' she insisted, 'and it can be all put right again.'

Boulte laughed grimly.

'It can't be Captain Kurrell! He told me that he had never taken the least the least interest in your wife, Mr. Boulte. Oh, do listen! He said he had not. He swore he had not,' said Mrs. Vansuythen.

The purdah rustled, and the speech was cut short by the entry of a little thin woman, with big rings round her eyes. Mrs. Vansuythen stood up with a gasp.

'What was that you said?' asked Mrs. Boulte. 'Never mind that man. What did Ted say to you? What did he say to you? What did he say to you?'

Mrs. Vansuythen sat down helplessly on the sofa, overborne by the trouble of her questioner.

'He said I can't remember exactly what he said but I understood him to say that is But, really, Mrs. Boulte, isn't it rather a strange question?'

'Will you tell me what he said?' repeated Mrs. Boulte. Even a tiger will fly before a bear robbed of her whelps, and Mrs. Vansuythen was only an ordinarily good woman. She began in a sort of desperation: 'Well, he said that the never cared for you at all, and, of course, there was not the least reason why he should have, and and that was all.'

'You said he swore he had not cared for me. Was that true?'

'Yes,' said Mrs. Vansuythen very softly.

Mrs. Boulte wavered for an instant where she stood, and then fell forward fainting.

'What did I tell you?' said Boulte, as though the conversation had been unbroken. 'You can see for yourself. She cares for him.' The light began to break into his dull mind, and he went on ' And he what was he saying to you?'

But Mrs. Vansuythen, with no heart for explanations or impassioned protestations, was kneeling over Mrs. Boulte.

'Oh, you brute!' she cried. 'Are all men like this? Help me to get her into my room and her face is cut against the table. Oh, will you be quiet, and help me to carry her? I hate you, and I hate Captain Kurrell. Lift her up carefully, and now go! Go away!'

Boulte carried his wife into Mrs. Vansuythen's bedroom, and departed before the storm of that lady's wrath and disgust, impenitent and burning with jealousy. Kurrell had been making love to Mrs. Vansuythen would do Vansuythen as great a wrong as he had done Boulte, who caught himself considering whether Mrs. Vansuythen would faint if she discovered that the man she loved had forsworn her.

In the middle of these meditations, Kurrell came cantering along the road and pulled up with a cheery 'Good-mornin'. 'Been mashing Mrs. Vansuythen as usual, eh? Bad thing for a sober, married man, that. What will Mrs. Boulte say?'

Boulte raised his head and said slowly, 'Oh, you liar!' Kurrell's face changed. 'What's that?' he asked quickly.

'Nothing much,' said Boulte. 'Has my wife told you that you two are free to go off whenever you please? She has been good enough to explain the situation to me. You've been a true friend to me, Kurrell old man haven't you?'

Kurrell groaned, and tried to frame some sort of idiotic sentence about being willing to give 'satisfaction.' But his interest in the woman was dead, had died out in the Rains, and, mentally, he was abusing her for her amazing indiscretion. It would have been so easy to have broken off the thing gently and by degrees, and now he was saddled with Boulte's voice recalled him.

'I don't think I should get any satisfaction from killing you, and I'm pretty sure you'd get none from killing me.'

Then in a querulous tone, ludicrously disproportioned to his wrongs, Boulte added

"Seems rather a pity that you haven't the decency to keep to the woman, now you've got her. You've been a true friend to her too, haven't you?'

Kurrell stared long and gravely. The situation was getting beyond him.

'What do you mean?' he said.

Boulte answered, more to himself than the questioner: 'My wife came over to Mrs. Vansuythen's just now; and it seems you'd been telling Mrs. Vansuythen that you'd never cared for Emma. I suppose you lied, as usual. What had Mrs. Vansuythen to do with you, or you with her? Try to speak the truth for once in a way.'

Kurrell took the double insult without wincing, and replied by another question: 'Go on. What happened?'

'Emma fainted,' said Boulte simply. 'But, look here, what had you been saying to Mrs. Vansuythen?'

Kurrell laughed. Mrs. Boulte had, with unbridled tongue, made havoc of his plans; and he could at least retaliate by hurting the man in whose eyes he was humiliated and shown dishonourable.

'Said to her? What does a man tell a lie like that for? I suppose I said pretty much what you've said, unless I'm a good deal mistaken.'

'I spoke the truth,' said Boulte, again more to himself than Kurrell. 'Emma told me she hated me. She has no right in me.'

'No! I suppose not. You're only her husband, y'know. And what did Mrs. Vansuythen say after you had laid your disengaged heart at her feet?'

Kurrell felt almost virtuous as he put the question.

'I don't think that matters,' Boulte replied; 'and it doesn't concern you.'

'But it does! I tell you it does' began Kurrell shamelessly.

The sentence was cut by a roar of laughter from Boulte's lips. Kurrell was silent for an instant, and then he, too, laughed laughed long and loudly, rocking in his saddle. It was an unpleasant sound the mirthless mirth of these men on the long white line of the Narkarra Road. There were no strangers in Kashima, or they might have thought that captivity within the Dosehri hills had driven half the European population mad. The laughter ended abruptly, and Kurrell was the first to speak.

'Well, what are you going to do?'

Boulte looked up the road, and at the hills. 'Nothing,' said he quietly; 'what's the use? It's too ghastly for anything. We must let the old life go on. I can only call you a hound and a liar, and I can't go on calling you names for ever. Besides which, I don't feel that I'm much better. We can't get out of this place. What is there to do?'

Kurrell looked round the rat-pit of Kashima and made no reply. The injured husband took up the wondrous tale.

'Ride on, and speak to Emma if you want to. God knows I don't care what you do.'

He walked forward, and left Kurrell gazing blankly after him. Kurrell did not ride on either to see Mrs. Boulte or Mrs. Vansuythen. He sat in his saddle and thought, while his pony grazed by the roadside.

The whir of approaching wheels roused him. Mrs. Vansuythen was driving home Mrs. Boulte, white and wan, with a cut on her forehead.

'Stop, please,' said Mrs. Boulte, 'I want to speak to Ted.'

Mrs. Vansuythen obeyed, but as Mrs. Boulte leaned forward, putting her hand upon the splashboard of the dog-cart, Kurrell spoke.

'I've seen your husband, Mrs. Boulte.'

There was no necessity for any further explanation. The man's eyes were fixed, not upon Mrs. Boulte, but her companion. Mrs. Boulte saw the look.

'Speak to him!' she pleaded, turning to the woman at her side. 'Oh, speak to him! Tell him what you told me just now. Tell him you hate him. Tell him you hate him!'

She bent forward and wept bitterly, while the sais, impassive, went forward to hold the horse. Mrs. Vansuythen turned scarlet and dropped the reins. She wished to be no party to such unholy explanations.

'I've nothing to do with it,' she began coldly; but Mrs. Boulte's sobs overcame her, and she addressed herself to the man. 'I don't know what I am to say, Captain Kurrell. I don't know what I can call you. I think you've you've behaved abominably, and she has cut her forehead terribly against the table.'

'It doesn't hurt. It isn't anything,' said Mrs. Boulte feebly. 'That doesn't matter. Tell him what you told me. Say you don't care for him. Oh, Ted, won't you believe her?'

'Mrs. Boulte has made me understand that you were that you were fond of her once upon a time,' went on Mrs. Vansuythen.

'Well!' said Kurrell brutally. 'It seems to me that Mrs. Boulte had better be fond of her own husband first.'

'Stop!' said Mrs. Vansuythen. 'Hear me first. I don't care I don't want to know anything about you and Mrs. Boulte; but I want you to know that I hate you, that I think you are a cur, and that I'll never, never speak to you again. Oh, I don't dare to say what I think of you, you man!'

'I want to speak to Ted,' moaned Mrs. Boulte, but the dog-cart rattled on, and Kurrell was left on the road, shamed, and boiling with wrath against Mrs. Boulte.

He waited till Mrs. Vansuythen was driving back to her own house, and, she being freed from the embarrassment of Mrs. Boulte's presence, learned for the second time her opinion of himself and his actions.

In the evenings it was the wont of all Kashima to meet at the platform on the Narkarra Road, to drink tea and discuss the trivialities of the day. Major Vansuythen and his wife found themselves alone at the gathering-place for almost the first time in their remembrance; and the cheery Major, in the teeth of his wife's remarkably reasonable suggestion that the rest of the Station might be sick, insisted upon driving round to the two bungalows and unearthing the population.

'Sitting in the twilight!' said he, with great indignation, to the Boultes. 'That'll never do! Hang it all, we're one family here! You must come out, and so must Kurrell. I'll make him bring his banjo.'

So great is the power of honest simplicity and a good digestion over guilty consciences that all Kashima did turn out, even down to the banjo; and the Major embraced the company in one expansive grin. As he grinned, Mrs. Vansuythen raised her eyes for an instant and looked at all Kashima. Her meaning was clear. Major Vansuythen would never know anything. He was to be the outsider in that happy family whose cage was the Dosehri hills.

'You're singing villainously out of tune, Kurrell,' said the Major truthfully. 'Pass me that banjo.'

And he sang in excruciating-wise till the stars came out and all Kashima went to dinner.

That was the beginning of the New Life of Kashima the life that Mrs. Boulte made when her tongue was loosened in the twilight.

Mrs. Vansuythen has never told the Major; and since he insists upon keeping up a burdensome geniality, she has been compelled to break her vow of not speaking to Kurrell. This speech, which must of necessity preserve the semblance of politeness and interest, serves admirably to keep alight the flame of jealousy and dull hatred in Boulte's bosom, as it awakens the same passions in his wife's heart. Mrs. Boulte hates Mrs. Vansuythen because she has taken Ted from her, and, in some curious fashion, hates her because Mrs. Vansuythen and here the wife's eyes see far more clearly than the husband's detests Ted. And Ted that gallant captain and honourable man knows now that it is possible to hate a woman once loved, to the verge of wishing to silence her for ever with blows. Above all, is he shocked that Mrs. Boulte cannot see the error of her ways.

Boulte and he go out tiger-shooting together in all friendship. Boulte has put their relationship on a most satisfactory footing.

'You're a blackguard,' he says to Kurrell, 'and I've lost any self-respect I may ever have had; but when you're with me, I can feel certain that you are not with Mrs. Vansuythen, or making Emma miserable.'

Kurrell endures anything that Boulte may say to him. Sometimes they are away for three days together, and then the Major insists upon his wife going over to sit with Mrs. Boulte; although Mrs. Vansuythen has repeatedly declared that she prefers her husband's company to any in the world. From the way in which she clings to him, she would certainly seem to be speaking the truth.

But of course, as the Major says, 'in a little Station we must all be friendly.'

THE HILL OF ILLUSION

What rendered vain their deep desire?
A God, a God their severance ruled,
And bade between their shores to be
The unplumbed, salt, estranging sea.

—Matthew Arnold.

He. Tell your jhampanies not to hurry so, dear. They forget I'm fresh from the Plains.

She. Sure proof that I have not been going out with any one. Yes, they are an untrained crew. Where do we go?

He. As usual to the world's end. No, Jakko.

She. Have your pony led after you, then. It's a long round.

He. And for the last time, thank Heaven!

She. Do you mean that still? I didn't dare to write to you about it all these months.

He. Mean it! I've been shaping my affairs to that end since Autumn. What makes you speak as though it had occurred to you for the first time?

She. I? Oh! I don't know. I've had long enough to think, too.

He. And you've changed your mind?

She. No. You ought to know that I am a miracle of constancy. What are your arrangements?

He. Ours, Sweetheart, please.

She. Ours, be it then. My poor boy, how the prickly heat has marked your forehead! Have you ever tried sulphate of copper in water?

He. It'll go away in a day or two up here. The arrangements are simple enough. Tonga in the early morning reach Kalka at twelve Umballa at seven down, straight by night train, to

Bombay, and then the steamer of the 21st for Rome. That's my idea. The Continent and Sweden a ten-week honeymoon.

She. Ssh! Don't talk of it in that way. It makes me afraid. Guy, how long have we two been insane?

He. Seven months and fourteen days, I forget the odd hours exactly, but I'll think.

She. I only wanted to see if you remembered. Who are those two on the Blessington Road?

He. Eabrey and the Penner Woman. What do they matter to us? Tell me everything that you've been doing and saying and thinking.

She. Doing little, saying less, and thinking a great deal. I've hardly been out at all.

He. That was wrong of you. You haven't been moping?

She. Not very much. Can you wonder that I'm disinclined for amusement?

He. Frankly, I do. Where was the difficulty?

She. In this only. The more people I know and the more I'm known here, the wider spread will be the news of the crash when it comes. I don't like that.

He. Nonsense. We shall be out of it.

She. You think so?

He. I'm sure of it, if there is any power in steam or horse-flesh to carry us away. Ha! ha!

She. And the fun of the situation comes in where, my Lancelot?

He. Nowhere, Guinevere. I was only thinking of something.

She. They say men have a keener sense of humour than women. Now I was thinking of the scandal.

He. Don't think of anything so ugly. We shall be beyond it.

She. It will be there all the same in the mouths of Simla telegraphed over India, and talked of at the dinners and when He goes out they will stare at Him to see how he takes it. And we shall be dead, Guy dear dead and cast into the outer darkness where there is

He. Love at least. Isn't that enough?

She. I have said so.

He. And you think so still?

She. What do you think?

He. What have I done? It means equal ruin to me, as the world reckons it outcasting, the loss of my appointment, the breaking off my life's work. I pay my price.

She. And are you so much above the world that you can afford to pay it. Am I?

He. My Divinity what else?

She. A very ordinary woman, I'm afraid, but so far, respectable. How d'you do, Mrs. Middle-ditch? Your husband? I think he's riding down to Annandale with Colonel Statters. Yes, isn't it divine after the rain? Guy, how long am I to be allowed to bow to Mrs. Middleditch? Till the 17th?

He. Frowsy Scotchwoman! What is the use of bringing her into the discussion? You were saying?

She. Nothing. Have you ever seen a man hanged?

He. Yes. Once.

She. What was it for?

He. Murder, of course.

She. Murder. Is that so great a sin after all? I wonder how he felt before the drop fell.

He. I don't think he felt much. What a gruesome little woman it is this evening! You're shivering. Put on your cape, dear.

She. I think I will. Oh! Look at the mist coming over Sanjaoli; and I thought we should have sunshine on the Ladies' Mile! Let's turn back.

He. What's the good? There's a cloud on Elysium Hill, and that means it's foggy all down the Mall. We'll go on. It'll blow away before we get to the Convent, perhaps. 'Jove! It is chilly.

She. You feel it, fresh from below. Put on your ulster. What do you think of my cape?

He. Never ask a man his opinion of a woman's dress when he is desperately and abjectly in love with the wearer. Let me look. Like everything else of yours it's perfect. Where did you get it from?

She. He gave it me, on Wednesday our wedding-day, you know.

He. The Deuce He did! He's growing generous in his old age. D'you like all that frilly, bunchy stuff at the throat? I don't.

She. Don't you?

Kind Sir, o' your courtesy,
　　As you go by the town,
　Sir, 'Pray you o' your love for me,
　　Buy me a russet gown, Sir.

He. I won't say: 'Keek into the draw-well, Janet, Janet.' Only wait a little, darling, and you shall be stocked with russet gowns and everything else.

She. And when the frocks wear out you'll get me new ones and everything else?

He. Assuredly.

She. I wonder!

He. Look here, Sweetheart, I didn't spend two days and two nights in the train to hear you wonder. I thought we'd settled all that at Shaifazehat.

She. (dreamily). At Shaifazehat? Does the Station go on still? That was ages and ages ago. It must be crumbling to pieces. All except the Amirtollah kutcha road. I don't believe that could crumble till the Day of Judgment.

He. You think so? What is the mood now?

She. I can't tell. How cold it is! Let us get on quickly.

He. 'Better walk a little. Stop your jhampanies and get out. What's the matter with you this evening, dear?

She. Nothing. You must grow accustomed to my ways. If I'm boring you I can go home. Here's Captain Congleton coming, I daresay he'll be willing to escort me.

He. Goose! Between us, too! Damn Captain Congleton.

She. Chivalrous Knight. Is it your habit to swear much in talking? It jars a little, and you might swear at me.

He. My angel! I didn't know what I was saying; and you changed so quickly that I couldn't follow. I'll apologise in dust and ashes.

She. There'll be enough of those later on Good-night, Captain Congleton. Going to the singing-quadrilles already? What dances am I giving you next week? No! You must have written them down wrong. Five and Seven, I said. If you've made a mistake, I certainly don't intend to suffer for it. You must alter your programme.

He. I thought you told me that you had not been going out much this season?

She. Quite true, but when I do I dance with Captain Congleton. He dances very nicely.

He. And sit out with him, I suppose?

She. Yes. Have you any objection? Shall I stand under the chandelier in future?

He. What does he talk to you about?

She. What do men talk about when they sit out?

He. Ugh! Don't! Well, now I'm up, you must dispense with the fascinating Congleton for a while. I don't like him.

She (after a pause). Do you know what you have said?

He 'Can't say that I do exactly. I'm not in the best of tempers.

She So I see, and feel. My true and faithful lover, where is your 'eternal constancy,' 'unalterable trust,' and 'reverent devotion'? I remember those phrases; you seem to have forgotten them. I mention a man's name

He. A good deal more than that.

She. Well, speak to him about a dance perhaps the last dance that I shall ever dance in my life before I, before I go away; and you at once distrust and insult me.

He. I never said a word.

She. How much did you imply? Guy, is this amount of confidence to be our stock to start the new life on?

He. No, of course not. I didn't mean that. On my word and honour, I didn't. Let it pass, dear. Please let it pass.

She. This once yes and a second time, and again and again, all through the years when I shall be unable to resent it. You want too much, my Lancelot, and, you know too much.

He. How do you mean?

She. That is a part of the punishment. There cannot be perfect trust between us.

He. In Heaven's name, why not?

She. Hush! The Other Place is quite enough. Ask yourself.

He. I don't follow.

She. You trust me so implicitly that when I look at another man Never mind. Guy, have you ever made love to a girl a good girl?

He. Something of the sort. Centuries ago in the Dark Ages, before I ever met you, dear.

She. Tell me what you said to her.

He. What does a man say to a girl? I've forgotten.

She. I remember. He tells her that he trusts her and worships the ground she walks on, and that he'll love and honour and protect her till her dying day; and so she marries in that belief. At least, I speak of one girl who was not protected.

He. Well, and then?

She. And then, Guy, and then, that girl needs ten times the love and trust and honour yes, honour that was enough when she was only a mere wife if if the other life she chooses to lead is to be made even bearable. Do you understand?

He. Even bearable! It'll be Paradise.

She. Ah! Can you give me all I've asked for not now, nor a few months later, but when you begin to think of what you might have done if you had kept your own appointment and your caste here when you begin to look upon me as a drag and a burden? I shall want it most then, Guy, for there will be no one in the wide world but you.

He. You're a little over-tired to-night, Sweetheart, and you're taking a stage view of the situation. After the necessary business in the Courts, the road is clear to

She. 'The holy state of matrimony!' Ha! ha! ha!

He. Ssh! Don't laugh in that horrible way!

She. I I c-c-c-can't help it! Isn't it too absurd! Ah! Ha! ha! ha! Guy, stop me quick or I shall l-l-laugh till we get to the Church.

He. For goodness sake, stop! Don't make an exhibition of yourself. What is the matter with you?

She. N-nothing. I'm better now.

He. That's all right. One moment, dear. There's a little wisp of hair got loose from behind your right ear and it's straggling over your cheek. So!

She. Thank'oo. I'm 'fraid my hat's on one side, too.

He. What do you wear these huge dagger bonnet-skewers for? They're big enough to kill a man with.

She. Oh! don't kill me, though. You're sticking it into my head! Let me do it. You men are so clumsy.

He. Have you had many opportunities of comparing us in this sort of work?

She. Guy, what is my name?

He. Eh! I don't follow.

She. Here's my card-case. Can you read?

He. Yes. Well?

She. Well, that answers your question. You know the other's man's name. Am I sufficiently humbled, or would you like to ask me if there is any one else?

He. I see now. My darling, I never meant that for an instant. I was only joking. There! Lucky there's no one on the road. They'd be scandalised.

She. They'll be more scandalised before the end.

He. Do-on't! I don't like you to talk in that way.

She. Unreasonable man! Who asked me to face the situation and accept it? Tell me, do I look like Mrs. Penner? Do I look like a naughty woman! Swear I don't! Give me your word of honour, my honourable friend, that I'm not like Mrs. Buzgago. That's the way she stands, with her hands clasped at the back of her head. D'you like that?

He. Don't be affected.

She. I'm not. I'm Mrs. Buzgago. Listen!

> Pendant une anne' toute entiŠre
> Le r,giment n'a pas r'paru.
> Au MinistŠre de la Guerre
> On le r'porta comme perdu.
> On se r'noncait . . . rtrouver sa trace,
> Quand un matin subitement,
> On le vit r'paraŒtre sur la place,
> L'Colonel toujours en avant.

That's the way she rolls her r's. Am I like her?

He. No, but I object when you go on like an actress and sing stuff of that kind. Where in the world did you pick up the Chanson du Colonel? It isn't a drawing-room song. It isn't proper.

She. Mrs. Buzgago taught it me. She is both drawing-room and proper, and in another month she'll shut her drawing-room to me, and thank God she isn't as improper as I am. Oh, Guy, Guy! I wish I was like some women and had no scruples about What is it Keene says? 'Wearing a corpse's hair and being false to the bread they eat.'

He. I am only a man of limited intelligence, and, just now, very bewildered. When you have quite finished flashing through all your moods tell me, and I'll try to understand the last one.

She. Moods, Guy! I haven't any. I'm sixteen years old and you're just twenty, and you've been waiting for two hours outside the school in the cold. And now I've met you, and now we're walking home together. Does that suit you, My Imperial Majesty?

He. No. We aren't children. Why can't you be rational?

She. He asks me that when I'm going to commit suicide for his sake, and, and I don't want to be French and rave about my mother, but have I ever told you that I have a mother, and a brother who was my pet before I married? He's married now. Can't you imagine the pleasure that the news of the elopement will give him? Have you any people at Home, Guy, to be pleased with your performances?

He. One or two. One can't make omelets without breaking eggs.

She (slowly). I don't see the necessity

He. Hah! What do you mean?

She. Shall I speak the truth?

He Under the circumstances, perhaps it would be as well.

She. Guy, I'm afraid.

He I thought we'd settled all that. What of?

She. Of you.

He. Oh, damn it all! The old business! This is toobad!

She. Of you.

He. And what now?

She. What do you think of me?

He. Beside the question altogether. What do you intend to do?

She. I daren't risk it. I'm afraid. If I could only cheat

He. A la Buzgago? No, thanks. That's the one point on which I have any notion of Honour. I won't eat his salt and steal too. I'll loot openly or not at all.

She. I never meant anything else.

He. Then, why in the world do you pretend not to be willing to come?

She. It's not pretence, Guy. I am afraid.

He. Please explain.

She. It can't last, Guy. It can't last. You'll get angry, and then you'll swear, and then you'll get jealous, and then you'll mistrust me you do now and you yourself will be the best reason for doubting. And I what shall I do? I shall be no better than Mrs. Buzgago found out no better than any one. And you'll know that. Oh, Guy, can't you see?

He I see that you are desperately unreasonable, little woman.

She. There! The moment I begin to object, you get angry. What will you do when I am only your property stolen property? It can't be, Guy. It can't be! I thought it could, but it can't. You'll get tired of me.

He I tell you I shall not. Won't anything make you understand that?

She. There, can't you see? If you speak to me like that now, you'll call me horrible names later, if I don't do everything as you like. And if you were cruel to me, Guy, where should I go? where should I go? I can't trust you. Oh! I can't trust you!

He. I suppose I ought to say that I can trust you. I've ample reason.

She. Please don't, dear. It hurts as much as if you hit me.

He. It isn't exactly pleasant for me.

She. I can't help it. I wish I were dead! I can't trust you, and I don't trust myself. Oh, Guy, let it die away and be forgotten!

He. Too late now. I don't understand you I won't and I can't trust myself to talk this evening. May I call to-morrow?

She. Yes. No! Oh, give me time! The day after. I get into my 'rickshaw here and meet Him at Peliti's. You ride.

He. I'll go on to Peliti's too. I think I want a drink. My world's knocked about my ears and the stars are falling. Who are those brutes howling in the Old Library?

She. They're rehearsing the singing-quadrilles for the Fancy Ball. Can't you hear Mrs. Buzgago's voice? She has a solo. It's quite a new idea. Listen!

Mrs. Buzgago (in the Old Library, con molt. exp.).

See-saw! Margery Daw!
Sold her bed to lie upon straw.
Wasn't she a silly slut
To sell her bed and lie upon dirt?

Captain Congleton, I'm going to alter that to 'flirt.' It sounds better.

He. No, I've changed my mind about the drink. Good-night, little
   lady. I shall see you to-morrow?
She. Ye es. Good-night, Guy. Don't be angry with me.
He. Angry! You know I trust you absolutely. Good-night and God
   bless you!

(Three seconds later. Alone.) Hmm! I'd give something to
discover whether there's another man at the back of all this.

A SECOND-RATE WOMAN

Est fuga, volvitur rota,
    On we drift: where looms the dim port?
One Two Three Four Five contribute their quota:
    Something is gained if one caught but the import,
Show it us, Hugues of Saxe-Gotha.

—Master Hugues of Saxe-Gotha.

'Dressed! Don't tell me that woman ever dressed in her life. She stood in the middle of the room while her ayah no, her husband it must have been a man threw her clothes at her. She then did her hair with her fingers, and rubbed her bonnet in the flue under the bed. I know she did, as well as if I had assisted at the orgy. Who is she?' said Mrs. Hauksbee.

'Don't!' said Mrs. Mallowe feebly. 'You make my head ache. I am miserable to-day. Stay me with fondants, comfort me with chocolates, for I am Did you bring anything from Peliti's?'

'Questions to begin with. You shall have the sweets when you have answered them. Who and what is the creature? There were at least half-a-dozen men round her, and she appeared to be going to sleep in their midst.'

'Delville,' said Mrs. Mallowe, '"Shady" Delville, to distinguish her from Mrs. Jim of that ilk. She dances as untidily as she dresses, I believe, and her husband is somewhere in Madras. Go and call, if you are so interested.'

'What have I to do with Shigramitish women? She merely caught my attention for a minute, and I wondered at the attraction that a dowd has for a certain type of man. I expected to see her walk out of her clothes until I looked at her eyes.'

'Hooks and eyes, surely,' drawled Mrs. Mallowe.

'Don't be clever, Polly. You make my head ache. And round this hayrick stood a crowd of men a positive crowd!'

'Perhaps they also expected '

'Polly, don't be Rabelaisian!'

Mrs. Mallowe curled herself up comfortably on the sofa, and turned her attention to the sweets. She and Mrs. Hauksbee shared the same house at Simla; and these things befell two seasons after the matter of Otis Yeere, which has been already recorded.

Mrs. Hauksbee stepped into the verandah and looked down upon the Mall, her forehead puckered with thought.

'Hah!' said Mrs. Hauksbee shortly. 'Indeed!'

'What is it?' said Mrs. Mallowe sleepily.

'That dowd and The Dancing Master to whom I object.'

'Why to The Dancing Master? He is a middle-aged gentleman, of reprobate and romantic tendencies, and tries to be a friend of mine.'

'Then make up your mind to lose him. Dowds cling by nature, and I should imagine that this animal how terrible her bonnet looks from above! is specially clingsome.'

'She is welcome to The Dancing Master so far as I am concerned. I never could take an interest in a monotonous liar. The frustrated aim of his life is to persuade people that he is a bachelor.'

'O-oh! I think I've met that sort of man before. And isn't he?'

'No. He confided that to me a few days ago. Ugh! Some men ought to be killed.'

'What happened then?'

'He posed as the horror of horrors a misunderstood man. Heaven knows the femme incomprise is sad enough and bad enough but the other thing!'

'And so fat too! I should have laughed in his face. Men seldom confide in me. How is it they come to you?'

'For the sake of impressing me with their careers in the past. Protect me from men with confidences!'

'And yet you encourage them?'

'What can I do? They talk, I listen, and they vow that I am sympathetic. I know I always profess astonishment even when the plot is of the most old possible.'

'Yes. Men are so unblushingly explicit if they are once allowed to talk, whereas women's confidences are full of reservations and fibs, except'

'When they go mad and babble of the Unutter-abilities after a week's acquaintance. Really, if you come to consider, we know a great deal more of men than of our own sex.'

'And the extraordinary thing is that men will never believe it. They say we are trying to hide something.'

'They are generally doing that on their own account. Alas! These chocolates pall upon me, and I haven't eaten more than a dozen. I think I shall go to sleep.'

'Then you'll get fat, dear. If you took more exercise and a more intelligent interest in your neighbours you would'

'Be as much loved as Mrs. Hauksbee. You're a darling in many ways, and I like you you are not a woman's woman but why do you trouble yourself about mere human beings?'

'Because in the absence of angels, who I am sure would be horribly dull, men and women are the most fascinating things in the whole wide world, lazy one. I am interested in The Dowd I am interested in The Dancing Master I am interested in the Hawley Boy and I am interested in you.'

'Why couple me with the Hawley Boy? He is your property.'

'Yes, and in his own guileless speech, I'm making a good thing out of him. When he is slightly more reformed, and has passed his Higher Standard, or whatever the authorities think fit to exact from him, I shall select a pretty little girl, the Holt girl, I think, and' here she waved her hands airily '"whom Mrs. Hauksbee hath joined together let no man put asunder." That's all.'

'And when you have yoked May Holt with the most notorious detrimental in Simla, and earned the undying hatred of Mamma Holt, what will you do with me, Dispenser of the Destinies of the Universe?'

Mrs. Hauksbee dropped into a low chair in front of the fire, and, chin in hand, gazed long and steadfastly at Mrs. Mallowe.

'I do not know,' she said, shaking her head, 'what I shall do with you, dear. It's obviously impossible to marry you to some one else your husband would object and the experiment might not be successful after all. I think I shall begin by preventing you from what is it? "sleeping on ale-house benches and snoring in the sun."'

'Don't! I don't like your quotations. They are so rude. Go to the Library and bring me new books.'

'While you sleep? No! If you don't come with me I shall spread your newest frock on my 'rickshaw-bow, and when any one asks me what I am doing, I shall say that I am going to Phelps's to get it let out. I shall take care that Mrs. MacNamara sees me. Put your things on, there's a good girl.'

Mrs. Mallowe groaned and obeyed, and the two went off to the Library, where they found Mrs. Delville and the man who went by the nick-name of The Dancing Master. By that time Mrs. Mallowe was awake and eloquent.

'That is the Creature!' said Mrs. Hauksbee, with the air of one pointing out a slug in the road.

'No,' said Mrs. Mallowe. 'The man is the Creature. Ugh! Good-evening, Mr. Bent. I thought you were coming to tea this evening.'

'Surely it was for to-morrow, was it not?' answered The Dancing Master. 'I understood I fancied I'm so sorry How very unfortunate!'

But Mrs. Mallowe had passed on.

'For the practised equivocator you said he was,' murmured Mrs. Hauksbee, 'he strikes me as a failure. Now wherefore should he have preferred a walk with The Dowd to tea with us? Elective affinities, I suppose both grubby. Polly, I'd never forgive that woman as long as the world rolls.'

'I forgive every woman everything,' said Mrs. Mallowe. 'He will be a sufficient punishment for her. What a common voice she has!'

Mrs. Delville's voice was not pretty, her carriage was even less lovely, and her raiment was strikingly neglected. All these things Mrs. Mallowe noticed over the top of a magazine.

'Now what is there in her?' said Mrs. Hauksbee. 'Do you see what I meant about the clothes falling off? If I were a man I would perish sooner than be seen with that rag-bag. And yet, she has good eyes, but Oh!'

'What is it?'

'She doesn't know how to use them! On my honour, she does not. Look! Oh look! Untidiness I can endure, but ignorance never! The woman's a fool.'

'Hsh! She'll hear you.'

'All the women in Simla are fools. She'll think I mean some one else. Now she's going out. What a thoroughly objectionable couple she and The Dancing Master make! Which reminds me. Do you suppose they'll ever dance together?'

'Wait and see. I don't envy her the conversation of The Dancing Master loathly man! His wife ought to be up here before long?'

'Do you know anything about him?'

'Only what he told me. It may be all a fiction. He married a girl bred in the country, I think, and, being an honourable, chivalrous soul, told me that he repented his bargain and sent her to her as often as possible a person who has lived in the Doon since the memory of man and goes to Mussoorie when other people go Home. The wife is with her at present. So he says.'

'Babies?'

'One only, but he talks of his wife in a revolting way. I hated him for it. He thought he was being epigrammatic and brilliant.'

'That is a vice peculiar to men. I dislike him because he is generally in the wake of some girl, disappointing the Eligibles. He will persecute May Holt no more, unless I am much mistaken.'

'No. I think Mrs. Delville may occupy his attention for a while.'

'Do you suppose she knows that he is the head of a family?'

'Not from his lips. He swore me to eternal secrecy. Wherefore I tell you. Don't you know that type of man?'

'Not intimately, thank goodness! As a general rule, when a man begins to abuse his wife to me, I find that the Lord gives me wherewith to answer him according to his folly; and we part with a coolness between us. I laugh.'

'I'm different. I've no sense of humour.'

'Cultivate it, then. It has been my mainstay for more years than I care to think about. A well-educated sense of humour will save a woman when Religion, Training, and Home influences fail; and we may all need salvation sometimes.'

'Do you suppose that the Delville woman has humour?'

'Her dress bewrays her. How can a Thing who wears her supplšment under her left arm have any notion of the fitness of things much less their folly? If she discards The Dancing Master after having once seen him dance, I may respect her. Otherwise '

'But are we not both assuming a great deal too much, dear? You saw the woman at Peliti's half an hour later you saw her walking with The Dancing Master an hour later you met her here at the Library.'

'Still with The Dancing Master, remember.'

'Still with The Dancing Master, I admit, but why on the strength of that should you imagine '

'I imagine nothing. I have no imagination. I am only convinced that The Dancing Master is attracted to The Dowd because he is objectionable in every way and she in every other. If I know the man as you have described him, he holds his wife in slavery at present.'

'She is twenty years younger than he.'

'Poor wretch! And, in the end, after he has posed and swaggered and lied he has a mouth under that ragged moustache simply made for lies he will be rewarded according to his merits.'

'I wonder what those really are,' said Mrs. Mallowe.

But Mrs. Hauksbee, her face close to the shelf of the new books, was humming softly: 'What shall he have who killed the Deer?' She was a lady of unfettered speech.

One month later she announced her intention of calling upon Mrs. Delville. Both Mrs. Hauksbee and Mrs. Mallowe were in morning wrappers, and there was a great peace in the land.

'I should go as I was,' said Mrs. Mallowe. 'It would be a delicate compliment to her style.'

Mrs. Hauksbee studied herself in the glass.

'Assuming for a moment that she ever darkened these doors, I should put on this robe, after all the others, to show her what a morning-wrapper ought to be. It might enliven her. As it is, I shall go in the dove-coloured sweet emblem of youth and innocence and shall put on my new gloves.'

'If you really are going, dirty tan would be too good; and you know that dove-colour spots with the rain.'

'I care not. I may make her envious. At least I shall try, though one cannot expect very much from a woman who puts a lace tucker into her habit.'

'Just Heavens! When did she do that?'

'Yesterday riding with The Dancing Master. I met them at the back of Jakko, and the rain had made the lace lie down. To complete the effect, she was wearing an unclean terai with the elastic under her chin. I felt almost too well content to take the trouble to despise her.'

'The Hawley Boy was riding with you. What did he think?'

'Does a boy ever notice these things? Should I like him if he did? He stared in the rudest way, and just when I thought he had seen the elastic, he said, "There's something very taking about that face." I rebuked him on the spot. I don't approve of boys being taken by faces.'

'Other than your own. I shouldn't be in the least surprised if the Hawley Boy immediately went to call.'

'I forbade him. Let her be satisfied with The Dancing Master, and his wife when she comes up. I'm rather curious to see Mrs. Bent and the Delville woman together.'

Mrs. Hauksbee departed and, at the end of an hour, returned slightly flushed.

'There is no limit to the treachery of youth! I ordered the Hawley Boy, as he valued my patronage, not to call. The first person I stumble over literally stumble over in her poky, dark little drawing-room is, of course, the Hawley Boy. She kept us waiting ten minutes, and then emerged as though she had been tipped out of the dirtyclothes-basket. You know my way, dear, when I am at all put out. I was Superior, crrrrushingly Superior! 'Lifted my eyes to Heaven, and had heard of nothing 'dropped my eyes on the carpet and "really didn't know" 'played with my cardcase and "supposed so." The Hawley Boy giggled like a girl, and I had to freeze him with scowls between the sentences.'

'And she?'

'She sat in a heap on the edge of a couch, and managed to convey the impression that she was suffering from stomach-ache, at the very least. It was all I could do not to ask after her symptoms. When I rose, she grunted just like a buffalo in the water too lazy to move.'

'Are you certain? '

'Am I blind, Polly? Laziness, sheer laziness, nothing else or her garments were only constructed for sitting down in. I stayed for a quarter of an hour trying to penetrate the gloom, to guess what her surroundings were like, while she stuck out her tongue.'

'Lu cy!'

'Well I'll withdraw the tongue, though I'm sure if she didn't do it when I was in the room, she did the minute I was outside. At any rate, she lay in a lump and grunted. Ask the Hawley Boy, dear. I believe the grunts were meant for sentences, but she spoke so indistinctly that I can't swear to it.'

'You are incorrigible, simply.'

'I am not! Treat me civilly, give me peace with honour, don't put the only available seat facing the window, and a child may eat jam in my lap before Church. But I resent being grunted at. Wouldn't you? Do you suppose that she communicates her views on life and love to The Dancing Master in a set of modulated "Grmphs"?'

'You attach too much importance to The Dancing Master.'

'He came as we went, and The Dowd grew almost cordial at the sight of him. He smiled greasily, and moved about that darkened dog-kennel in a suspiciously familiar way.'

'Don't be uncharitable. Any sin but that I'll forgive.'

'Listen to the voice of History. I am only describing what I saw. He entered, the heap on the sofa revived slightly, and the Hawley Boy and I came away together. He is disillusioned, but I felt it my duty to lecture him severely for going there. And that's all.'

'Now for Pity's sake leave the wretched creature and The Dancing Master alone. They never did you any harm.'

'No harm? To dress as an example and a stumbling-block for half Simla, and then to find this Person who is dressed by the hand of God not that I wish to disparage Him for a moment, but you know the tikka dhurzie way He attires those lilies of the field this Person draws the eyes of men and some of them nice men? It's almost enough to make one discard clothing. I told the Hawley Boy so.'

'And what did that sweet youth do?'

'Turned shell-pink and looked across the far blue hills like a distressed cherub. Am I talking wildly, Polly? Let me say my say, and I shall be calm. Otherwise I may go abroad and disturb Simla with a few original reflections. Excepting always your own sweet self, there isn't a single woman in the land who understands me when I am what's the word?'

'T^te-f^l,e,' suggested Mrs. Mallowe.

'Exactly! And now let us have tiffin. The demands of Society are exhausting, and as Mrs. Delville says ' Here Mrs. Hauksbee, to the horror of the khitmatgars, lapsed into a series of grunts, while Mrs. Mallowe stared in lazy surprise.

"'God gie us a guid conceit of oorselves,'" said Mrs. Hauksbee piously, returning to her natural speech. 'Now, in any other woman that would have been vulgar. I am consumed with curiosity to see Mrs. Bent. I expect complications.'

'Woman of one idea,' said Mrs. Mallowe shortly; 'all complications are as old as the hills! I have lived through or near all all All!'

'And yet do not understand that men and women never behave twice alike. I am old who was young if ever I put my head in your lap, you dear, big sceptic, you will learn that my parting is gauze but never, no never, have I lost my interest in men and women. Polly, I shall see this business out to the bitter end.'

'I am going to sleep,' said Mrs. Mallowe calmly. 'I never interfere with men or women unless I am compelled,' and she retired with dignity to her own room.

Mrs. Hauksbee's curiosity was not long left ungratified, for Mrs. Bent came up to Simla a few days after the conversation faithfully reported above, and pervaded the Mall by her husband's side

'Behold!' said Mrs. Hauksbee, thoughtfully rubbing her nose. 'That is the last link of the chain, if we omit the husband of the Delville, whoever he may be. Let me consider. The Bents and the Delvilles inhabit the same hotel; and the Delville is detested by the Waddy do you know the Waddy? who is almost as big a dowd. The Waddy also abominates the male Bent, for which, if her other sins do not weigh too heavily, she will eventually go to Heaven.'

'Don't be irreverent,' said Mrs. Mallowe, 'I like Mrs. Bent's face.'

'I am discussing the Waddy,' returned Mrs. Hauksbee loftily. 'The Waddy will take the female Bent apart, after having borrowed yes! everything that she can, from hairpins to babies' bottles. Such, my dear, is life in a hotel. The Waddy will tell the female Bent facts and fictions about The Dancing Master and The Dowd.'

'Lucy, I should like you better if you were not always looking into people's back-bedrooms.'

'Anybody can look into their front drawingrooms; and remember whatever I do, and whatever I look, I never talk as the

Waddy will. Let us hope that The Dancing Master's greasy smile and manner of the pedagogue will soften the heart of that cow, his wife. If mouths speak truth, I should think that little Mrs. Bent could get very angry on occasion.'

'But what reason has she for being angry?'

'What reason! The Dancing Master in himself is a reason. How does it go? "If in his life some trivial errors fall, Look in his face and you'll believe them all." I am prepared to credit any evil of The Dancing Master, because I hate him so. And The Dowd is so disgustingly badly dressed '

'That she, too, is capable of every iniquity? I always prefer to believe the best of everybody. It saves so much trouble.'

'Very good. I prefer to believe the worst. It saves useless expenditure of sympathy. And you may be quite certain that the Waddy believes with me.'

Mrs. Mallowe sighed and made no answer.

The conversation was holden after dinner while Mrs. Hauksbee was dressing for a dance.

'I am too tired to go,' pleaded Mrs. Mallowe, and Mrs. Hauksbee left her in peace till two in the morning, when she was aware of emphatic knocking at her door.

'Don't be very angry, dear,' said Mrs. Hauksbee. 'My idiot of an ayah has gone home, and, as I hope to sleep to-night, there isn't a soul in the place to unlace me.'

'Oh, this is too bad!' said Mrs. Mallowe sulkily.

"Cant help it. I'm a lone, lorn grass-widow, dear, but I will not sleep in my stays. And such news too! Oh, do unlace me, there's a darling! The Dowd The Dancing Master I and the Hawley Boy You know the North verandah?'

'How can I do anything if you spin round like this?' protested Mrs. Mallowe, fumbling with the knot of the laces.

'Oh, I forget. I must tell my tale without the aid of your eyes. Do you know you've lovely eyes, dear? Well, to begin with, I took the Hawley Boy to a kala juggah.'

'Did he want much taking?'

'Lots! There was an arrangement of loose-boxes in kanats, and she was in the next one talking to him.'

'Which? How? Explain.'

'You know what I mean The Dowd and The Dancing Master. We could hear every word, and we listened shamelessly 'specially the Hawley Boy. Polly, I quite love that woman!'

'This is interesting. There! Now turn round. What happened?'

'One moment. Ah h! Blessed relief. I've been looking forward to taking them off for the last half-hour which is ominous at my time of life. But, as I was saying, we listened and heard The Dowd drawl worse than ever. She drops her final g's like a barmaid or a blue-blooded Aide-de-Camp. "Look he-ere, you're gettin' too fond o' me," she said, and The Dancing Master owned it was so in language that nearly made me ill. The Dowd reflected for a while. Then we heard her say, "Look he-ere, Mister Bent, why are you such an aw-ful liar?" I nearly exploded while The Dancing Master denied the charge. It seems that he never told her he was a married man.'

'I said he wouldn't.'

'And she had taken this to heart, on personal grounds, I suppose. She drawled along for five minutes, reproaching him with his perfidy, and grew quite motherly. "Now you've got a nice little wife of your own you have," she said. "She's ten times too good for a fat old man like you, and, look he-ere, you never told me a word about her, and I've been thinkin' about it a good deal, and I think you're a liar." Wasn't that delicious? The Dancing Master maundered and raved till the Hawley Boy suggested that he should burst in and beat him. His voice runs up into an impassioned squeak when he is afraid. The Dowd must be an extraordinary woman. She explained that had he been a bachelor she might not have objected to his devotion; but since he was a married man and the father of a very nice baby, she considered him a hypocrite, and this she repeated twice. She wound up her drawl with: "An' I'm tellin' you this because your wife is angry with me, an' I hate quarrellin' with any other woman, an' I like your wife. You know how you have behaved for the last six weeks. You shouldn't have done it, indeed you shouldn't. You're too old an' too fat." Can't you imagine how The Dancing Master would wince at that! "Now go away," she said. "I don't want to tell you what I think of you, because I think you are not nice. I'll stay he-ere till the next dance begins." Did you think that the creature had so much in her?'

'I never studied her as closely as you did. It sounds unnatural. What happened?'

'The Dancing Master attempted blandishment, reproof, jocularity, and the style of the Lord High Warden, and I had almost to pinch the Hawley Boy to make him keep quiet. She grunted at the end of each sentence and, in the end, he went away swearing to himself, quite like a man in a novel. He looked more objectionable than ever. I laughed. I love that woman in spite of her clothes. And now I'm going to bed. What do you think of it?'

'I shan't begin to think till the morning,' said Mrs. Mallowe, yawning. 'Perhaps she spoke the truth. They do fly into it by accident sometimes.'

Mrs. Hauksbee's account of her eavesdropping was an ornate one, but truthful in the main. For reasons best known to herself, Mrs. 'Shady' Delville had turned upon Mr. Bent and rent him limb from limb, casting him away limp and disconcerted ere she withdrew the light of her eyes from him permanently. Being a man of resource, and anything but pleased in that he had been called both old and fat, he gave Mrs. Bent to understand that he had, during her absence in the Doon, been the victim of unceasing persecution at the hands of Mrs. Delville, and he told the tale so often and with such eloquence that he ended in believing it, while his wife marvelled at the manners and customs of 'some women.' When the situation showed signs of languishing, Mrs. Waddy was always on hand to wake the smouldering fires of suspicion in Mrs. Bent's bosom and to contribute generally to the peace and comfort of the hotel. Mr. Bent's life was not a happy one, for if Mrs. Waddy's story were true, he was, argued his wife, untrustworthy to the last degree. If his own statement was true, his charms of manner and conversation were so great that he needed constant surveillance. And he received it, till he repented genuinely of his marriage and neglected his personal appearance. Mrs. Delville alone in the hotel was unchanged. She removed her chair some six paces towards the head of the table, and occasionally in the twilight ventured on timid overtures of friendship to Mrs. Bent, which were repulsed.

'She does it for my sake,' hinted the virtuous Bent.

'A dangerous and designing woman,' purred Mrs. Waddy.

Worst of all, every other hotel in Simla was full!

'Polly, are you afraid of diphtheria?'

'Of nothing in the world except small-pox, Diphtheria kills, but it doesn't disfigure. Why do you ask?'

'Because the Bent baby has got it, and the whole hotel is upside down in consequence. The Waddy has "set her five young on the rail" and fled. The Dancing Master fears for his precious throat, and that miserable little woman, his wife, has no notion of what ought to be done. She wanted to put it into a mustard bath for croup!'

'Where did you learn all this?'

'Just now, on the Mall. Dr. Howlen told me. The manager of the hotel is abusing the Bents, and the Bents are abusing the manager. They are a feckless couple.'

'Well. What's on your mind?'

'This; and I know it's a grave thing to ask.

Would you seriously object to my bringing the child over here, with its mother?'

'On the most strict understanding that we see nothing of the Dancing Master.'

'He will be only too glad to stay away. Polly, you're an angel. The woman really is at her wits' end.'

'And you know nothing about her, careless, and would hold her up to public scorn if it gave you a minute's amusement. Therefore you risk your life for the sake of her brat. No, Loo, I'm not the angel. I shall keep to my rooms and avoid her. But do as you please only tell me why you do it.'

Mrs. Hauksbee's eyes softened; she looked out of the window and back into Mrs. Mallowe's face.

'I don't know,' said Mrs. Hauksbee simply.

'You dear!'

'Polly! and for aught you knew you might have taken my fringe off. Never do that again without warning. Now we'll get the rooms ready. I don't suppose I shall be allowed to circulate in society for a month.'

'And I also. Thank goodness I shall at last get all the sleep I want.'

Much to Mrs. Bent's surprise she and the baby were brought over to the house almost before she knew where she was. Bent was devoutly and undisguisedly thankful, for he was afraid of the infection, and also hoped that a few weeks in the hotel alone with

Mrs. Delville might lead to explanations. Mrs. Bent had thrown her jealousy to the winds in her fear for her child's life.

'We can give you good milk,' said Mrs. Hauksbee to her, 'and our house is much nearer to the Doctor's than the hotel, and you won't feel as though you were living in a hostile camp. Where is the dear Mrs. Waddy? She seemed to be a particular friend of yours.'

'They've all left me,' said Mrs. Bent bitterly. 'Mrs. Waddy went first. She said I ought to be ashamed of myself for introducing diseases there, and I am sure it wasn't my fault that little Dora '

'How nice!' cooed Mrs. Hauksbee. 'The Waddy is an infectious disease herself "more quickly caught than the plague and the taker runs presently mad." I lived next door to her at the Elysium, three years ago. Now see, you won't give us the least trouble, and I've ornamented all the house with sheets soaked in carbolic. It smells comforting, doesn't it? Remember I'm always in call, and my ayah's at your service when yours goes to her meals, and and if you cry I'll never forgive you.'

Dora Bent occupied her mother's unprofitable attention through the day and the night. The Doctor called thrice in the twenty-four hours, and the house reeked with the smell of the Condy's Fluid, chlorine-water, and carbolic acid washes. Mrs. Mallowe kept to her own rooms she considered that she had made sufficient concessions in the cause of humanity and Mrs. Hauksbee was more esteemed by the Doctor as a help in the sick-room than the half-distraught mother.

'I know nothing of illness,' said Mrs. Hauksbee to the Doctor. 'Only tell me what to do, and I'll do it.'

'Keep that crazy woman from kissing the child, and let her have as little to do with the nursing as you possibly can,' said the Doctor; 'I'd turn her out of the sick-room, but that I honestly believe she'd die of anxiety. She is less than no good, and I depend on you and the ayahs, remember.'

Mrs. Hauksbee accepted the responsibility, though it painted olive hollows under her eyes and forced her to her oldest dresses. Mrs. Bent clung to her with more than childlike faith.

'I know you'll make Dora well, won't you?' she said at least twenty times a day; and twenty times a day Mrs. Hauksbee answered valiantly, 'Of course I will.'

But Dora did not improve, and the Doctor seemed to be always in the house.

'There's some danger of the thing taking a bad turn,' he said; 'I'll come over between three and four in the morning to-morrow.'

'Good gracious!' said Mrs. Hauksbee. 'He never told me what the turn would be! My education has been horribly neglected; and I have only this foolish mother-woman to fall back upon.'

The night wore through slowly, and Mrs. Hauksbee dozed in a chair by the fire. There was a dance at the Viceregal Lodge, and she dreamed of it till she was aware of Mrs. Bent's anxious eyes staring into her own.

'Wake up! Wake up! Do something!' cried Mrs. Bent piteously. 'Dora's choking to death! Do you mean to let her die?'

Mrs. Hauksbee jumped to her feet and bent over the bed. The child was fighting for breath, while the mother wrung her hands despairingly.

'Oh, what can I do? What can you do? She won't stay still! I can't hold her. Why didn't the Doctor say this was coming?' screamed Mrs. Bent. 'Won't you help me? She's dying!'

'I I've never seen a child die before!' stammered Mrs. Hauksbee feebly, and then let none blame her weakness after the strain of long watching she broke down, and covered her face with her hands. The ayahs on the threshold snored peacefully.

There was a rattle of 'rickshaw wheels below, the clash of an opening door, a heavy step on the stairs, and Mrs. Delville entered to find Mrs. Bent screaming for the Doctor as she ran round the room. Mrs. Hauksbee, her hands to her ears, and her face buried in the chintz of a chair, was quivering with pain at each cry from the bed, and murmuring, 'Thank God, I never bore a child! Oh! thank God, I never bore a child!'

Mrs. Delville looked at the bed for an instant, took Mrs. Bent by the shoulders, and said quietly, 'Get me some caustic. Be quick.'

The mother obeyed mechanically. Mrs. Delville had thrown herself down by the side of the child and was opening its mouth.

'Oh, you're killing her!' cried Mrs. Bent. 'Where's the Doctor? Leave her alone!'

Mrs. Delville made no reply for a minute, but busied herself with the child.

'Now the caustic, and hold a lamp behind my shoulder. Will you do as you are told? The acid-bottle, if you don't know what I mean,' she said.

A second time Mrs. Delville bent over the child. Mrs. Hauksbee, her face still hidden, sobbed and shivered. One of the ayahs staggered sleepily into the room, yawning: 'Doctor Sahib come.'

Mrs. Delville turned her head.

'You're only just in time,' she said. 'It was chokin' her when I came, an' I've burnt it.'

'There was no sign of the membrane getting to the air-passages after the last steaming. It was the general weakness I feared,' said the Doctor half to himself, and he whispered as he looked, 'You've done what I should have been afraid to do without consultation.'

'She was dyin',' said Mrs. Delville, under her breath. 'Can you do anythin'? What a mercy it was I went to the dance!'

Mrs. Hauksbee raised her head.

'Is it all over?' she gasped. 'I'm useless I'm worse than useless! What are you doing here?'

She stared at Mrs. Delville, and Mrs. Bent, realising for the first time who was the Goddess from the Machine, stared also.

Then Mrs. Delville made explanation, putting on a dirty long glove and smoothing a crumpled and ill-fitting ball-dress.

'I was at the dance, an' the Doctor was tellin' me about your baby bein' so ill. So I came away early, an' your door was open, an' I I lost my boy this way six months ago, an' I've been tryin' to forget it ever since, an' I I I am very sorry for intrudin' an' anythin' that has happened.'

Mrs. Bent was putting out the Doctor's eye with a lamp as he stooped over Dora.

'Take it away,' said the Doctor. 'I think the child will do, thanks to you, Mrs. Delville. I should have come too late, but, I assure you' he was addressing himself to Mrs. Delville 'I had not the faintest reason to expect this. The membrane must have grown like a mushroom. Will one of you help me, please?'

He had reason for the last sentence. Mrs. Hauksbee had thrown herself into Mrs. Delville's arms, where she was weeping bitterly, and Mrs. Bent was unpicturesquely mixed up with both, while from the tangle came the sound of many sobs and much promiscuous kissing.

'Good gracious! I've spoilt all your beautiful roses!' said Mrs. Hauksbee, lifting her head from the lump of crushed gum and calico atrocities on Mrs. Delville's shoulder and hurrying to the Doctor.

Mrs. Delville picked up her shawl, and slouched out of the room, mopping her eyes with the glove that she had not put on.

'I always said she was more than a woman,' sobbed Mrs. Hauksbee hysterically, 'and that proves it!'

Six weeks later Mrs. Bent and Dora had returned to the hotel. Mrs. Hauksbee had come out of the Valley of Humiliation, had ceased to reproach herself for her collapse in an hour of need, and was even beginning to direct the affairs of the world as before.

'So nobody died, and everything went off as it should, and I kissed The Dowd, Polly. I feel so old. Does it show in my face?'

'Kisses don't as a rule, do they? Of course you know what the result of The Dowd's providential arrival has been.'

'They ought to build her a statue only no sculptor dare copy those skirts.'

'Ah!' said Mrs. Mallowe quietly. 'She has found another reward. The Dancing Master has been smirking through Simla, giving every one to understand that she came because of her undying love for him for him to save his child, and all Simla naturally believes this.'

'But Mrs. Bent '

'Mrs. Bent believes it more than any one else. She won't speak to The Dowd now. Isn't The Dancing Master an angel?'

Mrs. Hauksbee lifted up her voice and raged till bed-time. The doors of the two rooms stood open.

'Polly,' said a voice from the darkness, 'what did that American-heiress-globe-trotter girl say last season when she was tipped out of her 'rickshaw turning a corner? Some absurd adjective that made the man who picked her up explode.'

'"Paltry,"' said Mrs. Mallowe. 'Through her nose like this "Ha-ow pahltry!"'

'Exactly,' said the voice. 'Ha-ow pahltry it all is!'

'Which?'

'Everything. Babies, Diphtheria, Mrs. Bent and The Dancing Master, I whooping in a chair, and The Dowd dropping in from the clouds. I wonder what the motive was all the motives.'

'Um!'

'What do you think?'

'Don't ask me. Go to sleep.'

ONLY A SUBALTERN

. . . Not only to enforce by command, but to encourage by example the energetic discharge of duty and the steady endurance of the difficulties and privations inseparable from Military Service.

—Bengal Army Regulations.

They made Bobby Wick pass an examination at Sandhurst. He was a gentleman before he was gazetted, so, when the Empress announced that 'Gentleman-Cadet Robert Hanna Wick' was posted as Second Lieutenant to the Tyneside Tail Twisters at Krab Bokhar, he became an officer and a gentleman, which is an enviable thing; and there was joy in the house of Wick where Mamma Wick and all the little Wicks fell upon their knees and offered incense to Bobby by virtue of his achievements.

Papa Wick had been a Commissioner in his day, holding authority over three millions of men in the Chota-Buldana Division, building great works for the good of the land, and doing his best to make two blades of grass grow where there was but one before. Of course, nobody knew anything about this in the little English village where he was just 'old Mr. Wick,' and had forgotten that he was a Companion of the Order of the Star of India.

He patted Bobby on the shoulder and said: 'Well done, my boy!'

There followed, while the uniform was being prepared, an interval of pure delight, during which Bobby took brevet-rank as a 'man' at the women-swamped tennis-parties and tea-fights of the village, and, I daresay, had his joining-time been extended, would have fallen in love with several girls at once. Little country villages at Home are very full of nice girls, because all the young men come out to India to make their fortunes.

'India,' said Papa Wick, 'is the place. I've had thirty years of it and, begad, I'd like to go back again. When you join the Tail Twisters you'll be among friends, if every one hasn't forgotten Wick of Chota-Buldana, and a lot of people will be kind to you for our sakes. The mother will tell you more about outfit than I can; but remember this. Stick to your Regiment, Bobby stick to your Regiment. You'll see men all round you going into the Staff Corps, and doing every possible sort of duty but regimental, and you may be tempted to follow suit. Now so long as you keep within your allowance, and I haven't stinted you there, stick to the Line, the whole Line, and nothing but the Line. Be careful how you back another young fool's bill, and if you fall in love with a woman twenty years older than yourself, don't tell me about it, that's all.'

With these counsels, and many others equally valuable, did Papa Wick fortify Bobby ere that last awful night at Portsmouth when the Officers' Quarters held more inmates than were provided for by the Regulations, and the liberty-men of the ships fell foul of the drafts for India, and the battle raged from the Dockyard Gates even to the slums of Longport, while the drabs of Fratton came down and scratched the faces of the Queen's Officers.

Bobby Wick, with an ugly bruise on his freckled nose, a sick and shaky detachment to man uvre inship, and the comfort of fifty scornful females to attend to, had no time to feel home-sick till the Malabar reached mid-Channel, when he doubled his emotions with a little guard-visiting and a great many other matters.

The Tail Twisters were a most particular Regiment. Those who knew them least said that they were eaten up with 'side.' But their reserve and their internal arrangements generally were merely protective diplomacy. Some five years before, the Colonel commanding had looked into the fourteen fearless eyes of seven plump and juicy subalterns who had all applied to enter the Staff Corps, and had asked them why the three stars should he, a colonel of the Line, command a dashed nursery for double-dashed bottle-suckers who put on condemned tin spurs and rode qualified mokes at the hiatused heads of forsaken Black Regiments. He was a rude man and a terrible. Wherefore the remnant took measures [with the half-butt as an engine of public opinion] till the rumour went abroad that young men who used the Tail Twisters as a crutch to the Staff Corps had many and varied trials to endure. However, a regiment had just as much right to its own secrets as a woman.

When Bobby came up from Deolali and took his' place among the Tail Twisters, it was gently but firmly borne in upon him that the Regiment was his father and his mother and his indissolubly wedded wife, and that there was no crime under the canopy of heaven blacker than that of bringing shame on the Regiment, which was the best-shooting, best-drilled, best-set-up, bravest, most illustrious, and in all respects most desirable Regiment within the compass of the Seven Seas. He was taught the legends of the Mess Plate, from the great grinning Golden Gods that had come out of the Summer Palace in Pekin to the silver-mounted markhor-horn snuff-mull presented by the last C.O. [he who spake to the seven subalterns]. And every one of those legends told him of battles fought at long odds, without fear as without support; of hospitality catholic as an Arab's; of friendships deep as the sea and steady as the fighting-line; of honour won by hard roads for honour's sake; and of instant and unquestioning devotion to the Regiment the Regiment that claims the lives of all and lives for ever.

More than once, too, he came officially into contact with the Regimental colours, which looked like the lining of a bricklayer's hat on the end of a chewed stick. Bobby did not kneel and worship them, because British subalterns are not constructed in that manner. Indeed, he condemned them for their weight at the very moment that they were filling with awe and other more noble sentiments.

But best of all was the occasion when he moved with the Tail Twisters in review order at the breaking of a November day. Allowing for duty-men and sick, the Regiment was one thousand and eighty strong, and Bobby belonged to them; for was he not a Subaltern of the Line the whole Line, and nothing but the Line as the tramp of two thousand one hundred and sixty sturdy ammunition boots attested? He would not have changed places with Deighton of the Horse Battery, whirling by in a pillar of cloud to a chorus of 'Strong right! Strong left!' or Hogan-Yale of the White Hussars, leading his squadron for all it was worth, with the price of horseshoes thrown in; or 'Tick' Boileau, trying to live up to his fierce blue and gold turban while the wasps of the Bengal

Cavalry stretched to a gallop in the wake of the long, lollopping Walers of the White Hussars.

They fought through the clear cool day, and Bobby felt a little thrill run down his spine when he heard the tinkle-tinkle-tinkle of the empty cartridge-cases hopping from the breech-blocks after the roar of the volleys; for he knew that he should live to hear that sound in action. The review ended in a glorious chase across the plain batteries thundering after cavalry to the huge disgust of the White Hussars, and the Tyneside Tail Twisters hunting a Sikh Regiment, till the lean lathy Singhs panted with exhaustion. Bobby was dusty and dripping long before noon, but his enthusiasm was merely focused not diminished.

He returned to sit at the feet of Revere, his 'skipper,' that is to say, the Captain of his Company, and to be instructed in the dark art and mystery of managing men, which is a very large part of the Profession of Arms.

'If you haven't a taste that way,' said Revere between his puffs of his cheroot, 'you'll never be able to get the hang of it, but remember, Bobby, 't isn't the best drill, though drill is nearly everything, that hauls a Regiment through Hell and out on the other side. It's the man who knows how to handle men goat-men, swine-men, dog-men, and so on.'

'Dormer, for instance,' said Bobby, 'I think he comes under the head of fool-men. He mopes like a sick owl.'

'That's where you make your mistake, my son. Dormer isn't a fool yet, but he's a dashed dirty soldier, and his room corporal makes fun of his socks before kit-inspection. Dormer, being two-thirds pure brute, goes into a corner and growls.'

'How do you know?' said Bobby admiringly.

'Because a Company commander has to know these things because, if he does not know, he may have crime ay, murder brewing under his very nose and yet not see that it's there. Dormer is being badgered out of his mind big as he is and he hasn't intellect enough to resent it. He's taken to quiet boozing, and, Bobby, when the butt of a room goes on the drink, or takes to moping by himself, measures are necessary to pull him out of himself.'

'What measures? 'Man can't run round coddling his men for ever.'

'No. The men would precious soon show him that he was not wanted. You've got to '

Here the Colour-Sergeant entered with some papers; Bobby reflected for a while as Revere looked through the Company forms.

'Does Dormer do anything, Sergeant?' Bobby asked with the air of one continuing an interrupted conversation.

'No, sir. Does 'is dooty like a hortomato,' said the Sergeant, who delighted in long words. 'A dirty soldier and 'e's under full stoppages for new kit. It's covered with scales, sir.'

'Scales? What scales?'

'Fish-scales, sir. 'E's always pokin' in the mud by the river an' a-cleanin' them muchly-fish with 'is thumbs.' Revere was still absorbed in the Company papers, and the Sergeant, who was sternly fond of Bobby, continued ' 'E generally goes down there when 'e's got 'is skinful, beggin' your pardon, sir, an' they do say that the more lush in-he-briated 'e is, the more fish 'e catches. They call 'im the Looney Fishmonger in the Comp'ny, sir.'

Revere signed the last paper and the Sergeant retreated.

'It's a filthy amusement,' sighed Bobby to himself. Then aloud to Revere: 'Are you really worried about Dormer?'

'A little. You see he's never mad enough to send to hospital, or drunk enough to run in, but at any minute he may flare up, brooding and sulking as he does. He resents any interest being shown in him, and the only time I took him out shooting he all but shot me by accident.'

'I fish,' said Bobby with a wry face. 'I hire a country-boat and go down the river from Thursday to Sunday, and the amiable Dormer goes with me if you can spare us both.'

'You blazing young fool!' said Revere, but his heart was full of much more pleasant words.

Bobby, the Captain of a dhoni, with Private Dormer for mate, dropped down the river on Thursday morning the Private at the bow, the Subaltern at the helm. The Private glared uneasily at the Subaltern, who respected the reserve of the Private.

After six hours, Dormer paced to the stern, saluted, and said 'Beg y' pardon, sir, but was you ever on the Durh'm Canal?'

'No,' said Bobby Wick. 'Come and have some tiffin.'

They ate in silence. As the evening fell, Private Dormer broke forth, speaking to himself

'Hi was on the Durh'm Canal, jes' such a night, come next week twelve month, a-trailin' of my toes in the water.' He smoked and said no more till bedtime.

The witchery of the dawn turned the gray river-reaches to purple, gold, and opal; and it was as though the lumbering dhoni crept across the splendours of a new heaven.

Private Dormer popped his head out of his blanket and gazed at the glory below and around.

'Well damn my eyes!' said Private Dormer in an awed whisper. 'This 'ere is like a bloomin' gallantry-show!' For the rest of the day he was dumb, but achieved an ensanguined filthiness through the cleaning of big fish.

The boat returned on Saturday evening. Dormer had been struggling with speech since noon. As the lines and luggage were being disembarked, he found tongue.

'Beg y' pardon, sir,' he said, 'but would you would you min' shakin' 'ands with me, sir?'

'Of course not,' said Bobby, and he shook accordingly. Dormer returned to barracks and Bobby to mess.

'He wanted a little quiet and some fishing, I think,' said Bobby. 'My aunt, but he's a filthy sort of animal! Have you ever seen him clean "them muchly-fish with 'is thumbs"?'

'Anyhow,' said Revere three weeks later, 'he's doing his best to keep his things clean.'

When the spring died, Bobby joined in the general scramble for Hill leave, and to his surprise and delight secured three months.

'As good a boy as I want,' said Revere the admiring skipper.

'The best of the batch,' said the Adjutant to the Colonel. 'Keep back that young skrim-shanker Porkiss, sir, and let Revere make him sit up.'

So Bobby departed joyously to Simla Pahar with a tin box of gorgeous raiment.

"Son of Wick old Wick of Chota-Buldana? Ask him to dinner, dear,' said the aged men.

'What a nice boy!' said the matrons and the maids.

'First-class place, Simla. Oh, ri ipping!' said Bobby Wick, and ordered new white cord breeches on the strength of it.

'We're in a bad way,' wrote Revere to Bobby at the end of two months. 'Since you left, the Regiment has taken to fever and is fairly rotten with it two hundred in hospital, about a hundred in cells drinking to keep off fever and the Companies on parade fifteen file strong at the outside. There's rather more sickness in the out-villages than I care for, but then I'm so blistered with prickly-heat that I'm ready to hang myself. What's the yarn about your mashing a Miss Haverley up there? Not serious, I hope? You're over-young to hang millstones round your neck, and the Colonel will turf you out of that in double-quick time if you attempt it.'

It was not the Colonel that brought Bobby out of Simla, but a much-more-to-be-respected Commandant. The sickness in the out-villages spread, the Bazar was put out of bounds, and then came the news that the Tail Twisters must go into camp. The message flashed to the Hill stations. 'Cholera Leave stopped Officers recalled.' Alas for the white gloves in the neatly-soldered boxes, the rides and the dances and picnics that were to be, the loves half spoken, and the debts unpaid! Without demur and without question, fast as tonga could fly or pony gallop, back to their Regiments and their Batteries, as though they were hastening to their weddings, fled the subalterns.

Bobby received his orders on returning from a dance at Viceregal Lodge where he had But only the Haverley girl knows what Bobby had said, or how many waltzes he had claimed for the next ball. Six in the morning saw Bobby at the Tonga Office in the drenching rain, the whirl of the last waltz still in his ears, and an intoxication due neither to wine nor waltzing in his brain.

'Good man!' shouted Deighton of the Horse Battery through the mist. 'Whar you raise dat tonga? I'm coming with you. Ow! But I've a head and a half. I didn't sit out all night. They say the Battery's awful bad,' and he hummed dolorously

Leave the what at the what's-its-name,
Leave the flock without shelter,
Leave the corpse uninterred,
Leave the bride at the altar!

'My faith! It'll be more bally corpse than bride, though, this journey. Jump in, Bobby. Get on, Coachwan!'

On the Umballa platform waited a detachment of officers discussing the latest news from the stricken cantonment, and it was here that Bobby learned the real condition of the Tail Twisters.

'They went into camp,' said an elderly Major recalled from the whist-tables at Mussoorie to a sickly Native Regiment, 'they went into camp with two hundred and ten sick in carts. Two hundred and ten fever cases only, and the balance looking like so many ghosts with sore eyes. A Madras Regiment could have walked through 'em.'

'But they were as fit as be-damned when I left them!' said Bobby.

'Then you'd better make them as fit as bedamned when you rejoin,' said the Major brutally.

Bobby pressed his forehead against the rain-splashed window-pane as the train lumbered across the sodden Doab, and prayed for the health of the Tyneside Tail Twisters. Naini Tal had sent down her contingent with all speed; the lathering ponies of the Dalhousie Road staggered into Pathankot, taxed to the full stretch of their strength; while from cloudy Darjiling the Calcutta Mail whirled up the last straggler of the little army that was to fight a fight in which was neither medal nor honour for the winning, against an enemy none other than 'the sickness that destroyeth in the noonday.'

And as each man reported himself, he said: 'This is a bad business,' and went about his own forthwith, for every Regiment and Battery in the cantonment was under canvas, the sickness bearing them company.

Bobby fought his way through the rain to the Tail Twisters' temporary mess, and Revere could have fallen on the boy's neck for the joy of seeing that ugly, wholesome phiz once more.

'Keep' em amused and interested,' said Revere. 'They went on the drink, poor fools, after the first two cases, and there was no improvement. Oh, it's good to have you back, Bobby! Porkiss is a never mind.'

Deighton came over from the Artillery camp to attend a dreary mess dinner, and contributed to the general gloom by nearly weeping over the condition of his beloved Battery. Porkiss so far forgot himself as to insinuate that the presence of the officers could do no earthly good, and that the best thing would be to send the entire Regiment into hospital and 'let the doctors look after them.' Porkiss was demoralised with fear, nor was his peace of mind restored when Revere said coldly: 'Oh! The sooner you go out the better, if that's your way of thinking. Any public school could send us fifty good men in your place, but it takes time, time, Porkiss, and money, and a certain amount of trouble, to make a Regiment. 'S'pose you're the person we go into camp for, eh?'

Whereupon Porkiss was overtaken with a great and chilly fear which a drenching in the rain did not allay, and, two days later, quitted this world for another where, men do fondly hope, allowances are made for the weaknesses of the flesh. The Regimental Sergeant-Major looked wearily across the Sergeants' Mess tent when the news was announced.

'There goes the worst of them,' he said. 'It'll take the best, and then, please God, it'll stop.' The Sergeants were silent till one said: 'It couldn't be him!' and all knew of whom Travis was thinking.

Bobby Wick stormed through the tents of his Company, rallying, rebuking, mildly, as is consistent with the Regulations, chaffing the faint-hearted; haling the sound into the watery sunlight when there was a break in the weather, and bidding them be of good cheer for their trouble was nearly at an end; scuttling on his dun pony round the outskirts of the camp, and heading back men who, with the innate perversity of British soldiers, were always wandering into infected villages, or drinking deeply from rain-flooded marshes; comforting the panic-stricken with rude speech, and more than once tending the dying who had no friends the men without 'townies'; organising, with banjos and burnt cork, Sing-songs which should allow the talent of the Regiment full play; and generally, as he explained, 'playing the giddy garden-goat all round.'

'You're worth half-a-dozen of us, Bobby,' said Revere in a moment of enthusiasm. 'How the devil do you keep it up?'

Bobby made no answer, but had Revere looked into the breast-pocket of his coat he might have seen there a sheaf of badly-written letters which perhaps accounted for the power that possessed the boy. A letter came to Bobby every other day. The spelling was not above reproach, but the sentiments must have been most satisfactory, for on receipt Bobby's eyes softened marvellously, and he was wont to fall into a tender abstraction for a while ere, shaking his cropped head, he charged into his work.

By what power he drew after him the hearts of the roughest, and the Tail Twisters counted in their ranks some rough diamonds indeed, was a mystery to both skipper and C. O., who learned from the regimental chaplain that Bobby was considerably more in request in the hospital tents than the Reverend John Emery.

'The men seem fond of you. Are you in the hospitals much?' said the Colonel, who did his daily round and ordered the men to get well with a hardness that did not cover his bitter grief.

'A little, sir,' said Bobby.

"Shouldn't go there too often if I were you. They say it's not contagious, but there's no use in running unnecessary risks. We can't afford to have you down, y'know.'

Six days later, it was with the utmost difficulty that the post-runner plashed his way out to the camp with the mail-bags, for the rain was falling in torrents. Bobby received a letter, bore it off to his tent, and, the programme for the next week's Sing-song being satisfactorily disposed of, sat down to answer it. For an hour the unhandy pen toiled over the paper, and where sentiment rose to more than normal tide-level, Bobby Wick stuck out his tongue and breathed heavily. He was not used to letter-writing.

'Beg y' pardon, sir,' said a voice at the tent door; 'but Dormer's 'orrid bad, sir, an' they've taken him orf, sir.'

'Damn Private Dormer and you too!' said Bobby Wick, running the blotter over the half-finished letter. 'Tell him I'll come in the morning.'

"E's awful bad, sir,' said the voice hesitatingly. There was an undecided squelching of heavy boots.

'Well?' said Bobby impatiently.

'Excusin' 'imself before'and for takin' the liberty, 'e says it would be a comfort for to assist 'im, sir, if '

'Tattoo lao! Get my pony! Here, come in out of the rain till I'm ready. What blasted nuisances you are! That's brandy. Drink some; you want it. Hang on to my stirrup and tell me if I go too fast.'

Strengthened by a four-finger 'nip' which he swallowed without a wink, the Hospital Orderly kept up with the slipping, mud-stained, and very disgusted pony as it shambled to the hospital tent.

Private Dormer was certainly "orrid bad.' He had all but reached the stage of collapse and was not pleasant to look upon.

'What's this, Dormer?' said Bobby, bending over the man. 'You're not going out this time. You've got to come fishing with me once or twice more yet.'

The blue lips parted and in the ghost of a whisper said, 'Beg y' pardon, sir, disturbin' of you now, but would you min'' oldin' my' and, sir?'

Bobby sat on the side of the bed, and the icy cold hand closed on his own like a vice, forcing a lady's ring which was on the little finger deep into the flesh. Bobby set his lips and waited, the water dripping from the hem of his trousers. An hour passed and the grasp of the hand did not relax, nor did the expression of the drawn face change. Bobby with infinite craft lit himself a cheroot with the left hand, his right arm was numbed to the elbow, and resigned himself to a night of pain.

Dawn showed a very white-faced Subaltern sitting on the side of a sick man's cot, and a Doctor in the doorway using language unfit for publication.

'Have you been here all night, you young ass?' said the Doctor.

'There or thereabouts,' said Bobby ruefully. 'He's frozen on to me.'

Dormer's mouth shut with a click. He turned his head and sighed. The clinging hand opened, and Bobby's arm fell useless at his side.

'He'll do,' said the Doctor quietly. 'It must have been a toss-up all through the night. 'Think you're to be congratulated on this case.'

'Oh, bosh!' said Bobby. 'I thought the man had gone out long ago only only I didn't care to take my hand away. Rub my arm down, there's a good chap. What a grip the brute has! I'm chilled to the marrow!' He passed out of the tent shivering.

Private Dormer was allowed to celebrate his repulse of Death by strong waters. Four days later he sat on the side of his cot and said to the patients mildly: 'I'd 'a' liken to 'a' spoken to 'im so I should.'

But at that time Bobby was reading yet another letter he had the most persistent correspondent of any man in camp and was even then about to write that the sickness had abated, and in another week at the outside would be gone. He did not intend to say that the chill of a sick man's hand seemed to have struck into the heart whose capacities for affection he dwelt on at such length. He did intend to enclose the illustrated programme of the forthcoming Sing-song whereof he was not a little proud. He also intended to write on many other matters which do not concern us, and doubtless would have done so but for the slight feverish headache which made him dull and unresponsive at mess.

'You are overdoing it, Bobby,' said his skipper. "Might give the rest of us credit of doing a little work. You go on as if you were the whole Mess rolled into one. Take it easy.'

'I will,' said Bobby. 'I'm feeling done up. somehow.' Revere looked at him anxiously and said nothing.

There was a flickering of lanterns about the camp that night, and a rumour that brought men out of their cots to the tent doors, a paddling of the naked feet of doolie-bearers and the rush of a galloping horse.

'Wot's up?' asked twenty tents; and through twenty tents ran the answer 'Wick, 'e's down.'

They brought the news to Revere and he groaned. 'Any one but Bobby and I shouldn't have cared! The Sergeant-Major was right.'

'Not going out this journey,' gasped Bobby, as he was lifted from the doolie. 'Not going out this journey.' Then with an air of supreme conviction 'I can't, you see.'

'Not if I can do anything!' said the Surgeon-Major, who had hastened over from the mess where he had been dining.

He and the Regimental Surgeon fought together with Death for the life of Bobby Wick. Their work was interrupted by a hairy apparition in a bluegray dressing-gown who stared in horror at the bed and cried 'Oh, my Gawd! It can't be 'im!' until an indignant Hospital Orderly whisked him away.

If care of man and desire to live could have done aught, Bobby would have been saved. As it was, he made a fight of three days, and the Surgeon-Major's brow uncreased. 'We'll save him yet,' he said; and the Surgeon, who, though he ranked with the Captain, had a very youthful heart, went out upon the word and pranced joyously in the mud.

'Not going out this journey,' whispered Bobby Wick gallantly, at the end of the third day.

'Bravo!' said the Surgeon-Major. 'That's the way to look at it, Bobby.'

As evening fell a gray shade gathered round Bobby's mouth, and he turned his face to the tent wall wearily. The Surgeon-Major frowned.

'I'm awfully tired,' said Bobby, very faintly. 'What's the use of bothering me with medicine? I don't want it. Let me alone.'

The desire for life had departed, and Bobby was content to drift away on the easy tide of Death.

'It's no good,' said the Surgeon-Major. 'He doesn't want to live. He's meeting it, poor child.' And he blew his nose.

Half a mile away the regimental band was playing the overture to the Sing-song, for the men had been told that Bobby was out of danger. The clash of the brass and the wail of the horns reached Bobby's ears.

Is there a single joy or pain,

That I should never kno ow?

You do not love me, 'tis in vain,

Bid me good-bye and go!

An expression of hopeless irritation crossed the boy's face, and he tried to shake his head.

The Surgeon-Major bent down 'What is it, Bobby?' 'Not that waltz,' muttered Bobby. 'That's our own our very ownest own. Mummy dear.'

With this he sank into the stupor that gave place to death early next morning.

Revere, his eyes red at the rims and his nose very white, went into Bobby's tent to write a letter to Papa Wick which should bow the white head of the ex-Commissioner of Chota-Buldana in the keenest sorrow of his life. Bobby's little store of papers lay in confusion on the table, and among them a half-finished letter. The last sentence ran: 'So you see, darling, there is really no fear, because as long as I know you care for me and I care for you, nothing can touch me.'

Revere stayed in the tent for an hour. When he came out his eyes were redder than ever.

Private Conklin sat on a turned-down bucket, and listened to a not unfamiliar tune. Private Conklin was a convalescent and should have been tenderly treated.

'Ho!' said Private Conklin. 'There's another bloomin' orf'cer da ed.'

The bucket shot from under him, and his eyes filled with a smithyful of sparks. A tall man in a blue-gray bedgown was regarding him with deep disfavour.

'You ought to take shame for yourself, Conky! Orf'cer? Bloomin' orf'cer? I'll learn you to misname the likes of 'im. Hangel! Bloomin' Hangel! That's wot'e is!'

And the Hospital Orderly was so satisfied with the justice of the punishment that he did not even order Private Dormer back to his cot.

IN THE MATTER OF A PRIVATE

Hurrah! hurrah! a soldier's life for me! Shout, boys,
shout! for it makes you jolly and free.

—The Ramrod Corps.

PEOPLE who have seen, say that one of the quaintest
spectacles of human frailty is an outbreak of hysterics in a girls'
school. It starts without warning, generally on a hot afternoon
among the elder pupils. A girl giggles till the giggle gets beyond
control. Then she throws up her head, and cries, "Honk, honk,
honk," like a wild goose, and tears mix with the laughter. If the
n,istres. be wise she will rap out something severc at this point O
check matters. If she be tender-hearted, and send for a drink of
water, the chances are largely in favor of another girl laughing at
the afflicted one and herself collapsing. Thus Lhe trouble spreads,
and may end in half of what answers to the Lower Sixth of a boys'
school rocking and whooping together. Given a week of warm
weather, two stately promenades per diem, a heavy mutton and rice
meal in the middle of the day, a certain amount of nagging from
the teachers, and a few other things, some amazing effects develop.
At least this is what folk say who have had experience.

Now, the Mother Superior of a Convent and the Colonel
of a British Infantry Regiment would be justly shocked at any
comparison being made between their respective charges. But it
is a fact that, under certain circumstances, Thomas in bulk can be
worked up into ditthering, rippling hysteria. He does not weep, but
he shows his trouble unmistakably, and the consequences get into
the newspapers, and all the good people who hardly know a Martini
from a Snider say: "Take away the brute's ammunition!"

Thomas isn't a brute, and his business, which is to look after the virtuous people, nemands that he shall have his am-munition to his hand. He doesn't wear silk stockings, and he really ought to he supplied with a new Adjective to help him to express his opinions; but, for all that, he is a great man. If you call him "the heroic defender of the national honor" one day, and "a brutal and licentious soldiery" the next, you naturally bewilder him, and he looks upon you with suspicion. There is nobody to speak for Thomas except people who have theories to work off on him; and nobody understands Thomas except Thomas, and he does not always know what is the matter with himself.

That is the prologue. This is the story:

Corporal Slane was engaged to be married to Miss Jhansi M'Kenna, whose history is well known in the regiment and elsewhere. He had his Colonel's permission, and, being popular with the men, every arrangement had been made to give the wedding what Private Ortheris called "eeklar." It fell in the heart of the hot weather, and, after the wedding, Slane was going up to the Hills with the Bride. None the less, Slane's grievance was that the affair would he only a hired-carriage wedding, and he felt that the "eeklar" of that was meagre. Miss M'Kenna did not care so much. The Sergeant's wife was helping her to make her wedding-dress, and she was very busy. Slane was, just then, the only moderately contented man in barracks. All the rest were more or less miserable.

And they had so much to make them happy, too. All their work was over at eight in the morning, and for the rest of the day they could lie on their backs and smoke Canteen-plug and swear at the punkab-coolies. They enjoyed a fine, full flesh meal in the middle of the day, and then threw themselves down on their cots and sweated and slept till it was cool enough to go out with their "towny," whose vocabulary contained less than six hundred words, and the Adjective, and whose views on every conceivable question they had heard many times before.

There was the Canteen, of course, and there was the Temperance Room with the second-hand papers in it; but a man of any profession cannot read for eight hours a day in a temperature of 96 degrees or 98 degrees in the shade, running up sometimes to 103 degrees at midnight. Very few men, even though they get a pannikin of flat, stale, muddy beer and hide it under their cots, can continue drinkmg for six hours a day. One man tried, but he died, and nearly the whole regiment went to his funeral because it gave them something to do. It was too early for the excitement of fever or cholera. The men could only wait and wait and wait, and watch the shadow of the barrack creeping across the blinding white dust. That was a gay life.

They lounged about cantonments-it was too hot for any sort of game, and almost too hot for vice-and fuddled themselves in the evening, and filled themselves to distension with the healthy nitrogenous food provided for them, and the more they stoked the less exercise they took and more explosive they grew. Then tempers began to wear away, and men fell a-brooding over insults real or imaginary, for they had nothing else to think of. The tone of the repartees changed, and instead of saying light-heartedly: "I'll knock your silly face in," men grew laboriously p0lite and hinted that the cantonments were not big enough for themselves and their enemy, and that there would he more space for one of the two in another place.

It may have been the Devil who arranged the thing, but the fact of the case is that Losson had for a long time been worrying Simmons in an aimless way. It gave him occupation. The two had their cots side by side, and would sometimes spend a long afternoon swearing at each other; but Simmons was afraid of Losson and dared not challenge him to a fight. He thought over the words in the hot still nights, and half the hate he felt toward Losson be vented on the wretched punkahcoolie.

Losson bought a parrot in the bazar, and put it into a little cage, and lowered the cage into the cool darkness of a well, and sat on the well-curb, shouting bad language down to the parrot. He taught it to say: "Simmons, ye so-oor," which means swine, and several other things entirely unfit for publication. He was a big gross man, and he shook like a jelly when the parrot had the sentence correctly. Simmons, however, shook with rage, for all the room were laughing at him—the parrot was such a disreputable puff of green feathers and it looked so human when it chattered. Losson used to sit, swinging his fat legs, on the side of the cot, and ask the parrot what it thought of Simmons. The parrot would answer: "Simmons, ye so-oor." "Good boy," Losson used to say, scratching the parrot's head; "ye 'ear that, Sim?" And Simmons used to turn over on his stomach and make answer: "I 'ear. Take 'eed you don't 'ear something one of these days."

In the restless nights, after he had been asleep all day, fits of blind rage came upon Simmonr and held him till he trembled all over, while he thought in how many different ways he would slay Losson. Sometimes he would picture himself trampling the life out of the man, with heavy ammunition-boots, and at others smashing in his face with the butt, and at others jumping on his shoulders and dragging the head back till the neckbone cracked. Then his mouth would feel hot and fevered, and he would reach out for another sup of the beer in the pannikin.

But the fancy that came to him most frequently and stayed with him longest was one connected with the great roll of fat under Losson's right ear. He noticed it first on a moonlight night, and thereafter it was always before his eyes. It was a fascinating roll of fat. A man could get his hand upon it and tear away one side of the neck; or he could place the muzzle of a rifle on it and blow away all the head in a flash. Losson had no right to be sleek and contented and well-to-do, when he, Simmons, was the butt of the room, Some day, perhaps, he would show those who laughed at the "Simmons, ye so-oor" joke, that he was as good as the rest, and held a man's life in the crook of his forefinger. When Losson snored, Simmons hated him more bitterly than ever. Why should Losson be able to sleep when Simmons had to stay awake hour after hour, tossing and turning on the tapes, with the dull liver pain gnawing into his right side and his head throbbing and aching after Canteen? He thought over this for many nights, and the world became unprofitable to him. He even blunted his naturally fine appetite with beer and tobacco; and all the while the parrot talked at and made a mock of him.

The heat continued and the tempers wore away more quickly than before. A Sergeant's wife died of heat—apoplexy in the night, and the rumor ran abroad that it was cholera. Men rejoiced openly, hoping that it would spread and send them into camp. But that was a false alarm.

It was late on a Tuesday evening, and the men were waiting in the deep double verandas for "Last Posts," when Simmons went to the box at the foot of his bed, took aut his pipe, and slammed the lid down with a bang that echoed through the deserted barrack like the crack of a rifle. Ordinarily speaking, the men would have taken no notice; but their nerves were fretted to fiddle-strings. They jumped up, and three or four clattered into the barrack-room only to find Simmons kneeling by his box.

"Owl It's you, is it?" they said and laughed foolishly. "We thought 'twas"—

Simmons rose slowly. If the accident had so shaken his fellows, what would not the reality do?

"You thought it was—did you? And what makes you think?" he said, iashmg himself into madness as he went on; "to Hell with your thinking, ye dirty spies."

"Simmons, ye so-oor," chuckled the parrot in the veranda, sleepily, recognizing a well-known voice. Now that was absolutely all.

The tension snapped. Simmons fell back on the arm-rack deliberately,—the men were at the far end of the room,—and took out his rifle and packet of ammunition. "Don't go playing the goat, Sim!" said Losson. "Put it down," but there was a quaver in his voice. Another man stooped, slipped his boot and hurled it at Simmon's head. The prompt answer was a shot which, fired at random, found its billet in Losson's throat. Losson fell forward without a word, and the others scattered.

"You thought it was!" yelled Simmons. "You're drivin' me to it! I tell you you're drivin' me to it! Get up, Losson, an' don't lie shammin' there-you an' your blasted parrit that druv me to it!"

But there was an unaffected reality about Losson's pose that showed Simmons what he had done. The men were still clamoring n the veranda. Simmons appropriated two more packets of ammunition and ran into the moonlight, muttering: "I'll make a night of it. Thirty roun's, an' the last for myself. Take you that, you dogs!"

He dropped on one knee and fired into the brown of the men on the veranda, but the bullet flew high, and landed in the brickwork with a vicious phant that made some of the younger ones turn pale. It is, as musketry theorists observe, one thing to fire and another to be fired at.

Then the instinct of the chase flared up. The news spread from barrack to barrack, and the men doubled out intent on the capture of Simmons, the wild beast, who was heading for the

Cavalry parade-ground, stopping now and again to send back a shot and a Lurse in the direction of his pursuers.

"I'll learn you to spy on me!" he shouted; "I'll learn you to give me dorg's names! Come on the 'ole lot O' you! Colonel John Anthony Deever, C.B.!"-he turned toward the Infantry Mess and shook his rifle-"you think yourself the devil of a man-but I tell 'jou that if you Put your ugly old carcass outside O' that door, I'll make you the poorest-lookin' man in the army. Come out, Colonel John Anthony Deever, C.B.! Come out and see me practiss on the rainge. I'm the crack shot of the 'ole bloomin' battalion." In proof of which statement Simmons fired at the lighted windows of the mess-house.

"Private Simmons, E Comp'ny, on the Cavalry p'rade-ground, Sir, with thirty rounds," said a Sergeant breathlessly to the Colonel. "Shootin' right and lef', Sir. Shot Private Losson What's to be done, Sir?"

Colonel John Anthony Deever, C.B., sallied out, only to be saluted by s spurt of dust at his feet.

"Pull up!" said the Second in Command; "I don't want my step in that way, Colonel. He's as dangerous as a mad dog."

"Shoot him like one, then," said the Colonel, bitterly, "if he won't take his chance, My regiment, too! If it had been the Towheads I could have under stood."

Private Simmons had occupied a strong position near a well on the edge of the parade-ground, and was defying the regiment to come on. The regiment was not anxious to comply, for there is small honor in being shot by a fellow-private. Only Corporal Slane, rifle in band, threw himself down on the ground, and wormed his way toward the well.

"Don't shoot," said he to the men round him; "like as not you'll hit me. I'll catch the beggar, livin'.'"

Simmons ceased shouting for a while, and the noise of trap-wheels could be heard across the plain. Major Oldyne Commanding the Horse Battery, was coming back from a dinner in the Civil Lines; was driving after his usual custom—that is to say, as fast as the horse could go.

"A orf'cer! A blooming spangled orf'cer," shrieked Simmons; "I'll make a scarecrow of that orf'cer!" The trap stopped.

"What's this?" demanded the Major of Gunners. "You there, drop your rifle."

"Why, it's Jerry Blazes! I ain't got no quarrel with you, Jerry Blazes. Pass frien', an' all's well!"

But Jerry Blazes had not the faintest intention of passing a dangerous murderer. He was, as his adoring Battery swore long and fervently, without knowledge of fear, and they were surely the best judges, for Jerry Blazes, it was notorious, had done his possible to kill a man each time the Battery went out.

He walked toward Simmons, with the intention of rushing him, and knocking him down.

"Don't make me do it, Sir," said Simmons; "I ain't got nothing agin you. Ah! you would?"—the Major broke into a run—"Take that then!"

The Major dropped with a bullet through his shoulder, and Simmons stood over him. He had lost the satisfaction of killing Losson in the desired way: hut here was a helpless body to his hand. Should be slip in another cartridge, and blow off the head, or with the butt smash in the white face? He stopped to consider, and a cry went up from the far side of the parade-ground: "He's killed Jerry Blazes!" But in the shelter of the well-pillars Simmons was safe except when he stepped out to fire. "I'll blow yer 'andsome 'ead off, Jerry Blazes," said Simmons, reflectively. "Six an' three is nine an one is ten, an' that leaves me another nineteen, an' one for myself." He tugged at the string of the second packet of ammunition. Corporal Slane crawled out of the shadow of a bank into the moonlight.

"I see you!" said Simmons. "Come a bit furder on an' I'll do for you."

"I'm comm'," said Corporal Slane, briefly; "you've done a bad day's work, Sim. Come out 'ere an' come back with me."

"Come to,"-laughed Simmons, sending a cartridge home with his thumb. "Not before I've settled you an' Jerry Blazes."

The Corporal was lying at full length in the dust of the parade-ground, a rifle under him. Some of the less-cautious men in the distance shouted: "Shoot 'im! Shoot 'im, Slane !"

"You move 'and or foot, Slane," said Simmons, "an' I'll kick Jerry Blazes' 'ead in, and shoot you after."

"I ain't movin'," said the Corporal, raising his head; "you daren't 'it a man on 'is legs. Let go O' Jerry Blazes an' come out O' that with your fistes. Come an' 'it me. You daren't, you bloomin' dog-shooter!"

"I dare."

"You lie, you man-sticker. You sneakin', Sheeny butcher, you lie. See there!" Slane kicked the rifle away, and stood up in the peril of his life. "Come on, now!"

The temptation was more than Simmons could resist, for the Corporal in his white clothes offered a perfect mark.

"Don't misname me," shouted Simmons, firing as he spoke. The shot missed, and the shooter, blind with rage, threw his rifle down and rushed at Slane from the protection of the well. Within striking distance, he kicked savagely at Slane's stomach, but the weedy Corporal knew something of Simmons's weakness, and knew, too, the deadly guard for that kick. Bowing forward and drawing up his right leg till the heel of the right foot was set some three inches above the inside of the left knee-cap, he met the blow standing on one leg—exactly as Gonds stand when they meditate—and ready for the fall that would follow. There was an oath, the Corporal fell over his own left as shinbone met shinbone, and the Private collapsed, his right leg broken an inch above the ankle.

"'Pity you don't know that guard, Sim," said Slane, spitting out the dust as he rose. Then raising his voice—"Come an' take him orf. I've bruk 'is leg." This was not strictly true, for the Private had accomplished his own downfall, since it is the special merit of that leg-guard that the harder the kick the greater the kicker's discomfiture.

Slane walked to Jerry Blazes and hung over him with ostentatious anxiety, while Simmons, weeping with pain, was carried away. " 'Ope you ain't 'urt badly, Sir," said Slane. The Major had fainted, and there was an ugly, ragged hole through the top of his arm. Slane knelt down and murmured. "S'elp me, I believe 'e's dead. Well, if that ain't my blooming luck all over!"

But the Major was destined to lead his Battery afield for many a long day with unshaken nerve. He was removed, and nursed and petted into convalescence, while the Battery discussed the wisdom of capturing Simmons, and blowing him from a gun. They idolized their Major, and his reappearance on parade brought about a scene nowhere provided for in the Army Regulations.

Great, too, was the glory that fell to Slane's share. The Gunners would have made him drunk thrice a day for at least a fortnight. Even the Colonel of his own regiment complimented him upon his coolness, and the local paper called him a hero. These things did not puff him up. When the Major offered him money and thanks, the virtuous Corporal took the one and put aside the other. But he had a request to make and prefaced it with many a "Beg y'pardon, Sir." Could the Major see his way to letting the Slane M'Kenna wedding be adorned by the presence of four Battery horses to pull a hired barouche? The Major could, and so could the Battery. Excessively so. It was a gorgeous wedding.

* * * * *

"Wot did I do it for?" said Corporal Slane. "For the 'orses O' course. Jhansi ain't a beauty to look at, but I wasn't goin' to 'ave a hired turn-out. Jerry Blazes? If I 'adn't 'a' wanted something, Sim might ha' blowed Jerry Blazes' blooming 'ead into Hirish stew for aught I'd 'a' cared."

And they hanged Private Simmons-hanged him as high as Haman in hollow square of the regiment; and the Colonel said it was Drink; and the Chaplain was sure it was the Devil; and Simmons fancied it was both, but he didn't know, and only hoped his fate would be a warning to his companions; and half a dozen "intelligent publicists" wrote six beautiful leading articles on "'The Prevalence of Crime in the Army."

But not a soul thought of comparing the "bloody-minded Simmons" to the squawking, gaping schoolgirl with which this story opens.

THE ENLIGHTENMENTS OF PAGETT, M.P.

"Because half a dozen grasshoppers under a fern make the field ring with their importunate chink while thousands of great cattle, reposed beneath the shadow of the British oak, chew the cud and are silent, pray do not imagine that those who make the noise are the only inhabitants of the field-that, of course, they are many in number or that, after all, they are other than the little, shrivelled, meagre, hopping, though loud and troublesome insects of the hour."-Burke: "Reflections on the Revolution in France."

THEY were sitting in the veranda of "the splendid palace of an Indian Pro-Consul"; surrounded by all the glory and mystery of the immemorial East. In plain English it was a one-storied, ten-roomed, whitewashed, mud-roofed bungalow, set in a dry garden of dusty tamarisk trees and divided from the road by a low mud wall. The green parrots screamed overhead as they flew in battalions to the river for their morning drink. Beyond the wall, clouds of fine dust showed where the cattle and goats of the city were passing afield to graze. The remorseless white light of the winter sunshine of Northern India lay upon everything and improved nothing, from the whining Peisian-wheel by the lawn-tennis court to the long perspective of level road and the blue, domed tombs of Mohammedan saints just visible above the trees.

"A Happy New Year," said Orde to his guest. "It's the first you've ever spent out of England, isn't it?"

"Yes. 'Happy New Year," said Pagett, smiling at the sunshine. "What a divine climate you have here! Just think of the brown cold fog hanging over London now!" And he rubbed his hands.

It was more than twenty years since he had last seen Orde, his schoolmate, and their paths in the world had divided early. The one had quitted college to become a cog-wheel in the machinery of the great Indian Government; the other more blessed with goods, had been whirled into a similar position in the English scheme. Three successive elections had not affected Pagett's position with a loyal constituency, and he had grown insensibly to regard himself in some sort as a pillar of the Empire, whose real worth would be known later on. After a few years of conscientious attendance at many divisions, after newspaper battles innumerable and the publication of interminable correspondence, and more hasty oratory than in his calmer moments he cared to think upon, it occurred to him, as it had occurred to many of his fellows in Parliament, that a tour to India would enable him to sweep a larger lyre and address himself to the problems of Imperial administration with a firmer hand. Accepting, therefore, a general invitation extended to him by Orde some years before, Pagett had taken ship to Karachi, and only overnight had been received with joy by the Deputy-Commissioner of Amara. They had sat late, discussing the changes and chances of twenty years, recalling the names of the dead, and weighing the futures of the living, as is the custom of men meeting after intervals of action.

Next morning they smoked the after breakfast pipe in the veranda, still regarding each other curiously, Pagett, in a light grey frock-coat and garments much too thin for the time of the year, and a puggried sun-hat carefully and wonderfully made. Orde in a shooting coat, riding breeches, brown cowhide boots with spurs, and a battered flax helmet. He had ridden some miles in the early morning to inspect a doubtful river dam. The men's faces differed as much as their attire. Orde's worn and wrinkled around the eyes, and grizzled at the temples, was the harder and more square of the two, and it was with something like envy that the owner looked at the comfortable outlines of Pagett's blandly receptive countenance, the clear skin, the untroubled eye, and the mobile, clean-shaved lips.

"And this is India!" said Pagett for the twentieth time staring long and intently at the grey feathering of the tamarisks.

"One portion of India only. It's very much like this for 300 miles in every direction. By the way, now that you have rested a little—I wouldn't ask the old question before—what d'you think of the country?"

'Tis the most pervasive country that ever yet was seen. I acquired several pounds of your country coming up from Karachi.

The air is heavy with it, and for miles and miles along that distressful eternity of rail there's no horizon to show where air and earth separate."

"Yes. It isn't easy to see truly or far in India. But you had a decent passage out, hadn't you?"

"Very good on the whole. Your Anglo-Indian may be unsympathetic about one's political views; but he has reduced ship life to a science."

"The Anglo-Indian is a political orphan, and if he's wise he won't be in a hurry to be adopted by your party grandmothers. But how were your companions, unsympathetic?"

"Well, there was a man called Dawlishe, a judge somewhere in this country it seems, and a capital partner at whist by the way, and when I wanted to talk to him about the progress of India in a political sense (Orde hid a grin, which might or might not have been sympathetic), the National Congress movement, and other things in which, as a Member of Parliament, I'm of course interested, he shifted the subject, and when I once cornered him, he looked me calmly in the eye, and said: 'That's all Tommy rot. Come and have a game at Bull.' You may laugh; but that isn't the way to treat a great and important question; and, knowing who I was. well. I thought it rather rude, don't you know; and yet Dawlishe is a thoroughly good fellow."

"Yes; he's a friend of mine, and one of the straightest men I know. I suppose, like many Anglo-Indians, he felt it was hopeless to give you any just idea of any Indian question without the documents before you, and in this case the documents you want are the country and the people."

"Precisely. That was why I came straight to you, bringing an open mind to bear on things. I'm anxious to know what popular feeling in India is really like y'know, now that it has wakened into political life. The National Congress, in spite of Dawlishe, must have caused great excitement among the masses?"

"On the contrary, nothing could be more tranquil than the state of popular feeling; and as to excitement, the people would as soon be excited over the 'Rule of Three' as over the Congress."

"Excuse me, Orde, but do you think you are a fair judge? Isn't the official Anglo-Indian naturally jealous of any external influences that might move the masses, and so much opposed to liberal ideas, truly liberal ideas, that he can scarcely be expected to regard a popular movement with fairness?"

"What did Dawlishe say about Tommy Rot? Think a moment, old man. You and I were brought up together; taught by the same tutors, read the same books, lived the same life, and new languages, and work among new races; while you, more fortunate, remain at home. Why should I change my mind our mind-because I change my sky? Why should I and the few hundred Englishmen in my service become unreasonable, prejudiced fossils, while you and your newer friends alone remain bright and open-minded? You surely don't fancy civilians are members of a Primrose League?"

"Of course not, but the mere position of an English official gives him a point of view which cannot but bias his mind on this question." Pagett moved his knee up and down a little uneasily as he spoke.

"That sounds plausible enough, but, like more plausible notions on Indian matters, I believe it's a mistake. You'll find when you come to consult the unofficial Briton that our fault, as a class—I speak of the civilian now-is rather to magnify the progress that has been made toward liberal institutions. It is of English origin, such as it is, and the stress of our work since the Mutiny—only thirty years ago—has been in that direction. No, I think you will get no fairer or more dispassionate view of the Congress business than such men as I can give you. But I may as well say at once that those who know most of India, from the inside, are inclined to wonder at the noise our scarcely begun experiment makes in England."

"But surely the gathering together of Congress delegates is of itself a new thing."

"There's nothing new under the sun When Europe was a jungle half Asia flocked to the canonical conferences of Buddhism; and for centuries the people have gathered at Pun, Hurdwar, Trimbak, and Benares in immense numbers. A great meeting, what you call a mass meeting, is really one of the oldest and most popular of Indian institutions In the case of the Congress meetings, the only notable fact is that the priests of the altar are British, not Buddhist, Jam or Brahmanical, and that the whole thing is a British contrivance kept alive by the efforts of Messrs. Hume, Eardley, Norton, and Digby."

"You mean to say, then, it s not a spontaneous movement?"

"What movement was ever spontaneous in any true sense of the word? This seems to be more factitious than usual. You seem to know a great deal about it; try it by the touchstone of subscriptions, a coarse but fairly trustworthy criterion, and there is scarcely the color of money in it. The delegates write from England that they are out of pocket for working expenses, railway fares, and stationery—the mere pasteboard and scaffolding of their show. It is, in fact, collapsing from mere financial inanition."

"But you cannot deny that the people of India, who are, perhaps, too poor to subscribe, are mentally and morally moved by the agitation," Pagett insisted.

"That is precisely what I do deny. The native side of the movement is the work of a limited class, a microscopic minority, as Lord Dufferin described it, when compared with the people proper, but still a very interesting class, seeing that it is of our own creation. It is composed almost entirely of those of the literary or clerkly castes who have received an English education."

"Surely that s a very important class. Its members must be the ordained leaders of popular thought."

"Anywhere else they might he leaders, but they have no social weight in this topsy-turvy land, and though they have been employed in clerical work for generations they have no prac. tical knowledge of affairs. A ship's clerk is a useful person, but he it scarcely the captain; and an orderly-room writer, however smart he may be, is not the colonel. You see, the writer class in India has never till now aspired to anything like command. It wasn t allowed to. The Indian gentleman, for thousands of years past, has resembled Victor Hugo's noble:

> 'Un vrai sire
> Chatelain
> Laisse ecrire
> Le vilain.
> Sa main digne
> Quand il signe
> Egratigne
> Le velin.

And the little egralignures he most likes to make have been scored pretty deeply by the sword."

"But this is childish and medheval nonsense!"

"Precisely; and from your, or rather our, point of view the pen is mightier than the sword. In this country it's otherwise. The fault lies in our Indian balances, not yet adjusted to civilized weights and measures."

"Well, at all events, this literary class represent the natural aspirations and wishes of the people at large, though it may not exactly lead them, and, in spite of all you say, Orde, I defy you to find a really sound English Radical who would not sympathize with those aspirations."

Pagett spoke with some warmth, and he had scarcely ceased when a well appointed dog-cart turned into the compound gates, and Orde rose saying:

"Here is Edwards, the Master of the Lodge I neglect so diligently, come to talk about accounts, I suppose."

As the vehicle drove up under the porch Pagett also rose, saying with the trained effusion born of much practice:

"But this is also my friend, my old and valued friend Edwards. I'm delighted to see you. I knew you were in India, but not exactly where."

"Then it isn't accounts, Mr. Edwards," said Orde, cheerily.

"Why, no, sir; I heard Mr. Pagett was coming, and as our works were closed for the New Year I thought I would drive over and see him."

"A very happy thought. Mr. Edwards, you may not know, Orde, was a leading member of our Radical Club at Switebton when I was beginning political life, and I owe much to his exertions. There's no pleasure like meeting an old friend, except, perhaps, making a new one. I suppose, Mr. Edwards, you stick to the good old cause?"

"Well, you see, sir, things are different out here. There's precious little one can find to say against the Government, which was the main of our talk at home, and them that do say things are not the sort o' people a man who respects himself would like to be mixed up with. There are no politics, in a manner of speaking, in India. It's all work."

"Surely you are mistaken, my good friend. Why I have come all the way from England just to see the working of this great National movement."

"I don't know where you're going to find the nation as moves to begin with, and then you'll be hard put to it to find what they are moving about. It's like this, sir," said Edwards, who had not quite relished being called "my good friend." "They haven't got any grievance—nothing to hit with, don't you see, sir; and then there's not much to hit against, because the Government is more like a kind of general Providence, directing an old—established state of things, than that at home, where there's something new thrown down for us to fight about every three months."

"You are probably, in your workshops, full of Eng'ish mechanics, out of the way of learning what the masses think."

"I don't know so much about that. There are four of us English foremen, and between seven and eight hundred native fitters, smiths, carpenters, painters, and such like."

"And they are full of the Congress, of course?"

"Never hear a word of it from year's end to year's end, and I speak the talk too. But I wanted to ask how things are going on at home—old Tyler and Brown and the rest?"

"We will speak of them presently, but your account of the indifference of your men surprises me almost as much as your own. I fear you are a backslider from the good old doctrine, Ed wards." Pagett spoke as one who mourned the death of a near relative.

"Not a bit, Sir, but I should be if I took up with a parcel of baboos, pleaders, and schoolboys, as never did a day's work in their lives, and couldn't if they tried. And if you was to poll us English railway men, mechanics, tradespeople, and the like of that all up and down the country from Peshawur to Calcutta, you would find us mostly in a tale together. And yet you know we're the same English you pay some respect to at home at 'lection time, and we have the pull o' knowing something about it."

"This is very curious, but you will let me come and see you, and perhaps you will kindly show me the railway works, and we will talk things over at leisure. And about all old friends and old times," added Pagett, detecting with quick insight a look of disappointment in the mechanic's face.

Nodding briefly to Orde, Edwards mounted his dog-cart and drove off.

"It's very disappointing," said the Member to Orde, who, while his friend discoursed with Edwards, had been looking over a bundle of sketches drawn on grey paper in purple ink, brought to him by a Chuprassee.

"Don't let it trouble you, old chap," 'said Orde, sympathetically. "Look here a moment, here are some sketches by the man who made the carved wood screen you admired so much in the dining-room, and wanted a copy of, and the artist himself is here too."

"A native?" said Pagett.

"Of course," was the reply, "Bishen Siagh is his name, and he has two brothers to help him. When there is an important job to do, the three go 'ato partnership, but they spend most of their time and all their money in litigation over an inheritance, and I'm afraid they are getting involved, Thoroughbred Sikhs of the old rock, obstinate, touchy, bigoted, and cunning, but good men for all that. Here is Bishen Singn-shall we ask him about the Congress?"

But Bishen Singh, who approached with a respectful salaam, had never heard of it, and he listened with a puzzled face and obviously feigned interest to Orde's account of its aims and objects, finally shaking his vast white turban with great significance when he learned that it was promoted by certam pleaders named by Orde, and by educated natives. He began with labored respect to explain how he was a poor man with no concern in such matters, which were all under the control of God, but presently broke out of Urdu into familiar Punjabi, the mere sound of which had a rustic smack of village smoke-reek and plough-tail, as he denounced the wearers of white coats, the jugglers with words who filched his field from him, the men whose backs were never bowed in honest work; and poured ironical scorn on the Bengali. He and one of his brothers had seen Calcutta, and being at work there had Bengali carpenters given to them as assistants.

"Those carpenters!" said Bishen Singh. "Black apes were more efficient workmates, and as for the Bengali babu-tchick!" The guttural click needed no interpretation, but Orde translated the rest, while Pagett gazed with in.. terest at the wood-carver.

"He seems to have a most illiberal prejudice against the Bengali," said the M.P.

"Yes, it's very sad that for ages outside Bengal there should he so bitter a prejudice. Pride of race, which also means race-hatred, is the plague and curse of India and it spreads far," pointed with his riding-whip to the large map of India on the veranda wall.

"See! I begin with the North," said he. "There's the Afghan, and, as a highlander, he despises all the dwellers in Hindoostan-with the exception of the Sikh, whom he hates as cordially as the Sikh hates him. The Hindu loathes Sikh and Afghan, and the Rajput—that's a little lower down across this yellow blot of desert—has a strong objection, to put it mildly, to the Maratha who, by the way, poisonously hates the Afghan. Let's go North a minute. The Sindhi hates everybody I've mentioned. Very good, we'll take less warlike races. The cultivator of Northern India domineers over the man in the next province, and the Behari of the Northwest ridicules the Bengali. They are all at one on that point. I'm giving you merely the roughest possible outlines of the facts, of course."

Bishen Singh, his clean cut nostrils still quivering, watched the large sweep of the whip as it traveled from the frontier, through Sindh, the Punjab and Rajputana, till it rested by the valley of the Jumna

"Hate—eternal and inextinguishable hate," concluded Orde, flicking the lash of the whip across the large map from East to West as he sat down. "Remember Canning's advice to Lord Granville, 'Never write or speak of Indian things without looking at a map.'"

Pagett opened his eyes, Orde resumed. "And the race-hatred is only a part of it. What's really the matter with Bisben Singh is class-hatred, which, unfortunately, is even more intense and more widely spread. That's one of the little drawbacks of caste, which some of your recent English writers find an impeccable system."

The wood-carver was glad to be recalled to the business of his craft, and his eyes shone as he received instructions for a carved wooden doorway for Pagett, which he promised should be splendidly executed and despatched to England in six months. It is an irrelevant detail, but in spite of Orde's reminders, fourteen months elapsed before the work was finished. Business over, Bishen Singh hung about, reluctant to take his leave, and at last joining his hands and approaching Orde with bated breath and whispering hum. bleness, said he had a petition to make. Orde's face suddenly lost all trace of expression. "Speak on, Bishen Singh," said he, and the carver in a whining tone explained that his case against his brothers was fixed for hearing b& fore a native judge and-here he dropped his voice still lower tid he was summarily stopped by Orde, who sternly pointed to the gate with an emphatic Begone!

Bishen Singh, showing but little sign of discomposure, salaamed respectfully to the friends and departed.

Pagett looked inquiry; Orde with complete recovery of his usual urbanity, replied: "It's nothing, only the old story, he wants his case to be tried by an English judge-they all do that-but when he began to hint that the other side were in improper relations with the native judge I had to shut him up. Gunga Ram, the man he wanted to make insinuations about, may not be very bright; but he's as honest as day-light on the bench. But that's just what one can't get a native to believe."

"Do you really mean to say these people prefer to have their cases tried by English judges?"

'Why, certainly."

Pagett drew a long breath. "I didn't know that before." At this point a phaeton entered the compound, and Orde rose with "Confound it, there's old Rasul Ah Khan come to pay one of his tiresome duty calls. I'm afraid we shall never get through our little Congress discussion."

Pagett was an aimost silent spectator of the grave formalities of a visit paid by a punctilious old Mahommedan gentleman to an Indian official; and was much impressed by the distinction of manner and fine appearance of the Mohammedan landholder. When the exhange of polite banalities came to a pause, he expressed a wish to learn the courtly visitor's opinion of the National Congress.

Orde reluctantly interpreted, and with a smile which even Mohammedan politeness could not save from bitter scorn, Rasul Ah Khan intimated that he knew nothing about it and cared still less. It was a kind of talk encouraged by the Government for some mysterious purpose of its own, and for his own part he wondered and held his peace.

Pagett was far from satisfied with this, and wished to have the old gentleman's opinion on the propriety of managing all Indian affairs on the basis of an elective system.

Orde did his best to explain, but it was plain the visitor was bored and bewildered. Frankly, he didn't think much of committees;

they had a Municipal Committee at Lahore and had elected a menial servant, an orderly, as a member. He had been informed of this on good authority, and after that, committees had ceased to interest him. But all was according to the rule of Government, and, please God, it was all for the best.

"What an old fossil it is!" cried Pagett, as Orde returned from seeing his guest to the door; "just like some old blue-blooded hidalgo of Spain. What does he really think of the Congress after all, and of the elective system?"

"Hates it all like poison. When you are sure of a majority, election is a fine system; but you can scarcely expect the Mahommedans, the mast mas terful and powerful minority in the country, to contemplate their own extinction with joy. The worst of it is that he and his co-religionists, who are many, and the landed proprietors, also, of Hindu race, are frightened and put out by this electiop business and by the importance we have bestowed on lawyers, pleaders, writers, and the like, who have, up to now, been in abject submission to them. They say little, hut after all they are the most important fagots in the great bundle of communities, and all the glib bunkum in the world would not pay for their estrangement. They have controlled the land."

"But I am assured that experience of local self-government in your municipalities has been most satisfactory, and when once the principle is accepted in your centres, don't you know, it is bound to spread, and these important—ah'm people of yours would learn it like the rest. I see no difficulty at all," and the smooth lips closed with the complacent snap habitual to Pagett, M.P., the "man of cheerful yesterdays and confident to-morrows."

Orde looked at him with a dreary smile.

"The privilege of election has been most reluctantly withdrawn from scores of municipalities, others have had to be summarily suppressed, and, outside the Presidency towns, the actual work done has been badly performed. This is of less moment, perhaps-it only sends up the local death-rates-than the fact that the public interest in municipal elections, never very strong, has waned, and is waning, in spite of careful nursing on the part of Government servants."

"Can you explain this lack of interest?" said Pagett, putting aside the rest of Orde's remarks.

"You may find a ward of the key in the fact that only one in every thousand af our population can spell. Then they are infinitely more interested in religion and caste questions than in any sort of politics. When the business of mere existence is over, their minds are occupied by a series of interests, pleasures, rituals, superstitions, and the like, based on centuries of tradition and usage. You, perhaps, find it hard to conceive of people absolutely devoid of curiosity, to whom the book, the daily paper, and the printed speech are unknown, and you would describe their life as blank. That's a profound mistake. You are in another land, another century, down on the bed-rock of society, where the family merely, and not the community, is all-important. The average Oriental cannot be brought to look beyond his clan. His life, too, is naore complete and self-sufficing, and less sordid and low-thoughted than you might imagine. It is bovine and slow in some respects, but it is never empty. You and I are inclined to put the cart before the horse, and to forget that it is the man that is elemental, not the book.

'The corn and the cattle are all my care, And the rest is the will of God.'

Why should such folk look up from their immemorially appointed round of duty and interests to meddle with the unknown and fuss with voting-papers. How would you, atop of all your interests care to conduct even one-tenth of your life according to the manners and customs of the Papuans, let's say? That's what it comes to."

"But if they won't take the trouble to vote, why do you anticipate that Mohammedans, proprietors, and the rest would be crushed by majorities of them?"

Again Pagett disregarded the closing sentence.

"Because, though the landholders would not move a finger on any purely political question, they could be raised in dangerous excitement by religious hatreds. Already the first note of this has been sounded by the people who are trying to get up an agitation on the cow-killing question, and every year there is trouble over the Mohammedan Muharrum processions.

"But who looks after the popular rights, being thus unrepresented?"

"The Government of Hcr Majesty the Queen, Empress of India, in which, if the Congress promoters are to be believed, the people have an implicit trust; for the Congress circular, specially prepared for rustic comprehension, says the movement is 'for the remission of tax, the advancement of Hindnstan, and the strengthening of the British Govemment.' This paper is headed in large letters-

'MAV THE PROSPEEITY OF THE EMPIRE OF INDIA ENDURE.'"

"Really!" said Pagett, "that shows some cleverness. But there are things better worth imi'ation in our English methods of-er-political statement than this sort of amiable fraud."

"Anyhow," resumed Orde, "you perceive that not a word is said about elections and the elective principle, and the reticence of the Congress promoters here shows they are wise in their generation."

"But the elective principle must triumph in the end, and the little difficulties you seem to anticipate would give way on the introduction of a well-balanced scheme, capable of indefinite extension."

"But is it possible to devise a scheme which, always assuming that the people took any interest in it, without enormous expense, ruinous dislocation of the administ:ation and danger to the public peace, can satisfy the aspirations of Mr. Hume and his following, and yet safeguard the interests of the Mahommedans, the landed and wealthy classes, the Conservative Hindus, the Eurasians, Parsees, Sikhs, Rajputs, native Christians, domiciled Europeans and others, who are each important and powerful in their way?"

Pagett's attention, however, was diverted to the gate, where a group of cultivators stood in apparent hesitation.

"Here are the twelve Apostles, hy Jove-come straight out of Raffaele's cartoons," said the M.P., with the fresh appreciation of a newcomer.

Orde, loth to be interrupted, turned impatiently toward the villagers, and their leader, handing his long staff to one of his companions, advanced to the house.

"It is old Jelbo, the Lumherdar, or head-man of Pind Sharkot, and a very' intelligent man for a villager."

The Jat farmer had removed his shoes and stood smiling on the edge of the veranda. His strongly marked features glowed with russet bronze, and his bright eyes gleamed under deeply set brows, contracted by lifelong exposure to sunshine. His beard and moustache streaked with grey swept from bold cliffs of brow and cheek in the large sweeps one sees drawn by Michael Angelo, and strands of long black hair mingled with the irregularly piled wreaths and folds of his turban. The drapery of stout blue cotton cloth thrown over his broad shoulders and girt round his narrow loins, hung from his tall form in broadly sculptured folds, and he would have made a superb model for an artist in search of a patriarch.

Orde greeted him cordially, and after a polite pause the countryman started off with a long story told with impressive earnestness. Orde listened and smiled, interrupting the speaker at 'times to argue and reason with him in a tone which Pagett could hear was kindly, and finally checking the flux of words was about to dismiss him, when Pagett suggested that he should be asked about the National Congress.

But Jelloc had never heard of it. He was a poor man and such things, by the favor of his Honor, did not concern him.

"What's the matter with your big friend that he was so terribly in earnest?" asked Pagett, when he had left.

"Nothing much. He wants the blood of the people in the next village, who have had smallpox and cattle plague pretty badly, and by the help of a wizard, a currier, and several pigs have passed it on to his own village. 'Wants to know if they can't be run in for this awful crime. It seems they made a dreadful charivari at the village boundary, threw a quantity of spell-bearing objects over the border, a buffalo's skull and other things; then branded a chamur—what you would call a currier—on his hinder parts and drove him and a number of pigs over into JelIno's village. Jelbo says he can bring evidence to prove that the wizard directing these proceedings, who is a Sansi, has been guilty of theft, arson, rattle-killing, perjury and murder, but would prefer to have him punished for bewitching them and inflicting small-pox."

"And how on earth did you answer such a lunatic?"

"Lunatic I the old fellow is as sane as you or I; and he has some ground of complaint against those Sansis. I asked if he would like a native superintendent of police with some men to make inquiries, but he objected on the grounds the police were rather worse than smallpox and criminal tribes put together."

"Criminal tribes-er-I don't quite understand," said Paget

"We have in India many tribes of people who in the slack anti-British days became robbers, in various kind. and preye on the people. They are being restrained and reclaimed little by little, and in time will become useful; citizens, but they still cherish hereditary traditions of crime, and are a difficult lot to deal with. By the way what; about the political rights of these folk under your schemes? The country people call them vermin, but I sup-pose they would be electors with the rest."

"Nonsense-special provision would be made for them in a well-considered electoral scheme, and they would doubtless be treated with fitting severity," said Pagett, with a magisterial air.

"Severity, yes-but whether it would be fitting is doubtful. Even those poor devils have rights, and, after all, they only practice what they have been taught."

"But criminals, Ordel"

"Yes, criminals with codes and rituals of crime, gods and godlings of crime, and a hundred songs and sayings in praise of it. Puzzling, isn't it?"

"It's simply dreadful. They ought to be put down at once. Are there many of them?"

"Not more than about sixty thousand in this province, for many of the trlbes broadly described as criminal are really vagabond and crimlnal only on occasion, while others are being settled and reclaimed. They are of great antiquity, a legacy from the past, the golden, glorious Aryan past of Max Muller, Birdwood and the rest of your spindrift philosophers."

An orderly brought a card to Orde who took it with a movement of irritation at the interruption, and banded it to Pagett; a large card with a ruled border in red ink, and in the centre in schoolboy copper plate, Mr. Dma Nath. "Give salaam," said the civilian, and there entered in haste a slender youth, clad in a closely fitting coat of grey homespun, tight trousers, patent-leather shoes, and a small black velvet cap. His thin cheek twitched, and his eyes wandered restlessly, for the young man was evidently nervous and uncomfortable, though striving to assume a free and easy air.

"Your honor may perhaps remember me," he said in Englisb, and Orde scanned him keenly.

"I know your face somehow. You belonged to the Shershah district I think, when I was in charge there?"

"Yes, Sir, my father is writer at Shershah, and your honor gave me a prize when I was first in the Middle School examination five years ago. Since then I have prosecuted my studies, and I am now second year's student in the Mission College."

"Of course: you are Kedar Nath's son-the boy who said he liked geography better than play or sugar cakes, and I didn't believe you. How is your father getting on?"

"He is well, and he sends his salaam, but his circumstances are depressed, and be also is down on his luck."

"You learn English idiom". at the Mission College, it seems."

"Yes, sir, they are the best idioms, and my father ordered me to ask your honor to say a word for him to the present incumbent of your honor's shoes, the latchet of which he is not worthy to open, and who knows not Joseph; for things are different at Sher shah now, and my father wants promotion."

"Your father is a good man, and I will do what I can for him."

At this point a telegram was handed to Orde, who, after glancing at it, said he must leave his young friend whom he introduced to Pagett, "a member of the English House of Commons who wishes to learn about India."

Orde bad scarcely retired with his telegram when Pagett began:

"Perhaps you can tell me something of the National Congress movement?"

"Sir, it is the greatest movement of modern times, and one in which all edvcated men like us must join. All our students are for the Congress."

"Excepting, I suppose, Mahommedans, and the Christians?" said Pagett, quick to use his recent instruction.

"These are some mere exceptions to the universal rule."

"But the people outside the College, the working classes, the agriculturists; your father and mother, for instance."

"My mother," said the young man, with a visible effort to bring himself to pronounce the word, "has no ideas, and my father is not agriculturist, nor working class; he is of the Kayeth caste; but he had not the advantage of a collegiate education, and he does not know much of the Congress. It is a movement for the educated young-man"-connecting adjective and noun in a sort of vocal hyphen.

"Ah, yes," said Pagett, feeling he was a little off the rails, "and what are the benefits you expect to gain by it?"

"Oh, sir, everything. England owes its greatness to Parliamentary institutions, and we should at once gain the same high position in scale of nations. Sir, we wish to have the sciences, the arts, the manufactures, the industrial factories, with steam engines, and other motive powers and public meetings, and debates. Already we have a debating club in connection with the college, and elect a Mr. Speaker. Sir, the progress must come. You also are a Member of Parliament and worship the great Lord Ripon," said the youth, breathlessly, and his black eyes flashed as he finished his commaless sentences.

"Well," said Pagett, drily, "it has not yet occurred to me to worship his Lord-ship, although I believe he is a very worthy man, and I am not sure that England owes quite all the things you name to the House of Commons. You see, my young friend, the growth of a nation like ours is slow, subject to many influences, and if you have read your history aright"-"Sir. I know it all-all! Norman Conquest, Magna Charta, Runnymede, Reformation, Tudors, Stuarts, Mr. Milton and Mr. Burke, and I have read something of Mr. Herbert Spencer and Gibbon's 'Decline and Fall,' Reynolds' Mysteries of the Court,' and Pagett felt like one who had pulled the string of a shower-bath unawares, and hastened to stop the torrent with a qtlestion as to what particular grievances of the people of India the attention of an elected assembly should be first directed. But young Mr. Dma Nath was slow to particularize. There were many, very many demanding consideration. Mr. Pagett would like to hear of one or two typical examples. The Repeal of the Arms Act was at last named, and the student learned for the first time that a license was necessary before an Englishman could carry a gun in England. Then natives of India ought to be allowed to become Volunteer Riflemen if they chose, and the absolute equality of the Oriental with his European fellow-subject in civil status should be proclaimed on principle, and the Indian Army should be considerably reduced. The student was not, however, prepared with answers to Mr. Pagett's mildest questions on these points, and he returned to vague generalities, leaving the M.P. so much impressed with the crudity of his views that he was glad on Orde's return to say good-bye to his "very interesting" young friend.

"What do you think of young India?" asked Orde.

"Curious, very curious-and callow."

"And yet," the civilian replied, "one can scarcely help sympathizing with him for his mere youth's sake. The young orators of the Oxford Union arrived at the same conclusions and showed doubtless just the same enthusiasm. If there were any political analogy between India and England, if the thousand races of this Empire were one, if there were any chance even of their learning to speak one language, if, in short, India were a Utopia of the debating-room, and not a real land, this kind of talk might be worth listening to, but it is all based on false analogy and ignorance of the facts."

"But he is a native and knows the facts."

"He is a sort of English schoolboy, but married three years, and the father of two weaklings, and knows less than most English schoolboys. You saw all he is and knows, and such ideas as he has acquired are directly hostile to the most cherished convictions of the vast majority of the people."

"But what does he mean by saying he is a student of a mission college? Is he a Christian?"

"He meant just what he said, and he is not a Christian, nor ever will he be. Good people in America, Scotland and England, most of whom would never dream of collegiate education for their own sons, are pinching themselves to bestow it in pure waste on Indian youths. Their scheme is an oblique, subterranean attack on heathenism; the theory being that with the jam of secular education, leading to a University degree, the pill of moral or religious instruction may he coaxed down the heathen gullet."

"But does it succeed; do they make converts?"

"They make no converts, for the subtle Oriental swallows the jam and rejects the pill; but the mere example of the sober, righteous, and godly lives of the principals and professors who are most excellent and devoted men, must have a certain moral value. Yet, as Lord Lansdowne pointed out the other day, the market is dangerously overstocked with graduates of our Universities who look for employment in the administration. An immense number are employed, but year by year the college mills grind out increasing lists of youths foredoomed to failure and disappointment, and meanwhile, trade. manufactures. and the industrial arts are neglected, and in fact regarded with contempt by our new literary mandarins in posse."

"But our young friend said he wanted steam-engines and factories," said Pagett.

"Yes, he would like to direct such concerns. He wants to begin at the top, for manual labor is held to be discreditable, and he would never defile his hands by the apprenticeship which the architects, engineers, and manufacturers of England cheerfully undergo; and he would be aghast to learn that the leading names of industrial enterprise in England belonged a generation or two since, or now belong, to men who wrought with their own hands. And, though he talks glibly of manufacturers, he refuses to see that the Indian manufacturer of the future will be the despised workman of the present. It was proposed, for example, a few weeks ago, that a certain municipality in this province should establish an elementary technical school for the sons of workmen. The stress of the opposition to the plan came from a pleader who owed all he had to a college education bestowed on him gratis by Government and missions. You would have fancied some fine old crusted Tory squire of the last generation was speaking. 'These people,' he said, 'want no education, for they learn their trades from their fathers, and to teach a workman's son the elements of mathematics and physical science would give him ideas above his business. They must be kept in their place, and it was idle to imagine that there was any science in wood or iron work.' And he carried his point. But the Indian workman will rise in the social scale in spite of the new literary caste."

"In England we have scarcely begun to realize that there is an industrial class in this country, yet, I suppose, the example of men, like Edwards for instance, must tell," said Pagett, thoughtfully.

"That you shouldn't know much about it is natural enough, for there are but few sources of information. India in this, as in other respects, is like a badly kept ledger-not written up to date. And men like Edwards are, in reality, missionaries, who by precept and example are teaching more lessons than they know. Only a few, however, of their crowds of subordinates seem to care to try to emulate them, and aim at individual advancement; the rest drop into the ancient Indian caste gr('ove."

"How do you mean?" asked he, "Well, it is found that the new railway and factory workmen, the fitter, the smith, the engine-driver, and the rest are already forming separate hereditary castes. You may notice this down at Jamalpur in Bengal, one of the oldest railway centres; and at other places, and in other industries, they are following the same inexorable Indian law."

"Which means?" queried Pagett.

"It means that the rooted habit of the people is to gather in small self-contained, self-sufficing family groups with no thought or care for any interests but their own-a habit which is scarcely compatible with the right acceptation of the elective principle."

"Yet you must admit, Orde, that though our young friend was not able to expound tbe faith that is in him, your Indian army is too big."

"Not nearly big enough for its main purpose. And, as a side issue, there are certain powerful minorities of fighting folk whose interests an Asiatic Government is bound to consider. Arms is as much a means of livelihood as civil employ under Government and law. And it would be a heavy strain on British bayonets to hold down Sikhs, Jats, Bilochis, Rohillas, Rajputs, Bhils, Dogras, Pahtans, and Gurkbas to abide by the decisions of a numerical majority opposed to their interests. Leave the 'numerical majority' to itself without the British bayonets-a flock of sheep might as reasonably hope to manage a troop of collies."

"This complaint about excessive growth of the army is akin to another contention of the Congress party. They protest against the malversation of the whole of the moneys raised by additional taxes as a Famine Insurance Fund to other purposes. You must be aware that this special Famine Fund has all been spent on frontier roads and defences and strategic railway schemes as a protection against Russia."

"But there was never a special famine fund raised by special taxation and put by as in a box. No sane administrator would dream of such a thing. In a time of prosperity a finance minister, rejoicing in a margin, proposed to annually apply a million and a half to the construction of railways and canals for the protection of districts liable to scarcity, and to the reduction of the annual loans for public works. But times were not always prosperous, and the finance minister had to choose whether be would bang up the insurance scheme for a year or impose fresh taxation. When a farmer hasn't got the little surplus he hoped to have for buying a new wagon and draining a low-lying field corner, you don't accuse him of malversation, if he spends what he has on the necessary work of the rest of his farm."

A clatter of hoofs was heard, and Orde looked up with vexation, but his brow cleared as a horseman halted under the porch.

"Helln, Orde! just looked in to ask if you are coming to polo on Tuesday: we want you badly to help to crumple up the Krab Bokbar team."

Orde explained that he had to go out into the District, and while the visitor complained that though good men wouldn't play, duffers were always keen, and that his side would probalny be beaten, Pagett rose to look at his mount, a red, lathered Biloch mare, with a curious lyre-like incurving of the ears. "Quite a little thoroughbred in all other respects," said the M.P., and Orde presented Mr. Reginald Burke, Manager of the Siad and Sialkote Bank to his friend.

"Yes, she's as good as they make 'em, and she's all the female I possess and spoiled in consequence, aren't you, old girl?" said Burke, patting the mare's glossy neck as she backed and plunged.

"Mr. Pagett," said Orde, "has been asking me about the Congress. What is your opinion?" Burke turned to the M. P. with a frank smile.

"Well, if it's all the same to you, sir, I should say, Damn the Congress, but then I'm no politician, but only a business man."

"You find it a tiresome subject?"

"Yes, it's all that, and worse than that, for this kind of agitation is anything but wholesome for the country."

"How do you mean?"

"It would be a long job to explain, and Sara here won't stand, but you know how sensitive capital is, and how timid investors are. All this sort of rot is likely to frighten them, and we can't afford to frighten them. The passengers aboard an Ocean steamer don't feel reassured when the ship's way is stopped, and they hear the workmen's hammers tinkering at the engines down below. The old

Ark's going on all right as she is, and only wants quiet and room to move. Them's my sentiments, and those of some other people who have to do with money and business."

"Then you are a thick-and-thin supporter of the Government as it is."

"Why, no! The Indian Government is much too timid with its money-like an old maiden aunt of mine-always in a funk about her investments. They don't spend half enough on railways for instance, and they are slow in a general way, and ought to be made to sit up in all that concerns the encouragement of private enterprise, and coaxing out into use the millions of capital that lie dormant in the country."

The mare was dancing with impatience, and Burke was evidently anxious to be off, so the men wished him good-bye.

"Who is your genial friend who condemns both Congress and Government in a breath?" asked Pagett, with an amused smile.

"Just now he is Reggie Burke, keener on polo than on anything else, but if you go to the Sind and Sialkote Bank to-morrow you would find Mr. Reginald Burke a very capable man of business, known and liked by an immense constituency North and South of this."

"Do you think he is right about the Government's want of enterpnse?"

"I should hesitate to say. Better consult the merchants and chambers of commerce in Cawnpore, Madras, Bombay, and Calcutta. But though these bodies would like, as Reggie puts it, to make Government sit up, it is an elementary consideration in governing a country like India, which must be administered for the benefit of the people at large, that the counsels of those who resort to it for the sake of making money should be judiciously weighed and not allowed to overpower the rest. They are welcome guests here, as a matter of course, but it has been found best to restrain their influence. Thus the rights of plantation laborers, factory operatives, and the like, have been protected, and the capitalist, eager to get on, has not always regarded Government action with favor. It is quite conceivable that under an elective system the commercial communities of the great towns might find means to secure majorities on labor questions and on financial matters."

"They would act at least with intelligence and consideration."

"Intelligence, yes; but as to consideration, who at the present moment most bitterly resents the tender solicitude of Lancashire for the welfare and protection of the Indian factory operative? English and native capitalists running cotton mills and factories."

"But is the solicitude of Lancashire in this matter entirely disinterested?"

"It is no business of mine to say. I merely indicate an example of how a powerful commercial interest might hamper a Government intent in the first place on the larger interests of humanity."

Orde broke off to listen a moment. "There's Dr. Lathrop talking to my wife in the drawing-room," said he.

"Surely not; that's a lady's voice, and if my ears don't deceive me, an American."

"Exactly, Dr. Eva McCreery Lathrop, chief of the new Women's Hospital here, and a very good fellow forbye. Good-morning, Doctor," he said, as a graceful figure came out on the veranda, "you seem to be in trouble. I hope Mrs. Orde was able to help you."

"Your wife is real kind and good,] always come to her when I'm in a fix but I fear it's more than comforting I want."

"You work too hard and wear yourself out," said Orde, kindly. "Let me introduce my friend, Mr. Pagett, just fresh from home, and anxious to learn his India. You could tell him something of that more important half of which a mere man knows so little."

"Perhaps I could if I'd any heart to do it, but I'm in trouble, I've lost a case, a case that was doing well, through nothing in the world but inattention on the part of a nurse I had begun to trust. And when I spoke only a small piece of my mind she collapsed in a whining heap on the floor. It is hopeless."

The men were silent, for the blue eyes of the lady doctor were dim. Recovering herself she looked up with a smile, half sad, half humorous, "And I am in a whining heap, too; but what phase of Indian life are you particularly interested in, sir?"

"Mr. Pagett intends to study the political aspect of things and the possibility of bestowing electoral institutions on the people."

"Wouldn't it be as much to the purpose to bestow point-lace collars on them? They need many things more urgently than votes. Why it's like giving a bread-pill for a broken leg."

"Er-I don't quite follow," said Pagett, uneasily.

"Well, what's the matter with this country is not in the least political, but an all round entanglement of physical, social, and moral evils and corruptions, all more or less due to the unnatural treatment of women. You can't gather figs from thistles, and so long as the system of infant marriage, the prohibition of the remarriage of widows, the lifelong imprisonment of wives and mothers in a worse than penal confinement, and the withholding from them of any kind of education or treatment as rational beings continues, the country can't advance a step. Half of it is morally dead, and worse than dead, and that's just the half from which we have a right to look for the best impulses. It's right here where the trouble is, and not in any political considerations whatsoever."

"But do they marry so early?" said Pagett, vaguely.

"The average age is seven, but thousands are married still earlier. One result is that girls of twelve and thirteen have to bear the burden of wifehood and motherhood, and, as might be expected, the rate of mortality both for mothers and children is terrible. Pauperism, domestic unhappiness, and a low state of health are only a few of the consequences of this. Then, when, as frequently happens, the boy-husband dies prematurely, his widow is condemned to worse than death. She may not re-marry, must live a secluded and despised life, a life so unnatural that she sometimes prefers suicide; more often she goes astray. You don't know in England what such words as 'infant-marriage, baby-wife, girl-mother, and virgin-widow' mean; but they mean unspeakable horrors here."

"Well, but the advanced political party here will surely make it their business to advocate social reforms as well as political ones," said Pagett.

"Very surely they will do no such thing," said the lady doctor, emphatically. "I wish I could make you understand. Why, even of the funds devoted to the Marchioness of Dufferin's organization for medical aid to the women of India, it was said in print and in speech, that they would be better spent on more college scholarships for men. And in all the advanced parties' talk-God forgive them—and in all their programmes, they carefully avoid all such subjects. They will talk about the protection of the cow, for that's an ancient superstition—they can all understand that; but the protection of the women is a new and dangerous idea." She turned to Pagett impulsively:

"You are a member of the English Parliament. Can you do nothing? The foundations of their life are rotten-utterly and bestially rotten. I could tell your wife things that I couldn't tell you. I know the life—the inner life that belongs to the native, and I know nothing else; and believe me you might as well try to grow golden-rod in a mushroom-pit as to make anything of a people that are born and reared as these—these things're. The men talk of their rights and privileges. I have seen the women that bear these very men, and again-may God forgive the men!"

Pagett's eyes opened with a large wonder. Dr. Lathrop rose tempestuously.

"I must be off to lecture," said she, "and I'm sorry that I can't show you my hospitals; but you had better believe, sir, that it's more necessary for India than all the elections in creation."

"That's a woman with a mission, and no mistake," said Pagett, after a pause.

"Yes; she believes in her work, and so do I," said Orde. "I've a notion that in the end it will be found that the most helpful work done for India in this generation was wrought by Lady Dufferin in drawing attention-what work that was, by the way, even with her husband's great name to back it to the needs of women here. In effect, native habits and beliefs are an organized conspiracy against the laws of health and happy life—but there is some dawning of hope now."

"How d' you account for the general indifference, then?"

"I suppose it's due in part to their fatalism and their utter indifference to all human suffering. How much do you imagine the great province of the Pun-jab with over twenty million people and half a score rich towns has contributed to the maintenance of civil dispensaries last year? About seven thousand rupees."

"That's seven hundred pounds," said Pagett, quickly.

"I wish it was," replied Orde; "but anyway, it's an absurdly inadequate sum, and shows one of the blank sides of Oriental character."

Pagett was silent for a long time. The question of direct and personal pain did not lie within his researches. He pre ferred to discuss the weightier matters of the law, and contented himself with murmuring: "They'll do better later on." Then, with a rush, returning to his first thought:

"But, my dear Orde, if it's merely a class movement of a local and temporary character, how d' you account for Bradlaugh, who is at least a man of sense taking it up?"

"I know nothing of the champion of the New Brahmins but what I see in the papers. I suppose there is something tempting in being hailed by a large assemblage as the representative of the aspirations of two hundred and fifty millions of people. Such a man looks 'through all the roaring and the wreaths,' and does not reflect that it is a false perspective, which, as a matter of fact, hides the real complex and manifold India from his gaze. He can scarcely be expected to distinguish between the ambitions of a new oligarchy and the real wants of the people of whom he knows nothing. But it's strange that a professed Radical should come to be the chosen advocate of a movement which has for its aim the revival of an ancient tyranny. Shows how even Radicalism can fall into academic grooves and miss the essential truths of its own creed. Believe me, Pagett, to deal with India you want first-hand knowledge and experience. I wish he would come and live here for a couple of years or so."

"Is not this rather an ad hminem style of argument?"

"Can't help it in a case like this. Indeed, I am not sure you ought not to go further and weigh the whole character and quality and upbringing of the man. You must admit that the monumental complacency with which he trotted out his ingenious little Constitution for India showed a strange want of imagination and the sense of humor."

"No, I don't quite admit it," said Pagett.

"Well, you know him and I don't, but that's how it strikes a stranger." He turned on his heel and paced the veranda thoughtfully. "And, after all, the burden of the actual, daily unromantic toil falls on the shoulders of the men out here, and not on his own. He enjoys all the privileges of recommendation without responsibility, and we-well, perhaps, when you've seen a little more of India you'll understand. To begin with, our death rate's five times higher than yours-I speak now for the brutal bureaucrat—and we work on the refuse of worked-out cities and exhausted civilizations, among the bones of the dead."

Pagett laughed. "That's an epigrammatic way of putting it, Orde."

"Is it? Let's see," said the Deputy Commissioner of Amara, striding into the sunshine toward a half-naked gardener potting roses. He took the man's hoe, and went to a rain-scarped bank at the bottom of the garden.

"Come here, Pagett," he said, and cut at the sun-baked soil. After three strokes there rolled from under the blade of the hoe the half of a clanking skeleton that settled at Pagett's feet in an unseemly jumble of bones. The M.P. drew back.

"Our houses are built on cemeteries," said Orde. "There are scores of thousands of graves within ten miles."

Pagett was contemplating the skull with the awed fascination of a man who has but little to do with the dead. "India's a very curious place," said he, after a pause.

"Ah? You'll know all about it in three months. Come in to lunch," said Orde.

FRANCE AT WAR

On the Frontier of Civilization

FRANCE*
BY RUDYARD KIPLING

Broke to every known mischance, lifted over all
By the light sane joy of life, the buckler of the Gaul,
Furious in luxury, merciless in toil,
Terrible with strength that draws from her tireless soil,
Strictest judge of her own worth, gentlest of men's mind,
First to follow truth and last to leave old truths behind—
France beloved of every soul that loves its fellow-kind.

Ere our birth (rememberest thou?) side by side we lay
Fretting in the womb of Rome to begin the fray.
Ere men knew our tongues apart, our one taste was
      known—
Each must mould the other's fate as he wrought his own.
To this end we stirred mankind till all earth was ours,
Till our world-end strifes began wayside thrones and
      powers,
Puppets that we made or broke to bar the other's path—
Necessary, outpost folk, hirelings of our wrath.
To this end we stormed the seas, tack for tack, and burst
Through the doorways of new worlds, doubtful which was
      first.
Hand on hilt (rememberest thou?), ready for the blow.
Sure whatever else we met we should meet our foe.
Spurred or baulked at ev'ry stride by the other's strength,
So we rode the ages down and every ocean's length;
Where did you refrain from us or we refrain from you?
Ask the wave that has not watched war between us two.
Others held us for a while, but with weaker charms,
These we quitted at the call for each other's arms.
Eager toward the known delight, equally we strove,

Each the other's mystery, terror, need, and love.
To each other's open court with our proofs we came,
Where could we find honour else or men to test the claim?
From each other's throat we wrenched valour's last reward,
That extorted word of praise gasped 'twixt lunge and
    guard.
In each other's cup we poured mingled blood and tears,
Brutal joys, unmeasured hopes, intolerable fears,
All that soiled or salted life for a thousand years.
Proved beyond the need of proof, matched in every clime,
O companion, we have lived greatly through all time:
Yoked in knowledge and remorse now we come to rest,
Laughing at old villainies that time has turned to jest,
Pardoning old necessity no pardon can efface—
That undying sin we shared in Rouen market-place.
Now we watch the new years shape, wondering if they
    hold
Fiercer lighting in their hearts than we launched of old.
Now we hear new voices rise, question, boast or gird,
As we raged (rememberest thou?) when our crowds were
    stirred.
Now we count new keels afloat, and new hosts on land,
Massed liked ours (rememberest thou?) when our strokes
    were planned.
We were schooled for dear life sake, to know each other's
    blade:
What can blood and iron make more than we have made?
We have learned by keenest use to know each other's
    mind:
What shall blood and iron loose that we cannot bind?
We who swept each other's coast, sacked each other's
    home,
Since the sword of Brennus clashed on the scales at
    Rome,
Listen, court and close again, wheeling girth to girth,
In the strained and bloodless guard set for peace on earth.

Broke to every known mischance, lifted over all
By the light sane joy of life, the buckler of the Gaul,
Furious in luxury, merciless in toil,

Terrible with strength renewed from a tireless soil,
Strictest judge of her own worth, gentlest of men's mind,
First to follow truth and last to leave old truths behind,
France beloved of every soul that loves or serves its kind.

*First published June 24, 1913.

I

ON THE FRONTIER OF CIVILIZATION

"It's a pretty park," said the French artillery officer. "We've done a lot for it since the owner left. I hope he'll appreciate it when he comes back."

The car traversed a winding drive through woods, between banks embellished with little chalets of a rustic nature. At first, the chalets stood their full height above ground, suggesting tea-gardens in England. Further on they sank into the earth till, at the top of the ascent, only their solid brown roofs showed. Torn branches drooping across the driveway, with here and there a scorched patch of undergrowth, explained the reason of their modesty.

The chateau that commanded these glories of forest and park sat boldly on a terrace. There was nothing wrong with it except, if one looked closely, a few scratches or dints on its white stone walls, or a neatly drilled hole under a flight of steps. One such hole ended in an unexploded shell. "Yes," said the officer. "They arrive here occasionally."

Something bellowed across the folds of the wooded hills; something grunted in reply. Something passed overhead, querulously but not without dignity. Two clear fresh barks joined the chorus, and a man moved lazily in the direction of the guns.

"Well. Suppose we come and look at things a little," said the commanding officer.

AN OBSERVATION POST

There was a specimen tree—a tree worthy of such a park—the sort of tree visitors are always taken to admire. A ladder ran up it to a platform. What little wind there was swayed the tall top, and the ladder creaked like a ship's gangway. A telephone bell tinkled 50 foot overhead. Two invisible guns spoke fervently for half a minute, and broke off like terriers choked on a leash. We climbed till the topmost platform swayed sicklily beneath us. Here one found a rustic shelter, always of the tea-garden pattern, a table, a map, and a little window wreathed with living branches that gave one the first view of the Devil and all his works. It was a stretch of open country, with a few sticks like old tooth-brushes which had once been trees round a farm. The rest was yellow grass, barren to all appearance as the veldt.

"The grass is yellow because they have used gas here," said an officer. "Their trenches are—. You can see for yourself."

The guns in the woods began again. They seemed to have no relation to the regularly spaced bursts of smoke along a little smear in the desert earth two thousand yards away—no connection at all with the strong voices overhead coming and going. It was as impersonal as the drive of the sea along a breakwater.

Thus it went: a pause—a gathering of sound like the race of an incoming wave; then the high-flung heads of breakers spouting white up the face of a groyne. Suddenly, a seventh wave broke and spread the shape of its foam like a plume overtopping all the others.

"That's one of our torpilleurs—what you call trench-sweepers," said the observer among the whispering leaves.

Some one crossed the platform to consult the map with its ranges. A blistering outbreak of white smokes rose a little beyond the large plume. It was as though the tide had struck a reef out yonder.

Then a new voice of tremendous volume lifted itself out of a lull that followed. Somebody laughed. Evidently the voice was known.

"That is not for us," a gunner said. "They are being waked up from—" he named a distant French position. "So and so is attending to them there. We go on with our usual work. Look! Another torpilleur."

"THE BARBARIAN"

Again a big plume rose; and again the lighter shells broke at their appointed distance beyond it. The smoke died away on that stretch of trench, as the foam of a swell dies in the angle of a harbour wall, and broke out afresh half a mile lower down. In its apparent laziness, in its awful deliberation, and its quick spasms of wrath, it was more like the work of waves than of men; and our high platform's gentle sway and glide was exactly the motion of a ship drifting with us toward that shore.

"The usual work. Only the usual work," the officer explained. "Sometimes it is here. Sometimes above or below us. I have been here since May."

A little sunshine flooded the stricken landscape and made its chemical yellow look more foul. A detachment of men moved out on a road which ran toward the French trenches, and then vanished at the foot of a little rise. Other men appeared moving toward us with that concentration of purpose and bearing shown in both Armies when—dinner is at hand. They looked like people who had been digging hard.

"The same work. Always the same work!" the officer said. "And you could walk from here to the sea or to Switzerland in that ditch—and you'll find the same work going on everywhere. It isn't war."

"It's better than that," said another. "It's the eating-up of a people. They come and they fill the trenches and they die, and they die; and they send more and *those* die. We do the same, of course, but—look!"

He pointed to the large deliberate smoke-heads renewing themselves along that yellowed beach. "That is the frontier of civilization. They have all civilization against them—those brutes yonder. It's not the local victories of the old wars that we're after. It's the barbarian—all the barbarian. Now, you've seen the whole thing in little. Come and look at our children."

SOLDIERS IN CAVES

We left that tall tree whose fruits are death ripened and distributed at the tingle of small bells. The observer returned to his maps and calculations; the telephone-boy stiffened up beside his exchange as the amateurs went out of his life. Some one called down through the branches to ask who was attending to—Belial, let us say, for I could not catch the gun's name. It seemed to belong to that terrific new voice which had lifted itself for the second or third time. It appeared from the reply that if Belial talked too long he would be dealt with from another point miles away.

The troops we came down to see were at rest in a chain of caves which had begun life as quarries and had been fitted up by the army for its own uses. There were underground corridors, ante-chambers, rotundas, and ventilating shafts with a bewildering play of cross lights, so that wherever you looked you saw Goya's pictures of men-at-arms.

Every soldier has some of the old maid in him, and rejoices in all the gadgets and devices of his own invention. Death and wounding come by nature, but to lie dry, sleep soft, and keep yourself clean by forethought and contrivance is art, and in all things the Frenchman is gloriously an artist.

Moreover, the French officers seem as mother-keen on their men as their men are brother-fond of them. Maybe the possessive form of address: "Mon general," "mon capitaine," helps the idea, which our men cloke in other and curter phrases. And those soldiers, like ours, had been welded for months in one furnace. As an officer said: "Half our orders now need not be given. Experience makes us think together." I believe, too, that if a French private has an idea—and they are full of ideas—it reaches his C. 0. quicker than it does with us.

THE SENTINEL HOUNDS

The overwhelming impression was the brilliant health and vitality of these men and the quality of their breeding. They bore themselves with swing and rampant delight in life, while their voices as they talked in the side-caverns among the stands of arms were the controlled voices of civilization. Yet, as the lights pierced the gloom they looked like bandits dividing the spoil. One picture, though far from war, stays with me. A perfectly built, dark-skinned young giant had peeled himself out of his blue coat and had brought it down with a swish upon the shoulder of a half-stripped comrade who was kneeling at his feet with some footgear. They stood against a background of semi-luminous blue haze, through which glimmered a pile of coppery straw half covered by a red blanket. By divine accident of light and pose it St. Martin giving his cloak to the beggar. There were scores of pictures in these galleries—notably a rock-hewn chapel where the red of the cross on the rough canvas altar-cloth glowed like a ruby. Further inside the caves we found a row of little rock-cut kennels, each inhabited by one wise, silent dog. Their duties begin in at night with the sentinels and listening-posts. "And believe me," a proud instructor, "my fellow here knows the difference between the noise of our shells and the Boche shells."

When we came out into the open again there were good opportunities for this study. Voices and wings met and passed in the air, and, perhaps, one strong young tree had not been bending quite so far across the picturesque park-drive when we first went that way.

"Oh, yes," said an officer, "shells have to fall somewhere, and," he added with fine toleration, "it is, after all, against us that the Boche directs them. But come you and look at my dug-out. It's the most superior of all possible dug-outs."

"No. Come and look at our mess. It's the Ritz of these parts." And they joyously told how they had got, or procured, the various fittings and elegancies, while hands stretched out of the gloom to shake, and men nodded welcome and greeting all through that cheery brotherhood in the woods.

WORK IN THE FIELDS

The voices and the wings were still busy after lunch, when the car slipped past the tea-houses in the drive, and came into a country where women and children worked among the crops. There were large raw shell holes by the wayside or in the midst of fields, and often a cottage or a villa had been smashed as a bonnet-box is smashed by an umbrella. That must be part of Belial's work when he bellows so truculently among the hills to the north.

We were looking for a town that lives under shell-fire. The regular road to it was reported unhealthy—not that the women and children seemed to care. We took byways of which certain exposed heights and corners were lightly blinded by wind-brakes of dried tree-tops. Here the shell holes were rather thick on the ground. But the women and the children and the old men went on with their work with the cattle and the crops; and where a house had been broken by shells the rubbish was collected in a neat pile, and where a room or two still remained usable, it was inhabited, and the tattered window-curtains fluttered as proudly as any flag. And time was when I used to denounce young France because it tried to kill itself beneath my car wheels; and the fat old women who crossed roads without warning; and the specially deaf old men who slept in carts on the wrong side of the road! Now, I could take off my hat to every single soul of them, but that one cannot traverse a whole land bareheaded. The nearer we came to our town the fewer were the people, till at last we halted in a well-built suburb of paved streets where there was no life at all . . .

A WRECKED TOWN

The stillness was as terrible as the spread of the quick busy weeds between the paving-stones; the air smelt of pounded mortar and crushed stone; the sound of a footfall echoed like the drop of a pebble in a well. At first the horror of wrecked apartment-houses and big shops laid open makes one waste energy in anger. It is not seemly that rooms should be torn out of the sides of buildings as one tears the soft heart out of English bread; that villa roofs should lie across iron gates of private garages, or that drawing-room doors should flap alone and disconnected between two emptinesses of twisted girders. The eye wearies of the repeated pattern that burst shells make on stone walls, as the mouth sickens of the taste of mortar and charred timber. One quarter of the place had been shelled nearly level; the facades of the houses stood doorless, roofless, and windowless like stage scenery. This was near the cathedral, which is always a favourite mark for the heathen. They had gashed and ripped the sides of the cathedral itself, so that the birds flew in and out at will; they had smashed holes in the roof; knocked huge cantles out of the buttresses, and pitted and starred the paved square outside. They were at work, too, that very afternoon, though I do not think the cathedral was their objective for the moment. We walked to and fro in the silence of the streets and beneath the whirring wings overhead. Presently, a young woman, keeping to the wall, crossed a corner. An old woman opened a shutter (how it jarred!), and spoke to her. The silence closed again, but it seemed to me that I heard a sound of singing— the sort of chant one hears in nightmare-cities of voices crying from underground.

IN THE CATHEDRAL

"Nonsense," said an officer. "Who should be singing here?" We circled the cathedral again, and saw what pavement-stones can do against their own city, when the shell jerks them upward. But there *was* singing after all—on the other side of a little door in the flank of the cathedral. We looked in, doubting, and saw at least a hundred folk, mostly women, who knelt before the altar of an unwrecked chapel. We withdrew quietly from that holy ground, and it was not only the eyes of the French officers that filled with tears. Then there came an old, old thing with a prayer-book in her hand, pattering across the square, evidently late for service.

"And who are those women?" I asked.

"Some are caretakers; people who have still little shops here. (There is one quarter where you can buy things.) There are many old people, too, who will not go away. They are of the place, you see."

"And this bombardment happens often?" I said.

"It happens always. Would you like to look at the railway station? Of course, it has not been so bombarded as the cathedral."

We went through the gross nakedness of streets without people, till we reached the railway station, which was very fairly knocked about, but, as my friends said, nothing like as much as the cathedral. Then we had to cross the end of a long street down which the Boche could see clearly. As one glanced up it, one perceived how the weeds, to whom men's war is the truce of God, had come back and were well established the whole length of it, watched by the long perspective of open, empty windows.

II

THE NATION'S SPIRIT AND
A NEW INHERITANCE

We left that stricken but undefeated town, dodged a few miles
down the roads beside which the women tended their cows, and
dropped into a place on a hill where a Moroccan regiment of many
experiences was in billets.

They were Mohammedans bafflingly like half a dozen of
our Indian frontier types, though they spoke no accessible tongue.
They had, of course, turned the farm buildings where they lay into
a little bit of Africa in colour and smell. They had been gassed in
the north; shot over and shot down, and set up to be shelled again;
and their officers talked of North African wars that we had never
heard of—sultry days against long odds in the desert years ago.
"Afterward—is it not so with you also?—we get our best recruits
from the tribes we have fought. These men are children. They make
no trouble. They only want to go where cartridges are burnt. They
are of the few races to whom fighting is a pleasure."

"And how long have you dealt with them?"

"A long time—a long time. I helped to organize the corps. I
am one of those whose heart is in Africa." He spoke slowly, almost
feeling for his French words, and gave some order. I shall not forget
his eyes as he turned to a huge, brown, Afreedee-like Mussulman
hunkering down beside his accoutrements. He had two sides to his
head, that bearded, burned, slow-spoken officer, met and parted
with in an hour.

The day closed—(after an amazing interlude in the chateau
of a dream, which was all glassy ponds, stately trees, and vistas of
white and gold saloons. The proprietor was somebody's chauffeur

at the front, and we drank to his excellent health)—at a little village in a twilight full of the petrol of many cars and the wholesome flavour of healthy troops. There is no better guide to camp than one's own thoughtful nose; and though I poked mine everywhere, in no place then or later did it strike that vile betraying taint of underfed, unclean men. And the same with the horses.

THE LINE THAT NEVER SLEEPS

It is difficult to keep an edge after hours of fresh air and experiences; so one does not get the most from the most interesting part of the day—the dinner with the local headquarters. Here the professionals meet—the Line, the Gunners, the Intelligence with stupefying photo-plans of the enemy's trenches; the Supply; the Staff, who collect and note all things, and are very properly chaffed; and, be sure, the Interpreter, who, by force of questioning prisoners, naturally develops into a Sadducee. It is their little asides to each other, the slang, and the half-words which, if one understood, instead of blinking drowsily at one's plate, would give the day's history in little. But tire and the difficulties of a sister (not a foreign) tongue cloud everything, and one goes to billets amid a murmur of voices, the rush of single cars through the night, the passage of battalions, and behind it all, the echo of the deep voices calling one to the other, along the line that never sleeps.

* * * * *

The ridge with the scattered pines might have hidden children at play. Certainly a horse would have been quite visible, but there was no hint of guns, except a semaphore which announced it was forbidden to pass that way, as the battery was firing. The Boches must have looked for that battery, too. The ground was pitted with shell holes of all calibres—some of them as fresh as mole-casts in the misty damp morning; others where the poppies had grown from seed to flower all through the summer.

"And where are the guns?" I demanded at last.

They were almost under one's hand, their ammunition in cellars and dug-outs beside them. As far as one can make out, the 75 gun has no pet name. The bayonet is Rosalie the virgin of Bayonne, but the 75, the watchful nurse of the trenches and little sister of the Line, seems to be always "soixante-quinze." Even those who love her best do not insist that she is beautiful. Her merits are French—logic, directness, simplicity, and the supreme gift of "occasionality." She is equal to everything on the spur of the moment. One sees and studies the few appliances which make her do what she does, and one feels that any one could have invented her.

FAMOUS FRENCH 75's

"As a matter of fact," says a commandant, "anybody—or, rather, everybody did. The general idea is after such-and-such system, the patent of which had expired, and we improved it; the breech action, with slight modification, is somebody else's; the sighting is perhaps a little special; and so is the traversing, but, at bottom, it is only an assembly of variations and arrangements."

That, of course, is all that Shakespeare ever got out of the alphabet. The French Artillery make their own guns as he made his plays. It is just as simple as that.

"There is nothing going on for the moment; it's too misty," said the Commandant. (I fancy that the Boche, being, as a rule methodical, amateurs are introduced to batteries in the Boche's intervals. At least, there are hours healthy and unhealthy which vary with each position.) "But," the Commandant reflected a moment, "there is a place—and a distance. Let us say . . ." He gave a range.

The gun-servers stood back with the bored contempt of the professional for the layman who intrudes on his mysteries. Other civilians had come that way before—had seen, and grinned, and complimented and gone their way, leaving the gunners high up on the bleak hillside to grill or mildew or freeze for weeks and months. Then she spoke. Her voice was higher pitched, it seemed, than ours—with a more shrewish tang to the speeding shell. Her recoil was as swift and as graceful as the shrug of a French-woman's shoulders; the empty case leaped forth and clanged against the trail; the tops of two or three pines fifty yards away nodded knowingly to each other, though there was no wind.

"They'll be bothered down below to know the meaning of our single shot. We don't give them one dose at a time as a rule," somebody laughed.

We waited in the fragrant silence. Nothing came back from the mist that clogged the lower grounds, though no shell of this war was ever launched with more earnest prayers that it might do hurt.

Then they talked about the lives of guns; what number of rounds some will stand and others will not; how soon one can make two good guns out of three spoilt ones, and what crazy luck sometimes goes with a single shot or a blind salvo.

LESSON FROM THE "BOCHE"

A shell must fall somewhere, and by the law of averages occasionally lights straight as a homing pigeon on the one spot where it can wreck most. Then earth opens for yards around, and men must be dug out,—some merely breathless, who shake their ears, swear, and carry on, and others whose souls have gone loose among terrors. These have to be dealt with as their psychology demands, and the French officer is a good psychologist. One of them said: "Our national psychology has changed. I do not recognize it myself."

"What made the change?"

"The Boche. If he had been quiet for another twenty years the world must have been his—rotten, but all his. Now he is saving the world."

"How?"

"Because he has shown us what Evil is. We—you and I, England and the rest—had begun to doubt the existence of Evil. The Boche is saving us."

Then we had another look at the animal in its trench—a little nearer this time than before, and quieter on account of the mist. Pick up the chain anywhere you please, you shall find the same observation-post, table, map, observer, and telephonist; the same always-hidden, always-ready guns; and same vexed foreshore of trenches, smoking and shaking from Switzerland to the sea. The handling of the war varies with the nature of the country, but the tools are unaltered. One looks upon them at last with the same weariness of wonder as the eye receives from endless repetitions of Egyptian hieroglyphics. A long, low profile, with a lump to one side, means the field-gun and its attendant ammunition-case; a circle and slot stand for an observation-post; the trench is a bent line, studded with vertical plumes of explosion; the great guns of position, coming and going on their motors, repeat themselves as scarabs; and man himself is a small blue smudge, no larger than a foresight, crawling and creeping or watching and running among all these terrific symbols.

TRAGEDY OF RHEIMS

But there is no hieroglyphic for Rheims, no blunting of the mind at the abominations committed on the cathedral there. The thing peers upward, maimed and blinded, from out of the utter wreckage of the Archbishop's palace on the one side and dust-heaps of crumbled houses on the other. They shelled, as they still shell it, with high explosives and with incendiary shells, so that the statues and the stonework in places are burned the colour of raw flesh. The gargoyles are smashed; statues, crockets, and spires tumbled; walls split and torn; windows thrust out and tracery obliterated. Wherever one looks at the tortured pile there is mutilation and defilement, and yet it had never more of a soul than it has to-day.

Inside—("Cover yourselves, gentlemen," said the sacristan, "this place is no longer consecrated")—everything is swept clear or burned out from end to end, except two candlesticks in front of the niche where Joan of Arc's image used to stand. There is a French flag there now. [And the last time I saw Rheims Cathedral was in a spring twilight, when the great west window glowed, and the only lights within were those of candles which some penitent English had lit in Joan's honour on those same candlesticks.] The high altar was covered with floor-carpets; the pavement tiles were cracked and jarred out by the rubbish that had fallen from above, the floor was gritty with dust of glass and powdered stone, little twists of leading from the windows, and iron fragments. Two great doors had been blown inwards by the blast of a shell in the Archbishop's garden, till they had bent grotesquely to the curve of a cask. There they had jammed. The windows—but the record has been made, and will be kept by better hands than mine. It will last through the generation in which the Teuton is cut off from the fellowship of mankind—all the long, still years when this war of the body is at an end, and the real war begins. Rheims is but one of the altars which the heathen have put up to commemorate their own death throughout all the world. It will serve. There is a mark, well known by now, which they have left for a visible seal of their doom. When they first set the place alight some hundreds of their wounded were being tended in the Cathedral. The French saved as many as they could, but some had to be left. Among them was a major, who lay with his back against a pillar. It has been ordained that the signs of his torments should remain—an outline of both legs and half a body, printed in greasy black upon the stones. There are very many people who hope and pray that the sign will be respected at least by our children's children.

IRON NERVE AND FAITH

And, in the meantime, Rheims goes about what business it may have with that iron nerve and endurance and faith which is the new inheritance of France. There is agony enough when the big shells come in; there is pain and terror among the people; and always fresh desecration to watch and suffer. The old men and the women and the children drink of that cup daily, and yet the bitterness does not enter into their souls. Mere words of admiration are impertinent, but the exquisite quality of the French soul has been the marvel to me throughout. They say themselves, when they talk: "We did not know what our nation was. Frankly, we did not expect it ourselves. But the thing came, and—you see, we go on."

Or as a woman put it more logically, "What else can we do? Remember, *we* knew the Boche in '70 when *you* did not. We know what he has done in the last year. This is not war. It is against wild beasts that we fight. There is no arrangement possible with wild beasts." This is the one vital point which we in England *must* realize. We are dealing with animals who have scientifically and philosophically removed themselves inconceivably outside civilization. When you have heard a few—only a few—tales of their doings, you begin to understand a little. When you have seen Rheims, you understand a little more. When you have looked long enough at the faces of the women, you are inclined to think that the women will have a large say in the final judgment. They have earned it a thousand times.

III

BATTLE SPECTACLE AND A REVIEW

Travelling with two chauffeurs is not the luxury it looks; since there is only one of you and there is always another of those iron men to relieve the wheel. Nor can I decide whether an ex-professor of the German tongue, or an ex-roadracer who has lived six years abroad, or a Marechal des Logis, or a Brigadier makes the most thrusting driver through three-mile stretches of military traffic repeated at half-hour intervals. Sometimes it was motor-ambulances strung all along a level; or supply; or those eternal big guns coming round corners with trees chained on their long backs to puzzle aeroplanes, and their leafy, big-shell limbers snorting behind them. In the rare breathing-spaces men with rollers and road metal attacked the road. In peace the roads of France, thanks to the motor, were none too good. In war they stand the incessant traffic far better than they did with the tourist. My impression—after some seven hundred miles printed off on me at between 60 and 70 kilometres—was of uniform excellence. Nor did I come upon any smashes or breakdowns in that distance, and they were certainly trying them hard. Nor, which is the greater marvel, did *we* kill anybody; though we did miracles down the streets to avoid babes, kittens, and chickens. The land is used to every detail of war, and to its grime and horror and make-shifts, but also to war's unbounded courtesy, kindness, and long-suffering, and the gaiety that comes, thank God, to balance overwhelming material loss.

FARM LIFE AMIDST WAR

There was a village that had been stamped flat, till it looked older than Pompeii. There were not three roofs left, nor one whole house. In most places you saw straight into the cellars. The hops were ripe in the grave-dotted fields round about. They had been brought in and piled in the nearest outline of a dwelling. Women sat on chairs on the pavement, picking the good-smelling bundles. When they had finished one, they reached back and pulled out another through the window-hole behind them, talking and laughing the while. A cart had to be maneuvered out of what had been a farmyard, to take the hops to market. A thick, broad, fair-haired wench, of the sort that Millet drew, flung all her weight on a spoke and brought the cart forward into the street. Then she shook herself, and, hands on hips, danced a little defiant jig in her sabots as she went back to get the horse. Another girl came across a bridge. She was precisely of the opposite type, slender, creamy-skinned, and delicate-featured. She carried a brand-new broom over her shoulder through that desolation, and bore herself with the pride and grace of Queen Iseult.

The farm-girl came out leading the horse, and as the two young things passed they nodded and smiled at each other, with the delicate tangle of the hop-vines at their feet.

The guns spoke earnestly in the north. That was the Argonne, where the Crown Prince was busily getting rid of a few thousands of his father's faithful subjects in order to secure himself the reversion of his father's throne. No man likes losing his job, and when at long last the inner history of this war comes to be written, we may find that the people we mistook for principals and prime agents were only average incompetents moving all Hell to avoid dismissal. (For it is absolutely true that when a man sells his soul to the devil he does it for the price of half nothing.)

WATCHING THE GUN-FIRE

It must have been a hot fight. A village, wrecked as is usual along this line, opened on it from a hillside that overlooked an Italian landscape of carefully drawn hills studded with small villages—a plain with a road and a river in the foreground, and an all-revealing afternoon light upon everything. The hills smoked and shook and bellowed. An observation-balloon climbed up to see; while an aeroplane which had nothing to do with the strife, but was merely training a beginner, ducked and swooped on the edge of the plain. Two rose-pink pillars of crumbled masonry, guarding some carefully trimmed evergreens on a lawn half buried in rubbish, represented an hotel where the Crown Prince had once stayed. All up the hillside to our right the foundations of houses lay out, like a bit of tripe, with the sunshine in their square hollows. Suddenly a band began to play up the hill among some trees; and an officer of local Guards in the new steel anti-shrapnel helmet, which is like the seventeenth century sallet, suggested that we should climb and get a better view. He was a kindly man, and in speaking English had discovered (as I do when speaking French) that it is simpler to stick to one gender. His choice was the feminine, and the Boche described as "she" throughout made me think better of myself, which is the essence of friendship. We climbed a flight of old stone steps, for generations the playground of little children, and found a ruined church, and a battalion in billets, recreating themselves with excellent music and a little horseplay on the outer edge of the crowd. The trouble in the hills was none of their business for that day.

Still higher up, on a narrow path among the trees, stood a priest and three or four officers. They watched the battle and claimed the great bursts of smoke for one side or the other, at the same time as they kept an eye on the flickering aeroplane. "Ours," they said, half under their breath. "Theirs." "No, not ours that one—theirs! . . . That fool is banking too steep . . . That's Boche shrapnel. They always burst it high. That's our big gun behind that outer hill . . . He'll drop his machine in the street if he doesn't take care . . . There goes a trench-sweeper. Those last two were theirs, but *that*"—it was a full roar—"was ours."

BEHIND THE GERMAN LINES

The valley held and increased the sounds till they seemed to hit our hillside like a sea.

A change of light showed a village, exquisitely pencilled atop of a hill, with reddish haze at its feet.

"What is that place?" I asked.

The priest replied in a voice as deep as an organ: "That is Saint—It is in the Boche lines. Its condition is pitiable."

The thunders and the smokes rolled up and diminished and renewed themselves, but the small children romped up and down the old stone steps; the beginner's aeroplane unsteadily chased its own shadow over the fields; and the soldiers in billet asked the band for their favourite tunes.

Said the lieutenant of local Guards as the cars went on: "She—play—Tipperary."

And she did—to an accompaniment of heavy pieces in the hills, which followed us into a town all ringed with enormous searchlights, French and Boche together, scowling at each other beneath the stars.

* * * * *

It happened about that time that Lord Kitchener with General Joffre reviewed a French Army Corps.

We came on it in a vast dip of ground under grey clouds, as one comes suddenly on water; for it lay out in misty blue lakes of men mixed with darker patches, like osiers and undergrowth, of guns, horses, and wagons. A straight road cut the landscape in two along its murmuring front.

VETERANS OF THE WAR

It was as though Cadmus had sown the dragon's teeth, not in orderly furrows but broadcast, till, horrified by what arose, he had emptied out the whole bag and fled. But these were no new warriors. The record of their mere pitched battles would have satiated a Napoleon. Their regiments and batteries had learnt to achieve the impossible as a matter of routine, and in twelve months they had scarcely for a week lost direct contact with death. We went down the line and looked into the eyes of those men with the used bayonets and rifles; the packs that could almost stow themselves on the shoulders that would be strange without them; at the splashed guns on their repaired wheels, and the easy-working limbers. One could feel the strength and power of the mass as one feels the flush of heat from off a sunbaked wall. When the Generals' cars arrived there, there was no loud word or galloping about. The lakes of men gathered into straight-edged battalions; the batteries aligned a little; a squadron reined back or spurred up; but it was all as swiftly smooth as the certainty with which a man used to the pistol draws and levels it at the required moment. A few peasant women saw the Generals alight. The aeroplanes, which had been skimming low as swallows along the front of the line (theirs must have been a superb view) ascended leisurely, and "waited on" like hawks. Then followed the inspection, and one saw the two figures, tall and short, growing smaller side by side along the white road, till far off among the cavalry they entered their cars again, and moved along the horizon to another rise of grey-green plain.

"The army will move across where you are standing. Get to a flank," some one said.

AN ARMY IN MOTION

We were no more than well clear of that immobile host when it all surged forward, headed by massed bands playing a tune that sounded like the very pulse of France.

The two Generals, with their Staff, and the French Minister for War, were on foot near a patch of very green lucerne. They made about twenty figures in all. The cars were little grey blocks against the grey skyline. There was nothing else in all that great plain except the army; no sound but the changing notes of the aeroplanes and the blunted impression, rather than noise, of feet of men on soft ground. They came over a slight ridge, so that one saw the curve of it first furred, then grassed, with the tips of bayonets, which immediately grew to full height, and then, beneath them, poured the wonderful infantry. The speed, the thrust, the drive of that broad blue mass was like a tide-race up an arm of the sea; and how such speed could go with such weight, and how such weight could be in itself so absolutely under control, filled one with terror. All the while, the band, on a far headland, was telling them and telling them (as if they did not know!) of the passion and gaiety and high heart of their own land in the speech that only they could fully understand. (To hear the music of a country is like hearing a woman think aloud.)

"What *is* the tune?" I asked of an officer beside me.

"My faith, I can't recall for the moment. I've marched to it often enough, though. 'Sambre-et-Meuse,' perhaps. Look! There goes my battalion! Those Chasseurs yonder."

He knew, of course; but what could a stranger identify in that earth-shaking passage of thirty thousand?

ARTILLERY AND CAVALRY

The note behind the ridge changed to something deeper.

"Ah! Our guns," said an artillery officer, and smiled tolerantly on the last blue waves of the Line already beating toward the horizon.

They came twelve abreast—one hundred and fifty guns free for the moment to take the air in company, behind their teams. And next week would see them, hidden singly or in lurking confederacies, by mountain and marsh and forest, or the wrecked habitations of men—where?

The big guns followed them, with that long-nosed air of detachment peculiar to the breed. The Gunner at my side made no comment. He was content to let his Arm speak for itself, but when one big gun in a sticky place fell out of alignment for an instant I saw his eyebrows contract. The artillery passed on with the same inhuman speed and silence as the Line; and the Cavalry's shattering trumpets closed it all.

They are like our Cavalry in that their horses are in high condition, and they talk hopefully of getting past the barbed wire one of these days and coming into their own. Meantime, they are employed on "various work as requisite," and they all sympathize with our rough-rider of Dragoons who flatly refused to take off his spurs in the trenches. If he had to die as a damned infantryman, he wasn't going to be buried as such. A troop-horse of a flanking squadron decided that he had had enough of war, and jibbed like Lot's wife. His rider (we all watched him) ranged about till he found a stick, which he used, but without effect. Then he got off and led the horse, which was evidently what the brute wanted, for when the man remounted the jibbing began again. The last we saw of him was one immensely lonely figure leading one bad but happy horse across an absolutely empty world. Think of his reception—the sole man of 40,000 who had fallen out!

THE BOCHE AS MR. SMITH

The Commander of that Army Corps came up to salute. The cars went away with the Generals and the Minister for War; the Army passed out of sight over the ridges to the north; the peasant women stooped again to their work in the fields, and wet mist shut down on all the plain; but one tingled with the electricity that had passed. Now one knows what the solidarity of civilization means. Later on the civilized nations will know more, and will wonder and laugh together at their old blindness. When Lord Kitchener went down the line, before the march past, they say that he stopped to speak to a General who had been Marchand's Chief of Staff at the time of Fashoda. And Fashoda was one of several cases when civilization was very nearly maneuvered into fighting with itself "for the King of Prussia," as the saying goes. The all-embracing vileness of the Boche is best realized from French soil, where they have had large experience of it. "And yet," as some one observed, "we ought to have known that a race who have brought anonymous letter-writing to its highest pitch in their own dirty Court affairs would certainly use the same methods in their foreign politics. *Why* didn't we realize?"

"For the same reason," another responded, "that society did not realize that the late Mr. Smith, of your England, who married three wives, bought baths in advance for each of them, and, when they had left him all their money, drowned them one by one."

"And were the baths by any chance called Denmark, Austria, and France in 1870?" a third asked.

"No, they were respectable British tubs. But until Mr. Smith had drowned his third wife people didn't get suspicious. They argued that 'men don't do such things.' That sentiment is the criminal's best protection."

IV

THE SPIRIT OF THE PEOPLE

We passed into the zone of another army and a hillier country, where the border villages lay more sheltered. Here and there a town and the fields round it gave us a glimpse of the furious industry with which France makes and handles material and troops. With her, as with us, the wounded officer of experience goes back to the drill-ground to train the new levies. But it was always the little crowded, defiant villages, and the civil population waiting unweariedly and cheerfully on the unwearied, cheerful army, that went closest to the heart. Take these pictures, caught almost anywhere during a journey: A knot of little children in difficulties with the village water-tap or high-handled pump. A soldier, bearded and fatherly, or young and slim and therefore rather shy of the big girls' chaff, comes forward and lifts the pail or swings the handle. His reward, from the smallest babe swung high in air, or, if he is an older man, pressed against his knees, is a kiss. Then nobody laughs.

Or a fat old lady making oration against some wicked young soldiers who, she says, know what has happened to a certain bottle of wine. "And I meant it for all—yes, for all of you—this evening, instead of the thieves who stole it. Yes, I tell you—stole it!" The whole street hears her; so does the officer, who pretends not to, and the amused half-battalion up the road. The young men express penitence; she growls like a thunderstorm, but, softening at last, cuffs and drives them affectionately before her. They are all one family.

Or a girl at work with horses in a ploughed field that is dotted with graves. The machine must avoid each sacred plot. So, hands on the plough-stilts, her hair flying forward, she shouts and wrenches till her little brother runs up and swings the team out of the furrow. Every aspect and detail of life in France seems overlaid with a smooth patina of long-continued war—everything except the spirit of the people, and that is as fresh and glorious as the sight of their own land in sunshine.

A CITY AND WOMAN

We found a city among hills which knew itself to be a prize greatly coveted by the Kaiser. For, truly, it was a pleasant, a desirable, and an insolent city. Its streets were full of life; it boasted an establishment almost as big as Harrod's and full of buyers, and its women dressed and shod themselves with care and grace, as befits ladies who, at any time, may be ripped into rags by bombs from aeroplanes. And there was another city whose population seemed to be all soldiers in training; and yet another given up to big guns and ammunition—an extraordinary sight.

After that, we came to a little town of pale stone which an Army had made its headquarters. It looked like a plain woman who had fainted in public. It had rejoiced in many public institutions that were turned into hospitals and offices; the wounded limped its wide, dusty streets, detachments of Infantry went through it swiftly; and utterly bored motor-lorries cruised up and down roaring, I suppose, for something to look at or to talk to. In the centre of it I found one Janny, or rather his marble bust, brooding over a minute iron-railed garden of half-dried asters opposite a shut-up school, which it appeared from the inscription Janny had founded somewhere in the arid Thirties. It was precisely the sort of school that Janny, by the look of him, would have invented. Not even French adaptability could make anything of it. So Janny had his school, with a faint perfume of varnish, all to himself in a hot stillness of used-up air and little whirls of dust. And because that town seemed so barren, I met there a French General whom I would have gone very far to have encountered. He, like the others, had created and tempered an army for certain work in a certain place, and its hand had been heavy on the Boche. We talked of what the French woman was, and had done, and was doing, and extolled her for her goodness and her faith and her splendid courage. When we parted, I went back and made my profoundest apologies to Janny, who must have had a mother. The pale, overwhelmed town did not now any longer resemble a woman who had fainted, but one who must endure in public all manner of private woe and still, with hands that never cease working, keeps her soul and is cleanly strong for herself and for her men.

FRENCH OFFICERS

The guns began to speak again among the hills that we dived into; the air grew chillier as we climbed; forest and wet rocks closed round us in the mist, to the sound of waters trickling alongside; there was a tang of wet fern, cut pine, and the first breath of autumn when the road entered a tunnel and a new world—Alsace.

Said the Governor of those parts thoughtfully: "The main thing was to get those factory chimneys smoking again." (They were doing so in little flats and villages all along.) "You won't see any girls, because they're at work in the textile factories. Yes, it isn't a bad country for summer hotels, but I'm afraid it won't do for winter sports. We've only a metre of snow, and it doesn't lie, except when you are hauling guns up mountains. Then, of course, it drifts and freezes like Davos. That's our new railway below there. Pity it's too misty to see the view."

But for his medals, there was nothing in the Governor to show that he was not English. He might have come straight from an Indian frontier command.

One notices this approximation of type in the higher ranks, and many of the juniors are cut out of the very same cloth as ours. They get whatever fun may be going: their performances are as incredible and outrageous as the language in which they describe them afterward is bald, but convincing, and—I overheard the tail-end of a yarn told by a child of twenty to some other babes. It was veiled in the obscurity of the French tongue, and the points were lost in shouts of laughter—but I imagine the subaltern among his equals displays just as much reverence for his elders and betters as our own boys do. The epilogue, at least, was as old as both Armies:

"And what did he say then?"

"Oh, the usual thing. He held his breath till I thought he'd burst. Then he damned me in heaps, and I took good care to keep out of his sight till next day."

But officially and in the high social atmosphere of Headquarters their manners and their meekness are of the most admirable. There they attend devoutly on the wisdom of their seniors, who treat them, so it seemed, with affectionate confidence.

FRONT THAT NEVER SLEEPS

When the day's reports are in, all along the front, there is a man, expert in the meaning of things, who boils them down for that cold official digest which tells us that "There was the usual grenade fighting at—. We made appreciable advance at—," &c. The original material comes in sheaves and sheaves, where individual character and temperament have full and amusing play. It is reduced for domestic consumption like an overwhelming electric current. Otherwise we could not take it in. But at closer range one realizes that the Front never sleeps; never ceases from trying new ideas and weapons which, so soon as the Boche thinks he has mastered them, are discarded for newer annoyances and bewilderments.

"The Boche is above all things observant and imitative," said one who counted quite a few Boches dead on the front of his sector. "When you present him with a new idea, he thinks it over for a day or two. Then he presents his riposte."

"Yes, my General. That was exactly what he did to me when I—did so and so. He was quite silent for a day. Then—he stole my patent."

"And you?"

"I had a notion that he'd do that, so I had changed the specification."

Thus spoke the Staff, and so it is among the junior commands, down to the semi-isolated posts where boy-Napoleons live on their own, through unbelievable adventures. They are inventive young devils, these veterans of 21, possessed of the single ideal—to kill—which they follow with men as single-minded as themselves. Battlefield tactics do not exist; when a whole nation goes to ground there can be none of the "victories" of the old bookish days. But there is always the killing—the well-schemed smashing of a full

trench, the rushing out and the mowing down of its occupants;
the unsuspicious battalion far in the rear, located after two nights'
extreme risk alone among rubbish of masonry, and wiped out as it
eats or washes itself; and, more rarely, the body to body encounter
with animals removed from the protection of their machinery,
when the bayonets get their chance. The Boche does not at all like
meeting men whose womenfolk he has dishonoured or mutilated,
or used as a protection against bullets. It is not that these men are
angry or violent. They do not waste time in that way. They kill
him.

THE BUSINESS OF WAR

The French are less reticent than we about atrocities committed
by the Boche, because those atrocities form part of their lives.
They are not tucked away in reports of Commissions, and vaguely
referred to as "too awful." Later on, perhaps, we shall be unreserved
in our turn. But they do not talk of them with any babbling heat
or bleat or make funny little appeals to a "public opinion" that,
like the Boche, has gone underground. It occurs to me that this must
be because every Frenchman has his place and his chance, direct or
indirect, to diminish the number of Boches still alive. Whether he lies
out in a sandwich of damp earth, or sweats the big guns up the crests
behind the trees, or brings the fat, loaded barges into the very heart
of the city, where the shell-wagons wait, or spends his last crippled
years at the harvest, he is doing his work to that end.

If he is a civilian he may—as he does—say things about his
Government, which, after all, is very like other popular governments.
(A lifetime spent in watching how the cat jumps does not make
lion-tamers.) But there is very little human rubbish knocking about
France to hinder work or darken counsel. Above all, there is a thing
called the Honour of Civilization, to which France is attached. The
meanest man feels that he, in his place, is permitted to help uphold
it, and, I think, bears himself, therefore, with new dignity.

A CONTRAST IN TYPES

This is written in a garden of smooth turf, under a copper
beech, beside a glassy mill-stream, where soldiers of Alpine

regiments are writing letters home, while the guns shout up and down the narrow valleys.

A great wolf-hound, who considers himself in charge of the old-fashioned farmhouse, cannot understand why his master, aged six, should be sitting on the knees of the Marechal des Logis, the iron man who drives the big car.

"But you *are* French, little one?" says the giant, with a yearning arm round the child.

"Yes," very slowly mouthing the French words; "I—can't—speak—French—but—I—am—French."

The small face disappears in the big beard.

Somehow, I can't imagine the Marechal des Logis killing babies—even if his superior officer, now sketching the scene, were to order him!

* * * * *

The great building must once have been a monastery. Twilight softened its gaunt wings, in an angle of which were collected fifty prisoners, picked up among the hills behind the mists.

They stood in some sort of military formation preparatory to being marched off. They were dressed in khaki, the colour of gassed grass, that might have belonged to any army. Two wore spectacles, and I counted eight faces of the fifty which were asymmetrical—out of drawing on one side.

"Some of their later drafts give us that type," said the Interpreter. One of them had been wounded in the head and roughly bandaged. The others seemed all sound. Most of them looked at nothing, but several were vividly alive with terror that cannot keep the eyelids still, and a few wavered on the grey edge of collapse.

They were the breed which, at the word of command, had stolen out to drown women and children; had raped women in the streets at the word of command; and, always at the word of command, had sprayed petrol, or squirted flame; or defiled the property and persons of their captives. They stood there outside all humanity. Yet they were made in the likeness of humanity. One realized it with a shock when the bandaged creature began to shiver, and they shuffled off in response to the orders of civilized men.

V

LIFE IN TRENCHES
ON THE MOUNTAIN SIDE

Very early in the morning I met Alan Breck, with a half-healed bullet-scrape across the bridge of his nose, and an Alpine cap over one ear. His people a few hundred years ago had been Scotch. He bore a Scotch name, and still recognized the head of his clan, but his French occasionally ran into German words, for he was an Alsatian on one side.

"This," he explained, "is the very best country in the world to fight in. It's picturesque and full of cover. I'm a gunner. I've been here for months. It's lovely."

It might have been the hills under Mussoorie, and what our cars expected to do in it I could not understand. But the demon-driver who had been a road-racer took the 70 h.p. Mercedes and threaded the narrow valleys, as well as occasional half-Swiss villages full of Alpine troops, at a restrained thirty miles an hour. He shot up a new-made road, more like Mussoorie than ever, and did not fall down the hillside even once. An ammunition-mule of a mountain-battery met him at a tight corner, and began to climb a tree.

"See! There isn't another place in France where that could happen," said Alan. "I tell you, this is a magnificent country."

The mule was hauled down by his tail before he had reached the lower branches, and went on through the woods, his ammunition-boxes jinking on his back, for all the world as though he were rejoining his battery at Jutogh. One expected to meet the little Hill people bent under their loads under the forest gloom. The light, the colour, the smell of wood smoke, pine-needles, wet earth, and warm mule were all Himalayan. Only the Mercedes was violently and loudly a stranger.

"Halt!" said Alan at last, when she had done everything except imitate the mule.

"The road continues," said the demon-driver seductively.

"Yes, but they will hear you if you go on. Stop and wait. We've a mountain battery to look at."

They were not at work for the moment, and the Commandant, a grim and forceful man, showed me some details of their construction. When we left them in their bower—it looked like a Hill priest's wayside shrine—we heard them singing through the steep-descending pines. They, too, like the 75's, seem to have no pet name in the service.

It was a poisonously blind country. The woods blocked all sense of direction above and around. The ground was at any angle you please, and all sounds were split up and muddled by the tree-trunks, which acted as silencers. High above us the respectable, all-concealing forest had turned into sparse, ghastly blue sticks of timber—an assembly of leper-trees round a bald mountain top. "That's where we're going," said Alan. "Isn't it an adorable country?"

TRENCHES

A machine-gun loosed a few shots in the fumbling style of her kind when they feel for an opening. A couple of rifle shots answered. They might have been half a mile away or a hundred yards below. An adorable country! We climbed up till we found once again a complete tea-garden of little sunk houses, almost invisible in the brown-pink recesses of the thick forest. Here the trenches began, and with them for the next few hours life in two dimensions—length and breadth. You could have eaten your dinner almost anywhere off the swept dry ground, for the steep slopes favoured draining, there was no lack of timber, and there was unlimited labour. It had made neat double-length dug-outs where the wounded could be laid in during their passage down the mountain side; well-tended occasional latrines properly limed; dug-outs for sleeping and eating; overhead protections and tool-sheds where needed, and, as one came nearer the working face, very clever cellars against trench-sweepers. Men passed on their business; a squad with a captured machine-gun which they tested in a sheltered dip; armourers at their benches busy with sick rifles; fatigue-parties for straw, rations, and ammunition; long processions of single blue figures turned sideways between the brown sunless walls. One understood after a while the nightmare that lays hold of trench-stale men, when the dreamer wanders for ever in those blind mazes till, after centuries of agonizing flight, he finds himself stumbling out again into the white blaze and horror of the mined front—he who thought he had almost reached home!

IN THE FRONT LINE

There were no trees above us now. Their trunks lay along the edge of the trench, built in with stones, where necessary, or sometimes overhanging it in ragged splinters or bushy tops. Bits of cloth, not French, showed, too, in the uneven lines of debris at the trench lip, and some thoughtful soul had marked an unexploded Boche trench-sweeper as "not to be touched." It was a young lawyer from Paris who pointed that out to me.

We met the Colonel at the head of an indescribable pit of ruin, full of sunshine, whose steps ran down a very steep hillside under the lee of an almost vertically plunging parapet. To the left of that parapet the whole hillside was one gruel of smashed trees, split stones, and powdered soil. It might have been a rag-picker's dump-heap on a colossal scale.

Alan looked at it critically. I think he had helped to make it not long before.

"We're on the top of the hill now, and the Boches are below us," said he. "We gave them a very fair sickener lately."

"This," said the Colonel, "is the front line."

There were overhead guards against hand-bombs which disposed me to believe him, but what convinced me most was a corporal urging us in whispers not to talk so loud. The men were at dinner, and a good smell of food filled the trench. This was the first smell I had encountered in my long travels uphill—a mixed, entirely wholesome flavour of stew, leather, earth, and rifle-oil.

FRONT LINE PROFESSIONALS

A proportion of men were standing to arms while others ate; but dinner-time is slack time, even among animals, and it was close on noon.

"The Boches got *their* soup a few days ago," some one whispered. I thought of the pulverized hillside, and hoped it had been hot enough.

We edged along the still trench, where the soldiers stared, with justified contempt, I thought, upon the civilian who scuttled through their life for a few emotional minutes in order to make words out of their blood. Somehow it reminded me of coming in late to a play and incommoding a long line of packed stalls. The whispered dialogue was much the same: "Pardon!" "I beg your pardon, monsieur." "To the right, monsieur." "If monsieur will lower his head." "One sees best from here, monsieur," and so on. It was their day and night-long business, carried through without display or heat, or doubt or indecision. Those who worked, worked; those off duty, not five feet behind them in the dug-outs, were deep in their papers, or their meals or their letters; while death stood ready at every minute to drop down into the narrow cut from out of the narrow strip of unconcerned sky. And for the better part of a week one had skirted hundreds of miles of such a frieze!

The loopholes not in use were plugged rather like old-fashioned hives. Said the Colonel, removing a plug: "Here are the Boches. Look, and you'll see their sandbags." Through the jumble of riven trees and stones one saw what might have been a bit of green sacking. "They're about seven metres distant just here," the Colonel went on. That was true, too. We entered a little fortalice with a cannon in it, in an embrasure which at that moment struck me as unnecessarily vast, even though it was partly closed by a frail packing-case lid. The Colonel sat him down in front of it, and explained the theory of this sort of redoubt. "By the way," he said to the gunner at last, "can't you find something better than *that?*" He twitched the lid aside. "I think it's too light. Get a log of wood or something."

HANDY TRENCH-SWEEPERS

I loved that Colonel! He knew his men and he knew the Boches—had them marked down like birds. When he said they were beside dead trees or behind boulders, sure enough there they were! But, as I have said, the dinner-hour is always slack, and even when we came to a place where a section of trench had been bashed open by trench-sweepers, and it was recommended to duck and hurry, nothing much happened. The uncanny thing was the absence of movement in the Boche trenches. Sometimes one imagined that one smelt strange tobacco, or heard a rifle-bolt working after a shot. Otherwise they were as still as pig at noonday.

We held on through the maze, past trench-sweepers of a handy light pattern, with their screw-tailed charge all ready; and a grave or so; and when I came on men who merely stood within easy reach of their rifles, I knew I was in the second line. When they lay frankly at ease in their dug-outs, I knew it was the third. A shot-gun would have sprinkled all three.

"No flat plains," said Alan. "No hunting for gun positions—the hills are full of them—and the trenches close together and commanding each other. You see what a beautiful country it is."

The Colonel confirmed this, but from another point of view. War was his business, as the still woods could testify—but his hobby was his trenches. He had tapped the mountain streams and dug out a laundry where a man could wash his shirt and go up and be killed in it, all in a morning; had drained the trenches till a muddy stretch in them was an offence; and at the bottom of the hill (it looked like a hydropathic establishment on the stage) he had created baths where half a battalion at a time could wash. He never told me how all that country had been fought over as fiercely as Ypres in the West; nor what blood had gone down the valleys before his trenches pushed over the scalped mountain top. No. He sketched out new endeavours in earth and stones and trees for the comfort of his men on that populous mountain.

And there came a priest, who was a sub-lieutenant, out of a wood of snuff-brown shadows and half-veiled trunks. Would it please me to look at a chapel? It was all open to the hillside, most tenderly and devoutly done in rustic work with reedings of peeled branches and panels of moss and thatch—St. Hubert's own shrine. I saw the hunters who passed before it, going to the chase on the far side of the mountain where their game lay.

* * * * *

A BOMBARDED TOWN

Alan carried me off to tea the same evening in a town where he seemed to know everybody. He had spent the afternoon on another mountain top, inspecting gun positions; whereby he had been shelled a little—*marmite* is the slang for it. There had been no serious *marmitage,* and he had spotted a Boche position which was *marmitable.*

"And we may get shelled now," he added, hopefully. "They shell this town whenever they think of it. Perhaps they'll shell us at tea."

It was a quaintly beautiful little place, with its mixture of French and German ideas; its old bridge and gentle-minded river, between the cultivated hills. The sand-bagged cellar doors, the ruined houses, and the holes in the pavement looked as unreal as the violences of a cinema against that soft and simple setting. The people were abroad in the streets, and the little children were playing. A big shell gives notice enough for one to get to shelter, if the shelter is near enough. That appears to be as much as any one expects in the world where one is shelled, and that world has settled down to it. People's lips are a little firmer, the modelling of the brows is a little more pronounced, and, maybe, there is a change in the expression of the eyes; but nothing that a casual afternoon caller need particularly notice.

CASES FOR HOSPITAL

The house where we took tea was the "big house" of the place, old and massive, a treasure house of ancient furniture. It had everything that the moderate heart of man could desire—gardens, garages, outbuildings, and the air of peace that goes with beauty in age. It stood over a high cellarage, and opposite the cellar door was a brand-new blindage of earth packed between timbers. The cellar was a hospital, with its beds and stores, and under the electric light the orderly waited ready for the cases to be carried down out of the streets.

"Yes, they are all civil cases," said he.

They come without much warning—a woman gashed by falling timber; a child with its temple crushed by a flying stone; an urgent amputation case, and so on. One never knows. Bombardment, the Boche text-books say, "is designed to terrify the civil population so that they may put pressure on their politicians to conclude peace." In real life, men are very rarely soothed by the sight of their women being tortured.

We took tea in the hall upstairs, with a propriety and an interchange of compliments that suited the little occasion. There was no attempt to disguise the existence of a bombardment, but it was not allowed to overweigh talk of lighter matters. I know one guest who sat through it as near as might be inarticulate with wonder. But he was English, and when Alan asked him whether he had enjoyed himself, he said: "Oh, yes. Thank you very much."

"Nice people, aren't they?" Alan went on.

"Oh, very nice. And—and such good tea."

He managed to convey a few of his sentiments to Alan after dinner.

"But what else could the people have done?" said he. "They are French."

VI

THE COMMON TASK OF A GREAT PEOPLE

"This is the end of the line," said the Staff Officer, kindest and most patient of chaperons. It buttressed itself on a fortress among hills. Beyond that, the silence was more awful than the mixed noise of business to the westward. In mileage on the map the line must be between four and five hundred miles; in actual trench-work many times that distance. It is too much to see at full length; the mind does not readily break away from the obsession of its entirety or the grip of its detail. One visualizes the thing afterwards as a white-hot gash, worming all across France between intolerable sounds and lights, under ceaseless blasts of whirled dirt. Nor is it any relief to lose oneself among wildernesses of piling, stoning, timbering, concreting, and wire-work, or incalculable quantities of soil thrown up raw to the light and cloaked by the changing seasons—as the unburied dead are cloaked.

Yet there are no words to give the essential simplicity of it. It is the rampart put up by Man against the Beast, precisely as in the Stone Age. If it goes, all that keeps us from the Beast goes with it. One sees this at the front as clearly as one sees the French villages behind the German lines. Sometimes people steal away from them and bring word of what they endure.

Where the rifle and the bayonet serve, men use those tools along the front. Where the knife gives better results, they go in behind the hand-grenades with the naked twelve-inch knife. Each race is supposed to fight in its own way, but this war has passed beyond all the known ways. They say that the Belgians in the north settle accounts with a certain dry passion which has varied very little since their agony began. Some sections of the English line have produced a soft-voiced, rather reserved type, which does its work with its mouth shut. The French carry an edge to their fighting, a precision, and a dreadful knowledge coupled with an insensibility to shock, unlike anything one has imagined of mankind. To be sure, there has never been like provocation, for never since the Aesir went about to bind the Fenris Wolf has all the world united to bind the Beast.

The last I saw of the front was Alan Breck speeding back to his gun-positions among the mountains; and I wondered what delight of what household the lad must have been in the old days.

SUPPORTS AND RESERVES

Then we had to work our way, department by department, against the tides of men behind the line—supports and their supports, reserves and reserves of reserves, as well as the masses in training. They flooded towns and villages, and when we tried short-cuts we found them in every by-lane. Have you seen mounted men reading their home letters with the reins thrown on the horses' necks, moving in absorbed silence through a street which almost said "Hush!" to its dogs; or met, in a forest, a procession of perfectly new big guns, apparently taking themselves from the foundry to the front?

In spite of their love of drama, there is not much "window-dressing" in the French character. The Boche, who is the priest of the Higher Counter-jumpery, would have had half the neutral Press out in cars to advertise these vast spectacles of men and material. But the same instinct as makes their rich farmers keep to their smocks makes the French keep quiet.

"This is our affair," they argue. "Everybody concerned is taking part in it. Like the review you saw the other day, there are no spectators."

"But it might be of advantage if the world knew."

Mine was a foolish remark. There is only one world to-day, the world of the Allies. Each of them knows what the others are doing and—the rest doesn't matter. This is a curious but delightful fact to realize at first hand. And think what it will be later, when we shall all circulate among each other and open our hearts and talk it over in a brotherhood more intimate than the ties of blood!

I lay that night at a little French town, and was kept awake by a man, somewhere in the hot, still darkness, howling aloud from the pain of his wounds. I was glad that he was alone, for when one man gives way the others sometimes follow. Yet the single note of misery was worse than the baying and gulping of a whole ward. I wished that a delegation of strikers could have heard it.

* * * * *

That a civilian should be in the war zone at all is a fair guarantee of his good faith. It is when he is outside the zone unchaperoned that questions begin, and the permits are looked into. If these are irregular—but one doesn't care to contemplate it. If regular, there are still a few counter-checks. As the sergeant at the railway station said when he helped us out of an impasse: "You will realize that it is the most undesirable persons whose papers are of the most regular. It is their business you see. The Commissary of Police is at the Hotel de Ville, if you will come along for the little formality. Myself, I used to keep a shop in Paris. My God, these provincial towns are desolating!"

PARIS—AND NO FOREIGNERS

He would have loved his Paris as we found it. Life was renewing itself in the streets, whose drawing and proportion one could never notice before. People's eyes, and the women's especially, seemed to be set to a longer range, a more comprehensive gaze. One would have said they came from the sea or the mountains, where things are few and simple, rather than from houses. Best of all, there were no foreigners—the beloved city for the first time was French throughout from end to end. It felt like coming back to an old friend's house for a quiet talk after he had got rid of a houseful of visitors. The functionaries and police had dropped their masks of official politeness, and were just friendly. At the hotels, so like school two days before the term begins, the impersonal valet, the chambermaid of the set two-franc smile, and the unbending head-waiter had given place to one's own brothers and sisters, full of one's own anxieties. "My son is an aviator, monsieur. I could have claimed Italian nationality for him at the beginning, but he would not have it." . . ."Both my brothers, monsieur, are at the war. One is dead already. And my fiance, I have not heard from him since March. He is cook in a battalion." . . ."Here is the wine-list, monsieur. Yes, both my sons and a nephew, and—I have no news of them, not a word of news. My God, we all suffer these days." And so, too, among the shops—the mere statement of the loss or the grief at the heart, but never a word of doubt, never a whimper of despair.

"Now why," asked a shopkeeper, "does not our Government, or your Government, or both our Governments, send some of the British Army to Paris? I assure you we should make them welcome."

"Perhaps," I began, "you might make them too welcome."

He laughed. "We should make them as welcome as our own army. They would enjoy themselves." I had a vision of British officers, each with ninety days' pay to his credit, and a damsel or two at home, shopping consumedly.

"And also," said the shopkeeper, "the moral effect on Paris to see more of your troops would be very good."

But I saw a quite English Provost-Marshal losing himself in chase of defaulters of the New Army who knew their Paris! Still, there is something to be said for the idea—to the extent of a virtuous brigade or so. At present, the English officer in Paris is a scarce bird, and he explains at once why he is and what he is doing there. He must have good reasons. I suggested teeth to an acquaintance. "No good," he grumbled. "They've thought of that, too. Behind our lines is simply crawling with dentists now!"

A PEOPLE TRANSFIGURED

If one asked after the people that gave dinners and dances last year, where every one talked so brilliantly of such vital things, one got in return the addresses of hospitals. Those pleasant hostesses and maidens seemed to be in charge of departments or on duty in wards, or kitchens, or sculleries. Some of the hospitals were in Paris. (Their staffs might have one hour a day in which to see visitors.) Others were up the line, and liable to be shelled or bombed.

I recalled one Frenchwoman in particular, because she had once explained to me the necessities of civilized life. These included a masseuse, a manicurist, and a maid to look after the lapdogs. She is employed now, and has been for months past, on the disinfection and repair of soldiers' clothes. There was no need to ask after the men one had known. Still, there was no sense of desolation. They had gone on; the others were getting ready.

All France works outward to the Front—precisely as an endless chain of fire-buckets works toward the conflagration. Leave the fire behind you and go back till you reach the source of supplies. You will find no break, no pause, no apparent haste, but never any slackening. Everybody has his or her bucket, little or big, and nobody disputes how they should be used. It is a people possessed of the precedent and tradition of war for existence, accustomed to hard living and hard labour, sanely economical by temperament, logical by training, and illumined and transfigured by their resolve and endurance.

You know, when supreme trial overtakes an acquaintance whom till then we conceived we knew, how the man's nature sometimes changes past knowledge or belief. He who was altogether such an one as ourselves goes forward simply, even lightly, to heights we thought unattainable. Though he is the very same comrade that lived our small life with us, yet in all things he has become great. So it is with France to-day. She has discovered the measure of her soul.

THE NEW WAR

One sees this not alone in the—it is more than contempt of death—in the godlike preoccupation of her people under arms which makes them put death out of the account, but in the equal passion and fervour with which her people throughout give themselves to the smallest as well as the greatest tasks that may in any way serve their sword. I might tell you something that I saw of the cleaning out of certain latrines; of the education and antecedents of the cleaners; what they said in the matter and how perfectly the work was done. There was a little Rabelais in it, naturally, but the rest was pure devotion, rejoicing to be of use.

Similarly with stables, barricades, and barbed-wire work, the clearing and piling away of wrecked house-rubbish, the serving of meals till the service rocks on its poor tired feet, but keeps its temper; and all the unlovely, monotonous details that go with war.

The women, as I have tried to show, work stride for stride with the men, with hearts as resolute and a spirit that has little mercy for short-comings. A woman takes her place wherever she can relieve a man—in the shop, at the posts, on the tramways, the hotels, and a thousand other businesses. She is inured to field-work, and half the harvest of France this year lies in her lap. One feels at every turn how her men trust her. She knows, for she shares everything with her world, what has befallen her sisters who are now in German hands, and her soul is the undying flame behind the men's steel. Neither men nor women have any illusion as to miracles presently to be performed which shall "sweep out" or "drive back" the Boche. Since the Army is the Nation, they know much, though they are officially told little. They all recognize that the old-fashioned "victory" of the past is almost as obsolete as a rifle in a front-line trench. They all accept the new war, which means grinding down and wearing out the enemy by every means and plan and device that can be compassed. It is slow and expensive, but as deadly sure as the logic that leads them to make it their one work, their sole thought, their single preoccupation.

A NATION'S CONFIDENCE

The same logic saves them a vast amount of energy. They knew Germany in '70, when the world would not believe in their knowledge; they knew the German mind before the war; they know what she has done (they have photographs) during this war. They do not fall into spasms of horror and indignation over atrocities "that cannot be mentioned," as the English papers say. They mention them in full and book them to the account. They do not discuss, nor consider, nor waste an emotion over anything that Germany says or boasts or argues or implies or intrigues after. They have the heart's ease that comes from all being at work for their country; the knowledge that the burden of work is equally distributed among all; the certainty that the women are working side by side with the men; the assurance that when one man's task is at the moment ended, another takes his place.

Out of these things is born their power of recuperation in their leisure; their reasoned calm while at work; and their superb confidence in their arms. Even if France of to-day stood alone against the world's enemy, it would be almost inconceivable to imagine her defeat now; wholly so to imagine any surrender. The war will go on till the enemy is finished. The French do not know when that hour will come; they seldom speak of it; they do not amuse themselves with dreams of triumphs or terms. Their business is war, and they do their business.

BIBLIOBAZAAR

The essential book market!

Did you know that you can get any of our titles in large print?

Did you know that we have an ever-growing collection of books in many languages?

Order online:
www.bibliobazaar.com

Find all of your favorite classic books!

Stay up to date with the latest government reports!

At BiblioBazaar, we aim to make knowledge more accessible by making thousands of titles available to you- *quickly and affordably*.

Contact us:
BiblioBazaar
PO Box 21206
Charleston, SC 29413

1080890

Made in the USA